TRANSITORY

Acclaim for J.M. Redmann's Micky Knight Series

Not Dead Enough

"Micky is the epitome of the anti-heroine, a woman with serious flaws who had a hard childhood and who paid a high price for her life achievements as an adult. The great thing about this character is that she seems so realistic in her self-deprecation, her sarcasm, even her loneliness. It's inevitable that your heart goes with her as life gives her yet another blow. I absolutely love this character with all her flaws and also her strengths."—*LezReviewBooks*

"The author kept me on my toes, divulging just enough to keep me in the throes of the various situations arising. When I thought I knew where things were going, the author changed direction with a few exploits that enhanced my reading pleasure."—*Dru's Book Musings*

"*Not Dead Enough* offers fresh character insight, a compelling mystery, and addictive pacing. Through it all, Micky Knight continues to impress. Sure she makes mistakes—both professional and personal—but she remains a character readers can champion, and this book proves just how resilient Micky is. It will be exciting to see where J.M. Redmann takes her as she heads toward a dozen novels in this first-class series." —*BOLO Books Review*

"Although the mystery itself is complex and has a big cast, Redmann juggles the elements with a sure hand, lingering long enough to either establish or embroider the characters while making sure we understand how they fit into the larger picture. The complexity builds without you realizing it until you're as deeply involved as Micky, no matter how much she doesn't want to be."—*Out In Print*

Girl on the Edge of Summer

"Excellent storytelling and a brilliant character. This is one of only a few series where I reread all the books when a new one comes out… FIVE STARS and recommended if you like crime fiction with a heart— you may fall for Micky too."—*Planet Nation*

"The two mysteries themselves are interesting and have twists and turns to keep the reader entertained, and there are the usual fast-paced dangerous scenes…Overall, an entertaining read charged with action."—*Lez Review Books*

"We get to enjoy some well-plotted mysteries, some life-and-death rescues, and some despicably seedy characters. Redmann works through her action scenes with precision and balance, never letting them drag or sputter. The YA characters here are also well-drawn. They sound like teenagers, not forty-year-olds, and they act age appropriately as well. But at the heart of it all is Mickey—mostly smart (but sometimes stupid), looking forward without forgetting her past, and trying to reassemble her life with some bent and abraded puzzle pieces."—*Out in Print*

Ill Will

Lambda Literary Award Winner
***Foreword* Magazine Honorable Mention**

"*Ill Will* is fast-paced, well-plotted, and peopled with great characters. Redmann's dialogue is, as usual, marvelous. To top it off, you get an unexpected twist at the end. Please join me in hoping that book number eight is well underway."—*Lambda Literary Review*

"*Ill Will* is a solidly plotted, strongly character-driven mystery that is well paced."—*Mysterious Reviews*

Water Mark

***Foreword* Magazine Gold Medal Winner**
Golden Crown Literary Award Winner

"*Water Mark* is a rich, deep novel filled with humor and pathos. Its exciting plot keeps the pages flying, while it shows that long after a front page story has ceased to exist, even in the back sections of the newspaper, it remains very real to those whose lives it touched. This is another great read from a fine author."—*Just About Write*

Death of a Dying Man

Lambda Literary Award Winner

"Like other books in the series, Redmann's pacing is sharp, her sense of place acute and her characters well crafted. The story has a definite edge, raising some discomfiting questions about the selfishly unsavory way some gay men and lesbians live their lives and what the consequences of that behavior can be. Redmann isn't all edge, however—she's got plenty of sass. Knight is funny, her relationship with Cordelia is believably long-term-lover sexy and little details of both the characters' lives and New Orleans give the atmosphere heft."—*Lambda Book Report*

"As the investigation continues and Micky's personal dramas rage, a big storm is brewing. Redmann, whose day job is with NO/AIDS, gets the Hurricane Katrina evacuation just right—at times she brought tears to my eyes. An unsettled Micky searches for friends and does her work as she constantly grieves for her beloved city."—*New Orleans Times-Picayune*

The Intersection of Law and Desire

Lambda Literary Award Winner
***San Francisco Chronicle* Editor's Choice for the year**

Profiled on *Fresh Air*, hosted by Terry Gross, and selected for book reviewer Maureen Corrigan's recommended holiday book list.

"Superbly crafted, multi-layered...One of the most hard-boiled and complex female detectives in print today."—*San Francisco Chronicle* (An Editor's Choice selection for 1995)

"Fine, hard-boiled tale-telling."—*Washington Post Book World*

"An edge-of-the-seat, action-packed New Orleans adventure... Micky Knight is a fast-moving, fearless, fascinating character...*The Intersection of Law and Desire* will win Redmann lots more fans." —*New Orleans Times-Picayune*

"Crackling with tension...an uncommonly rich book...Redmann has the making of a landmark series."—*Kirkus Review*

"Perceptive, sensitive prose; in-depth characterization; and pensive, wry wit add up to a memorable and compelling read."—*Library Journal*

"Powerful and page turning...A rip-roaring read, as randy as it is reflective...Micky Knight is a to-die-for creation...a Cajun firebrand with the proverbial quick wit, fast tongue, and heavy heart."—*Lambda Book Report*

Lost Daughters

"A sophisticated, funny, plot-driven, character-laden murder mystery set in New Orleans...as tightly plotted a page-turner as they come... One of the pleasures of *Lost Daughters* is its highly accurate portrayal of the real work of private detection—a standout accomplishment in the usually sloppily conjectured world of thriller-killer fiction. Redmann has a firm grasp of both the techniques and the emotions of real-life cases—in this instance, why people decide to search for their relatives, why people don't, what they fear finding and losing…and Knight is a competent, tightly wound, sardonic, passionate detective with a keen eye for detail and a spine made of steel."—*San Francisco Chronicle*

"Redmann's Micky Knight series just gets better…For finely delineated characters, unerring timing, and page-turning action, Redmann deserves the widest possible audience."—*Booklist, starred review*

"Like fine wine, J.M. Redmann's private eye has developed interesting depths and nuances with age…Redmann continues to write some of the fastest –moving action scenes in the business…In Lost Daughters, Redmann has found a winning combination of action and emotion that should attract new fans—both gay and straight—in droves."—*New Orleans Times Picayune*

"…tastefully sexy…"—*USA Today*

"An admirable, tough PI with an eye for detail and the courage, finally, to confront her own fear. Recommended."—*Library Journal*

"The best mysteries are character-driven and still have great moments of atmosphere and a tightly wound plot. J.M. Redmann succeeds on all three counts in this story of a smart lesbian private eye who unravels the fascinating evidence in a string of bizarre cases, involving missing children, grisly mutilations, and a runaway teen driven from her own home because she is gay."—*Outsmart*

By the Author

The Micky Knight Mystery Series:

Death by the Riverside

Deaths of Jocasta

The Intersection of Law and Desire

Lost Daughters

Death of a Dying Man

Water Mark

Ill Will

The Shoal of Time

The Girl on the Edge of Summer

Not Dead Enough

Transitory

Women of the Mean Streets: Lesbian Noir
edited with Greg Herren

Men of the Mean Streets: Gay Noir
edited with Greg Herren

Night Shadows: Queer Horror
edited with Greg Herren

As R. Jean Reid, the Nell McGraw mystery series

Roots of Murder

Perdition

TRANSITORY

by

J.M. Redmann

2023

TRANSITORY

ISBN 13: 978-1-63679-251-4

This Trade Paperback Original Is Published By
Bold Strokes Books, Inc.
P.O. Box 249
Valley Falls, NY 12185

First Edition: September 2023

CREDITS

EDITORS: GREG HERREN AND STACIA SEAMAN
PRODUCTION DESIGN: STACIA SEAMAN
COVER DESIGN BY TAMMY SEIDICK

Acknowledgments

Let's be real, probably the first people I need to thank are my cancer care team at Froedtert Medical Center. Due to their excellent care, I am alive, and now cancer free. Hard to finish writing a book if you're dead. There are a plethora of people who pulled me thought this, from online to real life. Too many for me to remember all the names I should remember. Just know I am thankful to you all. Special thanks to my sister Connie, for coming over and helping out.

I also need to thank the writing community, especially the mystery and the queer writing communities. From a lunch date to coffee to online chats to brief words of encouragement, we all help each other through the long slogs of writing books. I especially want to thank Anne Laughlin of Sisters in Crime, Midwest chapter; Paul Willis, Executive Director of Saints and Sinners Literary Festival; Rob Byrnes and Carol Rosenfeld of the Publishing Triangle; Margery Flax and Donna Andrews of Mystery Writers of America; Queer Crime Writers; Bold Strokes Books; Golden Crown; PI Writers; and others my brain is not thinking of with a deadline looming. Also, thanks to Michele Karlsberg for her unstinting support of the LGBTQ writing community and for her friendship.

I also need to thank all my writer friends who struggle to get the words on the page amidst everything else life throws at us. Greg, Cheryl, Jesse, Kay, Carsen, Ali, Anne, VK, 'Nathan, Jeffrey, Rob, Fay, Isabella, K.G., Jerry, Lucy, David, Thomas, Dean, Barb, Mary, and I know I'm forgetting some of y'all. You keep me sane, or as close to it as I'm likely to get. Also, thanks to the authors who started so many of us on this journey and have been kind and generous to me, Ellen Hart, Katherine V. Forrest, Barbara Wilson, Dorothy Allison, Jewelle Gomez, and so many others. You gave us lesbian heroes at a time when lesbians weren't supposed to be heroes.

As always, a major thanks to Greg Herren for his editorial work, and his calm demeanor, especially about those pesky deadlines and all the shenanigans in New Orleans. What was the final Bloody Mary count?

I'm no longer there, now retired, but thanks to many people at my former day job at CrescentCare—Narquis, Joey, Chris, Diane, Jasmine, Blayke, Kyle and all the members of the Prevention Department. Y'all all gave me a great workplace and do important work.

Huge thanks to Radclyffe for making Bold Strokes what it is. Ruth, Sandy, Stacia, and Cindy for all their hard work behind the scenes and everyone at BSB for being such a great and supportive publishing house. Also, big thanks to Hanlon, my sensitivity reader, for helping me to get it right. However, the book is mine and any mistakes are mine as well.

And my partner in life and legally sanctioned marriage, Gillian, for all the help in getting me through the rough patch, cooking all the boring bland food when it was all I could eat. No more white rice ever again. We are looking forward to spending days at our respective offices working on our respective books. She makes me appreciate not having to do footnotes, an index, and stick to facts.

To Ellen Hart. Her books helped start and sustain me on this journey. Author of the Jane Lawless series, one of the first mystery series to feature a lesbian protagonist. Winner of the Mystery Writers of America Grand Master, one of the most prestigious honors in the crime-writing community. Someone I greatly admire and am fortunate to call a friend.

CHAPTER ONE

Blinding, blue, white. A spit of dark. Jarring, off and on. I stared at the police car parked half-on, half-off the road. The blinding, nauseating lights were better than looking at the woman on the ground.

Thirty minutes ago, she had been alive.

The glare did nothing for the roiling in my stomach.

Thirty minutes ago, I had been crossing Rampart Street, leaving the French Quarter to head back to my house in Tremé.

Thirty minutes ago—no, thirty-five now, I was mellow, enjoying the steps back to a normal life, returning from one of my favorite bars, showing the card to prove I'd been vaccinated.

A toned-down celebration. Like the previous plague, not everyone survived, and even those of us who did had our scars—loss of a loved one, of a friend, of the people we got used to seeing on a regular basis, a favorite waiter, store clerk, loss of income, a job, a home.

But it was supposed to be a night to see and laugh and hug one another, the tipping point to going back to normal, or creating what would be normal now.

New Orleans is a city with a dream that stopped at a bar along the way. No, not the raucous tourist joints on Bourbon Street, but a bar of storytellers, lazy fans swirling in the ceiling, a door wide open to the street, sultry air mixing with the chill of the bar, like a portal from one world to another. A scratched and beat-up bar, tales of hearts broken and hearts mended told over and over like it was the first time. Air thick with desperation and courage, a place where time seems slowed, even gentle. One low step from the entry to the sidewalk, to trip you if you're not careful, just like life. I've lived in New Orleans most of my years, and I think I've been in that bar for a good part of it.

A short wait for a shower to pass, a cool, rain-washed night, a lingering summer finally turning to fall in this subtropical city. A saunter from the bright lights of the Quarter, greeting strangers on the street because this is New Orleans, and it's what we do.

Two blocks from my house. Crossing Rampart, past the final lights of the gas station.

A roar of engine stopped me on the neutral ground. Someone speeding.

The car gunned by, only to screech to a halt just beyond me.

The door flung open and the woman was pushed out, into the middle of the street.

Into an oncoming vehicle, either a large boxy truck or an SUV.

It didn't stop.

The first car sped away, the door hanging open. It tailed the SUV, at first as if trying to catch it, flying through the just red light at Esplanade, but then both turned like they were traveling together.

The woman in the street was screaming, an incoherent cry of pain.

I pulled out my phone as I jumped into the street, frantically waving to halt oncoming cars. The next car stopped, seeing me, seeing the woman.

I was yelling at the 9-1-1 operator. Telling her to get help as quickly as possible.

Then telling her about the cars and where they were headed.

On my knee next to the woman. I didn't dare do anything; even moving her was dangerous.

"Help is coming," I told her. Over and other again. Sirens in the distance. *Help is coming.*

She looked at me, reaching her hand to mine. At first touch, the grip was strong, desperate.

But her fingers loosened, strength slipping away.

Her lips moved. I leaned closer.

"Why? Why do this? I wasn't going to…"

"I don't know," I answered. "Save your strength. Stay with us."

Other cars stopped. Some honking, some helping. A crowd around us.

Her fingers let go, her hand dropping to the pavement. I picked it up again, holding it tightly, as if that could keep her from slipping away.

"Don't let them get away…" A bare, harsh whisper.

A ragged breath, another. Another. Nothing.

"Stay with us," I begged her.

Another blur, the police and EMTs pushed through the crowd. I stood back. She was only a few breaths away from living. If they could start her heart and lungs again, she could hold on to life.

The seconds slipped into minutes. Then more minutes. The clock moved relentlessly.

The EMTs backed away.

The police took over.

I stared at the blinding lights.

The cop in charge had ordered me to remain; they wanted to talk.

I wanted to stumble the last few blocks to my house, crawl in bed, and pretend this was all a dream; walk away from it until I was sober and the sun chased away the night and I could carry the grief of a stranger who crossed my path.

I took a few careful steps back, but the closest cop glanced my way as if knowing what I wanted to do and watching me to make sure I didn't.

Time slipped away, marking only by my realizing I was chilly and tired. The sun might be coming up any minute for all I knew.

I pulled out my phone to check the time.

"Don't take pictures," the close cop barked at me.

"Just checking the time," I answered. One hour. Just one hour.

The cops had blocked the street, clearing the traffic. The mere onlookers had been sent away.

The morgue truck and the ME arrived.

The cops backed away, talking as if the night were still crowded and noisy.

"Yeah, sad, but that's what usually happens to guys like that," the younger one said.

The older one shook his head and replied, "Almost asking for it, if you ask me. Something wrong with him to dress like that."

Her. I was silent.

"Hey, you should get out more, check out a drag show. They can be pretty good," the younger cop said.

"No, thanks, got a wife and kids at home. That's enough for me."

I wanted to tell them she wasn't a drag queen. She was dressed in clothing that any woman could wear in a mall, not the flamboyant camp of drag. A sedate navy dress, cowl collar, elbow-length sleeves, sensible black kitten heels. A reasonable amount of makeup, nothing over-the-top. Not drag, not even close. Not working the streets, not the kind of look that would make a car stop. She was just a woman.

But I was alone, not as sober as I needed to be, and they didn't seem like the kind of people I could explain gender and sexuality to.

A man in a rumpled suit jacket sauntered over to them. He had a badge on his belt. "Any idea what this might be for?" He showed them a card in an evidence bag.

The older cop read, "Gender at CC with CJ, Monday at 10 a.m."

"Some appointment, maybe?" the younger cop said.

"Obviously, but where?" the detective said. "No ID on him that we could find. Just this crumpled up in his pocket. Isn't that something you'd put in your purse?"

"Maybe he was too butch to carry a purse," the older cop said.

They laughed.

I coughed, trying to clear my throat. The nausea wasn't going away. I had a guess, a strong guess, but that's not the same things as knowing, is it? A local community health clinic called CrescentCare did specialty work with the transgender community, running a gender clinic. My ex was their chief medical officer. Her initials were C.J.

New Orleans can be such a small town.

I didn't know that for sure, certainly not sure enough to tell these cops. I wanted a time of clear thinking to decide if it would help find her killers or be a tangled mess for the clinic that did no good for anyone. In any case, I didn't want to be the one who made the connection for the police unless I had to. There wasn't much Cordelia would thank me for, but landing the police on her doorstep without warning to interrogate her about a murdered patient would not be one of them.

"Who's that?" the detective asked the cops, pointing in my direction.

"A witness," the younger one said.

He strolled over to me. "What are you doing here?"

The question was suspicious, not friendly. Not a good sign. "I live close by. I was walking home."

"Home from where?"

"A bar about eight blocks away."

"Which one? Or can you even remember?"

No nice cop here. He had ideas about me, and he didn't like those ideas.

I'm a woman in my late forties, hair on the short side now, since I was finally able to get it cut. Black and curly—well, a lot of gray in the black now. Olive skin from my Greek mother and Cajun father. I'm white, but I don't look as white as some people think I should look.

A little taller than he was. Black leather jacket. Well-worn jeans, not fashionably aged. A purple T-shirt that read "Still, She Persisted."

"Q Carré," I said. His eyes narrowed even more. Q was well known as a hangout for the rainbow spectrum. I'd just outed myself, not that I was very far in. It's on the Rampart edge of the French Quarter, also known as the Vieux Carré, hence the name.

"You know him?" he asked, shrugging his shoulder in the direction of the women.

"No, I don't know her." I stared coolly at him.

He asked for my ID.

I gave him my driver's license. He didn't need to see my PI license.

"Michele Knight," he read, then my address, asking if I still lived there.

I just said yes, not pointing out that if I didn't live there, why was I walking there.

Only answer what's asked, and even then, keep it to a minimum.

I gave him the best description I could of the car and SUV, how both turned off at the same street.

"Yeah, well, maybe it was coincidence," he said.

"Both going the wrong way down a one-way street?" I countered.

He looked at me. "So?"

Damn, I was trying not to talk and had backed myself into talking. "It didn't seem like the SUV tried to stop. One car pushes her out, the second runs over her."

He kept staring at me. Then he sighed and said, "Yeah, right, you've been watching too much TV. He was working the streets. His customer got a nasty surprise under the dress and pushed him out. Bad luck he got hit be a car. It happens to those types all the time."

Don't get angry. It won't help. "She wasn't a prostitute."

"Yeah? Thought you didn't know him?"

"I don't. But she was wearing a dress with pockets, high neck, low heels, only basic makeup. Not the kind of look that gets a car to stop."

"Maybe she works by appointment, for the kind that like that look."

"Maybe you should keep an open mind and get actual facts before you make assumptions."

"You want to come down to the station and tell me how to do my job?"

I did manage to not say, "Why, would it do any good?" Instead shaking my head. Kept my mouth shut.

He stared at me, as if he wanted a fight.

"Is there anything else you'd like to ask me?" I said, in as bland a voice as I could.

He glared a moment longer. "No," he spat out, then spun away.

I backed up slowly, trying to leave without anyone noticing. He hadn't given me permission exactly. I was afraid if I left too abruptly, it would be an excuse for him to call me back. I edged away from them. It was the wrong direction, but getting away from them, the blinding lights, was all that mattered.

Finally, slow step by slow step, it was dark enough and I was far enough away to turn and walk as fast as my nausea would allow, cutting up side streets to detour around the police.

Tomorrow, I chanted to myself. Tomorrow will be daylight. You'll be sober and you can think through what you can do. If anything.

I managed to get the door to my house closed and locked before running to the bathroom and throwing up, slumping on the cold bathroom floor after the final empty heave.

I woke up, cramped, still on the floor, the night still dark. Managed to rinse out my mouth and stumble to bed, into the oblivion of sleep and dark.

Chapter Two

The morning brought light, a blinding headache, and a stomach that said it was starving and didn't want to eat anything. I'd had bad dreams, a restless night, thunder and lightning in the early hours of the morning.

I shambled to the bathroom to brush my teeth.

The night came back to me.

The woman left to die in the street.

The dismissive cops, laughing. She was Black, with genitals they thought were male. Not a death for them to worry about.

I spat out the toothpaste, splattering it all over the sink.

You don't know her and it's not your case, I told my reflection in the mirror.

I stared at myself, the lines that time had given me, at the eyes, a furrow at the brow. Laughing and crying, etching my face. Today my olive complection was sallow, the brown eyes red. More gray in my black hair.

Or maybe it was the light.

I again rinsed out my mouth, no longer looking at myself.

Kitchen and coffee were next.

Two slices of toast. Plain, not even butter. I wasn't sure my stomach could handle it even then.

I sat at the small breakfast nook. A tentative sip of coffee, followed by a nibble of toast.

Who was she and why was she thrown out of the car?

Had it been coordinated? The car pushes her out, claiming he was surprised by what was under the dress? The second car runs her over and he claims (she?—why did I think it was he?) it was an accident.

Complicated and messy. Maybe I had been watching too much TV.

And it's not your case.

But if I was right, they would get away with murder.

I finished my coffee and one piece of toast. So far, so good.

Another cup of coffee and I started on the second piece of toast.

What do I do?

You don't need to do anything. You gave your statement to the police. They're the professionals; they get to handle it their way.

Plus, it was Saturday, no one around until Monday except the cops already working on this, and they'd heard enough from me.

I finished the second piece of toast and second cup of coffee, staring at the shimmer of light on the plants and flowers on our small patio.

My small patio. Cordelia had done most of the gardening, picking out what would work well together, what needed the light in the back and what would do okay with the shade by the wall separating us from the neighbors. I had laid the brick for the seating area. It had been a quiet place for coffee on weekend mornings or wine in the evening.

Time for a shower.

Cleanliness didn't get me closer to godliness, not a single sin washed away.

But I was clean, and the coffee and toast had gone down and stayed there.

In a fit of pretending I was doing something without actually doing anything, I got dressed and headed down to my office.

Both my house and my office had been purchased when Tremé (where I live) and Bywater (where I work) were working-class neighborhoods, if not downright poor. I bought in the uncertain years after Katrina, after the attention of the world had moved on and we were still a city struggling to survive.

Now both areas were trendy, rapidly gentrifying, prices rising at dizzying speed. Luck had been with me and maybe some smarts, but mostly it was the pragmatic reality that I needed a place to live and a place to work.

It was about a seven-minute drive to my office, five if I gunned it and caught the lights right. I was still a mostly solo shop, mainly working on missing persons and security systems for small businesses, a lot of gay bars back when it was easier to deal with a lesbian than the macho straight guys out in the burbs. I called in assistance as needed, mainly from the computer grannies, who rented the second floor of my office building. They were a bunch of older women who had discovered they could sit in air-conditioned comfort and make decent money cruising the web, certainly better than supplementing their retirement by greeting shoppers at big box stores. I gave them a break on the rent, and they put my requests at the front of the line. The building was three stories, an old warehouse from back in the days when river cargo wasn't housed in shipping containers. It had character and the expenses that go with an old building. I rented the first floor to a trendy coffee shop, one that served the new people living in the neighborhood, and the increasing number of short-term renters. "I am not your Uber and get out of my way before I run over your toes" was becoming my mantra.

But I was still paying down the loan to upgrade the air system for the building, and a major roof repair was looming.

My one point of pride was that I never bought coffee from them. I wasn't going to contribute to the rent they paid me.

As usual, it was a busy Saturday late-ish morning, the block all parked up. I could typically find a spot in the street, but not today. There was a small parking pad in back. I just had to nose my car into the drive, get out, unlock the rusty lock and shove open the not-as-oiled-as-it-should-be gate, carefully navigate down the very narrow drive to not take out a side mirror, park, then walk back to the front of the building to close the gate.

As I was doing so, another car, a too-large SUV, was trying to shove in. I stood in the drive, shaking my head at them, motioning to back out. I considered letting them try, knowing they were too big, but that would still be my problem. The last thing I wanted to do was assist an entitled idiot into backing out and explain I wasn't going to pay for the scratch on the side of their vehicle.

"There is no parking on the street," the driver yelled at me. Why can jerks like that own an SUV that had to be around the 50K mark?

"Private property," I retorted.

"But there is no place to park. We need our coffee."

This is why I rarely carry my gun. I'd have been tempted to pull it out, aim it dead at him, and tell him this is private property—get out or get shot.

Instead, I stood directly in front, blocking his way, pulled out my phone like I had better things to do, and ignored him while checking the weather.

He honked.

Cool front, lows in the fifties, chance of showers.

He honked again.

Then he gunned his engine and inched forward.

"Private property, back off," I growled.

"I'm a lawyer, I know what private property is. I'm trying to go to the coffee shop, and this is their property."

"No, it's not. Tell them if they want to use this area, they can double their rent. Right now, they only pay for the inside area. Off-limits."

He fumed. Honked again.

I didn't move. Moving would most likely be to kick in his grill. Better for both of us that I stay put.

He seemed to be conferring with the women in the passenger seat. Trendy blonde with enough makeup on that she'd clearly already had coffee for the hour it would have taken her to put it on.

He backed out enough to completely block the sidewalk. She opened her door, took long enough with getting her purse and putting on her sunglasses. A group of people had to walk into the street to get around.

He backed out jerkily, almost hitting an oncoming car, pulling out anyway and making them wait.

She needed her sunglasses on a cloudy day for the ten-foot walk to the coffee shop.

I closed the gate, locking it from inside.

This is why I usually park on the street.

Instead of going in the front, I retreated to the back entrance, a heavy fire/burglar door with two locks on it and an alarm that had a short timer. Not my preferred way to enter since I had to remember the code in about two seconds or face a shrieking siren, pry open two rarely used locks, and get the creaky door to open and shut before resetting the alarm.

But I really wanted to avoid Mr. Privileged Parking Space. Why further ruin an already ruined day?

I made my way from the cluttered back hallway—too many boxes of coffee supplies stored here made it a fire hazard. Another reason not to go this way. If I didn't know, I didn't have to deal with telling the coffee shop dudes not to be jerks and ignore safety codes they were well aware of.

It's a busy weekend, leave it until Monday, I bargained as I headed for the staircase that would take me to my third-floor lair.

Just as Mr. PP entered, huffing about the lack of parking amenities. Yes, he actually used the phrase "parking amenities."

I hurried up the stairs, ignoring his complaining voice.

"I hope they overcharge you," I muttered as I unlocked my door.

I locked it behind me. I wasn't open for business and wanted no one exploring up the stairs to interrupt.

And why was I here?

Last night.

Not your case. Do some filing and paperwork and leave it alone.

I checked the local news.

No mention of it.

Maybe it had been a drunken nightmare?

Except I'd picked a pile of still damp clothes off the bathroom floor this morning. I can have vivid dreams, but never yet ones with actual wet rain.

I stared at the files but did nothing with them.

This case would rapidly grow cold. The cops had their easy version: Unfortunate accident; a little hanky-panky, the guy gets freaked when he realizes she's not as biological a woman as he thought and shoves her out of the car. She gets hit by another car. Too bad, but oh, well, to be expected for people like that. Sign the file and put in on the shelf.

I was sure that wasn't what happened. She wasn't a sex worker. No sex worker dresses like a librarian. A date and they finally got to third base? Also not likely. No one would want to risk that kind of surprise in the heat of passion. A boyfriend who decided a transgender partner was too risky? Came up with a convenient plan to get rid of her? But he'd have to have an accomplice in the second car—or wait until an innocent driver was in the right position.

Both cars fled the scene. If the second driver had nothing to do with it, was just a wrong place/wrong time thing, why not stop? They'd done nothing wrong, except maybe hadn't hit the brakes in a split second, but that's human, not criminal.

They both turned down the same street, heading back to the interstate.

I got up, made coffee, and told myself again it wasn't my case.

Call Joanne or Danny. Joanne was a homicide detective and a good friend. Danny was also a good friend, a long-ago ex, now happily married to her wife Elly and also an assistant DA. We'd bonded over being lesbian and being—in various ways—in law enforcement. They had been my social circle for a long time. Now we traded off. Alex, Joanne's partner (they hadn't gotten married yet) and Cordelia were best friends from way back in grade school. When Cordelia and I had been a couple, we often got together. Now it was unspoken that they'd do things with Cordelia and Nancy her gal-pal (not married—I am a PI, after all, and know how to look up things like that—not a crazed stalker, mind you, just an occasional curious glance) and then separate things with me. It was an awkward dance, especially given how small a town New Orleans really is.

So, I sat, pondering just about everything there is to ponder—if I should call Joanne and Danny now, friendly weekend chat and then slip in an "oh, by the way, there is a case you might wat to know about" or leave it until Monday and make it business. That I was here alone argued that they were doing something social with Cordelia. Which meant they probably wouldn't want to talk shop.

How easy it is to talk ourselves out of doing something we don't want to do.

And then I considered where was I going with my life—forties, on the later side, with the half-century mark the next big one. Fairly successful in work—a decent living doing work I liked and answering only to myself (and my bills). Disaster in my private life—blew up the one long-term relationship I'd managed to keep. Sparse dating because usually by the time you're my age, you're with someone or there is a good reason you're not.

I wondered if it was too early to spike my coffee with something stronger. And that led me to consider I was drinking, well, somewhere on the line between having a drinking solution and a drinking problem—enough to get through the insanity of the last few years or enough to blur the world and keep it at bay? A glass or two of Scotch in the evening helped the day slide away into the night. But sometimes it became a glass or three. Maybe for Lent this year, I'd stop drinking just to prove I could. Maybe.

I wasn't doing anything useful here. I started to leave, then went to the window overlooking the street below. Still fully parked up. At the end of the street, too close to the corner to be legal, was the big dark SUV. It looked familiar.

The second vehicle had been a dark, boxy car, an SUV or truck.

Or did it seem familiar because that was the car Mr. Privileged Parking tried to jam in here?

I went back to my desk, grabbed a small pair of binoculars, went back to the window, and jotted down the license plate. Not likely, but you never know.

Then I sat back down at my desk.

Write it down, write down every detail from last night, I told myself, before things grow fuzzy and crowded out by the rhythms of everyday life.

The time had been a little after eleven p.m. I had left the bar just around eleven, I remembered Rob joshing me about it being early, calling me a lightweight and offering a go-cup. I'd had three drinks already, more than I was used to with only bar snacks to eat. Plus, it had been a long day and I was tired. I also was still adjusting to going out in public, not used to being around people I didn't know without masks. Proof of vaccination was required to enter, of course. But I was ready to go home before it got too rowdy.

The night had been cool, a burst of rain just ending. I wanted to get out before the next round of showers arrived.

Walking along Rampart Street, transformed from being the seedy edge of the Quarter to now a bustling strip, I was in a mellow mood, happy to have seen friends, to feel the buzz of people around and be in a place I belonged. Happy to still be here and healthy.

Rampart is a wide street, the dividing line between the French Quarter and Tremé, two lanes on either side and a wide neutral ground (or median in the rest of the world). We call them neutral grounds because that's how much the French and the new Americans liked each other back in the day.

Easy crossing the first two lanes, no traffic coming. I was across most of the neutral ground when I heard the rumble of the car. I held that moment—I'd heard, not seen, the car. I'd probably been looking at the ground—people walked their dogs there—not really looking at traffic until I was ready to cross.

I don't remember seeing headlights. Was I not looking, not paying attention, or were they off? I focused on the picture in my head. Past the last oasis of lights at the gas station at the corner of Gov. Nicholls. A rainy night, so no moon to cut the dark. Streetlights, of course, but still it was a darker-than-usual area.

Did they not have their lights on?

And if not, what did it mean? Like me, less than sober (but unlike me, driving a car), and they forgot to turn them on?

Or not wanting to be seen?

The sound of the engine, a car driving too fast, had caught my attention, so I stopped to wait. People tend to speed on this stretch of Rampart because there's no light from the other side of Armstrong Park to the corner of Esplanade.

It was a light car, new and sleek, a blur as it went past, stopping abruptly, the one moment I saw it clearly. The door thrust open and the woman tumbling out, hitting the pavement hard as if she'd been shoved forcefully. It was the back door, not the front door. It had all been both fast and unexpected, a jumble of split seconds. She had been pushed out in the middle of the street.

Had she opened the door to get out and been pushed? Had someone in the back thrown her out? An argument? I tried to puzzle out how—someone sitting next to the door, had pulled her over them and then out? Or reached to open her door and then pushed her out?

The people in the car were vague shapes at best. I'd focused on her, so couldn't even be sure how many there were in the car or any description—male, female, young, old. Nothing. Only that another person had to be in the car because it drove away.

The first car was a creamy white car whose make and model I hadn't recognized. Probably a luxury model, a larger sedan. Big enough to have a back seat people actually could sit in.

The sickening thud of her landing, then her scream, no words, just pain.

Then another shape in my vision. I had been staring at the woman, so I only saw the next car as it came by. Probably an SUV or an extended cab truck—charcoal gray or even black, a boxy shape. But it didn't stop, also driving too fast.

Another even more sickening thump as it ran over her.

I swallowed hard to keep my coffee down.

Got up and walked around the room, taking several deep breaths.

Looked back out the window. The SUV was still illegally parked.

Then I sat back down at my desk.

The SUV didn't stop, didn't slow, even though the light in the next block was well into the yellow range.

It barely made it through the changing light, but the cream sedan followed, also not stopping even through the light had changed.

That was it; the second car not slowing or stopping. Maybe an innocent person would panic and keep driving, but not likely they wouldn't stop or at least slow—a hesitation of uncertainty before panic set in and they hit the accelerator. They both plowed through the light, refusing to be stopped. Two cars involved in a hit-and-run, and both fled the scene as quickly as they could.

The woman in the street. She would have been bruised and scraped from being thrown out of the first car. Being hit by the second killed her.

A brief second before impact, she held her hand up as if to beg it to stop. And then…she was lost under the wheels, her crumpled and bloody form spat out by the back tires.

Her face was bewildered and hurt and in pain. "Why would they do this?" Her whispered last words. "Don't let them get…" *Away with this?*

She knew them. No, I couldn't prove it, but my instinct was that she was asking why someone she knew—maybe trusted—would do this to her. Not anger at being thrown out and hit by a random car, but by a "they."

If I were a police detective, I would track down everyone she knew and recreate her steps that night. Check for security footage and get the license numbers of both cars, if possible.

But I wasn't, and it wasn't my case. I'd talk to Joanne and Danny on Monday. But it wasn't their case either.

I sighed, took another sip of coffee only to realize I was down to the dregs of the cup.

One more cup or should I get out of here?

My phone rang. The office phone. It's Saturday, no one should be calling me here. Then I noticed I had left my cell phone over by the coffeepot and couldn't remember turning the volume back on. I keep it by my bed since it's my only home phone now, but always turn off the volume to avoid getting unwanted notice dings (I'm sleeping—I don't care that it's going to rain in fifteen minutes). I'm not good about remembering to turn the sound back on.

Given the most likely possibility was that someone I knew well enough to know I might leave my cell off and also might be here was the caller, I picked up.

"You took your time answering." Not a voice I recognized.

"I'm sorry, who is calling?"

"Is this the M. Knight Private Investigator agency?"

"Yes, this is."

"Then it would be helpful if you would answer the phone that way."

"It is a Saturday and I just happened to be in the office; I answered because I expected someone's call."

"Do you want my business or not?"

Did I want to say no? You bet I did. But the pandemic times had been slow, and I couldn't afford to be too snooty about what I did. I could at least hear her out. "I'm happy to talk to you about what your concern is. Why don't we set up a time on Monday—"

"I'm a busy woman. I have time today. I only just decided to go ahead with this, and I might change my mind by Monday."

"Okay," I answered, going for the neutral business voice. "Can you give me some idea of what this is about?"

"I'm looking for my grandson."

She might be a righteous rhymes with witch, but she at least had enough of a heart to care about a grandkid.

And cash flow is never a bad thing. "Do you want to come to my office and discuss—"

"I want you to come to my house. I don't care to be gallivanting all over the city. Can you be here in half an hour?"

"It would take about an hour," I hedged. I needed to assert some boundaries.

"It shouldn't take that long to get here."

I had no idea where "here" was, so wasn't going to agree with that. "I have a few things I need to finish up before I can leave. What is your address?"

She rattled off a fancy Garden District location. I agreed to be there in an hour.

"I will see you then," she said. "Don't come in the front entrance, come around to the side on Second. There should be plenty of parking on the street." She hung up.

Come in through the servants' entrance. Loud and clear.

I got another cup of coffee and sat back down at my desk. Part of me wanted to blow this off—she was too much of a pain in the posterior. "Sorry, something else came up, but you didn't give me your phone number so I couldn't call to cancel." A big part of me. But I was also slightly intrigued to see what she really wanted. And my phone wasn't exactly ringing off the hook (did anyone under thirty even know what that meant anymore?) with other social engagements.

I could call this work and avoid the housecleaning waiting for me back at home. Or the filing I really should do if I stayed here.

Or staring at the walls and wondering if this was really the life I wanted.

My best option on a Saturday afternoon was to head uptown and use the servants' entrance.

Chapter Three

It was a big, ponderous mansion on a corner lot, designed to demonstrate how important the builder was. Painted bright white, door white with a big brass lion's head knocker—the one not for the likes of me—a wide veranda spanning at least three sides of the house, with the floor a light gray color, a nod to the reality that people might be walking with less than pristine shoes there. It was a good three stories tall, the bottom two with grand windows and a wraparound balcony jutting off the second floor. The third floor was presumably for the servants and didn't need large windows or any outdoor space. The yard matched the house, landscaped as if awaiting a photographer from a gardening magazine, hedges perfectly clipped and ringing the perimeter just inside the tall wrought iron fence—a double barrier to tell people to stay out if they didn't belong there.

After driving around the block to case the house, I found street parking and headed for the servants' entrance, as ordered. Still grand on a relative scale, with ornate woodwork framing it, but nowhere near as tall and wide as the front with only a prosaic doorbell, no gleaming brass to announce oneself.

It was an hour and three minutes after she called when I rang the doorbell. Three minutes in New Orleans traffic is a miracle worthy of canonization. Still, no one hurried to answer it. I watched a full sixty seconds tick by, mostly because I had nothing else to do except stare at my watch. Debated whether to ring again or take this as a sign of divine intervention and walk away.

Just as my finger was poised over the doorbell in indecision, the door opened. An older African American woman in a maid's uniform stood before me. Well, older as in about my age.

I tried to not let my jaw drop at stepping back into the fifties. I hope you're paid very, very well, I thought, knowing that wasn't likely. She also seemed flustered, as if seeing herself through the glance of a stranger.

"Can I help you?" she asked.

"I have an appointment with..." I realized she hadn't even given me her name, just this address. "The lady of the house." The words felt archaic as I said them. I hurried on to cover. "My name is Michele Knight, I'm a private detective and am here about a missing grandson?" I'd been told to use the servants' entrance, not that I couldn't state why I was here.

"Oh, yes, Mrs. D'Marchant did mention an appointment at three. Please follow me," she said as she turned to lead the way.

I discreetly checked my phone to make sure I hadn't been sucked into a time warp and landed in a different century. Same date and year as the day had started.

The servants' entrance led into a large pantry that had enough staples to last through another War of Northern Aggression, as I suspected it would be called here. It opened to a large kitchen, one clearly used for preparing meals out of sight of the guests, no white cabinets or granite countertops, but a large industrial stove, a long line of hanging pots and pans, and a large sink that could easily soak a gumbo pot. From there, we went into a liquor pantry with hundreds of bottles of wine in racks and just about every kind and shade of booze on the other side of the room.

Finally, I was led into a parlor/sitting room. The furnishings were older, with a few nicks and scars. High quality, probably moved here after they'd aged too much to be shown to true guests but still good enough for the help.

"Can I get you any refreshment?" she asked.

I briefly considered asking for one of their single malts—it might be the only compensation I'd get—but I wasn't going to put her to the trouble. I might have gotten away with it if I were a man, but a woman asking for hard liquor in the middle of the day just wasn't done in this world.

"No, thank you, I'm fine." A polite lie we both recognized. "What name should I call you by?"

She hesitated, unused to people treating her like she had a name. "I'm Dottie," she answered.

"Thank you, Dottie. Please call me Micky."

"I'll let Mrs. D'Marchant know you're here."

I waited fifteen minutes, long enough to regret not asking for the Scotch.

The woman who entered, Mrs. D'Marchant, first name unknown, was short and solid, her back rigid straight as if taking as much space as possible. She wore a rustling black silk dress, designed more to conceal than reveal her figure, providing a deep background for the jewelry she wore. A large shining necklace, diamonds and pearls, which seemed a bit much for a meeting with the help. Her hair was silver, probably natural, but its shine and gloss indicated it was well cared for.

"You are Michele Knight?" she asked, the rasp of age in her voice, but still strong and commanding. "You may go, Dottie," she dismissed her servant.

"Thank you," I said to her as she left. She gave a slight nod in acknowledgment, her footsteps silent as she exited.

"Yes, I'm Michele Knight." I remained standing, knowing the rules of this game well enough to know the servants didn't sit before the lady of the house did.

She bluntly stared at me, finally saying, "Well, you're not what I expected." She sat down.

I didn't ask her what she'd expected. Blond, blue eyed with the skin color to match? I doubted it was wearing a trench coat and fedora. I'm white, raised by white people, as a white person. But people make assumptions. My coloring was dark enough for a lot of assumptions.

I sat. "Why are you interested in hiring me?" I wanted to take control of this meeting—or at least not let her run it her way.

"I don't know that I am, but I wanted to explore possibilities."

Okay, that's the game we're playing. I come to your territory on my own dime and time, most likely a waste. I make a point of glancing at my watch.

"You have other places to go?"

"Yes, I do," I answered. Might as well let her know I wasn't dedicating my free afternoon to her.

"Where do you have to go?" she demanded.

"Why don't you tell me what this is about so you—and I—can decide if there is anything I can do for you. Tell me about the grandson you're looking for." Making it clear I was not the kind of "servant" she could ask what I was doing. Especially if she wasn't paying me.

"I got your name from other people I asked about this, I think it was Scotty Bradley. He said you were good." She hit "he said" just enough to let me know she was dubious.

Thanks, Scotty. Payback for the case I pawned off on you about the guy who was sure Nazi subs came up the Mississippi and some of the sailors got off at Canal Street and were still living here.

"Scotty and I have worked together a number of times." I left it at that. Scotty and I had mostly worked at hoisting a beverage of our choice and talking shop.

She sighed, then said, "My grandson Peterson Greyson D'Marchant has...drifted away from the family. I believe that is unfortunate and would like to find him and bring him back into the fold."

What she'd said wasn't very helpful, but what wasn't said was screaming. He was gay and had been thrown out a while back when gay wasn't okay. But now that all her friends were hooked on *Queer Eye*, it was acceptable to have a gay grandson. I doubted he drifted. He probably hightailed it away from this toxic family and never looked back. She'd hit up Scotty and then me, meaning she was trying to hire a PI who could work the queer side of town. And people don't just drift away from wealthy relatives. They show up for holidays, birthdays, and funerals.

Unless there is a good reason, like they were kicked out and told never to "darken their door again."

I was going to get a very sanitized version of that story.

Or an outright lie.

"Aren't you going to take notes?"

"Are you hiring me to search for your grandson?"

"We are here discussing that possibility. Hiring remains to be seen."

"Your grandson is named Peterson Greyson and he is missing. At this point, notes don't seem necessary."

"How long would it take you to find him? If I hire you, that is."

"There is no set formula or timetable to finding someone," I answered. "I've found people in a few days in some cases, and others have taken months. It may depend on why they are missing. Do they not want to be found? If they have changed their name and identity and moved far away, it may be hard."

"I can't imagine he would change his name—it's a distinguished one."

"It may also depend on why and how he is missing. Moving a long way away—distance always makes it harder. He could be in jail. Or dead."

"He is too young."

"Even young people can die, sadly."

The look on her face told me that wouldn't happen to anyone with her lineage. "So, you are saying that it can take anywhere from two days to six months? With me paying you the entire time?"

"I charge by the hour. You only pay for the hours I work on your case. The ones that take longer usually do take more of my time, but some of that is how long it can take for records or replies to come back to me. If I'm waiting and not actively working on your case, I'm not charging you."

A bare nod of her head was the only sign she was somewhat mollified by my answer.

"What do you do to find a missing person?" she asked.

"A lot of boring records searches."

"In other words, things I could do myself."

"Possibly, but as a professional I subscribe to multiple data sources. It makes financial sense for me since I use them for many things. That would be costly—searching for just one person. Plus, I know which ones are the most helpful. I also know where the shortcuts are, which need experience with them and their quirks. You would first have to do the research just to know which data sources to use, then learn how to use them. I have everyone on speed dial." I kept my tone professional and dispassionate. Maybe she was trying to push me, maybe she was just scared and that read as arrogance. She wasn't friendly, but that had nothing to do with me. Maybe she hated having to ask a dyke PI for help, and this was what she needed to do to swallow her pride.

"I see. I pay you for the convenience of your doing it for me."

"No, you pay me for my knowledge and expertise. I have tracked down hundreds of people and have over twenty years in the field. However, you are certainly welcome to do it yourself, if that's what you prefer." I again looked at my watch.

She would be a decent poker player, not a great one. Her displeasure showed in a bare downturn at one corner of her lips. She could dismiss me and keep going on the search. Or she could admit she needed me when she had been trying get me to sound like I wanted it.

"How do I know you're doing what you say you're doing?"

"I wouldn't still be working and getting recommendations if I took people's money and ran off with it."

"Can you guarantee you will find my grandson?"

"No, I can't. He may not want to be found. Maybe he expatriated to a place that is impossible to search. Or if he wanted to disappear, he may have covered his tracks well enough that he can't be found—it's hard, but not impossible. You need to consider what I might find as well. Occasionally my searches lead to a graveyard. Are you okay with that? Or even if I find him, he may not want to reconnect. I can't promise I'll find him. I can't promise happy endings. I can promise that I will use my knowledge and experience to do what I can to locate him."

She stared at me for a moment, like I'd veered off script and she needed to remember her next line. Finally, she said, "Well, at least you're honest. If I hire you, what would you charge?"

I was honest. I quoted my standard rate, mentioned up front expenses might be part of it.

"So, you might fly off to Las Vegas and charge it to me?"

"Not quite. Not a big fan of gambling. If I found information that he might be in Las Vegas, I would consult you first, explain why it would be helpful for me to go there, and let you decide whether it was worth it to you. I will report regularly. The interval will be dependent on what you prefer and also on what I have to report. I can do daily reports, but that's usually not necessary. Things don't happen that quickly. And the time I spend reporting is part of the time working on your case."

"And I'll be paying for it."

"Yes. You get to decide how much reporting you'd like and how much you want to pay for."

"I do want to find my grandson and I really don't have the time to do it." She made it sound both important and dismissive, vital it be done but the minutiae beneath her. "Can I hire you for two hours and see what the results are?"

She had liquor bottles that cost more than a week of full time from me. I raised an eyebrow. "My minimum is eight hours. Two would barely get me into about half the data sources I'd need to consult." Maybe the display of wealth was hiding a crumbling façade and she really was hard up, but my guess was this was just her way of keeping control.

"Do you need to consult them all?"

"No, I can do them one at a time, but that will take longer. For example, if I find an address and then go to that address only to find they no longer live there, which another search would have told me. Better to have several searches bringing in as much information as possible. It's often finding different clues—an old address, then a not so old address that I can use to find a newer address, that sort of thing." I felt like looking at my watch again but didn't want to overdo it. "We can start with eight hours of my time, but that is the least amount I'll agree to." Take it or leave it remained unsaid. Business was slow, but this was edging into not being worth it.

"Very well, then. Let us hope you can find him within eight hours."

I considered pointing out that I'm not doing a Google search. It's not just putting his name into a database and up he pops. Sometimes that happens, but usually it does take multiple searches. People move, marry and divorce (even queers do that, with new, combined names). They can move down the street or across the country—and then back again to farther down the street. Once I've amassed enough information to feel like I know where they are, then I have to make contact. It's usually best to do that when they have time, not in the morning when they're rushing off to work or at their workplace. Eight hours was possible. Usually it took longer, even working as hard and fast as I could.

I had a messenger bag with me, carting around what I might reasonably need. (Flashlight, yes; gun, no.) I reached into it and pulled out a printed contract, two copies. I handed one to her.

"This is my standard agreement. We can put in eight hours with an option for more, if you choose."

"I do expect you to find him in eight hours," she said as she fumbled in the drawer of a side table for reading glasses.

"I'll do my best, but I make no promises." I managed not to sigh, instead was quiet and let her read. She seemed to be scrutinizing every word.

She finally looked up. "I'd like my lawyer to look this over."

It would probably cost more for the lawyer than my eight hours, but you do you. Blandly, I said, "That's fine. Let me know what your decision is." I started to get up.

"When will you start?" she demanded.

"When we have a signed agreement." I was standing.

She sighed. "You drive a hard bargain."

"I drive an honest bargain. I work when I'm paid for my work. If you want to hire me, you need to do so. Right now, this is my free time—free to you and time that could be spent doing other things that pay me. You're welcome to hire someone else if you don't like my terms."

"And you leave."

"Yes. Like you, I don't appreciate my time being wasted."

"You think I brought you into my home to waste your time?"

I didn't need to get into an argument with her and waste more of my time. "No, I assume you wanted to meet with me to discuss finding your grandson. If you want, I can send additional references. You can have your lawyer look over the agreement. We can discuss this again next week. But now my free time is coming to an end. I do have other things I need to do today."

She motioned for me to sit back down. Either I had made my point or she was determined to waste more minutes of my day.

But I sat. The minutes would pass here or aimlessly driving around or staring at the walls at home.

"I will hire you for eight hours." She made it sound like it was her decision and hers alone. "I expect at least two progress reports in that time, as I'm assuming it won't be just one eight-hour day."

"That is correct. I have other jobs and try to arrange my schedule so that I work for you when there is work to be done. I will give you a report midweek after about four hours and one after eight hours."

"I suppose I sign here?" she asked, pointing to the clearly marked signature line on the second page.

"Yes, but first let me fill out the specifics we agreed to. And I'll need you to fill out the contact info on both." I first filled in the one I had, then gave it to her in exchange for the one she had. I put in the eight hours and two reports on both. Once we both signed, I handed her a copy. "As I'm sure you noticed, I do ask for half up front."

She sighed again, took a bell out of the side table door, and rang it.

A few moments later, Dottie appeared.

"I need my checkbook," she ordered.

With a silent nod, Dottie left the room.

"What can you tell me about your grandson?" I asked.

"I've told you his name and that he's missing. What else do you need to know?"

"The more information I have, the easier it is for me to do my search. And the less time I take."

"If you do it in six hours, do I get my money back?"

"Usually not, a minimum is a minimum. However, if that happens,

I'll consider it." It was about as likely as a zebra running down St. Charles Avenue. But if by some stroke of luck it took me that short a time, it might be easier to give her the money back rather than argue. She seemed like a woman who liked to argue.

"Do you know any of his friends? Anyone he might have kept in touch with?"

"If I knew that, I would have contacted them myself," she retorted.

"What about his parents? Can I contact them?"

Again, a slight downturn of the lips. "I'd prefer not. My son, his father, is divorced from the mother. We are not in contact."

"With your son?"

"No, but my son is busy, works in finance. We haven't kept contact with his ex-wife."

"She had custody?"

A twitch of the lips was my hint she didn't want to talk about the messy divorce and how little her son was involved with his children. "They shared, but the courts favored the mother, so my son had limited contact."

"Any siblings?"

"No, not from that marriage. No one he would be in contact with."

I didn't ask how many marriages her son was on. "School? College?"

"No, not really."

"He was homeschooled?" I asked.

More of a downturn. "He went for a year to Tulane, his father's alma mater, but didn't do well. Then UNO part-time."

Pride goeth before a fall. Clearly, she considered our local state school beneath her family. It's perfectly fine, but a commuter school for a large part, and didn't show up on "snooty college" lists. I wrote it down. I could check there. Colleges fund-raise, and fundraisers are good at tracking down people.

"What else can you tell me about him?"

She stared at me as if I'd asked an impertinent question.

"I've told you more than enough," she retorted.

"You've told me very little. How old is he? What does he look like? Do you have a recent picture? Any of his old addresses? How long has he been estranged from the family? Did he work—high school job, for example? What were his interests—did he belong to any social organizations or Mardi Gras krewes?"

"Why is any of this relevant?" she demanded.

"He may still be involved, have friends who can help me find him. Tracking down one good friend could be the key to finding him."

She again sighed and rang the bell. A few seconds passed, and she rang it again. Dottie appeared. "Dottie, can you bring me the family photo album from upstairs?"

"Which one, ma'am? I believe there are several."

"Bring them all."

"Do you need help?" I offered.

"No, she can do it," Mrs. D'Marchant answered for her. "I don't want strangers in the family quarters." She made it clear I was definitely strange.

Dottie left silently.

I prompted her. "How old is he now?"

"Twenty-seven, I believe."

"What's his birthday?"

"Why do you need to know that? To wish him happy birthday?"

"It can help me narrow it down. If I find ten Peterson G. D'Marchants, but only one with his birthday, for example."

"It's in April, but I'll have to look up the exact date."

Ah, she didn't know, hadn't wanted to be exposed as the not-so-doting grandmother.

"He did some work with his uncle. His mother's brother, so we no longer have contact with him. I don't know of any social clubs or hobbies of his, other than his collecting occasional coins as a child."

"What kind of work did his uncle do?"

Tight, compressed lips. "He worked on Mardi Gras floats and things like that. Not exactly a respectable career."

Ah, he worked with his gay uncle. I could ask Torbin, my cousin. We were the lavender sheep of the family. His superpower was knowing anyone and everyone in gay New Orleans and always being on top of the best gossip—deep chocolate, top soil dirt.

She fidgeted, turning to look where Dottie had exited. She wanted her grandson found, but discreetly, no family secrets revealed. People go missing for reasons, and those reasons usually aren't pretty. I try to talk to clients about the possible consequences—to be careful what they ask for.

"No chance you know his Social Security number?"

"None," she said flatly. "I don't know if he has one."

If he worked anywhere, he had one, but it wasn't my job to enlighten her on employment law.

Dottie returned, out of breath and carrying a stack of heavy photo albums. Mrs. D'Marchant pointed to a place on the floor by her feet.

Slowly, trying to balance the heavy load, Dottie put them on the floor. Then she took the checkbook balanced on top and gave it to Mrs. D'Marchant.

"Hand me the top one," Mrs. D'Marchant instructed, putting the checkbook aside.

Dottie did, before retreating back a few, respectful paces.

Mrs. D'Marchant flipped impatiently through the pages, getting almost to the end of the book before pausing. She removed a photo, then handed it to me.

It was a posed, formal portrait. Senior year of high school? College? A blue background, heavy paper, a suit and tie that looked like they had been picked out—or required—by adults.

"Senior year in high school," she said, forestalling my questions. "It's the most current one I have."

I looked at the photo. Combed, dark blond hair, wide blue eyes. If he were a girl, he'd be called pretty. Long lashes, high cheekbones, and a slight dimple in his chin. The eyes were looking beyond the camera, as if unwilling to confront it and going instead into a daydream.

Even as formal a portrait as this pinged my gaydar. The tie was neat and perfectly knotted, not the usual sloppy ties of high school boys. The haircut was edgy and fashionable, clipped closely on the sides but almost too long on top. Don't make assumptions, I warned myself. Even obvious ones like this one can be wrong.

"Can I keep this?" I asked.

"Yes, I have several," she answered, glancing at her watch.

"A few more questions," I said. I should be wearing a rumpled trench coat. "Was he ever arrested or in trouble with the law?"

"Certainly not!" she retorted.

"I know some of these questions are difficult, but they can be important in finding people."

"We are a law-abiding family," she clarified, in case I'd missed how fine and upstanding they were. "Is there anything else you need to know?" She again looked at her watch.

"What was the reason for the loss of contact?"

She looked away; a slight twitch of her lips told me she was about to lie. "There is no reason, we just drifted apart after the divorce and it's time we reconnect. Family is the most important thing."

She wasn't going to say it. So I did. "He's gay and his father broke off contact."

She whipped her head back to look at me. This was a house of secrets, and she wanted to keep it that way.

"Just an argument and your grandson left, or did he get thrown out?" I persisted.

"I don't know why the past is important," she said.

She didn't deny it, so bull's-eye for me.

"What if he doesn't want to reconnect?" I asked.

"We're family. Of course he'll want to be part of this family."

I nodded in acknowledgment, not agreement. "I'll do what I can to find him. I can't promise a happy ending. When you start on this journey, you need to think about how it will end."

"We are family," she insisted. She turned to Dottie and pointed to the photo albums.

I reached down, picked them up, and handed them to her. I do twice weekly arm and core strength workouts, might as well use those hard-earned muscles.

Dottie took them from me and exited.

"When can you start?"

I wanted to say "when the check clears," but I'd been blunt enough for one day. She wouldn't like me questioning a law-abiding family's finances. "I can start making inquiries shortly," I said. "Do you prefer to pay up front by check or credit card?" I was a tradesman; we were doing trade, and money was part of that.

"Check will be fine," she said as if telling me what to do. She held up the checkbook. I handed her my card so she could make it to my business name, M. Knight Detective Agency, and read out the amount from the contract.

"I expect to hear from you by midweek," she said, handing me the check.

"That sounds fine. My contact information is on the card and the contract." I stood up. I recognized a dismissal when I heard one.

"Dottie will see you out," she said, but Dottie entered the room before she had a chance to ring the bell again.

I heard voices from the way I'd come. The next round of servants to see the lady of the house?

But her lips turned down and she frowned before catching herself.

"Dottie, take this woman out. I'll see to Brice."

"Yes, ma'am," Dottie said. She nodded at me to follow her.

Mrs. D'Marchant was right behind me, hurrying us out.

There were three young men in the liquor room, perusing the shelves.

"Oh, Gram," one said. "We didn't mean to disturb you."

It was an awkward dance. They were taking up space as young men do, making it hard for Dottie and me to get past them.

The one who spoke seemed the youngest of the three, hair a little long, wearing an expensive leather jacket that was too big for him, sleeves to his knuckles. The family resemblance was clear, the same shade of blue in the eyes—hers icy and controlling, his watery and diffident. Hair was light brown, thick and full as her silver hair was. He was about my height, so short of the six feet required of men in this family.

"Mrs. D'Marchant! How lovely to see you," the oldest, tallest one said. He gave her a broad smile as if she was delighted to see him. He was tall and broad shouldered, maybe mid-twenties. He also wore a leather jacket, but his had probably fit a few six-packs—or bourbon binges—ago.

She might be old and she might even be an old fool, but I doubted she was fooled by his smarmy charm. "Garland, and Hugh," nodding to the third man, "how nice to see you here," she said, her smile tight. "Are you returning the bottles you borrowed earlier?" Smile even tighter. She was good at that Southern politeness that could be so nice it was rude.

"Oh, yes," Garland said, broadening his smile as if his charm could fix everything, even raiding Granny's liquor cabinet. "I'm working on it. Supply chain issues, but the two bottles are on order."

"And the champagne?" she asked, adding in an aside to Dottie, "Please see Miss Knight out."

Dottie edged around the boys, having to thread between them. I just pushed through. There was room for them to step aside if they wanted to.

"Oh, yes," Garland said as we entered the kitchen. "That's on the list. I just need to borrow one more bottle, have a special client to meet with."

"Really?" Mrs. D'Marchant said. "Why don't you take the one on the lower shelf? The one in your hand is for a special occasion."

"Oh, sure, no problem," he replied. His tone was flat, disappointed his charm wasn't enough to get him the good bourbon.

Dottie led me through the kitchen, aware that we weren't supposed to overhear this.

Softly, I asked, "Another grandson?"

She nodded. Not a good poker face or she clearly didn't care I could tell she didn't like him and his friends. No words, just her expression.

As we walked through the kitchen, she paused long enough to grab several of the freshly baked cookies, wrap them in a paper napkin, and hand them to me. "Those boys will just take them. Might as well go to some good use."

"Thank you," I said, "I did notice the smell when I came in, and considered snatching one." I smiled to reinforce the compliment.

She walked me out the door.

I turned to her and asked, "Did you know Peterson? The missing grandson?"

She nodded, with a look at the door to make sure no one was in the kitchen. Even so, she pitched her voice low. "Yes, and you got it right. Big fight, and his daddy told him to get out." She looked again at the door.

"I'd like to talk to you about him, but this probably isn't the best time. I'm happy to meet you wherever it's convenient."

"I'm off tomorrow, if you want to meet up."

"That would be great. Thank you." It turned out she lived only a few blocks from where I did. We agreed on after church at around one p.m.

I again said thank you, holding the cookies aloft so she would know it was for them, too.

Then I went back to my not-good-enough-for the driveway car.

I didn't immediately start it. I try to be a bit choosy about the cases I take, but bills have to be paid. This one was definitely in the pay-the-bills pile. I'm not a great believer in happy endings. There are happy moments and happy times, but not happily ever after. I wasn't as sure as Mrs. D'Marchant was that her grandson wanted to reconnect. She'd never been an outcast and couldn't imagine someone turning their back on what she had to offer. I might find her grandson in the sad places—a grave, jail, addiction. It does happen. People disappear for a reason, and sometimes it's because they can't reappear. He might well not want to reconnect to the family that threw him out. We queers have our chosen family—the people who welcome and love us for who we are. I'm close to Torbin, but the rest of the family who raised me and made me feel like I wasn't good enough, would never be good enough? I'm polite to them when our paths cross at the few funerals I attend. Biology doesn't make a family. Love and trust do. Mrs. D'Marchant might learn that lesson from her grandson.

It was time to get back to doing what I wanted to do with my day. I started my car and headed home.

CHAPTER FOUR

I headed home instead of my office, although I planned to do some preliminary work. Even before COVID, I had a serviceable workstation at home—if you're your own boss you don't need to go into the office unless you want to. With COVID, I'd upped my game, better chair and a new, bigger monitor.

The first steps would not go into my case notes. I learned the hard way that even a check clearing isn't enough to avoid trouble. New clients? I check them out.

I could tell by the lack of their cars on the street that Torbin and Andy weren't home. Torbin drives a distinctive red Mini Clubman. We live at opposite ends of the same block. Often convenient and occasionally annoying—he has been known to lift my garbage can lid to check how many liquor bottles are there.

My first choice would have been to hit them up to see if they knew the grandson or the gay uncle.

Instead, I was staring at my big screen, reading through what could have been an episode of *The Real Housewives of New Orleans*— uptown version. Yes, it had been a juicy divorce about eighteen years ago—first mutual accusations of infidelity, which escalated to kinky infidelity, him accusing her of being a dominatrix and her counter that he had talked her into the rubber suit. At the penultimate moment, they managed a soupçon of adulthood, getting out of the newspapers and into a sealed agreement in court.

He was remarried in three months (divorced four years later), so he was either a fast worker or already had wife number two picked out.

No records of her remarrying—hinting that the settlement was a nice one—but she did move to the West Coast. First Los Angeles, then Palm Springs, her last known address in Las Vegas.

I doubted Mrs. D'Marchant would approve me flying out to Vegas to talk to her, so I'd have to try a phone call and give her the easy option of hanging up on me.

Peterson was their only child.

Wife number two produced two more, daughters, both young enough not to be scandal material yet unless they worked hard at it. Only a brief notice about them being maids at one of the Carnival balls. Yeah, we still do that kind of thing down here.

Mrs. D'Marchant herself was properly widowed from her only marriage. She'd lost her husband about a year ago. Maybe that had promoted this search? Even if it's long, life can be short, and people are gone quickly. She had three children: Grayson Peterson, the son who had produced the missing grandchild; and a daughter, married after the requisite debut and typical maid of Rex duties and moved to the North Shore, the other side of Lake Pontchartrain. A twenty-four-mile causeway with tolls separated her from the riffraff of the city. There was also a younger son, the father of Brice. Also divorced, but his wife seemed to have been the breadwinner in the house. He drifted from typical well-to-do white boy failing up jobs: a bank, then a development firm, before finally real estate, anywhere from three to five years in each job. Fraud and embezzlement or just incompetent? Never succeeded but never really failed, either. White boy affirmative action, the most active kind.

I didn't pursue it since it wasn't relevant to this case.

She owned the Garden District mansion free and clear, a beach house in Waveland on the Mississippi coast, and a house north of Baton Rouge, presumably the hurricane hideaway. It meant her check would likely clear. It also meant she had a worldview at odds with mine.

I glanced at my watch. It was late enough in the day for a cocktail and to stop working this only-pays-the-bills case. I made a pomegranate Cosmo since it would pair well with fresh-baked chocolate chip cookies.

If I threw in an apple, I could call it supper.

Cocktail and cookies in hand, I ambled to the comfortable couch in the front parlor. No, it's not fancy, it's just the way this house is—a front double parlor including working pocket doors.

A flash of red went by in the street. Torbin's Mini.

With a sigh, I put the cookies and Cosmo down and headed out to catch him.

He and Andy were out and juggling containers of the kind that carried food. Back from a party?

"Oh, hi!" Torbin greeted me, a little too cheery. He must have been with Cordelia and her new girlfriend.

Torbin was also not a good poker player.

"Back from a party hearty?" I asked, flashing a big smile back at him to let him know I knew.

"No, not really, just a few friends, still being cautious about how raucous a crowd we mingle with."

I considered asking more pointed questions, then decided there was no point.

"Any leftovers?"

"Only salad," Andy said.

"Well, I wouldn't want to deprive you of leftover salad. Odd, that such a healthy bunch would leave salad." Another big smile to drive in the knife that I knew he'd been cavorting with my ex, whom he met through me. Bitter? Nah, only slightly snarky.

"But we can order pizza if you want to hang out," Torbin offered.

"Good pizza or the chain stuff?" I bargained.

"Only the best for you."

I followed them into their house, even carrying one of the serving trays. More proof that I'm not bitter at all.

Once in their kitchen, I said, "No pizza necessary. Just want to consult you in the gay gossip area."

"For that I might need pizza and a cocktail," Torbin said.

"Ah, an afternoon party of mostly salad and hummus?" I said. Snark is my second language.

Torbin didn't answer, just took one of the takeout menus stuffed between cookbooks and handed it to me.

I handed it back and said, "The usual." Half supreme and half veggie because we liked to pretend to be healthy.

"What cocktail would you like?" Andy asked.

"I left a perfectly good pomegranate Cosmo back at home to run here to catch you."

"If you bring the pomegranate juice, I can whip up some," he said.

So, back home to snag both the pomegranate juice and my freshly made cocktail. That way I could drink while he was making new ones. I didn't have to drive home, after all.

Torbin wasn't going to let me drink alone, so he took a sip of mine before asking, "What do you need in the way of queer community gossip?"

"Peterson D'Marchant," I said.

Torbin cocked his head, took the glass out of my hand for another sip, and waited for more.

"Do you know him?" I'd brought the photo with me, and showed it to him.

"Jailbait?"

"No, late twenties by now. The family only had this high school photo," I explained. "Dear Daddy kicked him out for being gay, and now Grammy wants to reconnect." Mrs. D'Marchant would hate being called "grammy," which was why I did it. I don't have to like my clients to take their money.

Torbin shook his head. "It doesn't seem possible, but I don't know him or of him. Maybe I'm past my prime?"

"Not likely," Andy said, giving us all new cocktails. "It's not possible to know every gay person in New Orleans. Some do live out in Metairie, after all," he added, naming the white bread suburb just over the Orleans Parish line.

"He has an uncle who works doing Mardi Gras stuff," I said.

"Well, that narrows it down," Torbin said sarcastically. Mardi Gras is a big business in this city. Floats are worked on all year long, and then there are the costumes and the sheer logistics of putting on the almost month-long onslaught of parades and parties. The pandemic had added house floats—houses decorated as floats for the years the parades didn't roll. People had so much fun they're still doing it during Carnival even though the parades are rolling again.

"Work with me, here," I said.

"Just a gay man who could be someone's uncle and works in something related to Mardi Gras doesn't give me a lot of work with."

I sighed. He was right. New Orleans is a quirky town. I can't tell people to look for the house with the purple door because there are three more purple doors on this block besides mine. Same with Mardi Gras. The uncle might not even be a paid employee. There were krewe captains and sub-captains, and parades throughout the area and surrounding parishes.

"So, you can't do anything to earn my high-class pomegranate juice?" I needled him.

"We're providing the pizza," he reminded me.

"He's the child of divorce, about eighteen years ago, a big juicy scandal in the uptown crowd."

"That narrows it down less than the gay uncle," Torbin answered.

"Accusations of kinky cheating," I added.

"Still not narrowing it down as much as you might think."

With that I got up. Cocktail firmly in hand, I went back to my house, grabbed my laptop, and then walked back to Torbin's.

I sat it down in front of him. "Greyson Peterson D'Marchant is the father."

Torbin perused the screen.

I sipped my cocktail.

"Ah," he said. "I do remember that one. As you know, the straight uptown folks are not my bailiwick. Did not know a gay son was involved. Shame on me for that one."

"He was on the young side during the divorce, so perhaps only proto-gay, occasionally playing with mama's shoes, but nothing more overt than that. Father kicked him out when he came out, somewhere in his early twenties."

"I know a lot of stories like that, sadly," he said, "but this specific one doesn't sound familiar. He may not have been part of the gay scene. Or he might have moved away too soon to be noticed."

I nodded. I'd been hoping that Torbin would say, "Oh, yeah, he's so and so's boyfriend. On my contact list," and I'd be done. And charging my eight-hour minimum. But it looked like I was right. This one would take at least that, if not more.

"Can you email me this?" Torbin asked.

"Sure," I said, taking back my laptop to do just that.

As I was emailing, I said, "Did you catch the murder last night? On Rampart?"

"What?" Torbin and Andy said almost together.

Andy continued, "I read a small blurb about a hit-and-run. Not a murder."

Of course the cops had called it an accident, and the newspapers were reporting it as such.

I told them my version.

"Oh, Micky," Torbin said as I finished, "I'm so sorry."

Andy refreshed my cocktail, adding, "That's awful for you."

"Not as bad as the victim. She wasn't a sex worker," I said, for the second time. "And she might be a patient of Cordelia's." I explained about the card the police found in her pocket.

"The newspaper said it was a man," Andy mentioned.

"A transgender woman," I corrected. "The cops misgendered her."

"Bastards," Torbin muttered. "If they're not real people, they don't have to work hard to solve the case."

"Yeah…but if you hear anything, let me know. I'll pass on what I know to Joanne and Danny. Maybe they can do something."

Torbin shook his head but said, "Yeah, maybe they can."

We were interrupted by the arrival of the pizza.

Torbin and I looked at each other as Andy went to open the door.

"But it's not my case. I have to walk away," I said softly.

"You do," he agreed. "You can't fix every broken thing."

Then it was time for pizza, another cocktail, and catching up on gossip that didn't involve this case.

At some point, Andy yawned. He's a computer nerd, does a lot of consulting work and sometimes keeps nine-to-five hours.

"I should be skedaddling," I said, getting up to help clear away the dishes, minimal as they were.

"Sorry," Andy apologized. "Big job this week and long hours, including weekends."

"I'm honored you made time for me," I said as we brought everything back into the kitchen.

"We had to eat; might as well eat with someone we like to eat with." But now Torbin had some semblance of a poker face. I couldn't tell if he was being general or referring to today's earlier company.

"So, how is Cordelia these days?" I asked. It was probably the fourth Cosmo that did it. "I mean, you were there earlier, right?" I blustered on.

Torbin and Andy shared a look.

"Busted," Torbin said. He added softly, "We are friends."

"You should be friends. I'm not asking anyone to choose."

"Good," he said, then gave me a hug. "I'd choose you if I had to, we've been family too long to ever let you go, but I'd prefer not to have to choose."

I hugged him back. Mostly because I needed a hug and partly to give me time to compose myself.

Torbin's not an idiot. He knows *in vodka veritas.*

I pulled away, turning from him. "Look, thanks for the pizza and the consulting. I should have paid and called it a business expense."

"Next time," Andy said.

I hugged Andy, grabbed my laptop and the cocktail glass I'd brought with me, and went out the door.

Halfway down the block, I turned back and waved. I knew they'd watch until I was safely home.

Another wave at the door and then I was inside.

Why the fuck had I said that?

Because you're the one who is alone.

Being lonely doesn't make you happy, and not being happy makes you do stupid things.

But both for my pride and for their comfort, I didn't pick at the wounds—the self-inflicted wounds—of our breakup. We'd been together for well over a decade. I lived in the house we'd shared (and still co-owned, which was another mess in the wind) with all the rooms and the memories in those rooms. Every time I came through the door, I remembered all the times we'd come through that door, or when I waited for her, or when she greeted me.

All the meals in the kitchen together. The bedroom.

All the memories. What do you do with memories you no longer want?

I eyed my Scotch bottle before remembering the multiple vodka drinks I'd already had.

Go to bed, just go to fucking bed, I told myself.

So, that's what I did.

But I didn't sleep well.

CHAPTER FIVE

I opened my eyes to bright sunshine, far later than I usually arose, even on Sunday. First panic—had I missed my meeting with Dottie?

But no, it was still mid-morning, and I had enough time for the coffee I would need.

Sleep had been fitful, my thoughts flitting from the dead woman to the grandson I was tasked to find to my life and what to do with it.

Maybe I should sell the house. That would be the simple way to solve the problem. Split the proceeds and walk away. Except I liked where I lived, just down the block from Torbin and Andy, a quick drive to my office, able to walk to the river and the French Quarter. Prices had shot up and I couldn't afford anything in this area now.

I shoved those thoughts aside and busied myself in the common morning tasks. Shower, coffee, something resembling breakfast, checking on the news to remind me how cruel the world can be and that my life could be a lot worse.

After one last check to make sure I looked like a respectable private detective, I headed out to meet Dottie. It was a short walk from my house, near the entrance to Armstrong Park where we were meeting.

I was a few minutes early, but she was already there when I arrived. She was sitting on a bench on a path that curved away from the entrance, far enough that no passing car could see us, her eyes closed, face up to the sun.

"Thank you for meeting me," I said as I joined her on the bench.

She slowly opened her eyes.

"It's my quiet time. When the weather is good, I come here when I can." She looked at me. "Not sure how much I can help. It's been a long time since I've seen Mr. Peter."

I wasn't expecting any great revelations from her. It was more my curiosity about this dysfunctional family as anything else. And why she worked there.

"Right now, I'm trying to get as much information as I can." I gave my standard line. "It's helpful to have multiple points of view. Did he go by Peter or Peterson? Or Pete?"

"I was to call him Mr. Peterson, but he told me to call him Peter. I never heard him go by Pete, but he probably wouldn't in his grandmother's house." That actually was helpful. Computers are fast but dumb. A variation of the name can throw a search off. Most likely he would be a Peter now.

"Mr. Peterson for a young boy sounds…rather formal," I said.

"Mrs. D'Marchant is set in her ways."

Dottie was at most five years younger than me. She shouldn't have to deal with this ancient level of "set in her ways."

"I know what you're thinking," she continued. "Why do I work there?"

"It crossed my mind. She doesn't seem like the most enlightened employer." I hastily added, "None of this will get back to her. She hired me to find her grandson, that's all. I'm just curious."

"She pays well. Demands a lot but pays for it."

She wasn't willing to share if there was an answer beyond that it. Why should she? I was a stranger, not someone she could trust. "What do you remember about Peter?"

She again closed her eyes, as if the sun's warmth could bring the memories back. "He was shy and quiet as a boy. Always polite, unlike, well, unlike some others. He liked to hang with me in the kitchen when his folks were visiting, like it was our special place."

"I bet he liked your cookies. I meant to eat just one but wound up finishing them."

She smiled. "Oh, he did, but he also liked making them, helping with the baking, like he wanted to know where the cookies came from. He didn't want to just take them after all the work was done."

"What happened? Why did the family lose touch?"

She kept her eyes closed but gave a quick shake of her head. "They think we don't hear, but we do. They didn't lose touch, they let it go, first with the divorce, like he was tainted since the wife wasn't good enough anymore. Then the whole gay thing. His father wasn't going to have 'one of those in the family.'" She did a very good imitation of what he probably sounded like.

"How about Mrs. D'Marchant, did she agree?"

"At the time, yes. He was her eldest son, after all. Her husband, he was still with us back then, and was even worse than the son. Hollering he'd cut him out of the will and never wanted to see him again. He got his wish. He passed and never laid eyes on him again. Never even spoke on the phone. They all agreed, no gay children in their family."

"Do you know if he ended up with his mother out on the West Coast?"

"When he was young, not after he came back here for school. She was a piece of work, and I don't see him running off to her. He was in his twenties, working in something to do with the coast and marine life. He explained it to me once, but that's all I got."

"Do you have any idea of his living situation when he was thrown out? Did he rent? Live with someone?"

"That was the nasty thing about it. He'd been renting some place that didn't work out. Lease wasn't in his name, so he had to leave with only about a week's notice. He was staying here and that's when they decided to tell him he could be gay or part of the family but not both." Again, mimicking the words she'd likely overheard.

"So, they literally kicked him out on the street."

"Just about. I asked him where he would go, and he said he had friends he could crash with until he figured it out. Then he walked out the door. They thought he would come back. That he'd learn his lesson, but I knew that boy had too much pride to return."

"Do you keep in contact?"

"Would have if I could. But I didn't have a phone number for him, and he wasn't going to call me and risk me getting in trouble. So, no. Regret that." She opened her eyes, looking at me for the first time.

"You can't fix other people," I said softly.

She just nodded.

"Why do you think Mrs. D'Marchant wants to connect now?"

"Lot of things, I suspect. Her husband passing, her son now married again to someone she's not fond of—says the new wife is eyeing the silver already. But mostly because of her ladies' club."

"Ladies' club?"

"Yes, they meet once a month, claim it's a reading club, but not too much book talk going on. Mrs. Fossett is one of the members, and she showed up one day, fashioned up the T's. New swanky dress, much better makeup. The other women commented, and she said she went shopping with her gay grandson, that he was into fashion and got her connected with all the glamorous shops in Dallas." Again, a look at me.

"If you ask me, it's because now having a gay grandson is the in thing with her circle."

"Do you think she cares for him? Or is it just trendy?"

She looked away, thinking, and finally said, "Probably somewhere under all that proper and family, she does. At least, I like to think that."

"What about the grandson we saw on the way out? Would he keep in touch with Peter?"

"Maybe...but not likely. They used to be friends, playing in the yard when they were there together. Peter was older and Brice looked up to him...but now..."

"Now?" I prompted.

"Now he hangs with a different bunch. Have to say I don't like them. All pretend tough boy and jawing on about how hard their life is—only because they mistake ordinary bumps as being hard."

"They can get a new car, but not the exact one they want," I said.

"That exactly. Girls don't go for them, like the girls owe them something. Nasty words about people like me."

"What? Where you can hear?"

"Just a servant, they forget we're around. But I hear. Brice apologized nice like, said they didn't mean me. But if they didn't mean me, who did they mean? Make other people small to make them feel big."

"But only small people need to do that."

"Sad to see. He used to be nice. Now I'm happy when him and his friends don't drop by."

"To help themselves to his grandmother's liquor supply."

"That, her cars, whatever they think they can get away with. She's not fooled, I'll say that, but she lets them get away with it. Family, you know."

"Yeah, I know," I said. Law and order was only for other families, not your own. This was off the subject, of course. I didn't need to know about the found but wayward grandson. I asked, "Is there anything else you can tell me about Peter?"

She had more stories of him in the kitchen, asking cooking questions, helping her. But despite Mrs. D'Marchant's claims of family, they didn't visit very often, just the required holidays, there a few hours and gone. She thought he was kind, one who didn't fit in well with the other boys, but little beyond that.

"Guess I haven't helped you much."

"You haven't given me an address, but you've given me

information that can be very helpful—that he goes by Peter and the kind of work he's doing. Those may be the key."

"Will you let me know?" she asked.

"Yes, I will," I said, realizing that Mrs. D'Marchant wouldn't keep Dottie apprised on so-called family matters.

I stood up to go. "Can I walk you anywhere?"

"No, sugar, I'm good. Going to sit in this nice sunshine for a bit more."

"Hey, did you happen to hear about the accident on Rampart right near here a few days ago?"

She opened her eyes and looked at me. "Read the paper. Sad business. They go way too fast along here."

"Any idea who she was?"

"She? Paper said it was he."

"I happened to be walking home when it happened. The woman was transgender."

"And the cops said it was a man." It wasn't a question.

"Yes, they labeled her a sex worker, but she wasn't dressed like that."

"Hate that. Had a brother, now have a sister, so I know a bit about the life. Says it's more who she is than ever being a boy. She left for Atlanta after Katrina, said it was better there. You looking into it?"

"Not really," I admitted. "But I was there, and I don't think the police care much about solving it."

"I'll keep an ear out. Might hear something."

"Thank you," I said and then left her to her sunshine.

I walked for a while, the quiet streets back here, letting my thoughts roam. With the birthdate from Mrs. D'Marchant, sent in a terse email this morning, along with what Dottie told me—that he likely used Peter as his name and worked in marine sciences—or had, that might be enough. I decided not to include my talk with Dottie in my billing—or my report. Mrs. D'Marchant didn't need to know her servants talked behind her back.

Chapter Six

A h, Monday, why do you have to show up every week without fail? I was up, sipping coffee at my usual weekday hours. I caught up on email and such at home while caffeinating myself and eating something resembling breakfast, not-completely-stale beignets that had been left in the refrigerator three days ago.

I needed to call Joanne or Danny today and I didn't want to. I made the bargain that it could wait until I was at my office, so I was safe if I stayed home.

But even I can't procrastinate the entire day away. I left a bit after nine, my rationale being to avoid rush-hour traffic, not that I was going the usual rush-hour way.

It was right on nine thirty when I got there.

As befits a later Monday morning, the street was quiet, lots of parking available. People on the way to work had already stopped for their coffee, and it was too early for the lunch crowd.

There were a few people in the shop. The slow sippers, taking their time.

I headed upstairs, one grudging step after another.

The computer grannies were already at work on the second floor. They were good at what they did and just ethical enough to suit me. I preferred walking the mean streets to staring at the mean screens. Well, the not-always-kind streets. I tried to stay away from truly mean ones.

But it was too early to give them this case. I needed to dig a bit more. The more info I gave them, the more easily they could search.

And then I was in my office, tasks looming over me.

Another pot of coffee had to be made first. More email, including reminders about bills. I started contemplating what I would do for lunch, but that was crossing the procrastination line.

I stared at my phone. Joanne, a detective in the NOPD, or Danny, an assistant DA.

I decided on Joanne finally because she would pay more attention to what I'd seen than that I was walking home drunk from a bar. Plus, she was a cop. Plus—and I hated to think this way—she was white. Danny was not. The detective on this case didn't strike me as being on the enlightened side. He was probably sexist, too, but they both were women. A woman would piss him off. Black and woman might bring out the Klan robes.

I dialed her office number. More likely to go to voice mail than her cell, and I could continue avoiding this while also doing the right thing.

She picked up. "Ranson."

Damn, I almost said aloud. I'd already been rehearsing the message I planned to leave. "Hey, Joanne, it's Micky."

"Bright and early on a Monday morning and on my work line. I can't wait for this."

I sighed, loud enough for her to hear it. "I know, sorry."

"You're calling about the transgender woman who was a hit-and-run Friday night," she stated, not even a question. She added, "I saw your name on the witness list."

"Has she been ID'ed?"

"No, not yet. Why?"

"I think the cops on the scene had it wrong."

"How so?"

"They labeled her a sex worker because she was trans, but she was dressed more like a social worker. And I think it may have been deliberate." I explained about the cars traveling together, how it seemed coordinated.

Joanne said when I finished, "Well, damn, it might be true, but it'll be hard to prove. I can nudge and prod a bit, but it's not my case. Even if it were, it would be challenging—only chance would be to track down the cars and see if anyone will talk." She took a long breath. "You've done your duty. If I hear anything more, I'll let you know."

"Um, there's more."

"Yes?"

"The cops found a card in her pocket."

"Not yours?"

"No, but it was for what looked like a medical appointment. Gender at CC with CJ."

Joanne was silent for a moment. "Well, fuck, when you said there was more, you delivered more. So, I need to call Cordelia and tell her a patient of hers was killed, might have been murdered, and you provided the link."

"You can leave out the last part. Just mention the card found on the woman."

"And this isn't even my case."

"You see why I dumped this one on you."

"I'll talk to Cordelia and leave you out of it." She sighed again. "Let's get Danny in on this. I think we need more brains."

I wanted to reply that my brain was already used up at this point, but couldn't very well walk away now. "Okay," I said. "Perhaps you should set it up with Danny?"

"So she can't ask you how you happened to be there at that time of night?"

"No," I lied, "so it comes through semi-official law enforcement channels instead of disreputable PI ones."

"I'll be in touch." She hung up.

I refilled my coffee.

Time to work on the case that was paying me.

I'm not a slouch at computer searches. It's a big part of what I do. I farm out work to the grannies when I don't want to do it—tedious title searches and the like—or when it does require more expertise than I have.

Lexis, Nexis, Sexis, Plexis, Hexis, Dildodexis—all the search tools I usually use. I'd spent the last three hours hunting for Peter D'Marchant, Peterson D'Marchant, P. D'Marchant, and even Pete D'Marchant.

And I'd found him. Up until two years ago. Before that there was the usual paper trail. Voter registration with an address, address change. He'd moved four times in the year after he was thrown out, then one place for a year, six months in Baton Rouge, then back here.

Then...nothing. Like Peter D'Marchant stopped existing. Death certificates, jail? Not there. Like he'd stepped through a portal into another world. Nothing, nada for two years.

He could have joined his mother out west. Or met someone in a different place, but there are forwarding addresses. Gone overseas? Met a surfer dude from New Zealand and gone there? International searches are for one very small needle in multiple haystacks.

Death and taxes are the two constants. Since he didn't seem to be dead, I'd check taxes, and financial records. I'd hand that over to the grannies. They're far better than me at trawling through places like that and at hiding their tracks. Ripping people off is wrong. Skirting a few rules for a good cause is the ethics the grannies and I agree on.

It was lunchtime. I was contemplating what to do about my growling stomach when my cell phone rang.

Joanne.

I stared at it for a second, wondering if I could claim I was in the bathroom. Then picked it up. She'd just call again. Joanne was a good police officer because she was oh so tenacious.

"Danny and I are meeting for a late lunch. Can you be uptown in half an hour?" As usual, she wasted no time with greetings.

"Depends on how far uptown."

"LPK at Carrolton and St. Charles."

"Any further uptown and we'd be out of the parish."

"We can meet without you, if you'd prefer."

It would solve the lunch problem, so I agreed.

And I was curious.

LPK is Louisiana Pizza Kitchen, one of those local places tourists pass by but those who live here know. New Orleans is a small city, and it's possible to be most places in about half an hour. Unless you get waylaid by a parade or second line. Those can leave you stuck sitting in your car for over an hour. But Mardi Gras chaos was over, and not too many second lines on Mondays.

The day was nice, our smug winter season, bright sunshine, blue sky. Had to throw on a light jacket. November, with what we call a cool front here.

Danny and Joanne were seated in a corner table away from the few other people in the place.

I waved my vaccine card and headed to their table, taking off my mask as I sat down.

"We ordered for you," Joanne told me.

"Do I get to know what or just wait until it's plopped in front of me?"

"Shrimp wrap," she replied.

Cops are observant; that was my usual order. My grumbling stomach was happy.

She laid a folder on the table. "I brought the scene photos," she said, opening it.

"So glad I didn't get anything with red sauce," I said, with only the barest glance at them. Once in real life was enough.

She and Danny looked them over while I stared out the window.

A waiter came to the table to take my drink order, only to beat a hasty retreat. After a few more minutes, they put them away.

Joanne turned to me and said, "Tell us what you saw."

I went over it again, why I thought she wasn't a sex worker, why it looked too neat to be an accident. "Think about it. You're going down Rampart, maybe a little too fast, and suddenly a car in the other lane stops and throws someone out right in front of you. Even if you panic and run, wouldn't you at least slow or stop for a second?" I finished.

"Yeah," Danny said. "Unless you're too drunk or high for what happened to register. It would be a clever way to kill someone, except you'd need several people involved."

"The more people, the more likely someone will talk," Joanne added.

"Maybe they swore a blood oath," I suggested.

"Honor among murderers? Not likely," Danny said. "People slip up, brag to someone they think they can trust, the girlfriend they're in love with at the time. Three months later after the breakup, she blabs to her best friend who tells her uncle the cop."

"Or her aunt the cop," Joanne said. "Assume at least three people—driver in the front car, someone to push her out from the back seat, and the driver for the second car. That's two people too many."

"So, y'all sit around and hope someone spills?" I asked.

"No," Joanne said. "First, we need to ID the woman. I've called Cordelia but haven't heard back yet."

"The best path right now is to investigate her friends and family," Danny said. "It may have been someone she knows. Someone who didn't want an ex-transgender lover in their life."

"Always check the husband or wife," I said.

"Exactly," Joanne agreed. "If it was murder, how likely is it that a random stranger picked her up only to do this to her?"

Danny and I looked at each other. I said it. "It could be a hate crime. Targeting a transgender woman."

Joanne nodded. "It could be. We can ask to monitor some of the usual idiot social media accounts, see if someone is bragging about this."

"Can you get what's-his-name, the detective on this to do any of this?" I asked.

Now Joanne and Danny shared a look.

This time Danny said it. "No. Or not likely. But I've put a word in to one of the special units and they're planning on taking over the investigation. Too many transgender women have been killed, and the higher-ups don't want to deal with being accused of bias."

"Or losing the LGBTQ votes in the next election," Joanne added.

Political memories are long here. A candidate for the city council lost her bid for reelection by twenty-some votes after voting against a gay rights ordinance. No one wanted to be that person.

We got the right outcomes, even if they were for the wrong reasons.

"I'm not sure just how or who will take it on," Danny said, "but asshole Melvin Landers is not the face the city wants on this case."

Our food arrived.

Joanne had just picked up a slice of her pizza (Greek with olives and spinach) when her phone rang. She glanced at it, then put her slice down and answered.

"Hey, sorry, but this is official. I'm here with Danny and—at lunch. Can we come by and talk to you this afternoon?"

Ah, Cordelia had called back.

I was hungry. I ate while listening to her and Joanne. Or Joanne's side of things.

"I'd prefer not to do this over the phone," Joanne said to her.

Cordelia believed in confidentiality, and Joanne knew well enough that she wouldn't give out patient information in a phone call. In person, Joanne might be able to convince her to give them a name to check out. If the patient was alive and well, then they moved on. But it was a murder investigation. And at least her family would know what happened to her.

I'd finished half my wrap before Joanne was able to get in her first bite.

Danny was eating a very healthy soup and salad combo. Her wife Elly was a nurse, and probably on her about her blood pressure.

There can be advantages to not being entangled. No one to nag me about a fried shrimp wrap. I considered ordering dessert just to be truly annoying.

"Cordelia can meet us around four," Joanne said with a glance at her watch.

Technically we had time for dessert, giving them about an hour to get there, but I knew better to dawdle when they had pressing things to do.

Danny also glanced at her watch, actually a fitness wrist monitor.

"Can we swing by my office on the way there? I need to run in and get a book I said I'd give to her, the latest Greg Herren."

"Sure," Joanne said between bites, making up for the lost eating time.

I refrained from being truly annoying by not mentioning that I really wanted to read the latest Greg Herren. Guess I'd have to do it the old-fashioned way: go to a bookstore and buy it.

"Thanks," Danny said, signaling to the waiter for the bill.

He checked to see that our table was free of crime scene photos before coming over.

I asked for a to-go container. I'd finish it later.

Joanne looked at me and said, "Can you come with us?"

I stared at her. "Me? Why?"

"You saw her. You can describe her in ways that Danny and I can't."

"And how will that help?" I demanded.

Another look between Joanne and Danny, then Danny said, "We may be friends, but we're asking her to break client confidentiality. If you describe the woman, it might rule in or out whether it's her patient or not."

"I can give you a description," I hedged. What part of keep-me-out-of-this did they not get? "She was about medium height with—"

"Not the same," Joanne said, finishing off another slice.

The waiter came over with the bill and my container.

Joanne took it from me and put the rest of her pizza in it before handing it back to me. Bribing me by with leftovers. I saw what they were doing. Points to them for wanting to keep this case active. If I was there in person describing what I'd seen, it put a lot more pressure on Cordelia to give them the name. Combining that with her seeing me in person, something we had been remarkably good at not doing, and hearing a first-person account of the woman's death would be much more emotional pressure than Joanne and Danny going over secondhand information.

"No to the no," I said. "I was an innocent bystander; I'd like to keep it that way."

Joanne nodded, like she knew that would be my answer.

"If she has questions, can we call you?" Danny pushed.

"I'd prefer you keep my name out of it."

"We'll do what we can. The reality is for this to get investigated the way it should be, your name will come up no matter what. It might be better to be open and honest up front," Joanne said, signing her credit card receipt.

When Cordelia found out later, in other words.

I sighed, deliberately obvious enough for them to hear. "If it is murder, I want them caught. I'll do what I have to—but can we make it 'have to'?"

"It would be really helpful," Joanne said.

I mouthed "no" to Danny in an attempt to enlist her help. A slight nod at me before saying, "Joanne is right, it would be helpful, but we'll try it your way."

Joanne nodded and stood up.

Danny and I joined her. I grabbed my to-go box, and as we walked out, I asked, "Any chance either of you have heard of a gay man by the name of Peter D'Marchant?"

"Of the great kinky sex divorce D'Marchant family?" Danny asked.

"Their son. Daddy could deal with rubber bondage outfits on his wife, but not having a gay son in the family. Grandmother hired me to find him."

"Didn't know there was a gay son involved," Danny said.

"Don't think he was officially gay at that point. The divorce happened when he was about ten."

"No, I don't, but there's a whole younger generation I don't know. Why is the grandmother looking for him if her son kicked him out?"

We stopped at her car, but she didn't get in.

"Not sure. I just cash the checks. Her husband died recently. It seems the ladies in her book club now all have gay grandsons who help them with fashion and makeup."

"Guess that's as good a reason as any," she said as she got into her car. "I'll keep an ear out for the name." She shut her door.

I walked Danny the extra ten yards to her car. We hugged, said good-bye, and she was on her way.

Then I was in my car and heading back downtown. I tried not to wonder what would have happened had I gone with them.

CHAPTER SEVEN

I stopped at the office long enough to make a list of everything I knew about Peter D'Marchant to give to the computer grannies. I also fetched a return address envelope and filled it out for the last address I had found for him. A long shot, but as I had told Mrs. D., best to try several things since you don't know when or where you're going to find the key.

I called the number I'd found for his mother in Las Vegas, but it was disconnected. I'd have to do more digging to see if I could find a working one.

I headed downstairs and popped into the grannies' office. They had hired a twenty-something man they called their Gal Friday, insisting that was the official job title for the position.

He was young and male enough to not know what real titles for secretary-adjacent type jobs actually were, so he'd put it on his business card. They'd approved the cards for that reason alone.

"Hi," he greeted me. He didn't seem to know my name. Which was fair since I didn't know his, either. I could argue I was the building owner and thus he should know mine, but I try not to enforce classist hierarchies.

"Is Lena or Clara around?" I asked. They were the ones I usually worked with.

"Just me and the office cat," he said. I wondered if he knew the cat's name. Maybe he was proper noun–impaired.

"When will they be back?"

"Uh…tomorrow?"

"I'll stop by then," I replied and walked back out, petting the cat on my way. I headed back upstairs and put the file away in the locked file cabinet.

I headed back down the stairs. I was my own boss; I could leave before five if I wanted to.

I looked at my watch while locking the front door behind me. Joanne and Danny would be talking to Cordelia now. Would it be brief? Would she refuse to give out patient information without more information and they would leave? Or would they say they understood, agree to let it go, and use being together as an excuse to go out to eat or get drinks together? Call Torbin and invite him and Andy? Add Cordelia's girlfriend?

You could have avoided this, I told myself, by going with them. It would have been a brief, professional meeting. There would be no talk of going out with me around.

I reminded myself that the scenario of them going out was in my head. It might not happen. I was making myself agitated on fantasy and assumptions. Rule one of being a PI is not making assumptions without good evidence.

I stared at my house. It could use a sweeping and general cleaning. But that could wait until the weekend. I was the only one here and the only one likely to be here for the foreseeable future.

I went upstairs to my bedroom and changed into sloppy at-home clothes—no bra, of course, torn T-shirt, faded baggy gym shorts. At least I could be comfortable.

Comfortable for doing the dishes. I can leave dust for a few days. It could be from the stars, after all. But I don't do unintended biology experiments in my kitchen. Most of them got tossed in the dishwasher— oh mighty modern convenience—and a few hand-washed.

I was about halfway through when there was a knock on my door. Either someone thinking this was their short-term rental ("no, wrong block") or Torbin. Maybe he had remembered something useful.

I opened the door.

Joanne.

Danny.

Cordelia.

Oh, fuck.

Instead of snarling "You could have warned me," I stood silently, nothing vaguely acceptable to say coming to mind.

"May we come in?" Danny asked. "We need to talk."

Still unable to think of anything to say, I stood aside and motioned them in. This was still partly Cordelia's house, after all.

"Sorry, wasn't expecting company," I mumbled as I grabbed the

pile of mail off the couch, indicating they should sit. Southern politeness kicked in. "Would you like something to drink? Water, wine,
something else?"

"No, thanks," Joanne said for everyone.

Danny sat. Joanne, Cordelia, and I remained standing.

I crossed my arms to hide my torn T-shirt that was showing more
than I wanted company to see.

Cordelia looked at Joanne for a moment before saying to me, "We
need to talk." Not waiting for an answer, she grabbed my elbow and
led me into the kitchen, leaving Danny and Joanne in the front parlor.

When we got to the breakfast nook at the back, I said, "I'm sorry,
I wasn't expecting this."

"Well, neither was I," she said. "Joanne and Danny said you
witnessed it."

"Is she a patient of yours?"

"Maybe." She brushed off my question. "Are you all right?"

"Yeah, I'm fine." I brushed off her question as well.

"You witnessed a woman being killed. We're still in a pandemic.
How is anyone okay?"

She was right and knew me too well. I wasn't okay but wasn't
going to let her know. She was going to leave soon, anyway.

"I'm okay, I didn't know her. It's horrible, but not a hole in my
life. Why are you here? Didn't Danny and Joanne give you what they
know?"

"Yes, but I have to be sure she's the victim before I release her
name." She pulled a folded piece of paper out of her back pocket and
showed it to me. It was a photocopy of a driver's license. "Is this the
woman you saw?"

I started at the picture. At least it was in color, but still not a great
image. The hair was different, but that changes. The nose and…a small
scar at the end of her left eyebrow. I'd barely noticed it during those
frantic moments, but it registered somewhere in my brain. I looked,
trying to match the rest of her face—the eyes, calm and bored in this
photo, with the painful wide-eyed expression I'd seen. One by one—
eyes, nose, chin—the memory matched the photo. I finally looked up at
Cordelia and nodded.

"Damn, damn, damn," she muttered. "Are you sure?" she asked.

"Yes, as sure as I can be. I remember the small scar. I'm sorry."

"Damn," she repeated. Then brushed her hand under her eyes to
catch a small tear.

I almost put my arms around her, but it wasn't my place anymore. Other arms would hold her now.

"Who is she?" I asked softly.

"Are you looking into this?" she asked.

"No, this is murder and a job for the police," I replied.

"The police don't care about Black transgender women," she said, with an angry shake of her head.

"Danny and Joanne?" I countered.

"This isn't their case. They can only do so much. They told me right now it's considered an accident, sex worker thrown out of a car at the wrong time."

"Was she a sex worker?"

"Is it important? If you're trans, it's hard to find work, and sometimes sex work is the only way to survive."

"I can't make this choice for you. Protect her and withhold, or tell and hope it helps catch who killed her instead of just smearing her name?"

"That's the choice, isn't it?" She looked out the window, at the blooming flowers she'd planted. "Can we make a deal?"

"It depends" was the only answer I could give.

"I'm not comfortable giving a patient file to the police. Can I just pass on anything that might help to you? You can decide whether or not to give it to the police?"

I stared at her.

"I know," she continued, "I'm asking a lot. Asking things I have... no right to ask."

"You're asking me to help find justice for a murdered woman. You have the right to ask that. I just need to consider if doing anything would help. If I can do it."

"I'm trying to do the right thing, but this...it's all so complicated and contradictory."

"It will help the police to know who she is. At least her family can be notified," I pointed out. "It's possible she was the random target of a hate crime, but that doesn't seem likely—she got in the car with them. My guess is she was killed by someone she knew. Even if she was doing sex work, she didn't deserve this. They only way to find who killed her is to investigate the people who knew her, were part of her life."

Cordelia nodded. "Still, would you consider my request?"

I made the decision I knew I would regret. "Yes, I'll do it. But it may not help, and it may get messy. How do I tell the cops how I found the information? What if I tell them something that backfires or that you didn't want them to know?"

"I don't have great answers, but I won't tell you anything I really don't want them to know, okay? And if it comes to that, yes, I'll take the consequences. And…you do investigations with the LGBTQ community on a regular basis, maybe you could claim to have stumbled over it on another case?"

"I can do that," I admitted. I knew enough to know the police wouldn't push too hard on where or how I found information they could use. "If they ask how, I can refuse to answer—take the info and leave me out of it or no info."

"Can you look into this as well?" she asked.

I looked at her. Hair was still the auburn it was when we met, but I suspected a good touch-up job. I'd really hate her if she was older and had less gray hair than me. More lines, on the brow and at the eyes, about twenty pounds lighter than when we had been together. More time at the gym? I'd put it down to less good food. Eyes still the clear blue of an autumn morning.

"I'll do what I can," I hedged. "Ask a few more questions here and there, follow up on some things. I have to be careful not to interfere with the police investigation."

"I understand. Would it help if I hired you? Paid you?"

"No," I said quickly. It was already messy enough. "Nothing on paper. I'm not sure how much I can do anyway."

She nodded. "Okay."

"What can you tell me about her?" I asked.

"Let me review her file first. I'll get in touch later. We need to get back to Joanne and Danny now."

"Can you tell them her name?"

"I'll do that, but that's all for now. I needed you to be sure it was her first." She nodded at me, although we hadn't really agreed to anything. At least, in my mind.

We headed back to the living room. On the way, I quickly grabbed an apron as a top to cover my ripped T-shirt. As I was tying it, I noticed it was the one that said, "Be nice. I can poison your food." Not appropriate, but neither was my torn shirt.

"I really appreciate how well you managed to keep my name out of this," I grumbled as we rejoined them.

Danny and Joanne exchanged sheepish looks. Danny said, "We

just said a mutual acquaintance witnessed it. Could have been Torbin or Andy."

"In which case you would have said so. Not saying meant it was me."

"They didn't mention your name," Cordelia said, "but, yes, I did guess it had to be you."

"Point taken," Joanne said. "Can we move on to the reason we're here? If we can get a name, the more likely we can get traction to move this case to someone who won't blow it off as a sex worker surprising a client. Are you willing to give us an ID?" she said to Cordelia.

Cordelia looked at me, wanting a final affirmation I'd recognized her.

I said, "The person I saw appears to be a client. A card in her pocket listed an appointment for today at 10:30. I'm guessing she didn't show."

Cordelia looked away. I couldn't tell if she was relieved or annoyed. Or both. She nodded slightly, then said softly, "Stella Houston didn't show today. She matches Micky's description of the woman she saw."

Danny asked gently, "Do you know what her...birth name was?"

"She legally changed her name. The name she was given a long time ago doesn't matter."

"I'm sorry I had to ask. Thank you, this is helpful," Danny said.

"If...if it is her, she was doing well. At Southern, getting a degree in social work."

"Do you have next of kin?" Joanne asked.

"Not here, not with me. And...I would need...something legal to do more. Than just this possible name. I want justice for her...but don't want to hurt other patients."

Joanne and Danny both nodded. They didn't push Cordelia for more information. The name was the most important thing. And if needed, they could get a search warrant for the medical records.

Danny said, "We understand. We'll try to leave both of you out of this as much as possible."

"But we can't make any promises," Joanne added. "I'm sorry."

They stood up.

Cordelia joined them. Her phone rang. She looked at the screen and answered. "I'm on my way home," she said as her greeting.

She headed for the door without looking back. Her conversation drifted back. "I stopped at Torbin's to drop off the book I promised him but am leaving now. Yes, I can pick that up on the way…" and then was out the door and I couldn't hear more.

"Someone's been using the location app," Danny mumbled.

She and Joanne headed out the door as well.

I was just taking off the apron when Joanne stuck her head in again. She held up a book. "Can you give this to Torbin?"

"And tell him if anyone asks, he got it from Cordelia?"

"Something like that." She handed me the book—the latest Greg Herren—then, as she was closing the door, added, "The apron didn't cover the rip."

Then I was home alone, in my torn T-shirt, wondering what the fuck to do now.

I should have had another drink that night. Another half hour or hour and I wouldn't have been a witness, wouldn't be involved at all.

Clearly, I needed to up my drinking habits.

Of course, had I stayed home and cleaned the house, same outcome.

The more drinks scenario was the more realistic one.

I went back to doing dishes, since they still needed to be done. And I needed to figure out what I'd gotten myself into and what I wanted to do about it.

When the dishes were clean, the only thought I'd come up with was, since I hadn't had that extra drink when it would have really helped, I might as well have one now. A hefty tumbler of Scotch and I could slide into a buzz and oblivion and the night would slide away.

Make it another blur of a day, a half-forgotten night, and avoid everything except a moment of feeling okay. Or feeling nothing. It was close to the same.

My phone rang.

I started at it. Take the five steps across the room to pick it up? Or pour the drink?

It was likely Joanne or Danny. Or Cordelia. Not answering would only make them call again.

I picked it up, playing phone roulette by not even looking at the number.

"Miss Micky?"

I didn't recognize the voice. "Hello?" I said. "Who is this?"

"Dottie. We met yesterday. I work for Mrs. D'Marchant."

"Dottie! Hi, I didn't recognize your voice. What can I do for you?"

"You were asking about what happened on Rampart the other night?"

"Yes?"

"Woman on the next over block from me is asking about her granddaughter. Said she didn't come home and that's not her way. Asking around if people know anything. She asked someone who knows me, and that's how I heard."

"She might want to call the police. It's possible it was her granddaughter."

"Said she read the story, but it said it was a man, working the streets, and her granddaughter wasn't that type, so it couldn't be her." She added softly, "But sometimes kids don't tell their grandmothers everything."

"And sometimes, the police lie. I saw the woman. She was not a sex worker. Not dressed for it. I think the cops took the easy answer."

"So, it could be her granddaughter?"

"I hope not…but it's someone's granddaughter."

"Can you talk to her?"

No, I can't! But I said instead, "It would be better if she talked to the authorities. I can give you a name of someone in the DA's office, a Black woman, if you'd like." Sorry, Danny.

"I hate to put this on you, but I told her you were okay. I think she just needs someone to listen."

I didn't sigh out loud. I get it, the Black community has an uneasy relationship with the police. I wasn't sure if even listening would help. The only thing I might accomplish would be connecting her to either Danny or Joanne.

Authorities who would listen.

But I was enough of a coward to hope even that wouldn't be necessary. "How about tomorrow in the evening? After you get off work, so you can introduce us?"

If her granddaughter was Stella Houston, the cops would be knocking on her door sooner than later. I was hoping that sooner would get me off the hook.

I've had to tell a few clients the person they were searching for was dead. But while those people had been lost, the looming possibility that they wouldn't return had been there. Those loved ones weren't still waiting for someone to come home like they did the day before. It's why I always broach the possibility that the person you're searching for might be in a grave to my clients. Maybe it helped prepare them for the worst. Maybe it helped me, letting me think I'd done what I could.

But this was different. Too new, too soon, no days and months or years of wondering what had happened. I desperately did not want to be the person caught so closely in this grief.

Joanne and Danny did it for a living. Even Cordelia. She was good at this kind of thing. Let one of them be the one to talk to this grandmother, not me.

"That seems so long. Any way you could come over now? She's close, just the other side of Claiborne from here."

No, I can't! Life's new rules: Don't answer the phone and keep drinking.

"I don't know…"

"Please. I think once she talks to you, she can do what's next. It's like she's holding on to signposts, just one step is all she can bear. I told her I'd do what I could to help."

Oh, fuck and damn. I owed Dottie. She had talked to me when it would have been more convenient and safer not to. "Okay, give me the address and I'll be there in an hour."

"I'll meet you there." It was close, one block over and just above Claiborne. An easy walk.

I called Danny.

"Fucking shit to hell, answer the phone!" I said as it kept ringing. It went to voice mail. "Damn," I muttered just before the beep, leaving the message, "Please call me back ASAP. It's urgent."

Carrying my phone with me, I headed upstairs. I'd requested an hour more to give me time to contact the people who should be there. Danny was my first choice. She was Black and wasn't a cop. I'd give her ten minutes to call back before moving on to Joanne.

I rummaged through my closet. Laundry would have to be done soon. But I managed to throw together the outfit I wore for what I considered my respectable clients. Black twill pants, a dark blue cotton sweater top, and a gray suit jacket. Maybe a bit heavy for the weather, but sober and professional.

Ten and a half minutes. No call back.

I dialed Joanne's number. Same result. Same message.

I debated calling Cordelia, but she was either picking something up or home. That was way beyond my comfort zone. Although out of all of us, she was probably the best at this.

I dithered, hoping for the phone to ring, giving it to the last possible minute before leaving. I even took the car, giving up the good parking space right in front of my house.

The phone remained silent as I pulled away from the curb.

Gentrification had crept across Claiborne. I-10 had been built over it, destroying a prosperous Black business stretch. Because the interstate was progress and a way for people to zoom through the city without having to drive by the people who lived there.

Now the houses were freshly painted, and new, more expensive cars dotted the block. The address Dottie had given me was a few streets away from Claiborne, a block with fewer new cars, and houses that still looked like they had been passed down through generations.

Still no return phone call. Damn my friends and their busy social life! Or work life. Or drinking-and-not-answering-the-phone-like-I-should-have-done life.

I parked across the street from the house. It was a tidy shotgun double, painted blue with cheery yellow shutters and door. Would need to be painted in a few years, but the small yard was neat, with trimmed bushes edging the house.

I looked at my watch. Just at an hour. Could I delay another five minutes?

No, I couldn't. Dottie was coming down the street and she had spotted me.

I waved back and got out of my car.

While I waited, I wondered at how jagged life can be. A day and everything as it's supposed to be. Another day, even a few minutes, and a hole gets ripped into your world. What was it like for a grandmother to be mourning for the granddaughter who was supposed to be the one mourning her? Not just the slash of loss but the whole order torn asunder, the old losing the young?

What possible words could I say to her? Even listening seemed feeble and inadequate.

"Thank you," Dottie said as she reached me.

"I'm not sure I can do much," I mumbled.

"She needs somebody to give her something," Dottie replied, leading me across the street.

I switched my phone to silent but kept it in a handy pocket. Danny or Joanne could at least give her official information. I just had a memory of what I'd seen.

I followed Dottie up the stairs to a small wooden porch.

She knocked softly, and the door opened immediately.

An older woman was there, late sixties or early seventies. She was short, but stood erect to meet life head-on. Her eyes were clear, with unshed tears glinting at the corners. Her granddaughter who always came home hadn't come home.

"This is the detective I told you about," Dottie said.

Guessing she wasn't sure of my name, I stepped in. "My name is Michele Knight. I'm a private detective, not police."

She was silent for a moment, just staring at me. There was hope in her eyes, but it didn't reach the rest of her face. I knew the look, waiting for the blow, the bad news, with just a skein of prayer that somehow, some way, what seemed so horribly wrong would be put right.

I couldn't make it right. It might not have been her granddaughter I'd seen killed, but that didn't explain why she didn't come home.

"May we come in?" I said, to break the silence, create movement and the customary act of welcoming people.

"Yes, of course," she said, backing away from the door and giving us space to enter.

The room was immaculate. Perhaps she had obsessively cleaned while she waited, a plea to fate that a perfect home was waiting.

Or maybe it was always this way.

"Please sit down." She motioned to a sofa and two side chairs. The furniture was old and worn but had clearly been good, like she'd held out for quality when she could. I glanced around, trying to guess which was her spot. A teacup indicated the chair facing the door.

I sat on the couch. Dottie joined me there.

"Most people call me Micky," I said.

That roused her to the polite routine. "I'm Estelle Houston," she said. "I appreciate you coming by. I'm fine to pay what I can," she added. Life didn't come free for her.

"No need. Dottie is a friend of mine, and I owe her. I don't live very far away. I don't know how much I can help, but will do my best to be honest with you."

The name Cordelia had given me was Stella Houston. The same last name, the similarities to the first. It would be easier for me to not know, to leave her in purgatory, unsure if this dead woman was her granddaughter. I could walk out and let someone else deliver the blow. But fate wasn't going to give me the coward's way out.

"It was her, wasn't it?" She had seen something in my face.

I hedged. "I'm not sure. But...it might be. I'm sorry." It is not a kindness to delay a blow that must fall. Grief is hard and brutal, but waiting for it is agony. "I witnessed a woman being pushed out of a car and then hit by another car. I stayed with her until the ambulance arrived."

She reached behind and picked up a photo in a frame. "Is this her?"

A dark night, the anguish of pain. The face in the photo was smiling and happy, dressed in a fancy, sparkly red dress, ready for a night on the town.

The small scar above the left eye.

I stared longer than I needed, to give me time to find words. But nothing other than simple ones came. "I think so. I'm sorry."

"But that was that accident on Rampart, the paper said a man had been killed," she said, grasping.

"They were wrong. The person I saw was a woman. Nicely dressed, a blue dress, low heels, like she'd come from class or work."

"They called her a man," she flatly stated. "They took away what her life was, didn't they?"

"Yes, they did. They have a...rigid way of looking at the world. She was transgender, wasn't she?" I asked gently.

"Yes, but that was so long ago, felt like I'd never had a grandson. She was always different, always knew who she should be..." Then Estelle Houston broke down in heaving sobs.

Dottie pulled a pack of tissues out of her purse, handing them to me to hand to her.

Grief is a blow, a slash, a tear, burning through the body.

Dottie and I sat silently while she let it rip though her, the heavy sobs finally slowing, replaced by a silent stream of tears.

The light outside changed, deepening into dusk. I didn't check my watch. Time wasn't a measure that mattered here.

Finally, I said, "Tell me about your granddaughter."

Estelle wiped her face, taking a sip of her now cold tea. "She kept me alive. I could exist without her, but she kept me alive. Always, always looking for how life could be good. Would find something funny, to laugh at, to get us through even the hard times. I'm a good cook and she was a better cook. We'd fry fish on Fridays and do plate lunches to help get by. She could crack a joke no matter how much the grease splattered." She paused to wipe her eyes again.

"Did you raise her?" I asked.

"No, not at first, but my son wasn't a great father. Streets and the needle called him too hard. His mother didn't know what to do with her. Thought she had a son and couldn't let her be that. After my son passed, her new man didn't want Stella around, so she came to me when she was about eleven. I told her she could dress however she wanted to, but had to clean her room and do her homework."

"What's her birthdate?" I asked.

She looked at me.

"We're going to need to know. The police messed up and we need to correct them."

"You mean they fucked up?" she said angrily.

"Yes, that's exactly what I mean."

She rattled off the birthdate. Unlike Mrs. D'Marchant, she knew it.

"She had some hard times, people wanted her to be one way and she wasn't that way. Sometimes they were…mean about it."

"Fucking bigots?" Dottie interjected.

"That's the word. But she was always welcome here, always had a home here."

"Had love here," I added.

"Yes, always love. Didn't always have much money. But always love."

"How did she struggle?"

"Is that important?"

"It shouldn't be," I answered. "But if she had an arrest record, it's going to come up. I'll do my best to keep that from mattering. It helps to know in advance."

"Yeah, some drugs. I think arrested twice. And…once for working the night. But that was all behind her, back when she was young, late teens. Nothing since. Working in a store, going to school part-time."

"What was she studying?"

"Social work at Southern. About to get her BSW. Already had plans to go on and get a master's."

That matched what Cordelia had told me. I suspected the things she'd hinted at were the sex work and drugs.

Survival in a harsh world.

"What else can you tell me? What should be known about her?" I asked.

Estelle looked at the door, as if seeing her come through it. Only tears, before she finally said, "She was a good person. Cared about people. Gave folks a chance. But not stupid about it. Had so many plans for the future. To support me, so I didn't have to work so much. To do social work with her community and help them in ways she needed to be helped. Keep them from the drugs and sex work. Keep people safe...so many plans." The tears came again. She took another tissue and wiped her face.

"I'm not official, so there are limits to what I can do," I said. I needed to be honest. Her granddaughter would be seen by too many as not human enough to care about.

"You've done more than anyone so far. Outside of those who know me," she added.

"I can't make promises," I hedged. Meaning I wanted my role to be passing her grief on to someone else, walk away from it. It hadn't been my tragedy, and I didn't want to know these people enough to let it become mine.

"Not asking for promise. Only honesty and kindness."

I wasn't sure if I could even do those. "I have friends who work with the DA's office and the police force. I'll contact them."

"Cops don't care. Called her a him, didn't bother to even find out who she was."

"The cops on the scene didn't care, but there are others who do. Not all cops are straight, white, and from the suburbs. We can try to put pressure on the cops so this is assigned to those who do care."

"Think that'll help?"

"It might help finding who did this to her. It might help the next person they try to hurt."

"But you can't make promises."

"No, I can't," I said softly. Stella would never walk back through that door.

"Okay, do what you can. You get hungry, you come over. I can at least cook."

"Thank you. I don't mind home cooking." I stood up.

There was a knock on the door. "Estelle? You in there?"

Dottie got up and opened the door. A group of women, some older, some younger, were on the porch.

The woman who had called out said, "You can't be alone right now. We're going to wait here with you."

"You can't be waiting for her alone," one of the other women added.

But the first woman saw her face and knew. "Oh, honey," she said, "we're going to be here with you. Come, let me hold you."

She was about Estelle's age, her body bountiful to Estelle's spare, a woman who could give a nourishing hug.

I took this as my cue to go. I was the stranger here. Her friends and family would be the ones to help her through this grief. I murmured, "I'm so sorry," and took my leave.

Dottie followed me out.

"That's a world of hurt," she said as we reached the street.

"Yes. I can't imagine losing a grandchild."

"First the son and now his child. A whole world of hurt."

"I came in my car. Can I give you a ride?" And can I change the subject?

"Naw, I'm a block back that way. Take me shorter to walk then you drive the one-way streets to get there." But she didn't move to walk home. "Thank you for doing this. I know you didn't want to."

"Would anyone want to? Give that kind of news?"

"Don't mean it's easy when you do it. You were about as kind as you can be. That's all you can do." She turned to walk away.

I couldn't resist. I had to ask. "How can you stand working for those uptown snobs? You are so much better than they are."

She turned and gave me a wry look. "They might disagree."

"I'm sure they would. But fuck them. They are wrong about so much."

She gave a small laugh. "Guess I'm in a rut. Worked as a maid and cook since high school. Studying wasn't my thing. Got this job a few years in, they paid a little more than the last place. Didn't ask me to stay and help with a party at the last minute. And…I just stayed. No clear path away, and I haven't bothered to make one."

"You are a very good cook. That's a prized skill in this town."

"You've only had my cookies. Hard to mess up cookies."

"Even harder to do this just right. Not just sweet, but a little salt, the flavors all balancing perfectly."

"Thank you. I owe you. I asked you to do something you didn't want to do, and you did it because I asked. That's a big favor. A favor worth a lot of cookies." She again turned away.

"Let me know if you want options. No promises, but I can help you explore other paths."

"Might take you up on that. Don't know you well, but I know

you're kind, and that matters more than most things. You take care of yourself." She walked away and I let her go.

I can fake kind pretty well. I'm much better at pushing the world away so I don't have to be kind to it.

I got in my car.

Physical pain leaves us. We remember the cut, the broken leg, but we can't call back the pain. Grief offers no such mercy; the loss lingers and can ambush us at any turn. How do we let go of the people, the places, even a cat or dog, the changes in life that can't be called back? I'm almost fifty, a half century. I didn't have an answer. In fifty years, you should.

A few weeks ago, one of Torbin's and Andy's cats died. I'm still crying over him. I'd done a lot of cat-sitting for them, enough to feel like I was part of the tribe. Torbin and Andy would carry them to my house, and they both were perfectly happy there with me. The black one, Mr. Squeaky, loved to be with humans, sitting on my lap for hours, following me to the bathroom in the middle of the night for a head rub. Just a cat. Torbin called me to say he wasn't doing well, likely bladder cancer. Did I want to be with him to say good-bye? Of course I did. And, of course, I didn't.

We went to the vet together. Petted him for what seemed like hours, and much too short a time. He was purring as we said good-bye.

I still tear up knowing he's never going to sit in my lap again. Just one cat. The burn of an ember, not the raging inferno of a person, a smiling granddaughter, someone who should be there for so many days and years. It was my closest grief, so I touched on it but knew it wasn't close to the deep, wide piercing grief Estelle was going through.

Why does it hurt so much? The stabbing pain of loss, of the days that will not, cannot return. All the spaces that are made in our lives. Is it selfish? To count on those moments—the people, the places, the pets, the jobs—keep them as solid ground under our feet? Or is it when they change, it's the tremble in the soil that says change will come for us, too?

Or maybe we mourn what we know the other person has lost? They loved coming in the door to tell us about their day. The moments of joy, of struggle together and triumph or just getting through. Maybe our mourning was less about us than about the enormity of what they lost. A grandchild who will never get out of their twenties.

Maybe grief was what they lost and what we lost all together.

And did it matter? It left the pain and empty places. I had no answers. Only the pull of life, not the big moments even, but the quotidian ones, having to do laundry, go to the grocery store, back to work, small moments, an hour, a day. Another day. A year.

When I was young, I was tall enough to get into the gay bars though I was underage. It was a sanctuary from my horrible home life and the brittle façade I had to wear at school. I knew I was queer, but no one else could know. Most of the time I went to the gay bars, with the men, safe to be lesbian, but out of the sexual tug and pull. Several of the bartenders took me under their wing. One wouldn't give me alcohol but handed me a free Coke and let me sit as long as I wanted. Talked to me about being gay, about his horrible high school years and how he had survived. He felt like one of the few friends I could be honest with. I noticed he was losing weight. And then the bruises. And one day I came in and a new bartender handed me a note. His good-bye. So many of those men—and a few women—young and gone. Our first modern plague.

I felt like I'd found a small, safe place only to lose the people who made it safe.

I pulled in front of my house. My parking spot was still there. (It helps to drive a car that only needs a small space in the world of large SUVs.)

I wiped the seeping tears off my face.

This is why the young should bear the hardest losses: parents, grandparents, those we have always known. The older you get, the more you lose, and they all come to haunt you. How many ghosts can we carry?

I'd lost my parents when I was young—my mother just left. My father when I was ten. Taken in by my prim and pious Aunt Greta and her husband, Uncle Claude, my father's younger brother, a man already defeated by life.

I got through each loss because the days passed. The transit of time, putting layers of padding—a day at school or work or traveling or doing chores—between me and the loss.

It's the only answer I have. Time.

What of people who didn't have time? Estelle Houston. Probably in her seventies. Old enough that her age wouldn't seem out of place in an obituary.

I got out of my car.

The world is broken in so many ways. I cannot fix them all.

It was well after five in this part of the world. I could make time pass, this day turn into another.

And then my phone rang.

"Finally!" I said, answering it as I put the key in my door.

Robocall about my car warranty.

"Fuck off!"

I entered, slammed the door behind me, and headed straight for the Scotch bottle.

And didn't pour it.

Grief is also part anger. How blistering angry you can be at what has been taken. A young woman, going through so much. Black, trans, all the ugliness the world can throw at you, and yet she still came through the door every day to a grandmother who loved her, to a life with meaning and momentum and potential.

Some motherfucker pushed her out of a car, into oncoming traffic.

I could drink a large tumbler of Scotch or I could do something about that.

CHAPTER EIGHT

And do what, my rational brain inquired. I had other things to do, other cases to take care of, the routine ones like bar security that were ongoing. Plus, all the paperwork, billing, and filing.

Joanne and Danny might get the case moved to someone who gave a damn. But would it go to someone who knew and understood the LGBTQ community? Especially the transgender community? No, I'm not trans, but at least I'm a lesbian.

Would a straight cop even get that far?

It was, at the very least, a criminal investigation into a hit-and-run. I believed it was planned and therefore murder, but might have to be content with the former.

I already knew what the cops didn't know. Stella Houston wasn't working the streets. She was about to graduate college and go on to graduate school.

Could I solve this? Probably not, I admitted reluctantly. We all want to be the hero but mostly settle for being occasionally useful.

I could work my contacts, use my skills as a private detective and possibly uncover information that the police wouldn't find. I'd be more trusted in the queer community than the cops. I've been out for years, put ads in the local community media—not that I get much business that way, but I want to be supportive. Been to too many gay Mardi Gras balls to count—and a lot of the bars, let's be honest. If they don't know me, they probably know someone who knows me, and that opens doors. People might talk to me in ways they won't to the police.

I might be able to find things to help point the police in the right direction. Or away from the wrong direction. Maybe I wouldn't find whoever killed Stella Houston, but at least I would be able to make her a real *person*, not what she was now to the cops—a sex worker who surprised a client and oh, well, too bad, any normal guy would react like that!

I didn't fight for her enough in life, but I could fight for her in death. And for the grandmother still living.

I threw together a plate of cheese and crackers. Got a glass of nice, healthy water and sat down at my computer.

Three hours later, I rubbed my eyes and ate the last cracker.

Stella Houston would have turned twenty-nine in two months. Was going to graduate with a BSW (Bachelor of Social Work) from Southern University–New Orleans in the spring. She had legally changed her name when she was twenty-one. She was almost nineteen when she graduated high school, probably missed some time. My guess was being bullied or dealing with who she was; her college grades were good, so it didn't look like she struggled academically. There were two arrest records: one for possession and one that seemed trumped up. Misdemeanor sex crime (aka prostitution), but the evidence cited was that she was carrying over ten condoms. The cops decided she was working; the judge gave her a slap on the wrist. Six months' probation and community service, like the judge was skeptical but didn't have time for anything other than a light enough sentence to get her to plead out.

The marijuana charge left her in jail for two months, and she was let go with time served.

Then working. First, with her grandmother in domestic service. Then sales clerk at the local food co-op, probably a crunchy enough place that they overlooked the arrests. Waiting tables, first at a pizza joint, then one of the nicer new restaurants down in the now trendy Bywater area. Not too far from my office, but I hadn't been because I bought down there before the area was trendy and was trying to ignore all the changes—and what that would do to my property tax when it was reassessed. Two jobs switched to one when she started school. She moved in with her grandmother a few months before she started. Stella was still doing the food co-op during the weekdays. She was working hard, not the streets.

The search showed me a picture that matched what her grandmother had said. Stella had a few missteps when she was young but had moved beyond them. She was willing to work hard and be smart about it—two jobs to save money, cutting expenses by living with her grandmother. She was doing well enough at Southern to have a scholarship there and also got a PFLAG award. Might not have covered all of her costs, but good for most of it. With her still working part-time and living with her grandmother in a house that was paid for, she should have been okay. No reason for her to make a bit more with sex work.

I had looked into Estelle Houston as well. Most of the time people are who they seem to be, with the polish we all put on for the public. I had no reason to think otherwise of her, but it never hurt to check. For most of her life she had worked as a domestic, but about ten years ago started a small business cleaning houses. She had done her homework and all the paperwork. She had three full-time employees and a number of part-timers. Again, smart move. As she was getting older, the work that takes a whole body would get harder. Better to hire the younger people and do the work to get them work. She seemed to be doing well, enough to make all the ends she needed to meet. A decent amount in a savings account, a little over twenty thousand. Not a retirement, but a cushion for the hard times.

I could find nothing that hinted at why Stella Houston was pushed out of that car. Schools of social work aren't known for that kind of violence. Nor are food co-ops, but who knows what kind of battles could be fought over organic broccoli?

I reminded myself that as wholesome as all this sounded, with no glaring clues otherwise, it gave me a picture of who she was. The more we knew about her, the more likely we were to find what out had happened. My gut said it was someone she knew, not something random. She'd gotten in that car. Not with a stranger, but someone she knew and trusted.

I shoved away from the computer. This wasn't really my case.

I went back to the kitchen and found the bottle of Scotch.

I could do a little digging, ask some questions. If I stumbled over anything, hand it over to the police.

My paying case, that of the missing gay grandson, would be reason enough to ask around in the LGBTQ community.

I took a sip of Scotch. I wanted to blur the grief I had seen on Estelle Houston's face.

CHAPTER NINE

You shouldn't have had that second drink. Or had it been the third? The morning sun was bright, high enough in the sky to find the slit in my shutters to hit me in the face.

Get up and get going and drink enough coffee to cure the hangover. I forced myself out of bed and into the shower.

Half an hour later I was heading to my office. Some days require motion as if it has meaning. I considered calling in sick, but my boss isn't very understanding about that. Not working means not making money, and my boss, aka my rational brain, liked to not worry about paying the piled-up bills.

I'd packed a big thermos of coffee and a couple of granola bars to not give myself an excuse to linger over breakfast at home. It took a lot of willpower to walk past the smells of fresh baked goods wafting in from the coffee shop. But buying from them meant paying them to help them pay me.

It took about half the thermos for me to do more than sit at my desk and do a desultory check of email and phone messages. I was still expecting phone calls and wondering why I hadn't had any. It took me a few more sips to remember I hadn't turned on the sound on my cell phone.

Two messages. One from Joanne. "Called you. Call me back," was hers. The second was about my car warranty. There was a text message from Danny. *Sorry got your call too late. Will call tomorrow.* Which was now today.

Another sip of coffee. Still waking up.

I heard a noise that didn't sound right. Now I was awake. Outside. From behind the building. I got up to look.

What the hell?

There are two ways to get to the back area. I can't call it a yard because it's mostly cracked asphalt, with only weeds hardy enough to poke through the broken parts. From inside, it's out the back hallway, past the coffee shop restrooms, past several storage closet doors, and through a clearly marked Emergency Exit Only door. Or by climbing over the heavy iron gate blocking the narrow driveway from the outside.

He had to have come from inside, since I would have heard the gate. Even climbing over it made it shake and creak (yes, I had tried it; no, I wasn't entirely sober).

Mr. Entitled SUV was nosing about the back of my building.

I needed more coffee for this. But it would have to wait.

This time I tucked my gun under my jacket and hastened down the stairs. I was going to need to explain private property to him again.

My annoyance hurried me down the stairs. An asshole to vent my frustration on could only make this day go better.

At the bottom of the stairs, I slung around the banister to head back instead of front. The back door was supposed to have an alarm on it, but the coffee shop folks snuck out to smoke and tended to leave it off during the day. I hadn't busted them on it because it was annoying to have to run downstairs only to find a sheepish barista trying to figure out how to turn off the alarm.

I slammed out the door, hoping the alarm was off and I wouldn't have to yell at him over the screech.

"What are you doing here?" I demanded.

"Was in the coffee shop, wanted some fresh air," he said. His smirk told me this was bullshit. He was pushing limits, and he knew he wasn't supposed to be here.

"Let me explain private property to you again," I said. "This is not part of the coffee shop, and they and their customers have no access to it. Including you."

"So, you're the owner of this building?"

"You're the person trespassing on private property. And do better next time. At least get a cup of coffee."

He didn't move. Another smirk. "I'm a private eye, just like you." He put his hand on his hip, pushing aside his jacket just enough for me to see he was armed.

"Private property, dude. Time for you to get back into public space."

"I looked you up. Michele Knight, right?"

"Last time you said you were a lawyer."

"Always a good one to use," he said, pleased with his tricks of the trade.

Not playing this game. "Private property. You need to exit stage right."

"Witness at a tragic accident a few days ago."

"You're right, I am a private eye. Enough of one to know it's not kosher to view police files."

He grunted a laugh. "Nothing like that. Buddies over beers. Detective Landers is an old family friend. My dad was his mentor in the police force, and he thought a lot of him."

The name was vaguely familiar. Right, Danny had mentioned him. He was the cop in charge at the scene.

"So? I did my job as a private citizen. Answered all questions asked of me."

"He's a good cop. But some people don't like honesty, and when the story doesn't match up to what they want to believe, they have to make a stink. Say the cops are corrupt."

"That doesn't change that *you* are a trespasser and need to leave. This may be the way you work, but I don't. You have something to say to me, make an appointment. Don't break and enter."

"I was curious to see what was back here, why you were so adamant no one could park here."

"Because the driveway is very narrow, and a big SUV like yours would have gotten stuck. I'd rather prevent stupid than have to fix it. As you can see, what's back here isn't a crime scene or even interesting." I pulled open the exit door as a signal that he needed to go through it and leave.

"I don't want my friend to get in trouble because some people don't like the way he's doing his job."

"Maybe your friend shouldn't be a bigoted asshole who jumps to the easiest answer even if the inconvenient facts don't fit."

"Hey, I wanted to just have a friendly conversation. See if we could work this out without making a mess."

"A woman died. I'm okay making a mess."

"Screw over a good cop, holler and make a fuss, and you'll still end up back with what it really was. A chick with a dick and an upset customer."

"Fine, you believe whatever the fuck you want to believe. If you don't leave right now, I'm having you arrested for B&E and trespass. You've been repeatedly asked to leave."

He didn't move. "I know a lot of cops. Good luck with that." Again, the smirk.

I sighed loud enough for him to hear. I let go of the door and it slammed shut. Then pulled my gun and aimed it dead center at his chest. "So I'll call the cops after I shoot an intruder. Private property."

That got the smirk off his face. He knew I could fire before he could draw.

"You don't need to be that way," he wheedled.

He was used to nice Southern women and expected me to back down. Yeah, I'm Southern, but nice is not in my genes. Especially for entitled jerks like him.

I aimed slightly lower. "Yes, I do need to be this way. I fire. I have a stranger who won't leave, who has invaded my property and threatened me. Count of three bang, bang."

He lifted his hands. Appeasement, not surrender. "I just want to talk. We can work this out."

"No, we can't. This case is a police matter. You and I aren't officially involved and we don't make the decisions. One."

"Just call off the woke mob."

"There is no woke mob. Can't call off what doesn't exist."

"Okay, the gay mafia, whatever. They're kicking Butch Landers to the curb, and he doesn't deserve that. Suggest he continue as lead and they can bring in some junior kid to listen to the queer community."

"Two. Being a patronizing dick isn't helping your case. In fact, I'm now assuming that you have it in for your so-called friend Butch—is that really his name?—Landers and you're making sure you screw him over as much as possible while being a two-faced jerk and claiming you did everything you could to help."

"What? No, I'm trying to help, just get this settled down." He genuinely seemed confused, not seeing that pissing me off wasn't the way he'd meant to help.

"Really? You have pretty much proven you're as much a bigoted jerk as your friend. If you don't want to pee in a bag for the rest of your life, leave. Not to mention the other things you won't be able to do. You and your friend are too blinded by your bigotry. Can't get why anyone would care that a Black transgender woman died."

"No, that's not true. I've even been to some of the drag brunches in the Quarter. Had a good time."

"You really are trying to make me pull the trigger. I'd prefer not to, just to avoid cleaning up the blood…"

"Okay, okay, okay. Can we put the gun down and talk?"

"No. You can leave or I can pull the trigger. Your choice."

"You're making a mistake." But he was finally moving, hands halfway in the air to make sure I wasn't going to damage the family jewels.

Rhinestones, I'd guess.

"Made lots of mistakes. Shooting you would be one of my lesser ones."

That got a frown, the smirk long gone. He jerked open the exit door, and I heard a muttered C-word from the hallway.

I stayed where I was, gun still raised, just in case he decided to come back, ready to fire.

My arm was getting tired. And my coffee, having gone in, now wanted to get out.

I slipped around the corner, out of sight from the door. I let my arm down and reminded myself the next time I worked out to focus on arms.

I checked my watch.

That had taken about fifteen minutes. And a year off my life.

What the hell was this? Okay, he was a PI and could easily look up who owned this building. Might have done so after I kicked him off the first time, so recognized my name when jawing with his cop buddy. A name with a big-L lesbian attached to it. That's not hard to find out either. Probably assumed he could come around and bully the dyke off the case. Show his gun and talk tough.

I suspected he was telling at least some version of the truth about being friends with the cop on the scene. Butch Landers. (The only men I knew who were actually named Butch were all gay.) I assumed that my going to Joanne and Danny had rippled through the ranks and ruffled feathers.

Why would his friend want to stay on the case? Ego? Not to be pushed out of the way? Wanting to make sure that straight white guys still got to define other people, with no one telling him his world view was as niche as everyone else's?

Something more sinister? Cops can be criminals, too. Even murderers. Was he involved? Someone he knew and was covering for?

Motherfucker, this was getting to be a complicated case.

One that isn't really yours, I reminded myself.

Mr. Big Shot PI was that truly annoying combination of idiot and asshole. That didn't mean he wasn't a problem or dangerous. Clever assholes might at least think through consequences and decide not to be stupid. Stupid assholes? Not a chance. I doubted he'd go away. He wasn't the type of man who would let an old woman like me get the best of him. He might even be stupid enough to pull the trigger of his gun, claim self-defense, and think his cop friends would let him get away with it.

On that cheery note, my bladder prompted action.

I carefully peeked around the corner. Nothing but a few bees at one of the hardier weeds.

I slowly moved across the yard, gun half-raised. I didn't want to be too trigger happy and shoot a bee. Or even a weed.

I jerked open the door, scaring one of the man-bunned baristas coming out of the bathroom. I just nodded, like I routinely checked the back yard while armed. "Snakes," I said as I passed him. That might keep them from sneaking out to smoke for a while.

I set the alarm in case Mr. Big Shot PI was stupid enough to repeat his first mistake.

Then I made my way to the stairs and hurried up them.

I locked my door once I was in my office.

My phone rang. I carried it with me to the bathroom.

"Sorry to be so long getting back to you." Danny. "Last night was a mess. Two serious crimes."

Okay, she had a job to do that didn't always promise regular hours. "Stella Houston's next of kin is her grandmother, Estelle Houston," I said as I did a one-handed unzip and sat down.

"Yeah, we were just following up on that. How did you find out?"

I told her about Dottie contacting me and what happened. I made a point of letting her know I'd tried to contact both her and Joanne beforehand. She let it go.

"That poor woman. We'll get someone over there as soon as we can."

I got up, flushed, and hastened out of the bathroom hoping she wouldn't hear. Don't ask me why, I just don't think it's polite to talk on the phone while peeing.

"I had even more fun today," I said, to further cover the toilet sounds. Old pipes can be so noisy. Then I told her about Mr. Big Shot PI and his warning to me.

"Wow, that's brazen," Danny said. "Melvin 'Butch' Landers wasn't happy about the suggestion that he's not the most sensitive guy," she added. "He's making a stink."

"Think it's they don't like being told there are things they don't know or understand? Or that they don't want anyone telling them they should understand people they don't care about?"

"Who knows?" Danny said. "Probably pissed that politics are no longer on their side. This is a big gay town. Plus over sixty percent Black. This case gets botched, two big constituent groups are pissed off. So, it's pretty much a done deal, and that's upset some people. Do you want to get a restraining order against him?"

I hadn't thought about that. "Maybe, but I don't even know his name. All he did was flash a brief glimpse of his gun. And tell me I was making a mistake."

"That might be hard. Need to find out who he is first."

"I have a license plate."

"Like a good PI."

I rummaged on my desk and found the slip of paper, then read it out to her.

"I'll see what I can do," Danny said. "Wanted to also give you a heads-up. The two cases from last night? Two gay men, drugs slipped in their drinks. When they woke up, they found their phones missing and any account on the phone maxed out."

"Wait, how?"

"Drugged them. Probably while they were out, the crooks used either fingerprint or facial recognition to open the phones. Both men were dumped on the sidewalk in the industrial area near the bridge over the Mississippi. I know you do security for some of the gay bars, so get the word out. Also, if you see anything on security tapes, let us know."

"Could they be linked?"

"Linked?"

"Stella Houston and these guys."

"In what way?"

"Both attacks on the queer community. Maybe there were trying it with her as well and it went badly. Or she found out something."

"Maybe," but her voice sounded skeptical.

Maybe I was seeing boogeymen everywhere after my unsettling morning.

"Look, if you want to, stay with me and Elly for a few days. We have a new puppy."

"House trained?"

"We're working on it."

Just what I wanted, to hang out with a peeing puppy. Danny was saying the unspoken. He would know where I lived as well. "Let me think about it," I hedged. Puppy piss wouldn't kill me.

Or it might lead him to her house.

He might be off drinking beers with his buddies, telling an alternative facts version of our encounter and smirking about living rent-free in my head.

"I'll be fine," I added, making the decision I wasn't going to let him jerk me around.

"Okay. I'll touch base later. I can't believe I'm saying this, but maybe hang out in the bars and check on them."

"I can't believe you're saying it either, but it sounds like good advice."

We hung up.

Do people still hang up with cell phones? Shouldn't it be swipe off?

It rang again just as I left it on my desk to get another needed cup of coffee.

Joanne. I picked it up and answered.

I opened with "I was just talking to Danny."

"Ah, good. She told you about the robberies?"

"Yes, even suggested that I hang out in bars."

"To see if you see anything?" Joanne said. "They could be dangerous." She was in cop mode.

"To get the warning out. Let bartenders and patrons know to watch their drinks."

"Okay, good. Call us if you see anything. No independent action."

"Will do. I've had enough excitement for the day." I told her the same story I had just told Danny.

"Well, fuck," was her response. "I heard he was upset. Didn't think he'd do anything this stupid."

"Wouldn't that be nice if stupid people stopped doing stupid things."

"Dumping on you was really stupid. Like you could change anything."

"I can't just wave my gay unicorn wand and control the world?"

"Not in this lifetime. Even if you hadn't said anything to Danny and me, it's likely he would have been reassigned. A trans woman was killed about six months ago. Her killer hasn't been found. Politics alone means we have to take this seriously and put effort into it. Melvin Landers as a TV face for the police would be a disaster. His idea of a joke is to leave taco wrappers for all the short-haired women and watermelon seeds for Black people. Got reamed out and did the usual song and dance of claiming it was all a joke and people don't have a sense of humor anymore."

"Lovely. How is he still on the police force?"

"Enough old guys doing things the old ways. He got a written reprimand and put on notice it had to stop."

"A slap on the hand."

"Yes and no. Officially it didn't do much, but he's slowly being squeezed out. Not assigned to mentor new officers, hours not as convenient. A not so gentle push to early retirement."

"Does this help the case? I'd like to see justice for her, or at least a real attempt."

"Can't hurt it. A new detective has been assigned. Edmont Thompson. I don't know him very well, but he seems smart and willing to do the work. Also, he's Black and gay."

"From here?"

"No, recently moved from Atlanta. Started about six months ago. Another reason Landers isn't happy."

"So, he would have been okay with an experienced white guy replacing him?"

"Who knows? I suspect not. Doesn't strike me as the kind of person to let go of anything that might be a slight."

"Did he leave taco wrappers for you?"

"No, I'm too old for him to consider I might have any sexuality. Plus, I outrank him. Kind of turd who punches down. Things should start moving. You can probably expect to hear from Thompson soon."

"What should I do about his attack dog?"

"If he really is a PI, he has a license."

"He didn't leave a card with me, but I did get his license plate. Already gave it to Danny."

"Good. Stay away from him."

"He came to my office, remember?"

"Yeah, but if you see him lurking around, don't confront him or engage. If he's trespassing, call 9-1-1. Treat him like any B&E. Landers isn't stupid. He has to know that going after you isn't going to help him."

"But Mr. Big Shot PI is stupid. That's what worries me. Plus…"

I debated letting her in on my suspicions. "Could they be in on it?

Something more than just ego? If Landers is investigating, he gets to decide who and what to investigate."

Joanne was silent just long enough to worry me. "Ego is the most likely. But…maybe we need to know more about why he's pushing back so hard."

"Covering for someone?"

"Let's not talk about this over the phone. Too many people around." Her voice became muffled, like she was covering the phone. "I'll get back to you later," she said. Clearly someone was in her office.

"Later," I said and she was off the line.

That did not improve my day. Maybe it was time to do a working bar crawl and not be at either my office or my home.

And it wasn't even lunchtime.

My phone rang, the official office one. I am supposed to be working, I reminded myself as I considered not answering.

It was probably either Mrs. D'Marchant, wanting to know why I hadn't found her grandson yet and if she could get any of her eight hours back, or Mr. Big Shot PI to curse me out.

Edmont Thompson. He wanted to set up a time to talk to me. We agreed on tomorrow at ten, here in my office. He was brisk and efficient, polite enough but no "how's your mama and dem" chat. I wasn't able to get much of a sense of him other than that. At least he was on the case and not wasting time.

I needed to finish my coffee. I made a list of all the bars I do security for. Some of them were one-time jobs—training or advice about security and what would work for them. Others were continuing—things like regular check-ins, reviewing security tapes to alert owners to things like ongoing drug dealing or underage drinking, being on call if an issue came up. I decided I could go to the bars to warn about patrons being drugged, ask about grandson Peter, and maybe see if anyone knew Stella and who she hung out with.

Detective Thompson was gay, but new in town and wouldn't be known in the LGBTQ community. Queer folks aren't always so chatty with the cops.

Don't do it, Micky. This is not your case. All you need to do is talk to the detective and pass it on. If you stumble over anything else, tell him or Danny or Joanne.

Justice is so elusive, one truth versus another. I wanted it for Stella Houston, for her grandmother.

For myself, for my friends. All of us, kicked out of homes or schools, bullied with the teacher laughing along. The laws that not only didn't include but were against us. I'm old enough to have committed felonies just for having sex with another woman. No, never arrested and charged, but the laws were there—an ambush that could destroy lives for wanting human touch.

Ask a few questions. When inquiring about Peter D'Marchant, ask about Stella Houston. Finding a friend who knew her, who would know others who knew her. Her last words to me weren't about a stranger but about someone she knew.

If I was lucky—and good—I might find that link and be able to give it to the police. I would hold myself to that and not impossible standards.

I grabbed my list of bars and headed out. Since I was going to the bars that evening, I could count that as work time and do needed things now, like going to the grocery and the workout I tried to do most days of the week.

After making groceries—forgetting the things I needed the most—and a quick lunch of greasy grocery store pizza, I changed to workout clothes and headed over to Torbin's. He, Andy, and I had gone in on an elliptical and some other workout gear when the gyms closed for the pandemic. We were still leery about being around sweaty, heavy-breathing people, some who might be of the stupid variety, so we'd kept it going even when things reopened. They had a shed in back for our new gym, small enough that a window AC unit was adequate for all but the worst days of our steamy summer.

I was also hoping to run into them, but it was probably too early in the day for either to be home. I hadn't asked Torbin about Stella Houston. It was easier to just do a "by the way" while passing rather than arranging a time. We were so used to seeing each other that we rarely planned anything.

I did an extra ten minutes, but that only helped my physique and not my curiosity. No Torbin, no Andy.

I left a note on their back door. *Call me when you get a chance.* I also wanted to alert him to the robberies.

Then I left, carefully scanning the street for Mr. Big Shot PI or his hulking SUV.

I showered and changed before driving out to the bars in the burbs. Two were out in Metairie, the suburb just upriver from Orleans Parish, and one on the West Bank, the other side of the Mississippi.

The visits were brief. There were few customers this early in the day. I talked to the bartender or manager on duty. It was likely the thieves weren't regulars, so I warned them to look out for new faces and watch the drinks.

Then back to the sanctity of Orleans Parish. People sometimes ask me why I don't live out there, where it's supposedly safer. Safer for whom? People who all look alike and think alike? New Orleans has its problems, but no one on my block cares that I wear pants and Torbin wears a dress. Do we help clean out the storm drains before hurricane season, or mind our parking spots and not take those in front of someone else's house? Do we put our garbage out where we're supposed to and pull the cans back in? Do we sit on the stoop and chat with whoever comes by? Share our beer when the second line comes?

The things that *should* matter. I don't want to live in a place where people hate or fear people like me. That's what I call not safe.

I headed to the bars with a mostly Black clientele. Sadly, the gay community has issues with racism. There was one on Tulane Avenue, a main artery that was nowhere near the uptown University. It was one of the first major highways from Baton Rouge, built by Huey Long and ending at the Roosevelt Hotel, his favorite watering hole. It had long been tawdry, known for low-rent sex work, but it changed as the city changed. More respectable, the houses around it more expensive. I wondered how long this bar could survive gentrification.

Everyone looked at me as I entered. Not unfriendly, just assuming I was in the wrong place.

The bartender asked, "Can I help you?"

I smiled. "Yes. Don't worry, I know where I am. I'm a lesbian, work as a private detective and know some of the queer cops. I wanted to alert you to what's going on." I then gave him the rundown of what Danny told me: spiked drinks and drugged patrons with their phone app accounts raided.

"Oh, shit, man, uh, woman," the bartender said when I finished. I guessed he was young, barely drinking age himself. "Haven't we got enough hassles without this shit?"

"You have, but assholes usually go after people the system doesn't protect."

One of the patrons said, "Think those guys in here the other night might be them?"

"Wait, who?" the bartender asked.

"Oh, not your night."

"What are you talking about?" the bartender asked.

"Some well-dressed folks that came in," he said.

"You mean white," the man next to him said. Older, probably late thirties.

"No, I mean what I mean. Yeah, they were white, but we get all kinds here. The smell of money and trouble on them."

"Trouble how?" I asked.

"Nothing I can name, just didn't feel right."

The older man added, "Looking around, like they were checking the joint. Didn't head for the bar like most people, like you did. Scoped us all out. Then went to the bar and took the seats next to Teddy. Picked him out because he was sitting alone and had on his nice leather jacket."

"What happened then?" I asked.

"Nothing, really. Teddy don't like being crowded when he wants to be left by himself, so half a split second after they sat down, he got up and left. Rest of us watched them until they ambled out," the older man said.

"They had one drink, expensive whiskey. Then left," the other patron added. "Top shelf stuff not too many people go for."

"Have any of you seen them before?" I asked. I got a chorus of no's.

"Can you describe them?"

"White, young," the first patron said.

"Hair color? Eye color? How were they dressed?"

"Not sure," he said. "Dark in here. Jeans, I think, the kind you spend money for to look beat up."

"Didn't think much of it," the older man said. "Lost tourists who wandered into this bar by mistake."

"Tourists up here?" I inquired.

"City changing. More new people up here," he replied. "Yeah, young side, not more than thirty. Hadn't stumbled enough to lose their arrogance. Probably brownish hair on them, but could have been dark blond to black. It was night and the lighting was moody enough to make the old mean dog in the corner look like a pretty perky poodle."

"How many of them?"

"Two," the first patron said.

"Three," the older man said at the same time.

"I just saw two."

"Three came in. One left right after."

"This important?" the bartender asked. He could see where this was going. "They didn't do anything worrying. Probably just the wrong bar. Or were looking for something—like drugs—and it wasn't here. Not good what's going on, but we don't want any trouble. Cops asking questions here is trouble."

"I'm not going to bring the cops here, okay? You're right, some out-of-place men here isn't much. Would you be willing to call me if you see something? If it's important, I can make sure only the right cops get involved."

The bartender hesitated before saying, "Yeah, sure," and took my card. The other patrons took one as well. Didn't mean they would call, though.

"You really a private dick?" the older man asked me.

"Yep, the real thing. Real isn't as exciting as the movies. Mostly I track down paper trails." I pulled out my license and showed it to him. He gave it a brief glance.

"Cool," he said, then turned back to his drink.

My cue to go.

The other reality is that I often chase a lot of dead ends. Maybe those out-of-place men were the criminals. More likely some suburb boys looking for something and found instead a standard bar, with sedate people drinking and talking about how awful the recent rain storm had been and if their street flooded. They got bored and left.

I continued on my mission. The day was turning cloudy, rains to come in the next twenty-four hours. I parked near my house, since the bars in the French Quarter would require walking no matter where I parked. If I got wet, at least I could get wet walking home. I could also have a drink or two at my last stop and not have to worry about driving.

It was a slow crawl. I had planned to leave a brief message, but people had questions. I didn't have many answers, but I did my best—just repeated the usual advice to watch their drinks, be cautious with strangers, the buddy system. But word was getting out, and people wanted to talk. I was discouraged that I seemed to be the most official person who'd come by the bars—I'm not at all official.

Like the bar on Tulane, some had seen new people come in. And new people were now suspicious. But these were French Quarter bars, and the area is tourist central, and that included gay tourists. Or closeted tourists who want to sneak away.

Or straight tourists making a mistake they'd laugh about when they got back home.

The gay bars should be our safe space. The place we don't need to worry if we're welcomed or not. Or called names. Spat on. Or worse. But even that safety was an illusion, one the thieves prayed on. They entered our safe space, so we assumed they were safe, one of us, seeking the same refuge we were.

Instead, they were hunting.

I trudged to the next bar. It was one of those New Orleans days where the temperature and the humidity were enough to be warm if moving and cold if standing. I was doing a lot of both. Walking to the next bar, then standing as the questions were being asked. Or listening to the latest rounds of rumors. Outlandish as some of them were—aliens from one grizzled beer guzzler, vampires from a gin imbiber—the tales often held tendrils of truth, an emotional reality if not a factual one. One rumor held it was a white militia up from the North Shore (of Lake Pontchartrain) to get gay money to buy weapons. Another was that it was the police, the pandemic bringing out new levels of corruption. Or the well-to-do gays were using their knowledge of the gay community to fund their lavish lifestyles.

Probably crazy, probably all wrong, just not irrational enough to totally dismiss. More dead ends.

At least no one suggested the lesbian mafia.

I had asked about Stella Houston and Peter D'Marchant. A few said the names sounded familiar but couldn't place them. Several of the older man remembered the messy divorce of his parents. Another claimed he'd dated Peter but needed money for any information. Not that I knew Peter well enough to say, but this guy didn't look like his type. "Did you know him as a bar dancer?" I asked. When he said he did, I knew he was lying and saved my money. Two made reference to the Barbara Stanwyck movie *Stella Dallas*. I just smiled and said no, it was a family name. One said he thought he knew a lesbian who had once been a roommate of someone of that same name—or similar. But he had to go home and find his address book to look up her name. Not on his phone, old school. "I like to write things down," he said, "Not have a machine remember it for me."

The lack of information told me that Stella was living as a woman and not doing drag. No sex work out of these bars. Indications her grandmother had been right—a hardworking student making up for youthful missteps.

By the time I trudged to the last few bars, I was tired and discouraged. I had wanted at least one "Eureka, I have found it" moment for Peter, Stella, or even the ID thieves. But nada. A few interesting things here and there, something that might lead to something or to another dead end. Unlike real life, the dead-end streets weren't labeled as such. Sometimes there were only dead ends, and always turning around.

I was heading to my last bar, Q Carré. It was my usual place, they had good burgers, and I was hungry. Plus, it was closest to my house.

It was also the one I'd been walking home from when I saw Stella Houston get killed.

It was starting to get crowded, but there were a few tables in the back. I staked out one, ordered an ooey-gooey cheeseburger with fries and a beer. I had worked out today after all, I rationalized. The extra ten minutes waiting in vain for Torbin to come home was worth at least the fry calories, I told myself. I would eat first and get new energy for the latest round of rumors. It wouldn't do to be as jaded and cynical as I was now and laugh in someone's face when they suggested some Confederate flag–waving militia cosplayers from a small town could walk into a New Orleans gay bar and not look like a timid deer in megawatt headlights.

The burger was hot, the beer was cold, I will survive. Yes, it was playing in the background.

I didn't even have to get up from my table. Rob, the bar owner, spotted me and came over.

"Our bar was one of the places they hit," he said as he sat down.

I have an ongoing security contract with him. He was within his rights to hit me up even as I was eating.

Neither Danny or Joanne had mentioned any specific names, so this was news.

"What happened?" I asked.

"I'm not sure. I wasn't here. It was a busy weekend night. A couple of conventions in town and a lot of new faces. I've tried to look at the tapes but haven't seen anything."

"How did you find out?"

"Guy came back Sunday morning, looking for his phone. The bartender who helped him got the story. He was in town for one of the conventions, came here, was having a good time, meeting new people…then he remembered getting in a cab and nothing after. Woke up on a bench by Armstrong Park by someone walking past. He still had his wallet, so went back to his hotel, crashed out. When he woke up again, he realized his phone was missing. Came back here to look for it."

"Did he find it?"

"No, it wasn't here. After closing we do a major cleaning of the bar. Only a ratty jacket was found."

"Was he robbed?"

"Not sure. Once he realized his phone was gone, he left."

"Do you know if he went to the police?"

"Again, not sure. He didn't leave his name, so no way to follow up."

"Would you be willing to go to the police?"

"And do what?"

"They could review your security tapes."

Rob sat back. "And let them fish through the whole weekend? I mean, I run a clean bar, but some things slip through. The police haven't exactly been friendly when they come around."

He had a point. Although they'd been overturned by the Supreme Court, Louisiana still had sodomy laws on the books, and some in law enforcement thought they should be the law of the land. If they found someone who looked underage and no proper ID check—it can happen on a busy night—or a drug deal, even if it had nothing to do with the bar, he might be shut down.

"I'll let you look at the tapes," he said. "If you see anything specific, then we can talk about releasing that to the cops."

"About how long ago was this?" I asked.

"This weekend. First, it wasn't a big deal, someone lost his phone and it wasn't here. Only after hearing about the others did it click in. I hope he wasn't cleaned out too badly."

"At least he woke up. Street drugs—wrong dose and they don't wake up."

"That's a happy thought."

"Anything unusual about that night? New faces?"

Rob shook his head. "Sorry, nothing I know of. By the time we figured out what probably happened, the night had blurred into all the others."

"It was Saturday, right?"

"It was a busy weekend, nice weather, COVID rates down, conventions finally back in the city. We assumed it was Saturday since he came in on Sunday, but maybe it was Friday. You see the problem?"

"Anything suspicious since then?"

"Outside of the usual suspicious?"

I knew what he meant—fake IDs, bad credit cards, sex or drugs, pickpockets, an idiot carrying a gun. "Even inside the usual—one kind of thief can easily be another kind of thief." They probably hadn't started with drugging and robbing but with smaller crimes, and probably already knew the gay bars. I hoped the police thought of that, since it wasn't my case.

"Oh, wait, we had the lines for the security cameras cut."

"What? You didn't call me?"

"No, it was an easy fix. I had three lesbian bartenders; they all carry Swiss army knives. Mary used some electrical tape and get it back working again. It was hard to tell if it was deliberate or if a rat nibbled on it. And it wasn't all the cameras, just the one out front and the one in the entrance. The ones in the main bar still worked."

Of course they did. I had wired them so if some failed, others worked.

"Do you know when that was?" I asked.

"Yeah, this last weekend...oh, shit. Mary noticed it when we opened Sunday at eleven. But as far as we knew, there was nothing that happened the night before. We got it fixed and forgot about it."

"Do you still have those tapes?"

"Computer files? Yeah. Since we upgraded during the quiet period, we keep about six months' worth."

I sighed and finished my final French fry. "I guess I know what I'm doing for the next few days."

"Well, is this for the bar or for the cops?"

It was a fair question. I charge by the hour, and those hours add up. "Let me look. I'll only charge for things that you should know about."

"Okay, I'll go with that. I'll even throw in another beer on the house."

"And a burger or two?"

"You drive a hard bargain, but yeah, when the grill is open."

"Deal," I said.

"The office is a bit of a mess, but you can move the piles."

He got up. The happy hour drinkers were crowding into the place. I headed to the hallway leading to the restrooms in the back of the house. I went up the back stairs. Upstairs was storage for things that weren't too heavy to come up stairs, a staff changing area, and the office.

It was a small space, more cramped by everything jammed into it: the messy desk, a couch and coffee table plus a few more chairs—castoffs from the bar but decent enough to hold someone—several file cabinets, a computer and monitor on the desk. Against the wall next to it was the security setup: a large computer, and screens showing all the feeds. What I was seeing now was live. I watched for a few minutes, but it seemed like a typical, even boring happy hour.

I tapped into the security computer. We had indeed updated when there wasn't much business. Video takes a lot of storage, and Rob wanted to be able to keep things longer and not have to constantly delate old images to make more room for new.

The system ran all the time, even when the bar was closed.

I scrolled back to the day the wire broke/was cut. Alas, a rat was a possibility. We have a lot of critters in this city. It may have been a raccoon. They are smart enough. An electrical substation was once taken out by a far too adventurous one. It was a duel to the death for them both.

But the current in the camera line wasn't that deadly.

I started late morning on that previous Friday. The system was mostly automatic. The opening crew are supposed to do a check, but that didn't always happen. After that they might not notice the screens were off unless someone was in the office and looking. There's a warning if the system loses power or goes offline completely.

But not if one wire out of five failed.

I set it to double speed. All the cameras were working at that time. There were two out front, aimed to cross to capture a good part of the street and sidewalk in front of the bar. Another in the entry area. Two on the bar, two more covering the rest of the space, and one in the back alley where the garbage was. That one also covered the back door.

The beer was making me sleepy. That, and the adrenaline of the day. Now the cameras were just showing an empty bar—lights dim, chairs on tables—and the cars on the street.

I must have nodded off because suddenly two of the screens were blank. I stopped the feed and scrolled back, going back a good ten minutes before the front cameras went off. Sometime Saturday morning, just before seven, after the bar closed.

I started again at normal speed.

Nothing, nothing.

A dark figure in the back. Hoodie, ball cap, mask. I froze the image and captured it. No way to ID, but I might get height, weight if I examined it more closely.

I started again. The wires were inside, except for the ones for the cameras outside.

The person was at the back door. They got in.

Key? That wasn't good.

Next, inside the bar and heading to the wire box tucked inside the bar in a far corner. They had to know where it was.

The front screens went out.

But did they intend to cut only the front cameras? Or did they not know enough about the security system to understand the wiring? It was a balance of safety and money—we had put the three from the front area on one wire because it saved running separate wires for a long distance.

I watched as the hooded figure scurried across to the back door and out. He disappeared into the street. The back area had a gate, but it wasn't locked. Who would want to steal garbage?

He. I'd thought of the figure as male. What had I seen that made me assume that? Not short, close to high five to almost six feet tall. I looked again at the saved image. Shoulders were broader than most women. No gloves. I zoomed in on the hands. Ah, hair on the knuckles. Coarse, dark hair.

I could safely eliminate half the population from my suspect pool.

I zoomed in on the face. Mostly hidden by the hood and the ball cap, but I could see small patches of skin above the mask. White. Pasty white, even. Or thoughtful enough to put on clown white for any showing skin.

White male, about five ten to six feet, normal weight, maybe a little paunchy, hard to tell with the hoodie, but not heavy. Nor skinny. Probably twenties, but that was a guess.

Why? Was it about the robberies? Something else? Hard to think there were two elaborate schemes going on at the same time in the small town that was the New Orleans gay community.

This fell into what Rob should know. Not good to have a loose key running around unchaperoned. I sent him a text: *come talk to me when you get a chance.*

I continued watching the tape.

One possible drug deal, a couple of clumsy and rejected pickups, a crowded bar with a lot of people I hadn't seen here before. A busy night. Busy enough that it was hard to cover everything. Losing the entry cameras made it harder; since they could be used to scan everyone as they came into the bar, to see who was alone and who was with someone, and then watch how they mingled.

I did notice one person against the wall, in a dark area, nursing a beer, wearing a ball cap obscuring his face. White and young was all I could discern. He seemed to be watching. Was he just shy, or did he just want to listen to the music and watch? Or was he looking for someone? He stayed almost two hours, on the same beer. Then he put the can down on the floor instead of bussing it and headed out. Being a jerk didn't make him a crook. He was too short and slight to be the hooded figure. I couldn't see him when he left or which way he was going.

I followed each camera instead of trying to scan the bar.

Someone took a couple of drinks off the bar, turning his back to the crowd and the camera. They were obvious—the point was to deter, not clean up later. Spiking a drink? I couldn't see what he was doing. He went back to a crowded table and passed the drinks around before going back to the bar for a second round. This time there was no turn.

I scrolled back and got screenshots of the men he gave the first round of drinks to. I'd have to interview the Sunday bartender who'd spoken to the lost phone man and see if any of these looked like him.

This is the boring stuff I do. Details and more details, sorting to see which, if any, mean anything. Ten steps to find a suspect. Or a dead end.

I followed the group at the table. They stayed for another round, then left at around two a.m. All of them seemed a bit drunk, no one noticeably out of it.

And it could be nothing, not the right group at all.

I continued watching. There is no legally mandated last call in New Orleans. Some bars go for twenty-four hours. Rob closed at six a.m., kind enough to wait until breakfast places were open for the greasy food to absorb the booze.

Around three, someone came in who looked familiar—but not from here. I froze and grabbed a screen shot of him. Nice leather jacket, open because it was probably now too tight for his paunch. Confident, even smug look. By himself. Then it clicked. He was the booze moocher I'd seen at Mrs. D'Marchant's house, the friend of her other grandson. I had pegged him as annoyingly straight, so what was he doing here?

He got a top shelf drink and starting chatting with the people around him at the bar. He stayed long enough to finish his drink.

Closeted? Or the kind of asshole who wanted to watch the "freak" show to reassure himself he was better? I'd judged him on a few minutes of interaction. Easy to misjudge when you make snap judgments. Even if I was right about him being an asshole, he could still be gay and just hanging out at the bar the same way I did.

Did he have anything to do with the robberies?

Or was my mind too suspicious? He had one drink, hands on the glass, didn't give anyone anything.

Three separate things, I reminded myself. Finding Mrs. D'Marchant's grandson. Asking about Stella Houston. The bar robberies, including one that might have happened here. New Orleans is a small city, but it is a city, about one million in the metro area. Plenty of space for multiple nefarious things to go on in the queer community at the same time.

Shortly after he left, a large group of mixed men and women came in. The women looked straight. Yeah, I know, lots of lesbians with long hair, but their energy was focused on the men. It's not really gaydar, just common sense for those of us who don't default to assume everyone is hetero. They had to push their way to the bar since it was so crowded. About seven of them. This didn't look like the first bar they'd been to—their gestures were sloppy and broad, and one of the women was tottering from a combination of high heels and too many high-octane cocktails. They were having a good time and wanted everyone else to know. They ordered well drinks—no high spenders here—of the boozy variety, like Hurricanes and daiquiris, about every color in the rainbow.

I can admit that I didn't like them because they're invading our space. Now that queers aren't the pariahs we used to be, straight woman have started coming to gay bars. I get it, they can dance and not have men constantly harassing them. But we've become aware of outsiders looking in at us. It's usually the men's bars, but New Orleans is small enough that some of them are more mixed. I had to confess I got so annoyed once at a bridal party that I rounded up all the butch women and we hit on them, using every obnoxious pickup line we could think of—"You come here often?" "What's your sign?" "How many cats do you have? You like pussies, don't you?" Yeah, I wasn't sober when I suggested it, but we had fun. I suspected they didn't. Go to the champagne bar next time, girls.

The group got their drinks, grabbed any empty chair, and made a seating circle for themselves, making everyone from the back tables and dance floor have to go around them to get to the bar.

Typical.

Another group came in, also mixed men and women, and mixed racially this time as well. Closer look said that at least one of the women was likely trans. Then I wondered why I assumed that. Taller than the average woman? But I'm taller, too. Facial structure? Early in transition, while the outer façade is catching up to the real person? A combination of things, including being in this bar?

Then I realized I don't know and I can't know. Most of the people I knew were transgender was because they told me. The markers of visible gender are fragile and easily changed—hair, makeup, clothing. I've been called "sir" more times than I can keep track of. Why? I'm tall and don't wear much makeup. Those assumptions were wrong and mine—and others'—could easily be as well. For a few people, I might make assumptions and I might be right, but that was at best a guess, based on little more than those who called me sir, a narrow and shallow view of gender.

Maybe the big question was why I wanted to know. Other people are making the same assumptions, I reminded myself, and I'm looking into the murder of a trans woman. Our assumptions might be wrong, but theirs might kill people; mine were merely boorish and nosy.

There were five in the group. When a spot opened at the bar, one of them took it to get everyone's drink order, the others waiting behind him. The energy of this group was different. Out to have a good time. Not sober, but not drunk enough to forget other people were there, too. They got their drinks and retreated to a just-vacated table. Two kept standing since there weren't enough chairs.

Other people drifted in and out. Some couples, some small groups of three or four.

The two larger groups converged at the bar, one with four of them all pushing in, the other with two, one at the bar and one behind to help carry drinks. One of the straight women sloshed her drink on one of the women from the other group.

The first woman apologized, grabbed napkins, and brought her another drink. Being nice? Then they started chatting together, first the two women, then others in the groups.

Everyone happy and having a good time, low light and high alcohol. I felt like a voyeur, outside their party but unseen, watching.

Focus, I reminded myself. These boisterous and loud people might be fun to watch, but I needed to look at the dark corners, to watch the people watching.

But I saw nothing. Well, I saw lots of things: People openly making out, hands on thighs. A couple of people swallowing a pill—could be anything from aspirin to something illegal. But it was self-administered, not slipped in a drink. Drinks were passed around, but nothing looked like anyone spiking someone else's drink.

A very faint glow showed at the camera out in back. Sunrise sneaking up on the revelers.

Someone cut the cords for a reason. I hadn't seen it. I didn't want to give this to the cops, even though they might be able to spot something I hadn't. I'd have to review them again before suggesting that to Rob.

I glanced at my watch to see what the time in real life was. Almost nine p.m. I was going to start yawning any moment.

Rob popped into the office. "I got your text. What's up?"

"It was a rat of the human variety," I said, then pulled up the saved clip of the man with the key he shouldn't have had.

"Well, I'll be fucked," Rob said at the end.

"Tell me about your keys."

"Four of us have keys. Me, Mary my head bartender, and Peg the assistant manager, aka chief cook and bottle washer. And you. All the other keys are kept here in the office."

"Any keys missing?" I asked.

Rob got up and opened a small locked key box beside his desk. It was metal and attached to the wall. "All seem to be here. We do a check at opening and closing. As needed, we hand out keys for each shift and collect them at the end. People need to get into storage or take garbage out, that sort of thing." He did a slow count. "They're all here."

I knew both Mary and Peg; they had worked here for years. And I also knew Rob and me.

"Could someone make a copy?" I asked.

Rob sat back. "Maybe. But they would have to leave here during their shift to get a key made. The rule is, if someone has to leave, they give the keys back. But I can't promise it happened every time."

"Any likely suspects?" I asked. "Current or past employees?"

"You think it was someone who worked here?"

"Likely. Much harder for a customer. Employees would know about the keys, and the security cameras, since checking them is part of the opening routine."

"No one comes to mind," he said, shaking his head. "I mean, people come and go, bartenders, barbacks."

"How about cleaning?"

"No, they're scheduled to come right at closing and are only here with other staff."

"Then we're back to employees."

"Fuck and damn. I'm going to have to pay you for this, aren't I?" But he said it with a rueful grin.

"Yep. You could call the police. It's B&E, but who's more likely to figure it out?" I continued, "You can do this quick and dirty, and change all the locks."

He groaned. All the doors here was keyed to one master key, so every lock would have to be rekeyed. That would be a pain and neither quick nor cheap.

"But that doesn't solve how someone got the key in the first place and if they could do it again," I pointed out.

"Okay, okay. I was hoping to drink most of my profits, but clearly, I'll be giving them to you instead."

"Sorry. I'll do this as quickly and as cheaply as I can. If I can't figure it out without an exhaustive investigation, I'll let you know and we can go from there."

He got up. "I can throw a padlock on the handles of the back-alley door," he said. "Key still works for the front, but it's bright and lot of people out there. I can't padlock both doors from inside and expect to get out."

"I'll come back tomorrow," I said. "I'd like to look at your employee files and also download the security tapes to my computer so I can review them at home."

"Sounds good. I'll be here by about eleven a.m. And thanks, Micky. I needed to know this."

"My day job," I said. "Oh, Rob, do you know a man named Peter D'Marchant or a woman named Stella Houston?"

He turned back and looked at me. "Yeah, I know Stella."

"You do? How?"

"She came in a while back, about four to six months ago, asking for a donation for a project to benefit trans women."

"Which one?"

"I'd have to look it up. She gave me a flyer. I liked her. She did it the right way, gave me all the details—which I've obviously forgotten—paperwork for tax purposes. It was a food donation for a fundraiser to help trans people with expenses. She explained it's costly to get a name change or things like hormones for those who don't have insurance to cover it."

"Did you donate?"

"Yeah, I did. Mostly I do, because you can't take it with you. I try to ask enough obnoxious questions to knock out the really sketchy ones. Get a number from the known community organizations, CrescentCare,

Project Lazarus, and the like. Some from the well-meaning, heart but not head in the right place. Stella had her shit together. Organized, a plan for exactly how things would be used."

"How much?"

"About five hundred in food and supplies, like paper plates and cups. I threw in an extra two-fifty in cash. What really impressed me is that she came back about a week after the fundraiser to tell me what they raised, how my stuff was used, and what they could do with the money—how many people they could pay name change expenses for, how they were channeling the hormone/medical money through medical providers who served the trans community. Asked me to get the word out for people in need."

"Bet you donated another chunk then?"

"Naw, I blew her off and told her to stop wasting my time."

"How much?"

"Okay, another five hundred. Louisiana makes it expensive to change your name. We talked about doing a big fundraiser here in the summer. Why are you asking about her? Don't tell me she's a scam artist."

"I wish that's what I was telling you," I said. "She was killed last weekend. The hit-and-run on Rampart."

"Wait, what? I read about this. It said it was a man who was killed."

"The police misgendered her."

"Oh, shit, hard to believe she could go like that. I ran into her on the street a little while back. She seemed so happy and alive." He shook his head sadly. "I guess only the good die young."

"I witnessed it as I was walking home," I said.

Rob looked shocked. I gave him the bare details—he knew her and didn't need to have the images in his head.

"You think it was murder?" he said when I finished.

"I don't know for sure, but it should be investigated. Negligent homicide if not intentional."

"Should I hire you to look into that as well? That happened pretty close to here, and that's bad for business."

I knew him well enough to know he wasn't worried about his bottom line. Rob played a cynical Chardonnay swiller, but he was one of the kindest and most generous men I knew.

"No, the police are looking into it."

"The same one who misgendered her?"

"No, they got pulled off the case. The new detective is a gay man."

"Maybe that will help. Well, fuck. Not a good news night. Thieves and murderers all around."

I couldn't disagree.

"What was the other person's name?" he asked, mostly to change the subject, I suspected.

"Peter D'Marchant. Of the uptown family. Thrown out for being gay, and now it's cool enough that grandma wants to reconnect." I pulled out the picture I had of him.

Rob examined it but finally shook his head. "Not familiar. Easy enough on the eyes I would have noticed him. I think. I might have, but then forgotten after the fourth glass."

Helpful only that it told me where not to look. If he was still in the area, he wasn't part of the gay social scene if nether Rob nor Torbin recognized him.

I headed home. The streets were quiet this time.

Chapter Ten

A nother day, another dollar. Although most of what I wanted to do today was head back to Rob's bar, I needed to go to my office to meet with the new detective assigned to Stella's case.

Shower, coffee, all the things that made me human. I was at my office a little before nine.

We'd agreed to meet at ten. I know better than early mornings. I have to have enough coffee in me to be awake enough to be polite.

He was right on time, carrying a large latte from the downstairs shop. At least I'd get something from this interview.

He was the opposite of the other detective. A well-fitting three-piece suit, light gray with a soft pattern, a navy dress shirt, perfectly tied tie that was bold with red and purples weaved in yet also matched his suit and shirt. Well-dressed and professional looking, with just enough flair to set him apart.

He introduced himself and put the coffee on my desk, He didn't immediately sit, instead walking about the office as if he needed to see everything.

I wondered when I'd last done a major cleaning. His looking made me notice the dusty shelf on the bottom on the bookcase, the water ring near my coffeepot, all the imperfections that had become so much a part of the everyday I didn't notice anymore.

"Thank you for meeting with me," he said as he sat down. "I'll try to be concise so I don't waste your time."

Or his time.

"What did you see?" he asked.

I went through it again with as much precise detail as I could, this time sharing with him my thoughts on how the two cars seemed to be traveling together. Stella would have been bruised but okay from being pushed out.

It was the second car that killed her.

He listened quietly, his face giving away nothing. He could still be interested in what I thought or already blown me off as a crank.

"That's very interesting," was his only comment when I had finished.

I continued, telling him about meeting her grandmother, asking around about her at the bars and that everything I found said the initial assessment of her being a sex worker was wrong. She was finishing her BSW, working and living with her grandmother.

"She has a record, you know," he interjected when I paused.

"I know, but it's old, back when she was a teenager. Sure, people can hide things, or get away with them, but so far, I've found no hint that she was still doing any of that. If she were a white girl from a nice family, would she be treated with the same suspicion?"

"By me, yes, she would. You do understand I have to keep an open mind and ask hard questions."

"I'm on board with that, as long as you ask the hard questions to the other cops as well as people like me."

"Fair enough," he answered. "Ms. Clayton mentioned you might have your own ideas. Which is fine. But ideas aren't evidence."

Ms. Clayton? Ah, Danny. "No, but I'm not just pulling ideas out of store-bought red beans and rice. I have things you don't have—witnessing her killing, seeing how she was dressed and what she said in that brief time. Meeting her grandmother, asking around in the community. There is no evidence proving she was a sex worker or did drugs, but there is definitely indicating she wasn't. That would change the motive for her killing."

"You're convinced it wasn't just a horrible hit-and-run?"

"No, not convinced, but if I had to pick, I'd choose premeditated murder over it being a surprised and disappointed john."

He nodded. "You do know this is a police investigation and you are not on the police force." His tone was neutral. I took it more as him defining boundaries then attempting to put me in my place.

"No argument there. Part of me really wishes I had walked home ten minutes later."

"You could have walked away right after," he said. "Given your statement and turned away."

"And left Stella to die in the street as a disposable person? Cops call her a man and blow it off as a sex worker? Let her grandmother and the people who loved her swallow another bitter pill? Think those cops would have treated a lesbian like me any better?" I was angry, but also saw what he was doing—deliberately throwing questions to make me angry and get me talking. The more he could see into me, the more he knew.

He leaned forward, put his coffee down, and said, "Look, girlfriend, they wouldn't be much nicer to me, either." The mask slipped, or maybe he chose to let it down.

"Except you wear a badge."

"True that, but it helps and it hurts. Lot of them straight, white boys really pissed with a Black, queer cop like me."

"Especially when they get pulled off a case?"

"Especially. Look, I'm going to be real with you, but I'm the law and you're not. Okay? I have to ask hard questions, not pursue an agenda."

"The only agenda I want is for Stella Houston to get the same kind of justice a blond white woman would get."

"That's my goal." He sat back up and took a sip of his coffee. "Hey, you heard anything in the bars about the drug and rob stuff?"

"Are you working on that, too?"

"It's on my desk."

"Yeah, I have. When I went to the bars, I was the first person to give them info other than rumors. Second, there are a lot of rumors, and now people are getting scared, pointing out everyone who is strange or acts in ways they don't like."

"Anything concrete? That evidence thing?"

"Evidence? No, nothing that I'd call even a decent hunch. Look, I'm not the cops, but I do a lot of security work in the local gay bars."

"And your point is?" He sat back and took a sip of his coffee.

He knew what my point was but wanted me to put it on the table. "I've lived in this city most of my life, been out as a lesbian before I was twenty. I've worked with several of the gay bars for years now. Who are people more likely to talk to? A new cop in town, or me? I know you have to ask your questions, but no question is any good if it's not answered."

"You want to be part of this investigation? Not going to happen."

"I don't want to be an official part and you don't want me to be.

But we can be a mutual aid society, so to speak. I have other work I'm doing, and if I hear things, I can let you know."

"What other things?"

"Private detective work. Hired by a grandmother to look for her missing gay grandson. Working with a bar about possible employee theft—too low level for y'all to do much with, but the owner wants it looked into."

"Which bar?"

"Nope, not going there."

He nodded as if expecting that. "Anything related to either Stella's death or the robberies, you let me know?"

It wasn't really a question, instead a polite imperative. "I'm not expecting you to keep me updated, but if there is something important, can you let me know?" Mine was a question.

"Like what?"

"You have a suspect, so I can head off witch hunts of innocent people. Or that they change their MO, so I can warn people. Or they escalate."

"You think that's likely?"

"Strange drugs in strange people—the robbers are likely more worried to make sure their mark is out than if he wakes up."

"They do it enough, they get unlucky."

"Their victims, for sure."

"No promises," he said. "You and I are mostly on the same side. But I'm new in town and this case might make or break me. If I screw up, I need to at least screw up by the book." He stood up to go.

I nodded in the direction of my trash can and he threw his cup in. As I let him out the door, I handed him my card.

He slipped it in his vest pocket. "Two flights of stairs, huh? Ever consider moving to a ground floor?"

"Nope, it helps keep me in shape and discourages the nut cases." Plus, the stairs are old and creaky. No one gets up here unnoticed.

He nodded and left.

I gave him about fifteen minutes—in case he stopped to get another cup of coffee—before heading out. Unless I was really lucky with parking, I would get to Rob's bar at around eleven a.m., our agreed-on meeting time.

I was not lucky on parking, one perfect space being snatched from me by a fool who U-turned against traffic to get it. Two more victims of stupid parking, people leaving three-quarters of a space in front of them and half a car behind. "If you can't park that big a thing, maybe you shouldn't drive it," I muttered at the second. I ended up about five blocks away.

The humidity was back, so I was glowing by the time I got to the bar.

Rob wasn't there yet, but Mary was. She waved a greeting at me. "You're here early."

"Alas, this is work."

"Bummer. But I feel your pain," she said as she wiped down the bar. So far, we were the only people here.

"Rob said you were here when the guy came in to report his phone missing?"

"Yeah. Third drink and things get lost easily. Not the first phone gone AWOL, so assumed it was the usual. Put it down or dropped it and forgot."

"What did he look like? Any of these him?" I pulled up the photos I'd clipped on my phone and handed it to her.

"Average," she said as she reviewed the faces. "Not too tall, but not short either, brown hair, just starting to thin, but could have been anywhere from late twenties to early forties—face a little pudgy so it both looked older and younger, if you know what I mean. I think it's this one." She pointed a finger at one of the photos and handed it back to me.

I looked at it. Her description was pretty good. The average man's average man. The picture wasn't great; security cameras aren't meant for taking portraits. Enough extra weight to make him look out of shape, but it also filled in wrinkles. "Did he give a name or his hotel? In case you stumbled over the phone?"

"Maybe," she said, pulling a small notebook from her back pocket. She flipped through it. "I have a note that says, 'Sammy, Hotel Monteleone,' but that's all. We do a pretty good job of cleaning the bar, plus I looked when he asked about it. I assumed it wasn't here and that would be the end of that."

I noted down his name and hotel. I couldn't do anything with it, but Detective Thompson might be able to. He could call the hotel and ask for their guest list. Well, I could, too, but they wouldn't give it to me.

"What did he tell you?" I asked.

She repeated what Rob had passed on. He was having a good time, drinking more than usual, and woke up on a park bench. Assumed it was the too-much-alcohol and stumbled home to his hotel. He had his wallet so didn't think he'd been robbed. Only later, awake and sober, did he realize he didn't have his phone.

But it wasn't here at the bar, so Mary thought that was the end of it.

"Okay, thanks," I said when she finished. "Any other things seem out of place or weird?"

She laughed. "This is a rainbow spectrum bar on the outside of the French Quarter. We make New Orleans weird look normal."

"True dat, but more like someone hunting, casing out the people around them."

"People always look for things here, someone to go home with, maybe even true love. Also for drugs, but we try to keep that out. How do you tell the difference?"

"Any that creep you out?"

"Sure, the older men cruising the really young ones, the cute boys taking advantage of it to get as many free drinks as possible. The ones looking for the impossible, love when they're unlovable, friends when they're not friendly. You see what I mean? People hunt all the time. It's not always easy to know what they're hunting for. Sometimes even they don't know."

What was I hunting for when I hung out in the bars? The motion and blur to pass the time? A place to end one day before sleep and the start of the next one? A chance to meet a stranger, chat for an hour. Or two. Sometimes they had a lot to say about Oshkosh—far more than I was interested in. The wheel of chance? Meet someone new, see something new, open doors of possibility? Most of them fantasy. I'd found only pleasant conversations, a few interesting passersby (not Oshkosh—sorry, I like cheese, just don't need to know that much about how it's made) some good times hanging with friends. Some not so good times, some wasted times with people I realized I didn't want to be with. And home alone after all of it.

What was the difference between those who hunted for fantasy and those who hunted for prey? I couldn't answer Mary's question.

"Anything about this person that's familiar?" I asked instead, showing her the screen shot of the person who'd entered with the stolen key.

She again carefully examined the picture, finally saying, "Hard to tell with the mask and the hat."

Rob joined us. "This the key thief?"

I nodded. He explained to Mary.

She looked again at the picture but still shook her head.

I thanked her and followed Rob upstairs to the office.

The beauty of the age of technology is that when things work, it's a major time-saver. I was able to download the security videos onto my computer as well as the employee files. I'm old enough to remember having to stand at a copy machine and feed everything through.

And taking breaks to add more paper and change the toner.

"Heard about the latest?" Rob said as I was waiting for files to save.

"Which latest? Life seems like a roller coaster of chaos now."

"They hit one of the straight bars on Bourbon Street."

"The phone robbers?"

"Yep, story is some young buck was in town, looking for fun, two women offered to take him back to their place, and he woke up in a strange and cheap hotel room."

"That's odd," I commented. "The same or copycat? It's a different MO, with women involved. If it's the same group, it means it's a larger operation."

"One guy hitting the gay bars and the two women hitting the straight bars?"

"Maybe, but those are two different social ecosystems. Would have to be familiar with them both."

"But a bar is a bar," Rob pointed out. "Yes, everyone is special and unique and all that, but it's basically a place anyone can walk in and buy drinks and see who else is there."

"True, but crooks read the papers, too. They might want to be on the cutting edge. I'm guessing the victim woke up."

"Yes, and rumor says he was first outraged at the cheap hotel and then even more outraged that both his phone and wallet were stolen."

"Interesting. The man Mary talked to said at first, he didn't think he'd been robbed because he still had his wallet."

"Still, doesn't mean much. Thieves might have decided that to get as much as they could. Or he had more in his wallet than on his phone."

"Maybe important, maybe not. Just interesting," I said. "Anything from the queer bars?"

"Not that I've heard."

My file finished saving. I clicked on the next one.

"Want a burger while you're waiting?" Rob asked.

To be healthy I opted for the chicken sandwich. Fried, yes, but chicken is better, right?

My lunch arrived just as I was downloading the final file. The lunchtime crowd was coming in, so Rob only dropped off the plate—and a beer—and left.

I contemplated what to do next as I munched and sipped. The obvious task—going home or to my office and staring at computer screens until my eyes bled—wasn't beckoning me with open arms.

I was waiting on the computer grannies to report on Peter D. to know what to do next there. I was sure Mrs. D. would be demanding a progress report any day now. Stella Houston wasn't my case, nor were the robberies. That left working on the not-my-cases or staring at the computer screen.

Maybe I should hang out here and have another beer.

And maybe I shouldn't. A long sigh and I decided to go back to my office. I had to admit that part of the decision was so people were around in case Mr. Big Shot PI decided he wanted to continue our discussion. Sure, people were around on my block at home, but at the office I had people in the building. Plus, the creaky stairs.

I waved good-bye to Rob and Mary and hiked to my car.

I was sweating by the time I got there. Fall in New Orleans can require air-conditioning. The day had warmed up and the computer was heavy. I'd had to choose between it being light or it doing a lot of things. I'm not on and off airplanes for work, so I'd chosen the latter.

It's your exercise for the day, I told myself as I got in and turned the AC to high.

Once in my office, I made coffee to counter sleepiness from the beer and fried chicken. While waiting for it to brew, I copied the files from my laptop to my desktop. So much of what I do these days is online, so it was a top-of-the-line one (and a tax deduction.) Plus, much bigger screen to see the details.

After fifteen minutes, I realized I could only watch for so long before my brain started drifting. It was oh so boring. People drinking. More people drinking. People talking. More people talking. No obvious drink spiking or even a quick slip of hands for a drug deal, no bar brawls. Just the same old, same old.

I took a break with a saunter around my office, then stared out the window for distance to readjust my eyes. A black SUV on the side street? But it was just a glimpse and it was gone.

Get organized, I told myself. Make a log of each day. I knew some of the regulars, but only those around when I was there. As a working girl, I wasn't part of the late-night crowd. Or morning/early afternoon crowd. I was probably looking for someone who visited a few times to check things out, found their victim, then didn't show for a while. I started a few weeks before the night the robbery likely happened.

The problem with a town like New Orleans and a bar in the French Quarter is there are a lot of people coming and going. Conventions, tourists. The churn of people provided lots of possible targets and made it hard to notice anyone different—too many were different.

Someone had a key to the bar, had broken in and cut the lines to the video cameras for one night. Why? I was guessing they were related, so the robberies might hold the key—pun intended—to who stole the key.

But the day was getting dark and I'd found nothing. I could come back to this tomorrow. I packed up my laptop—if I was really ambitious, I might do a few more days this evening at home.

I checked in with the computer grannies on my way out. Lena, the ringleader, aka COO on official company letterhead, handed me a file. "This is what we found. Not great. He seems to have disappeared about two years ago. Bank accounts closed, like it was intentional."

"Moved away?"

"Hard to know. We can dig more, but it's not going to be one of the easy ones."

"Okay, thanks. Go a little deeper and see if you can find anything."

I headed down the stairs. The coffee shop was busy—they did a good business with people picking up food to go, having expanded to offering pizzas. It all smelled good, but I had food at home.

Like two-days-expired yogurt. Milk that was turning to sour cream. A banana more brown than yellow.

I put my stuff down, threw on workout clothes, and headed over to Torbin's. Ostensibly to work out, but more to catch them at home to ask them about Stella. Also, to see if they were cooking something I might wrangle an invitation to.

Mercifully, ten minutes into my workout, Torbin popped his head into the shed.

"Thought I heard you out here."

Not so mercifully, he was here to work out, too. Since I was on the elliptical, he started with the weights.

I gave it another ten minutes, then got off. Like I was courteously vacating it for him.

He gave a grunt as he finished his reps, then said, "Did cardio this morning, so only doing weights."

To show I wasn't a slacker, I picked up some weights as well. We could chat over bicep curls.

"Heard anything more about the robberies?" I asked.

"Other than it's a right-wing militia from the North Shore?"

"Other than that." I grunted. It had been a while since I'd done a good bicep workout.

"No. I did disable fingerprint and facial recognition from my phone."

"You're not a likely target," I pointed out.

"Maybe," he said.

"Unless you lead a double life. You go out with Andy or me or other friends. They're not targeting someone with friends. Likely a single person, especially a tourist by themselves."

"True, but better safe than sorry," he said. He put down the dumbbell and strapped on ankle weights. "Are you looking into it?"

I switched to one-arm rows. "No, not officially, at any rate. Some weird stuff at one of the bars I work with, and I'm looking into that. Might be related."

"Stay safe. These sound like nasty dudes."

"Why do you say that?" I agreed, but was curious.

"They're drugging strangers, then dumping them. Lot of possible harm along the way."

"They might not wake up."

"Or get attacked while they're out."

I switched to my other arm. I was going to be sore tomorrow. "Do you know someone named Stella Houston?"

"Stella? Why?"

"You know her?"

"Yes, I did drag for a couple of her fundraisers for her transgender support projects. A real go-getter." I kept my face neutral, but Torbin knew me too well. "What's happened?"

"The hit-and-run I witnessed? It was her."

"Oh, shit." He stopped working out. "I didn't know her well, but she struck me as both hardworking and fun. Like she had found the path she wanted to be on and was smart enough to have fun on the way."

"Did you meet any of her friends? People she knew?"

"You're looking into this one, right?"

"Not officially. It's a police investigation."

"I saw that horrible quote from the detective. Claiming it was a sex crime, upset customer. Nothing to worry about for respectable citizens." Torbin took off his ankle weights and threw them in the weight pile. Then he got up and stacked them in their rack.

"He's off the case."

"Good."

"New cop is gay and Black. Came here from Atlanta."

"So he won't know the community. I hate that these motherfuckers might get away with this."

"They might," I admitted. "But they might not. It wasn't a sex crime. I think it was someone she knew. That's why I'd like to talk to her friends. I know a lot of them might not go to the police, but if I can find things that police should know—"

"You act as a go-between," Torbin cut in. "Most trans people, especially POC, don't view the police as their protectors. The opposite, in fact."

"Yes. Sadly, for good reason. Stella gets killed and the first thing the cops do is throw asshole assumptions and blame her and misgender her."

"I might have phone numbers from the drag show I did for them. A friend of hers, I think. Desiree. I'll have to dig, and see if I kept it."

"Trans woman or a woman?"

"Does it matter?"

"No," I realized. "It doesn't."

"I'm a man. I'm queer as a purple dyed three-dollar bill but never thought I was anything other than male. How do we know that?" Torbin said, wiping the sweat off his face.

"It just seems like we always do. When I was young, I sometimes wanted to be a boy, but not the gender, just the privilege. Be able to wear pants, or play outside instead of playing house."

"I remember Stella saying she never felt like a boy, like something vital wasn't the way it should be."

"Why do people care so much? Why is gender such a lockbox?" I asked.

"It's one of the verities we're raised with. Pink for girls, blue for boys, everything divided into gender categories—toys, shoes, clothes. Gifts for her. Gifts for him."

"And a rift in the world opens up if those certainties are questioned," I added.

"Sad that we have to fit people into categories that don't really matter," Torbin said. "Unless you're a doctor or a sex partner, why do you need to know about someone's genitals?"

"Because we need to put people into a hierarchy," I speculated. "It's how we're taught to see the world, to judge people and know where they fit."

"Just judge them on who they are."

"Too much work. You're a woman—you're weak, emotional, can be treated ways you don't treat men. It's control. You think you know something by knowing someone's gender."

Torbin nodded, then said, "I think I'm done exercising for the day. We're not going to solve this. Or we can try the Nick and Nora method and have a cocktail."

I readily agreed. I probably need a leg workout as well, but it could wait until tomorrow. I might need to come back here again around dinnertime.

CHAPTER ELEVEN

Andy made a big batch of lasagna, enough for unexpected guests, and even gave me a generous serving to take home.

With cocktails, eating, and talking, it was almost ten p.m. by the time I got home. I wasn't quite ready for bed, so I tackled another hour of watching the security tapes.

Boring, boring, boring.

Until the last five minutes of the time I'd allotted as my limit. Out on the street. Two cars, one a sleek white sedan and the other a boxy SUV. They drove slowly by the bar. The car in front, the SUV following. The shapes, the colors. Familiar. From the night Stella was killed.

But this wasn't the right night, about a week before.

There are lots of cars in this city; have to be hundreds that look like the blurs I saw.

I rewound the tape and slowed it down. They were going slowly, prowling. Rampart is a four-lane street, and cars usually go at a good clip.

Unless they're looking for parking. Or lost tourists, I reminded myself.

I watched the tape again in slow motion. There was an open space just beyond the bar, but neither car slowed. Okay, cross off parking. The picture wasn't great, but the license looked like the right style and color for Louisiana plates.

They were close together, both going the same slow speed.

Damn. I sat back after the fourth view. I didn't have the equipment to enhance the photos. The grainy images hinted, but I couldn't confirm. Shiny and new, expensive. Maybe a Mercedes or other high end for the sedan. The SUV was boxy and large. Maybe a Range Rover? A Lincoln

Navigator? Two expensive cars. Possibly the same ones I'd seen with Stella.

Was I seeing what I wanted to see? If they were together like this before her death, it meant I might be right that the two were working together.

Making it murder.

"Damn it," I cursed out loud. Tendrils and mist. Two cars that *might* be similar to the ones I'd seen that night, in that blurred moment. Or they might be just two random cars on a busy street. I could clip this footage and give it to Detective Thompson. He might blow it off.

Or might believe me but be where I am now—a hint and a hunch, but nothing useful.

"Well, fuck," I said to the expectant computer screen. At best a tattered thread to follow that might lead nowhere. Nor had I accomplished anything on my two paying cases. Two cars in the street didn't help to identify the Q Carré key thief or find a missing grandson. I had planned to skim what the computer grannies had given me, but it was late.

I'd do it and the employee files in the morning. Tomorrow, after all, is another day.

A rainy, messy day. We can do gentle sprinkles here but have a climate that is very good at drenching downpours. I'd get soaked getting from my door to my car.

Cold and wet? Was that how I wanted to start my day? I could review files and the camera footage here.

I had a better, faster computer at my office. Everyone else had to go to work, I might as well, too. The deciding factor? I had toaster pastries in my office. That was as close as I was going to get to a warm and comforting breakfast. Only cereal and the mushy banana awaited me here.

I was right about the cold and wet.

I was also right about the toaster pastries. Strawberry with white frosting and sprinkles. It was hurricane food—you buy crazy things because they can be eaten out of the box, no refrigeration or cooking required. I popped two into the office microwave to warm while I toweled dry my hair. I put coffee on as well, although I'd brought a go-mug with me. I needed caffeine to drive in this city.

Warm gooey goodness and coffee and I was ready to sit at my desk.

First, I tackled the file on Peter D'Marchant. If I was really lucky, I could get a progress report to Mrs. D. before she demanded one.

The computer grannies were correct. The usual trail until about two years ago: bank accounts, work, addresses. Then nothing. Bank accounts closed. Job ended. He had been doing what I considered work that paid well and ate the soul, some sort of marine science for one of the big energy companies. I hoped he'd put away a bunch of money and was now traveling Europe. Good for him, but it made him hard to find.

I called the company, but it was big enough I'd get nothing more than dates of employment. Didn't get even that. I was only able to leave a message for HR. They would call me back. Not holding my breath for that one.

I addressed a bunch of "return address requested" for the old addresses. If I was lucky, I might get something back with a newer address. Maybe even the right one.

I then called the man who said he knew someone who might have been his roommate. Again, had to leave a message.

Next step was a progress report for Mrs. D'Marchant. Or lack of progress report. I had to both make it look long and detailed and avoid details that she could nitpick or think she could have done herself to save my exorbitant fee. Like sending the return request mail. Yeah, easy, once you have the old address, but those had probably taken the computer grannies an hour or two of searching to find, and they are good at this. I emailed her a copy, even though she had let me know she did not regularly check her email, using it only to receive pictures of her grandchildren. I also put a copy in the mail.

Those tasks had taken me to lunchtime. Or what my stomach considered lunchtime. But all I had here was a second round of toaster pastry. I did a quick check of the weather. There was a slight break in the clouds. I decided to run to the post office, drop off the mail, and do a much-needed grocery run. Middle of a rainy day was probably a good time to go. The only way to eat and avoid the rain was to get something at the coffee shop downstairs, and a little rain wasn't going to make me break my vow. Admittedly it was tacking on the mail and the groceries that made it worthwhile going out. And the break in the clouds. It looked like it would rain the rest of the afternoon, and wet people and crowded grocery stores are a mixture for murder.

No one was killed. Mail sent, groceries procured, mushy banana in the garbage. Lunch was a store-bought half a muffuletta; I'd worked out yesterday, after all.

Now the Q Carré employee files stared at me.

It's helping to pay the bills, I reminded myself, after several squint-eyed reads of bad handwriting on applications. Rob had done a good job of collecting and organizing everything. All employees had to fill out an application, have references, and have a criminal background check. The form for the last stated that a criminal record wasn't an automatic disqualification but would be taken into consideration. You don't hire someone convicted of fraud to handle your books, for example. One of his longtime bartenders had a record for car theft. Can't steal a car when you're behind a bar.

The employees tended to fall into three groups: the ones who stayed, like Mary and Peg; the ones who worked while going to college or trade school before moving on; and the ones who lasted a few months or weeks. Or just a day or two in some cases—the ones who discovered the experiential way that this was not the career for them.

I doubted it was any of the long-term employees but couldn't rule them out completely. I had to make some choices. They had easy access to the bar and keys; why sneak in when they could open or close and be the only ones there? Maybe to put suspicion on someone else, but that seemed far-fetched. If the robberies hadn't happened, it was likely that the cut wires would have been blown off to a hungry mouse, fixed and forgotten.

But the long-term employees were the smallest pile, eight of them. The other piles added up to sixty-two, going back two years.

I put those over a year old to the side. Why hold on to a key for over a year? Something that small that I didn't use in over a year wasn't likely to be found again.

I also put aside those who were working while going to school. They had plans and were moving on to other things, less likely to break the law. That took away thirty-two.

That left the people who'd come and left.

Again, on guesses and hunches, I put aside those who had lasted only a few days. Less likely to have had a chance to take a key, make a copy, and return it.

I had winnowed the pile down to twenty-three. Still a hefty pile.

Now what? Look at the employee photos and see if anyone looked guilty? I decided to put aside those who had been gone at least three months before the break-in. This was organized, but not likely to be organized enough to be planned out that far in advance. My guess was probably a window of a week or two. Maybe a month. That's a long time in crook world. People don't steal because they're good at long-term goals.

That got me to a pile of fourteen.

On a sexist whim, I took out the women. Less likely to be engaged in criminal activity, especially the kind that involved breaking and entering. That cut the pile in half. Seven.

I reread their files. No smoking gun in the pages, but I hadn't expected any. One of them was in his forties. Life hadn't been kind to him. He had a record for dealing. His previous employment history was sketchy, at most a year at the previous jobs listed. The kind of person to lead a robbery ring?

No, he'd been busted for dealing about three months ago, unable to make bail, waiting in jail for his trial. Life wasn't going to be any kinder to him.

The other six were all in their early to mid-twenties. Young, flailing around, trying to get through the days, meet those adult bills on their own. An easy time to fall in with their peers, still new to consequences and how far they could reverberate.

I had been lucky more than good at that age. High school had scarred me. I knew I was queer and I knew most of the kids in my class would hate me if they knew. I made few friends. I snuck into the bars to not feel so achingly alone. But even there, pretending to be older, to know what I wanted instead of being pulled along with what was offered. Going home with older women, ones I couldn't be honest with and let them know they were sleeping with a seventeen-year-old. Always hiding part of me.

An older lesbian couple took me in, paying for me to go to college, which my blood family wouldn't do. After those four years in New York—freeing and challenging—I came back here. I knew I didn't want to work in an office, although I did for about a year. But so many other paths were daunting. What if I'd come to a bar like Q Carré, found people who were fun and took me in? Would I have slipped and fallen if they'd asked me to? What do we do to find acceptance? Or more, what do we do to keep it once we're found it?

Had that happened to one of these men? Boys in so many ways, but men in age.

I made a list of the names. I considered handing them to the computer grannies, but I wasn't sure what to tell them to search for. I'd also told Rob I'd try to do this as inexpensively as possible, and that was an added cost. I'd do the quick and dirty search and see if I found anything. And go from there.

Reading and sorting the files had eaten the afternoon. I stayed until after six to make up for the errands in the middle of the day.

A lot of what people pay me for is to do very boring things—carefully read and reread files, find the few things that are useful and discard the rest of a huge pile.

It was time to head home. I could do some more work this evening, but my eyes and shoulders needed to do something else besides stare at a computer screen.

Plus, I had actual food at home. Even if I had to do it myself, a home-cooked meal sounded nice.

Shrimp and grits. It's a luxury to live in a place where shrimp is inexpensive enough to be a weeknight throw-together meal.

"I should do this more often," I announced to the empty house. Should, but wouldn't. For just me, it was easier to throw together a salad or a sandwich or do takeout. The effort of cooking a whole meal seemed too much for just one. When Cordelia and I had been together, we cooked most nights. Someone to share the food with—and the chores. We would talk while I cooked (mostly, although she did on weekends when she had more time), and she cleaned up afterward and we continued talking. It was our way of winding down the day.

But now I had no one to talk to, and the lengthy moments in the kitchen seemed too empty. Better to grab a quick meal, turn on the TV or keep on working. The time passed more gently.

I wondered how Estelle Houston was passing the evening. I hoped she had people she cared about with her, to help her through the long hours, to cook her a good meal, clean the kitchen. Fill the silence.

I didn't wonder about Mrs. D'Marchant. Maybe she did truly miss her grandson and regret what had happened. But she had lived for many years without him in her life. And even if he came back, he would never be part of her daily life, expected in the door each evening.

I put away enough leftovers for another meal, then debated hate-watching new home buyers on TV or doing some more work.

I opted for the latter. Rob and his bar had been violated, and until we knew who it was, it could happen again. The two cars also nagged at me. I needed to see if I could find anything else, maybe catch them driving by on other nights to get a better picture, maybe even a license plate.

Since Rob was paying me, I continued work on the employee files. Seven names.

I put them into search engines one by one.

Boring. I started with the obvious, checking criminal records. Yes, Rob had done that for employment, but it never hurt to do it again; something might have come up after they started.

Nothing new, nothing to indicate they were in the habit of stealing.

Two of them weren't good drivers, with several tickets each, and even one totaled car. Single-car accident. DUI? But nothing came up.

Two of them no longer lived here; one to Houston, one to Pittsburgh. I took them off the list.

One was still bartending at another bar and going to UNO part-time. He lived in Gentilly, an easy commute to both where he worked and school. No car registered, so he might be using public transportation. Less likely to be prowling the French Quarter at all hours. Public transit isn't kind during the late hours. And not great during regular hours.

One was apprenticing as a plumber. A job I'm happy to pay people to do. Lot of hours, also less likely to be haunting bars late at night.

A third was now driving the tourist mule buggies and a walking ghost tour guide.

The fourth didn't seem to have another job, and his mail drop was a PO box. I couldn't find an address for him.

And the fifth listed his address in the Garden District, coincidentally about a block away from Mrs. D'Marchant. I cross-checked. He was the bad driver who had totaled his car. Likely this was his parents' address, and if they lived there, they could take care of any mess baby boy got himself into.

My top two were Mr. No Address No Job and Mr. Ghost Tour. The first because he was either hiding something or was living on couches and likely desperate for money. Mr. Ghost Tour because he was rambling around the area, the work could be hit or miss, he would know where the big tourist events were in town, big conventions and the like.

I'd continue looking at the others but dig deeper on these two.

Social media.

Gawd, people, it's not just your best friends checking out what you post. Too many people post pictures of their new shiny toy—computer, big screen TV, expensive deer hunting rifle—then two weeks later how excited they are to be going on their Bahamas vacation. I'm always amazed at what I find. A quick snapshot? It gives background, who you're with, possible location, possible things to steal. At least lock down your account so only people you choose can see what you post.

Mr. No Address seemed to be hustling dodgy supplements promising a great sex life or CBD to help you forget you didn't have a great sex life. He had few personal details but a lot of promises about how buying these things from him would transform your life. Snake oil salesman. Selling crap that hurts people (even if only in their pocketbook) makes you a scummy person. The kind of person who would steal a key. Maybe with a plan and maybe with just a vague idea it could be useful.

Kevin Jordan. I wondered if it was his real name. Not clearly fake, but only idiots use clearly fake names. I searched some more, but he had been smart enough to limit his online presence to his snake oil—I mean, fantastic sex supplements—sales. I'd give his name to the computer grannies tomorrow.

I did a quick search on the others. Lots of bad photographs. Oh, *special* if you're in them and it's your memory, but out of focus, bad framing, bad lighting. Special to you, boring for someone who doesn't know you (and frankly, doesn't want to).

Ghost Tour guy did a much better job. He had an agenda, to make you want to ride his buggy and take his tour, so he put effort into the photos he posted. A great shot of Jackson Square on a foggy morning. A night shot of the wrought iron balconies of the French Quarter, with the flicking gaslights. An arty shot of the river, catching the curve that gave us the name Crescent City. Organized and ambitious. Albert St. James. A good name for a ghost tour guide. I'd give his to the grannies as well.

Mr. Likely DUI was Hugh Melancon. His social media was mostly of either bottles of alcohol or a new gun. He seemed to have more than he needed of both. Some out-of-focus bar shots, including one that looked like Q Carré—which tracked since he'd worked there. No captions or explanations. I'd keep him in reserve—try the first two with the computer grannies and drop him in if nothing turned up. He didn't seem to need money; the guns and booze weren't cheap. But he might be the type who thinks the rules don't apply to him.

I'd have to talk to the longtime staff who had worked with them. The files did have photo ID but told me nothing about height, and a face was only a hint of weight. I'd need to know that to see if they matched the figure on the video. If they were very tall or short, it might rule them out.

I rubbed my eyes and looked at the clock. A little past nine, too early for bed. Not too early for a drink. I settled on wine, a nice Malbec. It would get me through more of the security footage.

I made it through another day—at fast forward—and most of the wine before I gave up. Nothing, no sign of the cars or anything other than a small crowd of people having a few drinks. It was a weeknight, a slow one.

A final sip of wine and it was time for bed.

Chapter Twelve

The rain had cleared and it was a beautiful day, sunny with the hint of cooler temperatures. Coffee, a decent breakfast of avocado toast, and I headed to my office.

On the way up the stairs, I handed the two names to the computer grannies. "See what you can dig up. Possible suspects in a bar robbery." I was calling it a robbery because that seemed the best shorthand. Only a key was stolen, but it was stolen for a purpose that didn't seem altruistic.

Then up to my office, with coffee put on to supplement the cup I'd had at home.

Now what?

I could contact Detective Thompson, give him the name of another victim. And possibly mention seeing the cars again. But the latter seemed too tenuous. I wanted more, to catch them again, get the license plate or at least a partial. Not close enough to evidence. It could take days to get through all the security tapes. Even then, a blink or a moment of inattention and I could miss it.

Or I could move on. Not my case, not my job to chase down all the dead ends.

Torbin and Rob both knew Stella.

I sighed, poured a big mug of coffee, and sat down at my computer screen.

It was almost lunchtime before I saw something that made me stop and review. What's-his-name was there again. The big guy cadging Mrs. D'Marchant for her booze. Chatting with the bartender who looked like Hugh Melancon, aka Ex-Employee. Seeing them together triggered my memory of the third man with him and grandson Brice.

A quick memory and a not great security tape, but they looked alike. What the hell?

I wrote down his name and went downstairs to the computer grannies to add it to the list. I don't like coincidences. They either mean something or they're a messy distraction.

I went back upstairs to my office and reran the tape in real time. The big guy came into the bar, ordered a drink from the bartender, one I was guessing was his friend. They chatted for less than a minute, then Ex-Employee had to take care of other customers. This went on for about half an hour, a brief chat interrupted by other customers. It seemed open and free, no leaning in to whisper; at one point another customer made a comment. They could have been talking about the latest Saints game or the weather.

Oh, wait, curiouser and curiouser. Mr. Big Shot PI joined them. Greetings and friendly handshakes all around. He only stayed long enough to get a drink, then drifted to a back table and the woman there. She was tall and blond and seemed happy for his company. Or for the drink he bought her. It was hard to tell if he just knew her in passing or if they were friends.

Then the big guy left. He didn't pay for his drink.

Nothing criminal, nothing suspicious. Except not paying for his drink. But even that was minor. Rob often comped me drinks. A lot of questions swirling around. Not a single bar of my gaydar had pinged around these guys, but then I'm a lesbian of a certain age, and things change, and they may have changed beyond me.

I needed their full names. I only had Ex-Employee's from his employee file.

Dottie might know, but I didn't want to call her during working hours when Mrs. D. might be around.

"Shit, piss and corruption," I muttered.

It was after twelve, so the Q Carré would be open. And maybe quiet enough that I could get in my questions over the phone instead of traipsing there.

Just as I was dialing, my cell phone rang.

An unfamiliar voice. "You asked me to call you?"

My brain scrambled to remember.

"You were looking for someone, and I thought I might know someone who knew him."

Ah, yes, the possible roommate of Peter D'Marchant.

"Yes, thank you so much for calling me back," I said in as friendly a voice as I could manage to make up for my earlier suspicion that it was another call about my bogus car warranty.

"My friend Sara Bayer roomed with someone with his name. Or something like it. I can't be sure. But she'll know." He gave me her name and number.

"How do you know Sara?" I asked. Partly to be friendly, partly to check her out. His lawyer or his occasional drinking buddy?

"She's my personal trainer. Does individual sessions, so I started with her when the gyms shut down. See her twice a week. Hate it, but it's good for me. Glutes are killing me right now." He said it in a cheery voice, proud of his hurting glutes.

I thanked him and hung up.

My office phone rang.

HR from big energy company. I hadn't expected them to actually call back.

"I'm seeking a reference for Peter D'Marchant," I said, using my most professionally busy voice.

"Who's calling?"

I was prepared for them. " Michele Landrieu, with Prejean Marine." If they asked, I'd say no, I was not related to the former mayor. But if they didn't ask, I was fine with letting them assume whatever they wanted. "Did Peter work for you?"

Evidently I'd passed muster. She answered yes and gave me his dates of employment. They matched what the grannies had supplied.

"Is he eligible for rehire?" I'd probably gotten all I was going to get, but this was the kind of question I'd ask if I was legit.

She hesitated, then cleared her throat. "Yes, although perhaps in a different position."

"Different position? Why?"

She again cleared her throat. "Well, the position he was in was out in the field a lot, rough conditions."

"And that wouldn't be appropriate now?"

She seemed to realize she had said more than the corporate mores allowed. "Well, that would be up to you. He left of his own choice. We didn't fire or harass him. Those are the only questions I can answer. Good luck with your hiring." She hung up.

That was interesting. I wondered if he had been outed and was no longer welcome on all-boy trips offshore.

I had been good and brought a turkey sandwich on whole wheat for lunch. If I went to Q Carré, I could report to Rob, see if he had any insight into the candidates I'd narrowed it down to, see if I could get a better physical description of them. And get one of their oh-so-good burgers.

It's good to be decisive sometimes.

I headed out. The parking gods were even kind, and I found a spot half a block away.

The bar wasn't crowded yet. Which was good. Rob wasn't there, which was not good. I didn't want to ask his employees suspicious questions without talking to him first. Even if I was right about the key thief being one of the three, I'd be wrong about two of them.

I ordered the burger at the bar, paid up front for it, then settled in a booth in the back.

I was checking the weather on my cell phone when I looked up and saw an unwelcome figure heading my way.

"You're easy to follow," he said as he heaved himself in the seat opposite me. Same smirk from when I'd last seen him behind my building.

"Black SUV. Yeah, I saw you but couldn't think why anyone would bother following me on my lunch break."

"I think we started off on the wrong foot," he said.

"We?"

He ignored me.

"I think we can work together."

"On what? And why on earth would we do that?"

"These robberies. There's now a fifty-thousand-dollar reward." He said it like he'd stated something obvious—that money would be enough to entice me to work with him.

"So?"

"We split it fifty-fifty."

"Uh-uh." I was hoping he'd notice the enthusiasm in my replies.

"It should be easy for the two of us. I have mad PI skills—and police contacts. You know the gay community. We work together and crack the case and pick up the reward."

"Yeah. Except I remember the last time we talked, you threatened me because a police contact friend of yours got reassigned. Like I have some magic wand to control them."

"Look, we all know you woke types have infiltrated things and work together. It was worth a try. He's a good friend."

"Got rid of a few white supremacists and you think that's woke? You want to work with someone who you think screwed over a good friend of yours?" There was as much verbal sarcasm in my tone as I could pack.

"Hey, just a working relationship. For the money."

It was possible he was interested in the money. It was also possible he was stupid and clueless enough to think one queer person could give him entrée to the entire LGBTQ community. His estimation of his PI skills was wildly overblown. I'm good at this, and I would never make the kinds of claims he was making. However, I doubted any of these were his only reasons for being here—following me in broad daylight in a straight line from my office to one of my frequent hangout spots. Not "mad wild" skill. He wanted to know what I was up to, probably to—in his mind—control what I did.

"You got to be kidding me," was the only response I could come up with.

"Look, I know you're a lesbian and you hate men, but we—"

I howled with laughter, loud enough to shut him up. "Hate men? Oh, honey, it has to be all about you, doesn't it? If we don't like you, we have to hate you, so you're still at the center of everything. I like some men, love some even, hate a few. But for the most part, just don't care. Don't expend an iota of love/lust energy on you. Hire a plumber, then he goes home and the toilet seat stays down like God intended."

His face was blank. Like this was something that had never occurred to him and it couldn't be right. Indifferent? To him? That wasn't a world he understood.

"Now, let me give you as much energy as I'm willing to give you. I do not want to chase down the robbers. Leave that for the police. I may not have mad skills, but I do well enough that I don't need to pursue unlikely rewards. So, no, we are not working together."

His face remained the same confused blank, like he hadn't considered this as a possible outcome and now he didn't know what to do.

Mary gave him a break by serving me my hamburger and giving him time to think.

He grabbed one of my French fries.

I moved the plate as far from him as I could.

"Not very friendly, are you?"

"I'm very friendly to my friends. You aren't one."

"Too bad, we could have had a sweet deal. Twenty-five grand for a few days' work."

"A few days? Are you smoking crack? Unless you're part of the gang and planning to rat out your friends."

The blank look disappeared. Just a blink. Anger? Fear? But it was gone, replaced by his usual smirk. Okay, he wasn't as stupid as I thought he was. I'd caught him off guard, but he'd recovered in a microsecond. The idiot I'd pegged him for couldn't do that. But why the reaction?

"Well, your loss," he said. "I can easily find other queers who'll want in on it. In fact, their cut will be smaller, so more for me." He reached to grab another fry, but his arm wasn't long enough. He bent up to get it.

I spit on them just as his fingers were closing in.

"Fucking dyke," he muttered, standing up and turning away. Over his shoulder he called, "Your loss!"

The first was for me, the last for the onlookers—if there were any—and his ego.

I let him go, much as I wanted to see how many curse words I could hurl his way before he reached the door.

"Friend of yours?" Mary came by with some extra ketchup.

"Not in this reality."

"Wondered," she said. "He doesn't seem like the type you'd hang with."

"He's been here before?"

"A few times. Not lately, though. Like he found what he was looking for."

"What was he looking for?"

"Someone to spend the night with. Maybe more."

"Gay? Or on the side?"

"He was looking for women. Ignored the men, but chatted up the women." At my look, she added, "Not the lesbians, the transgender women."

"Can you remember about when he was last here?"

"Not really, wasn't paying that much attention."

"A few days? Or weeks?"

"Probably weeks at least, maybe a month or so."

"Within the last six months?" I asked.

"Likely, but I can't pin it down."

"What kind of customer was he?"

She shrugged. "Okay, I guess."

"Top shelf? Bargain basement? Tipped well?"

"He liked the good stuff, not a great tipper, but okay. Well, if people were watching. One time a friend cajoled him to leave a better tip. He occasionally got his drink, wandered away, and didn't tip at all. Does this matter?"

This time I shrugged. "I don't know. He wanted to team up with me to solve the identity theft robberies and said we could split the reward. I turned him down."

"Sounds like a good decision. He was a glad-hander. My niece just graduated from the police academy and he was there, schmoozing with the cops. He saw me, then looked like he didn't know me. You know the type."

"You do remember a lot."

She smiled, a small one. "Maybe I do after thinking about it for a bit."

"What else can you tell me about him?"

"Won't help, but I didn't much like him. He seemed too…needy isn't the right word, like he wanted what he wanted too much. To get someone to go home with him, to be the center of attention. That sort of thing."

"You and I agree on that. I don't like him either. You remember any of the women he went home with?"

"Yeah, some come here on occasion. But I can't remember names, just faces," she finished as if knowing my next question.

"Might be interesting to talk to them. If you see them again, can you give them my info and ask them to call? Tell them I'm lesbian and they don't have to answer anything they don't want to." I gave her several of my cards.

"I'll try. It might take a while. Never know when people will show up."

I saw Rob come in and waved at him.

"I need to get back to the bar," Mary said. She greeted Rob as they passed.

He sat down in the booth.

"Can I have a fry?" he asked.

I told him I'd spit on them and then had to explain why.

"Don't know the guy," he said when I'd finished.

"Don't think you want to know him. He may be a distraction."

I pulled out the paperwork on the three ex-employees and handed it to him. I did a quick explanation of why I had singled them out.

While Rob looked them over, I was finally able to eat a few fries. Even managed a bite of my burger.

"No bells ringing," Rob said when he put the papers down. "I vaguely remember them—through a Chardonnay glass darkly. I let the supplement guy go because he was hawking his junk while on the clock."

"He angry about that?"

"Maybe, but he didn't show it. More like he knew he was over the line and had gotten busted. Almost like he was expecting it. Just shrugged, asked for his last paycheck—I paid him in cash—and left. Mary said he came by later and asked if she could pass on his contact info if people came to look for him."

"Do you still have that?"

"She said yes, but mostly to avoid the confrontation. She handed it to me and I threw it in the trash."

I nodded, mostly expecting that. Then I asked if his vague memory could call up what they looked like. "Really tall? Or short? Anything stand out about them?"

"The supplement guy was a bit cross-eyed. But he was average height. Maybe just a bit shorter than I am. Maybe."

"Weight?"

"Again, average. Supplement guy was skinny, like he was either always active or hyped on something. Tour guide was in decent shape. He had a lot of fans as a bartender. He left on his own choice, said his tours were picking up and he didn't have time. The other guy…a baby beer belly. He kind of drifted away. No show, no call, for one shift. Called a few days later with a lame excuse. We let him come back but didn't put him on the busy times. He called in sick, Mary told him to call when he thought he could work again, and he never did."

"Anything from them that was suspicious or odd?"

"Not that I can think of."

"Like wanting to work on the slow shifts by themselves. Or asking about the security here?"

Rob shook his head. "No one works alone. We always have at least two people here, even in the dead times. New employees don't get to close or open for at least six months. We go over the security, along with everything else when we start, but it's basic—more what to do with an unruly customer, when to call the police, how to handle drug deals. That sort of stuff. I don't show them how things are wired, or even where the cameras are."

"They should be able to spot them."

"They should," Rob agreed. "But they'd have to look up."

"Would you want to consider hidden cameras?" I asked. Our original decision had been to make them obvious, so people would know there were on candid camera. The point being to keep people in line instead of catching them after they'd stepped over.

Rob sighed. "I hate to think what that would cost me."

"More than a burger and fries," I took another bite, "but not horrible. Could do it for as little as a few hundred, depending on how many you want."

"What would that tell us? And who would have time to review the footage?"

Two valid points. "I'm not sure, and probably no one unless something happened."

"I'll think about it," he said. "Let me see what this is going to cost me before digging into the blind, orphaned puppies fund."

I nodded.

"What do we do now?" he asked.

I wasn't quite sure. "Let me keep digging. I'd like to narrow it down more if I can. Helpful if we can rule anyone out. Keep the door padlocked."

Rob nodded and left me to finish my burger in peace.

What did I need to do next, I contemplated as I ate the now lukewarm fries. I had the names of the three ex-employees. I could try to talk to them. Not that they would admit to stealing the key, but people reveal things—expressions, tone, their choice of words.

This was the paying case.

Mr. Big Shot PI hooked up with women he thought were transgender.

Stella Houston was killed by someone she knew.

Why had he reacted to my comment about being in league with the robbers? I had also made the comment about being on crack. Maybe he had a drug problem? Was he newly clean? I couldn't be sure what he'd reacted to, nor what his reaction meant.

I knew his offer hadn't been legit. More likely meant to both distract me and keep tabs on what I was doing. To keep me from doing anything more about Stella Houston? He drove a dark SUV. Was that the second car I'd seen? If he was the killer, of course he'd want his friend investigating the case.

The bar was getting busier and noisier. I needed quiet time to think.

I bussed my plate back to the bar, waved good-bye to Mary, and headed out. As I exited, I scanned the area for his SUV.

Ah, parked about a block down in a No Parking zone.

I sauntered to my car as if I didn't have a care in the world and drove at a leisurely pace back to my office.

I didn't stop, instead turning at the next block and speeding up, turning again at the next block. I kept this up until I had wound my way to St. Claude, the major thoroughfare in this part of town.

I picked up speed, crossed over the Industrial Canal bridge into the Lower Ninth Ward. Devastated during Katrina, it was bouncing back with new construction and gentrifiers. I again did the block-by-block turns, even going around several blocks twice. The second time, I caught sight of the dark SUV again, but now I was behind him. He seemed not to have considered I'd just loop the block. I watched him take the turn, slowed as I drove to it, but this time I kept going straight.

I kept to the side streets, taking St. Claude into Chalmette, a town just downriver from New Orleans in the next parish, St. Bernard. It was a working-class area, fishing and oil. I found a suitable shopping strip and pulled in.

Waited.

No sign of his SUV. I hoped he was still lost in the Lower Ninth.

After about fifteen minutes of checking email on my phone—mostly deleting spam—I headed back to the safety of Orleans Parish.

I was both triumphant that I had eluded him and annoyed that I wasted time doing so.

I still wasn't sure what to do next.

Follow the threads. Get to the dead ends to cross them off. Get lucky and find one or two that aren't dead ends.

I headed home, but not in a direct way. I parked about a block away from my house. My car is a nondescript gray Mazda, but he knew what it looked like and probably my license plate number as well. I sat, scanning the block.

I did not need this complication. Maybe it was just harassment. Or him trying to prove how great a PI he was by being able to tail me. Not that great since I'd lost him. But maybe he was the killer, or part of the robbery gang. Or both. The more time I had to spend evading him, the less time I could use for anything else.

I wasn't investigating either the robberies or Stella's death officially. But I was close to, or over, the line not so officially. The missing key might be connected to the robberies. Searching for Peter D'Marchant wasn't a link, but it still had me asking around in the LGBTQ community.

A big SUV was gliding down the block. I watched it in my side mirror.

It parked two spots in front of me. A couple got out, letting out a shaggy dog and grabbing several grocery bags from the back. They looked suspiciously at me. The man took out his phone and took a photo. Torbin had mentioned they'd moved here from Brooklyn and hadn't adjusted to living in a city where people talked to each other on the streets and hung out on their stoops. Torbin said they even complained about a second line parade coming by.

I held up my phone as if videoing them. Let the suspicion flow both ways.

I exited my car, ignoring their outraged stares. Too bad I don't play the tuba or trombone, otherwise I'd blow the horn while sauntering home. Less out of place in this neighborhood than them.

Instead of going home, I stopped at Torbin's and Andy's. Torbin wasn't there, but Andy waved me in.

"Don't want to disturb you," I said. Andy was a computer nerd and often worked from home.

"Not in the least. I was desperately looking for an excuse to take a break, and you're better than cleaning the stove."

"I have an odd question," I started.

"I'd expect nothing less from you," he said with a smile.

"I have to review a pile of security camera footage. Is there any way to find specific people more quickly?"

Andy considered for a moment, then said, "Maybe, but facial recognition isn't as good as in the spy movies. Different angles, different lighting can fool it. Also, it's better with people who fit a certain demographic—that of those who have done most of the development."

"White people."

"Yep. Can it search fairly quickly? Yes, but you might recognize someone from behind and it might not."

"That's less than helpful."

"Yes, agreed. Tech is great when it works, frustrating when it doesn't—the story of my life. What are you looking for?"

I told him. Luckily I was only partway through when Torbin arrived, so I didn't have to repeat everything for him.

"Three computers, three sets of eyes," Torbin said when I'd finished.

Andy gave him a dirty look.

"But you're buying dinner," he added.

Andy seemed mollified.

"And making the cocktails," Torbin added.

I was happy to agree to both.

I pulled up my laptop, showed them the various images I was looking for. The three ex-employees at the top. Also, anything that looked like spiked drinks, people who didn't arrive together leaving together. I pulled a picture of Mr. Big Shot PI from the security footage and threw that in. And, in a final thought, the images of the two cars.

I got them started, giving them different days, then had to run to my house to get a full bottle of vodka and some mixers. Pomegranate Cosmo sounded good.

Dinner had been ordered and eaten (po-boys; oyster for me, shrimp for Torbin, and roast beef for Andy, with bread pudding for dessert, of which we could only eat about a bite apiece) before anything interesting showed up.

Mr. Supplement working the bar looked like he was spiking a drink. We slowed the tape and watched it on Andy's large screen.

False alarm. The customer seemed fine, stayed with his friends and left with them.

I made another cocktail.

And another. I might need to run out and get another bottle of vodka. Three people can drink a lot more than one.

"Wait," Torbin said. "Those cars."

Both Andy and I stopped and looked at his screen.

It was the two cars, driving close together as if they wanted to make sure no one got between them. The images weren't great, but good enough to see it was them.

Andy glanced at the time stamp. "That was the day of one of the robberies."

"How do you know that?" I asked.

"I've made a chart, times, locations, what we know."

"Trying to be a detective?"

"Not really," Torbin answered. "He's good at spreadsheets. This might help us, our friends, stay safe."

"I wanted to do something. It's not like the police have advised the community."

I nodded. He was right.

"Follow me on a hunch," I said. "Look at your spreadsheet and let's see if we can see these cars at any of the other times."

We finished the bread pudding and had switched to coffee before we found another hit.

Of the five robberies we knew of, we could see the cars in Q Carré's security cameras on two of them. Both of the robberies were in the area. Of the other five, one was out in the suburb of Metairie, one was in the Mid-City area, and the third in a bar in the Marigny. Rampart Street is the top perimeter, dividing the French Quarter from Tremé. With four lanes, it's the fastest way to get uptown or downtown in the area. Streets in the Quarter are slow, packed with traffic, including mule-drawn buggies and wandering tourists.

"What are the odds?" Torbin asked me as he sat back.

"Hard to say," I answered. "Could be coincidence. We could be seeing similar but different cars. How often do we take Rampart to get where we're going?"

"I can do an image match, see if it just looks like them or is likely to be them," Andy offered.

"That would be great. It's getting late," I said. "Let's call it a night. Are y'all willing to meet again Monday? I'll buy dinner and provide drinks again."

"Sure," Andy said. "This might be more useful than my spreadsheet."

"Your spreadsheet was the key. I might not have made the connection. You did."

It was past eleven p.m. and we all had worked a long week. I bid their yawning faces good-bye. I walked back to my car, moving it to in front of my house. I didn't want to wake up in the morning and think it had been stolen.

As I let myself in, I considered what we had found. As I told them, it was odd, but no real proof. Were they the same cars I'd seen? I needed to look at the footage for that time. Maybe Rob's street cameras had caught them. The bar was about six blocks uptown on Rampart.

If they were the same, what did it mean?

If I searched those cameras for my car, I'd find it as well. Probably more than once. But I live a block away from Rampart, and it's a main street.

I didn't have an answer.

CHAPTER THIRTEEN

The weekend blurred by. I had agreed to go camping with people I didn't know well enough to go camping with. Older lesbians, all single, but seemed sane. I was trying to expand my circle of friends, meet new people, all the healthy social activity we're told we should do. Of course it rained. Of course I was in the leaky tent. Of course the duo doing breakfast were ardent tea drinkers with a nod to coffee drinkers by bringing cheap store instant. Lesson learned and circle of friends not expanded. Just a pile of dirty clothes that took all Sunday evening to do.

Then it was Monday. Coffee, lots of coffee.

I had tossed and turned last night, almost getting up to review more of the footage, but managed to roll over and finally fall asleep.

I was meeting Torbin and Andy this evening. They both had their regular work until then. But my hours were much more flexible.

I took a long, looping route to my office. No sign of anyone following and no dark SUV. I even went through the annoying process of parking in the back, keeping my car out of sight.

Maybe it was too early for Mr. Big Shot PI to be awake after walking the mean streets.

There was an ostensibly polite email from Mrs. D'Marchant, asking for another update. I'd get to her later. Maybe by then I'd have something more to update.

The first thing I wanted to do was review the bar security tapes from the night Stella was killed. Maybe the cameras caught an image of the cars. I was crossing Rampart when I'd seen them. The bar was about six blocks up the street, making it likely they had come that way.

I started the footage at about half an hour before it had happened, running it at normal speed to not miss anything.

About five minutes in, I spotted what looked like the cars, but they were on the far side of the street, going in the uptown direction. Because of the distance, the images were indistinct, more shapes and colors. It was only a few seconds of them passing. I saved that clip, then resumed watching.

I saw them again, this time going downtown, closer to the cameras. I stopped the scroll, staring at them. Zoomed in as much as I could. Three silhouettes in the front car. It looked like two in back and one in front. I couldn't make out more than that. A driver, Stella, and someone else in back? Odd grouping. But someone had to push Stella out. A passenger sitting next to her, able to struggle and shove without losing control of the car.

You're making assumptions, I reminded myself.

But the timing was too close. In a few seconds they would have passed the bar and arrived where I was crossing the street. These had to be the cars I saw, both following closely as I'd seen the other times. I stared at the frozen image with both in the frame, the light sedan and the dark, boxy SUV. The color was a dark gray, maybe charcoal. Mr. Big Shot PI's was black, the shape slightly different.

Maybe he was smart enough not to drive his own vehicle when committing murder.

I rolled the clip again, at normal speed. The sedan seemed to be speeding up, putting distance between it and the SUV. Enough distance for the SUV to arrive just as Stella was pushed out?

I saved the clip and emailed it to Detective Thompson, along with the info about Sammy who'd stayed at the Monteleone. All I said was I'd found the clip on security footage from one of the bars I worked with. He would likely want more, but I wanted to talk to Rob first before I did anything else. Detective Thompson might be able to enhance the footage and get more from it than I was able to. He could get started on that.

I got up to get more coffee and my phone rang. I reached across my desk to answer it, hoping it wasn't Mrs. D. following up on her email.

"Hey, my friend Leland said to call you. Something about an old roommate of mine?" Then, to someone else, "You can start with twenty squats."

"Yes, I'm searching for Peter D'Marchant," I said. The background was noisy. Leland said he knew her from training. "Leland said you might have been roommates?"

"Yeah, a while back. What's this about?"

"His grandmother hired me to find him. She wants to reconnect. I gather he didn't get along with his father?"

"Yeah, that'd be true." To her trainee, "Try to get lower, work your glutes."

"Any idea of how to contact him?"

"I lost my phone a few days ago. Have to replace it and see if I can restore my contacts."

Damn, but didn't say it. "Anything you can tell me would be helpful."

"Like what?" Then, "Bicep curls into shoulder press. Twenty."

"Does he still live in the city?"

"Yeah, somewhere in the Bywater, I think."

"Can you remember the street?"

"Not offhand. Wait, I was going through stuff and found a Christmas card. If you give me a few, I can dig it up. Was piling stuff up to save or throw out, so it's in my office."

"That would be great."

She put the phone down. I could hear more muffled directions for the next exercise. And even more muffled, grunts of exertion in the background.

It took a few minutes and several rounds of exercises—body rows, one leg balance, sit-ups—before she came back on the line.

She read me the address and broke off to say, "No, work your shoulder muscles." Then to me, "Sorry, got to go. Hope this helps."

It made me glad that Torbin and I could set our own pace for working out. On the other hand, being pushed might not be a bad thing.

I stared at the address. It was about ten blocks from where my office was. Middle of the day now, not likely anyone would be home.

On the other hand, I had agreed to meet Torbin and Andy that evening. I could try later afternoon, on my way home to meet them. Maybe I'd get lucky and solve Mrs. D.'s case today.

Okay, one paying case close to being solved. I needed to concentrate on the other one.

Why did the thief take the key? Maybe if I could figure out the why, it would tell me the who. So far, the only use of it we'd seen had been coming in to cut wires to the security cameras. Did he mean to cut them all? Or just the ones out front?

It was the street cameras that had shown us the two cars. The ones that killed Stella had been in the vicinity of the two robberies in the area. Were they connected? Stella learned something about the robberies and they silenced her?

But why those cameras, that night?

My cell phone rang again.

I almost didn't answer it. Cordelia.

But I wanted to know why she was calling, so picked up.

"Hello," I said. I thought about answering "M. Knight Detective Agency," my usual office greeting, to pretend she wasn't still on my contacts list, but caught myself. That would be obnoxious. And untrue.

"Micky, hi."

"Hi," I answered. She called me; she needed to be the one talking.

Why do emotions ambush us so suddenly? Her voice, calling me in the middle of the day, so common when we'd been together. A brief prosaic contact about picking up something for dinner, maybe get cat litter, or just to say hi. A reminder someone was waiting for me to come through the door.

But it had been a long time since anyone had called me like that.

We had not talked, just the two of us, since the breakup. Our paths had crossed. In this small city, with our circle of mutual friends, it was inevitable. Mostly these meetings had been polite and cordial and superficial.

Her voice, me sitting in my office picking up the phone, all so familiar. A past that caught in my throat.

"I'm calling to see if you've heard anything…about Stella." Her voice was halting, hushed, like this was a forgotten path she hadn't traveled on in a long time. She cleared her throat, which I knew meant she was gathering her thoughts. "I've talked to Joanne and Danny, and they mostly say it's an ongoing investigation. They told me the case had been reassigned to someone else. I caught the TV clip of the original detective and it was awful. He said something like 'It's too bad, but this kind of thing often happens to she-men.'"

"He said that on TV?"

"I don't remember the whole thing, but that phrase stuck with me."

"Yes, they have reassigned the case. I talked to the new detective, and he seems good. He's gay but only recently moved here from Atlanta."

"You talked to him?"

"As a witness, not as a PI," I clarified. "I'm not getting much more from the official sources than you are."

"What about unofficial sources?"

She knew me well enough to ask that question.

"Have you heard about the identify theft robberies?"

"Something vaguely on the news. Why?"

"Targeting the gay community. Get friendly with someone at a bar, spike their drink. While they're out, use fingerprint or facial recognition to clean out all their accounts."

"Wait, what? I'm part of the gay community and I haven't heard about that. At least, not the part that they're targeting gay bars."

"Not sure why it hasn't been well publicized. Maybe the police want to keep details to themselves."

"Or maybe it's they don't care as much if it's targeting gay men."

"Maybe. Anyway, I've been looking into it for one of the bars. Since I'm already asking around, I'm asking questions about Stella."

"What have you found?"

"Not much," I had to admit. "Tendrils that might dissolve into mist. Some background on her—a striving student, well beyond the missteps of her youth. Not a sex worker, like the original detective alleged."

"I knew that."

"But hidden behind medical confidentiality."

"Well, true."

"I managed to find security camera footage of the cars. I don't have the equipment, but the police might be able to enhance the images, maybe even get a license plate."

"You gave it to them?"

"Yes. There are things they can do that I can't."

"Is that all?"

"No, more bits and pieces, but nothing that's evidence. I may have a suspect even, an obnoxious guy who dates trans women."

"A suspect?"

"Really a hunch," I admitted. "Found out he's hit on trans women and he's been very interested in what I'm doing. Another PI. He offered to work with me to get the rewards for the robberies. But that's not evidence."

"I don't think Stella was dating anyone, and obnoxious doesn't seem her type."

"He may not have been obnoxious to her," I pointed out.

"Point taken."

"Besides, there can sometimes be a rakish charm with obnoxious people." I liked to think I managed it. Sometimes.

"Hmm, I suppose. Especially if they're obnoxious on your behalf." Then she seemed to remember we needed to veer away from these areas. "What are you doing next?"

"I think whoever killed her was someone she knew. It would be helpful if I could talk to people around her. Did she mention anyone to you? Come in with friends? In a support group?"

Silence for a moment, then, "Even if I did know, I can't tell you."

"I don't expect you to." I knew that would be her answer. I can skate ethical lines if I think the end is worth it. Cordelia doesn't. Confidentially was sacrosanct. "Ask if they'll talk to me, give them my name and number. I won't know who they are unless they make the choice."

"Okay," she said slowly. "Some of my clients are reluctant to go to the police. How will you protect them?"

"I'm not the police. I want to find her killer. But...the living people need to be protected, too. If I have to choose, I'll choose those still breathing. If they tell me anything useful, I'll try to find other sources—even make them up, if need be. I won't give anyone's name to the police unless they give the explicit okay."

I heard a muffled "I'll be with you in a minute," then it was back to me. "Thank you. I know I can trust you. I just...this has been hard on a lot of people she knew. I can't promise anyone will talk to you."

"Tell them I'm a lesbian, not a cop. A PI who isn't going to follow the official rules if they might hurt people who shouldn't be hurt."

"Obnoxious, I see." But there was a smile in her voice. "I'll do what I can. I've got to go."

The line went silent.

We'd fallen into our usual rhythm, an ease of long knowing one another. Maybe we both needed to stay away from this. I was staring at the phone, as if it held promise and pain.

I sat back. I could call and update her.

Not a good idea, Micky. It's only going to remind you that you're single and she's not.

I had met her new partner. We didn't like each other. My reasons were valid. She didn't like me because I was Cordelia's ex and they had another nine years to go before the two of them would spend the same amount of time together as we had. One glaring issue Cordelia and I had yet to resolve was the house. We had bought it together; now I lived in it alone. I paid the entire mortgage at this point. But on paper, she owned half.

Nancy, her new partner, really liked the house and the neighbor-hood, hinting that I should vacate and let them live it in. Two of them and one of me and all that.

Cordelia hadn't pushed the issue. She was a community health center doctor, so was doing okay. Not well enough for an Uptown mansion, but well. Best I could tell, Nancy was content to be a domestic goddess. She had been a nurse so could easily find a job, but I'd seen no evidence of her having one. I can easily look those things up, and I'm nosy enough on a slow afternoon to do it. My interactions with her had been stiff and, as we are wont to do in the South, so polite as to be rude.

Yes, I can be obnoxious.

Let it go. Focus on the work in front of you.

I needed to review more of the security footage, see if I could find Mr. Big Shot PI with Stella. A long shot—it was only one bar and they could meet anywhere. Also, who did he hang out with? If it *was* him, he hadn't done it alone. He knew one of the ex-employees. I needed to dig further into that. Two people in the first car, one in the second. I needed to figure out who those people might be.

And it was lunchtime. I'd filled my stomach with coffee and needed something to sop it up.

I retrieved the turkey sandwich I'd brought the other day. It would do. With delectable toaster pastry for dessert.

Turkey sandwich, drink, ready to eat. Phone call, of course. Joanne.

"Hey, what's up?"

"License plate registered to Reginald Reine. His has a PI license. Thought you should know."

"Thanks," I said.

"Gotta go."

I would look him up but was going to eat lunch first.

I'd just taken a large bite when my phone rang. I picked it up and managed to mumble, "M. Knight Detective Agency," around a mouthful of turkey and bread. I hadn't put enough mustard on it, so it was dry.

"Which bar?"

"Who is this?" Although I knew who it was. Bright and eager NOPD Detective Edmont Thompson. "Client confidentiality," I muttered as I finished swallowing.

"Don't make me subpoena your ass."

"I have to talk to the bar owner. Will get back to you by tomorrow."

"Not good enough. Shit has hit the wind turbine."

"What happened?"

"Shouldn't tell you, but it'll be in the news in a hot minute. One of the victims didn't make it. Missing for several days. They found the body dumped in an overgrown lot."

"Oh, shit. Where?"

"So, if I can't move on Stella Houston's murder, it'll get pushed aside. Can't tell you, so you heard it on the news, abandoned lot in the Lower Ninth."

"But it's just another gay man," I said sarcastically.

"A pretty well-to-do one from Boston. Husband didn't hear from him; he didn't come home when he was scheduled to. Alarms went off. It's shifting into high gear. We know it's him, still had his wallet. Phone gone. Don't have cause of death yet, but if he was drugged, it's the same MO and there will be press howling, which means the powers that be want it solved pronto."

"Okay, but I'd still like to contact the bar first. Cops aren't always welcome."

"I get that, but I need to be moving to keep moving."

"Can you do anything to enhance the video?"

"Not without some verification it's authentic. Too easy to fake things these days."

"Later this afternoon."

He gave me his cell number and said to call ASAP.

I took another bite of turkey sandwich. After chewing my food, I called Q Carré, but Rob wasn't there. I left a message for him to call me as soon as he could.

Then I finished my sandwich.

I sent Rob the same footage I'd sent Detective Thompson, with an explanation and another request to call me. He might read his email before he got the message from the bar.

I was discombobulated, first by the phone call from Cordelia and now that someone had died from the spiked drinks. What would it be like? Waiting at home, expecting a phone call? Excusing the first missed call because he was traveling, then maybe he lost his phone. Then not arriving on his expected flight. Yes, the police and the media would be on this. Well-to-do, out of town, only lacking being a pretty blond woman to hit the trifecta of media bait.

Not my case.

Images of Mr. Big Shot PI, with Stella. I didn't recall her being there, but I didn't know her when she was alive, and the bar is open many more hours than I'm there. Or she might never have come in.

Time to search for him. Reginald Reine was, as he claimed, a private investigator. Flunked out after one year in law school at Loyola. Business degree from UNO. Married, two children, both daughters. Lived out in the safe suburbs, solidly middle-class area. No criminal record, not surprising since he was licensed. Boring, except for hassling me.

I sighed and did a quick search of evenings in the three weeks before Stella was killed. If they met at Q Carré, this was a likely time. I started with the times from seven p.m. to midnight. She was a student and working, so likely not out too late. I watched the figures going by at double speed.

First week, nothing.

Second week, Mr. Big Shot PI showed up, with his ex-employee friend, now on the buying side of the bar. They got drinks and hogged several barstools. Mary was serving them. Her expression was neutral, meaning she preferred they drink elsewhere. No smile or chitchat as she served them. That seemed to be the point. They could be here and there was nothing she could do about it except frown. They were chatting, got another drink. After about an hour, their other friend joined them, the one I'd seen at Mrs. D.'s place. They had been saving the barstool for him. Not polite to hold a seat in a busy bar for an hour. Once the three of them were there, they got another round of drinks. Then they started looking around the bar.

Hunting. But for what? Or whom?

It took only a few minutes for the answer.

A group of women came in. Two of them were tall, around six feet—all but one was on the tall side for women. When straight women come into a bar like this as a large group, they act like this is a novel and fun experience just for them. That's biased, I reminded myself; there were a number of regulars who were straight but worked either in the bars or restaurants or do-gooder social services so were cool with everyone but assholes. I've hung out with several of them on occasions, enjoying bitching about the potholes and the politics.

Two topics that never run dry in New Orleans.

These women had a different energy. Bright and happy, as if they'd entered a space where they knew they would be welcome and safe.

There were four in this group. Stella wasn't there.

How could she still be alive, like I might see her on the tape, and not be alive in real life?

I refocused on the scene. Mr. Big Shot PI sauntered over to them and started talking. Frustrating that I could only see and not hear. They laughed a few times, more polite than hearty. Or maybe the jokes weren't that funny. He seemed to be motioning for them to join him at the bar. A little back-and-forth. He pointed to their drinks as if offering to buy a round. After about another minute, they followed him back to the bar. Introductions, handshakes, some nodding. Ex-Employee even got off his stool and offered it to one of them. Drinks were ordered.

Mr. Big Shot PI seemed to be flirting with the shortest of the bunch. Mr. Booze Boy was interested in her, too, but also working the others. Maybe more interested in the attention than anything else. He seemed to do most of the talking. Ex-Employee was mostly drinking and dutifully laughing at his friends' jokes.

Second drink in, they started getting hands on. First Mr. Big Shot put an arm around his target's shoulder. Booze Boy tried to put his hand on the thigh of the woman next to him, only to have it playfully swatted away. Ex-Employee was content to be a gentleman, at least in this crowd.

Stop judging, I reminded myself. These are all consenting adults. I'd flirted in bars, gone home with women I'd met there. This was no different. Except it was. When I did it, we were both women, for the most part close in age, only well off enough to buy the bottom-line beer. In this case, the men were well dressed, probably making money (perhaps not Mr. Ex-Employee, but his parents were rich). They were hitting on African American trans women. It might be consenting adults, but consent was slippery when power is out of balance.

The two women not being pawed—I mean, hands-on flirting— left, heading for the bathroom.

Just at the edge of this camera, Mary beckoned them over at the far end of the bar. I pulled up that screen. Mary said something to them. They nodded, looked like the fun had gotten less fun. I wondered if Mary was warning them off. One of them leaned over and kissed Mary on the cheek, and they continued on to the bathroom.

I was right. When they came back from the bathroom, they rejoined their friends and make the classic "but we have to run" motions. Smiling and laughing but making it clear that they had all forgotten they had to be at work tomorrow at eight and needed to go.

Mary and one of the other bartenders chose that time to stand at this part of the bar, clearly watching. Booze Boy gave her his charming smile like he just knew that was the key to making friends and influencing people. Didn't seem to be working.

The women made their escape.

The three men finished their drinks, scanning the bar the whole time but finding nothing to their liking. Mary handed them the bill. Booze Boy handed it to Ex-Employee for his rich parents to pay. He looked sheepish as he handed her his credit card. Booze Boy and Mr. Big Shot PI were already out the door when he got it back.

I hoped he tipped well.

I saved the footage in a separate file.

What did it tell me? A lot of men like what they consider exotic or forbidden. There is a lot of so-called kink in the world, a good deal of it hidden. I doubted Mr. Big Shot PI mentioned any of this to his police contact friends. But this wasn't evidence of anything other than these three straight white boys liked to come downtown. Consenting adults all around.

I wondered what Mary had warned them about. I'd have to ask her.

I looked at the time. If I wanted to knock on Peter D'Marchant's door before meeting Torbin, I'd have to head there now. I needed to make sure I had enough time in case he was there. A strange PI telling you your estranged grandmother wants to reconnect wasn't likely to be a brief conversation.

The address wasn't very far from my office, in an area real estate salespeople are calling New Marigny, trying to get people to forget that it's been called the Seventh Ward for generations. It's across St. Claude Avenue, which used to be a hard dividing line between working-class whites nearer the river and working-class Blacks. Gentrification was insidious like that. The bartenders, waiters, artists, and musicians who used to live in the Marigny and Bywater areas got priced out, so they moved to where they could afford. They made it seem cool and hip—and safe—so the middle managers moved in. And the people who lived there got pushed out. Lather, rinse, repeat. I suspected Peter was living where he could afford to live and where it was as safe as possible to be gay. It's why I'd moved to my neighborhood—it was queer friendly, there were already other gay people on the block, and I could afford it. We're each a drop, just trying to live our lives, in a river of hard change.

I headed for a light to cross St. Claude. The evening traffic was starting up. It can be a busy four-lane road. In that quirky New Orleans fashion, Rampart slides into it, the four lanes switching from Rampart to St. Claude. Rampart became a smaller side street.

Peter's was the first block in, on Marais Street. It used to be swamp in bygone eras before effective pumping stations.

His house was a turquoise and salmon single shotgun, narrow and long. It wasn't the most colorful house on the block. The paint was starting to fade but would be okay for a few more years. I found parking across the street and walked back to his door.

Fingers crossed this would solve a well-paying case. Not long and lucrative, but decent bucks for the time spent. I wasn't charging Rob as much as I'd charge Mrs. D'Marchant. First, because she fell into the oh-shit cases, ones I only took for the money. Also, she was a one-time client and Rob was ongoing. And I liked Rob.

I knocked on the door.

Knocked again and was about to assume no one was home when it opened.

A short man, not Peter, opened it.

"Don't need religion, nor can we help your husband who needs gas money to get to the hospital," he greeted me.

"None of the above." I pulled out my license and showed it to him. "I'm looking for Peter D'Marchant."

He narrowed his eyes. "What's this about?"

Ah, bingo! He knew the name, otherwise he would have looked blank, not wary.

"His grandmother hired me to find him." I don't always tell the truth, but in this case, it seemed the most useful.

He scrutinized my license, then looked at me. I was wearing black jeans, a V-neck blue T-shirt to make it look classy, and a denim jacket.

I heard a voice from inside asking what was going on.

The man called back, "Someone here looking for you, using your deadname."

Oh, shit, oh, shit. Now I knew why I couldn't find Peter.

A tall, blond woman came to the door. One who looked like Peter D'Marchant.

"I'm sorry," I blurted out, "I didn't know."

"It's okay," she said. "What's this about my grandmother?" She motioned me in.

The living room was like the outside of the house, colorful, a little worn, and comfortable looking.

"Would you like something? Coffee, tea, water?" the woman asked.

I didn't even know her real name.

"You don't need to do that," the man muttered.

"Thank you, no," I answered.

He sat down on the end of the couch and she sat next to him. I took the chair opposite.

I handed her my license. "My name is Michele Knight. I'm a private detective. Your grandmother hired me to locate you. The information she gave me was what I've been using. I apologize for using your deadname."

"It's okay, how could you know?"

The man snorted. "So, what do you want?" he said.

"James, it's okay," she said to him.

"Is it? This is your past, and you put it behind you," he said.

"Let's hear what Ms. Knight has to say," she answered.

"Your grandmother has had a change of heart," I said, "and wants to reconnect. She hired me to search for you. She said the family had lost contact."

"Lost contact?" James interjected. "That's what they said?"

"That's the version your grandmother told me," I said. This was their family drama, and they carried the emotions, not me. "Because she wants contact doesn't mean you need to accept it."

"So, we can tell them to fuck off?" James said.

"If you choose," I said. "Are you okay giving me your names? I'd like something other than your deadname."

"Why should we do that?" James said.

I guessed they were a couple, and he was being protective. It made me like him.

"You don't need to. You can tell me to leave, and I will."

"It's okay. My name is Audra D'Marc. Got so used to writing the 'D apostrophe M' that I kept it. This is my partner, James Davis."

"I'm pleased to meet you," I said. "I know this might feel like a bolt of lightning, me showing up on your doorstep and pulling you back into what sounds like a painful time in your life. As I said, you don't need to talk to me, and you don't need to make any decisions now. You have time to think about this."

"If we tell you to leave, what do you do?" James asked.

"I leave. I'll tell your grandmother that I found you. You are alive and doing well, but wish no further contact."

"That's it?"

"Pretty much. And hope she pays the bill."

"Knowing your grandmother, she won't," he muttered.

"At this point, I no longer know what she would do," Audra said. "You're right, this is unexpected and I'm not sure what to think. I'm guessing she wanted to find her gay grandson, not a granddaughter."

"From the information she gave me, that's likely. But I can't predict if that will make a difference."

"Did she say why she wants to connect now? I haven't been hidden, exactly. My mother knows where I am. But it was a bitter divorce, so I can see them hiring someone rather than asking her," Audra said.

"Like the lady says, you can think about this," James said.

Lady? Me? I let it pass.

"I am thinking about it. It was both horrible and freeing. They kicked me out of the house, gave me barely time to throw things into a suitcase. I was between jobs, so I had to beg couches from friends."

"That was horrible," I acknowledged. "What was freeing?"

"I didn't need to try to be what they wanted me to be anymore. I could go on my own journey. I could be as gay as I wanted, didn't have to hide. I was finally open enough with myself to know what I should have known all along, more of me is a woman than a man. I was able to live my truth." She smiled radiantly, as if remembering the weight that had been lifted.

"What do you know about being trans?" James asked.

"Not enough," I admitted.

"Do you even know any gay people?" he challenged.

"What? How dare you assume I'm straight! Most people take one look and go right to dyke."

Audra laughed. James scowled before allowing a small, sheepish smile.

"Yes, I'm lesbian, pretty much out since high school. Started sleeping with women when marriage was in the when-pigs-fly category."

"Look, sorry," he said. "We're both trans and…well, you know."

"The world isn't kind to people who are different," I said.

"Does my grandmother know you're a lesbian?" Audra asked.

"I assumed that's why she hired me."

"Takes one to find one?" James said.

"She might think that way," I said.

"A long time. It's been over five years," Audra said. "She could have looked for me anytime she wanted to. Did she say why now?"

"Not directly. I think some of it is the changing times. More of her friends are accepting gay family members. Peer pressure, so to speak. Plus, she's getting older, the years left fewer. Maybe she wants to see a younger generation moving on in the world, to be there when she's gone."

Audra nodded. "I guess the question I have to ask myself is whether I'll lose my freedom, tamp myself down to fit their expectations."

"Don't do that," I said. "If it costs you that, maybe it's not worth it. I think we know better than most that sometimes you have to leave your birth family for your family of choice."

"Yes." She looked at James with a joyful smile.

He returned that smile, with a look of adoration on his face.

I've always appreciated short men who love tall women.

"I don't want to take up more of your time. You might want to talk this through. Or pour a stiff drink."

"Or both," she said. "What should we do next? Do I contact you with my decision?"

"If you'd like. You can just call your grandmother if you want. I don't need to be the middleman anymore."

"Middle person," James said.

I nodded. He was right, we gender language in too many ways.

"I do need time to think. If I keep you in the middle, can you charge my grandmother more?" Audra asked, with a smile.

"I do charge for time," I said. "But you should do what's best for you."

"I don't think I want to just show up. I don't think I'm ready for that," she said.

"Okay, think about it," I said. "Contact me when you're ready." I pulled out two cards and gave them each one. "I've done this before and can help you through it—whether you want to make contact or not."

"Help us how?" James asked.

"Finding missing persons is a lot of what I do. Some want to be found, reconnected. Some don't. Some for good reason and some not so good. Sometimes, it's a happy ending. But only sometimes. Families can be messy, as you know. I try to prepare both the people searching and the people they're searching for with realistic expectations."

Audra nodded. "Realistic endings. Maybe that will help."

I had one more question. "Did either of you know Stella Houston?"

"The woman who was killed the other night?" James said. "Why do you ask?"

"I was walking home when it happened. I was a witness. While I'm working on other things, I'm asking around. People might talk to a lesbian PI in ways they won't talk to the police."

Audra and James exchanged a look.

"It would take a murder for us to call them," James said. "Not exactly trans allies."

"We both knew Stella," Audra answered. "Not well. Not come over and have a drink well, mostly like mentoring newly trans folks, working on projects like a website for the community. It hit us all hard when she died."

"Don't believe it was an accident like the cops claim," James said.

"Why do you think that?" I asked.

"Active, making-waves trans woman in good health dies. We can live to a ripe old age, as long as no one kills us." he said.

"Anything beyond that?"

"No," he admitted.

"It's hard to think Stella could have something stupid and random like that happen to her, but life is full of shit," Audra said.

"I think she was killed," I said. "I saw what happened. Maybe it was an unlucky accident, but it could have been planned."

"Don't encourage James and his theories," Audra said, smiling at him.

"Not my goal. Just want to find the truth. There were two cars involved and they seemed to be traveling together. One pushed her out, the second ran over her."

Audra covered her mouth. "That's what happened? That's horrible!"

"Evil," James seconded.

"I don't have proof. And may never find it. But I'd like to keep looking."

"What can we do?" Audra asked.

"Just what I'm doing. It might have been someone she knew."

"Stella would not get in a car with a stranger," James said. "We did workshops together and she was big into safety. Even said that—don't get in cars or go places with people you don't know."

"Was she dating anyone? Had a falling-out with someone? Anyone angry at her?"

"We can ask. Like you said, they might talk to us."

"Call me if you find anything."

They both nodded.

I stood up, glancing at my watch.

"In a hurry?" James asked.

"Sorry. I'm supposed to meet my cousin Torbin in about fifteen minutes with dinner in tow," I said. "But I can tell him I'll be late if you want to talk more."

"Torbin? Torbin Robideaux?" Audra asked.

"Yes. You know him?"

"Everyone knows Torbin," James said. "Wait, you're his cousin Micky?"

"Yep, that's me."

"Would have been nicer if I'd known that," he said.

I grinned. "Hazards of the PI trade."

"We'll have a stiff drink next time," Audra said. "I'll be in touch."

I waved good-bye as I went down the stairs. Out of habit, I scanned the street. No boxy black SUVs. Once in my car I texted Torbin, saying I'd be a little late and asking if burgers from Q Carré would do for dinner.

I'd just gotten my seat belt on when he texted back their order. Grilled chicken for Andy, and he was fine with the burger. Extra order of fries and one serving of the praline bacon brownie—if we shared, we could claim there weren't enough calories to count.

I texted *OK* and headed for the bar.

Parking was kind, a spot right in front. What Cordelia and I used to call Doris Day parking.

It was slow, happy hour not yet happy. I went to the bar and placed my order.

"My, you must be hungry," Mary said.

"For three of us, not just me."

She nodded as she passed the order to the grill.

"Do you have time for a couple of questions?" I asked. I'd deliberately not called in the order, wanting an excuse to hang around.

"Sure, for you anything. Especially when it's slow like this. The robberies and now the murder might be keeping people away."

"What have you heard?"

"Mostly what's on the news. Somebody dead, likely from the drugs he was given. Wondering if he was here."

"That possible?"

"I hope not. But it's too real. Was that your question?"

"No, I want to see if you can recognize some faces."

She nodded, put up a finger to say wait while she served a customer. I swiped through my phone and pulled up the pictures to show her.

"What do you know about these guys?" I asked, showing her the group of Mr. Big Shot PI, Booze Boy, and Ex-Employee.

She looked at the picture, frowning. "They come in from time to time."

"Not your favorites?"

She pointed to Ex-Employee. "He used to work here. Think it was more of a lark for him. Didn't take it seriously, almost like playing at being an adult. Forgot he was supposed to serve drinks, not chat with his friends. Okay sort, mostly friendly and cheerful, until you reminded him to do his job, then he could be surly. Needed to grow up. He only lasted a few weeks, then left. Came back about a month later as a customer. So many other bars in this city and he comes here."

"How about the other two?"

She pointed to Mr. Big Shot PI. "Likes to boast, but tips well if you listen. Suspect he has a wife and two kids in the suburbs, and coming here is his early midlife crisis."

"Any problems or issues with him?"

"Not that I know of, other than him bothering you."

"He thinks he's a better PI than I am."

"Not a chance."

"What's going on here?" I swiped to the screen capture of her warning the women.

She again looked at the photo.

I clarified, "They were talking to those men, went to the bathroom, and you said something to them. When they rejoined the group, the women left pretty quickly."

"Oh, yes, I told them that he," pointing to Mr. Big Shot PI, "has lots of cop friends. Brags about working with them. Thought they might need to know that."

"Why?" I had an idea but wanted her answer.

"It's hard being queer sometimes, especially if you're Black and transgender. These two," she pointed to two of the women, "have sometimes done less-than-legal things to survive. Minor as far as I know, low-level dealing and occasional sex work. They keep it out of here, so no problem. That and cops don't mix."

"Have these men come in before and tried to hit on trans women?"

"Don't think they're regulars, or at least not when I'm here. Maybe come in once a month, every few weeks at most. Have a few drinks, sometimes chat with some of the other customers. Trying to remember if I saw them leave with anyone." She thought for a moment, and shook her head. "Only when it's slow like this would I notice. Most of the time, it's too busy to see more than who needs the next drink."

"Can you remember the last time they were here?"

"Not sure, not that long ago. Only noticed because only one of them got a drink and he didn't stay long. In a hurry, like."

Rob entered the bar and headed straight for me. "I got your messages. What's up?"

"Did you look at the photo?" I asked.

"Yes. Guessing it's going to the police, and you wanted to be nice enough to let me know."

"Pretty much."

"They were here earlier."

"They were?"

"Yeah, new detective on the case." He fumbled in his jacket pocket to pull out Detective Thompson's card. "Also, some fresh new lesbian cop."

"Did you get her name?"

"She's too young for you. And way too earnest."

"Not for dating, so I know who's working on this. What did they want?"

"Pretty much what you gave them. Any security footage from the times of the robberies around here."

"What did you tell them?"

"That we are law-abiding citizens and will be glad to cooperate. Going to ask you to pull the footage. I have the list of what they asked for." He pulled a folded sheet of paper from the same jacket pocket and handed it to me.

"On your dime?"

"Free burgers for the next year?" he joked.

"Burgers don't pay the mortgage. And one a day would not be good for my waistline."

"I suppose. Gotta keep your girlish figure. Yeah, add it all to the bill."

"I was reviewing them anyway, this shouldn't be too much beyond that. Do you want to review anything first?"

"Do I want needles in my eyes? No, unless you see something that might cause me to lose my license or end up in jail."

"You're law-abiding, so no need to worry."

"Got your order," Mary interrupted us. "Sorry about the brownies. We just did a new batch and had three left from the old one, so we're putting them all in."

"Breakfast of champions," I said, taking the fragrant bag from her. It had bacon in it, after all.

I waved good-bye and left.

As I exited the bar, I noticed Booze Boy and Ex-Employee on the far side of the street. They were posing and mugging near the entrance to Armstrong Park. Someone with his back to me was filming them with a cell phone. The other grandson? Skinny, too-big leather jacket, but I couldn't see his face. Booze Boy had a new jacket, one that was a better fit—didn't hide the encroaching beer belly, but shaped it better.

I started to cross the street to talk to them, but reconsidered. The three of them together would be hard to get much from. If I was going to question them, better to do it when they weren't in a pack. Besides, cold French fries was a sin Torbin would never forgive.

I headed to Torbin's and Andy's place.

"Where are the cocktails?" he asked as I put the food on his kitchen counter.

"Go ahead and eat the food before it gets cold, I can microwave mine after I run back to my house, get the cocktail stuff, and get back here."

Torbin mimed a tiny violin.

Andy had empathy. "It's not a problem. We have plenty of stuff here. Let's eat first and decide drinks later." He began taking the food out of the bag and distributing it.

"I had to take three bacon brownies as they were the end of a batch and they already had a new one in the oven. I'll take the extra two home with me, so don't you worry."

"We can't allow you to absorb the calorie burden," Torbin informed me. "We will all do our part."

I would have to find something else for breakfast tomorrow.

After we had eaten and were again in front of our computers, I pulled out the list Rob had given me. "We need to make separate files of these times and dates," I said, showing it to them.

"What's this?" Torbin asked.

"Police asked for security footage from the times of the robberies. Rob gave me permission to take from his stuff and give it to them."

"Cool! Official police list of the robberies," Andy said, taking the sheet from me. He immediately started checking it against his spreadsheet.

I had a slight qualm about giving him information I didn't have permission to hand out, but it passed. Andy's spreadsheet had already been helpful. No one said I couldn't share it, and they were helping me. And as for the police, who were they really here to protect and serve? We had to pressure them to assign a detective who'd take Stella's death seriously, and the first robberies were blown off as just drunk gay men. We could ask them for justice but might have to seek what we could find on our own. I left Andy to it.

If Mr. Big Shot PI and his cop friends were involved in Stella's death, who would they protect?

After a few minutes, he said, "This added three to what I have. Interesting."

"Anything particular?" I asked.

"Not yet, let me look at the footage," he answered.

We each started working on our assigned times and days.

About an hour in, we all decided it was time for alcohol. To be moderate—by New Orleans standards—we settled on wine, a nice Shiraz.

Nothing. And nothing. No sign of who I was now thinking of as the big three. Just people having a jolly good time, silent laughter flowing on the screen, a busy bar and happy people.

I had clipped three sections, all of them innocuous as far as I could tell. Torbin emailed me two he'd found, with a brief note saying he saw nothing suspicious in them. The list they sent had eight total on it. The robberies out in the suburbs weren't included. That made ten total.

Torbin and I were debating the wisdom of a second bottle of wine when Andy said, "I think I have something."

"Let's see," I said.

"It's what's not there," he answered. "The list they gave us added an early one and the most recent one. The early is too early. The recent... was the one where the man died."

"Was murdered," I said.

"Yes," Andy agreed. "The night the camera feed was cut."

"Wait, what? Are you sure?" I said. But of course he was sure.

"The police haven't released that," Torbin said.

"Not to the papers," Andy replied. "Can't be sure, but either they left him off, or this is it."

"The night the cameras were cut," I mused. "But they didn't get all the cameras, just the outside and front entrance. If he came in the bar, the other cameras would have caught it."

"Let's look," Torbin said.

We all put that night on our computers.

People at the bar, drinks being poured. Three blank panes from the two street cameras and the one front entrance. I focused on the bar one that overlapped slightly with the front. The front had a short hall, better to control the flow and scrutinize anyone who came in. The bar camera only showed just outside the hall.

Booze Boy came in. Got a drink, was looking around, looking at his phone several times as if checking for a message. Chugged his drink in a hurry. Then he left.

"That's him, right?" Torbin asked over my shoulder.

"Yes, one of them."

I slowed the speed down to see it again. He was there about ten minutes. Bought a drink, left a ten on the bar, didn't get change. Kept looking at his phone. Looked at it one more time, finished his drink, then left. As far as I could tell, he was by himself.

Torbin got another bottle of wine and poured us each a glass.

"What the hell does this mean?" he said.

"I don't know," I admitted. "Maybe nothing. I can see if the police have a more precise time."

"What would that tell us?"

"Was it around the time Booze Boy was in the bar? Waiting for the others to contact him? Maybe the police can pull his phone records."

"Based on what?" Andy pointed out.

I sighed. "That I don't like him isn't enough?" He'd gone into a bar and checked his phone. Not exactly probable cause.

"They didn't try to destroy footage after, but stopped it before," Torbin said. "Which means it was planned. They knew they would be robbing someone that night and didn't want cameras on."

"On what, though?" Andy asked. "Rampart Street is pretty busy. Even if the cameras were cut, could they kidnap someone and throw him in a car without being seen?"

"True," I said. "The bar cameras would be the least of their worries."

"Wait, what's this?" Torbin said. He pointed to a tall, skinny man who appeared in the bar.

I looked at the time stamp. Around four a.m., late enough things were slowing down.

"What?" both Andy and I asked.

"Off-duty," Torbin said. "I was walking with some friends, and he pulled up next to us. To warn us about being gay and out in public. 'Bad things can happen to boys like you. Might want to tone it down.' That kind of bullshit. Gave us all the creeps."

"You're not a boy," I pointed out. "You have more gray in your hair than I do. If you didn't dye it."

"Randy and Darren were with us. He might have meant them."

"Racist and homophobic," I said.

"So, what is he doing here?" Torbin asked.

"Warning everyone to be careful?" Andy said sarcastically.

We watched the footage. He walked around the bar, looking everything over, scrutinizing everyone. He finally came back to the bar and ordered a drink. Peg, one of the late-night bartenders, served him. He sipped his drink, still staring around the bar. Nothing overt, just the hint of a sneer, his bold stare, as if he had the right to watch everyone.

I didn't like him either.

He finished his drink, got another. Then he saw someone enter and went to her. She was dressed for a night on the town. She tried to step around him, but he grabbed her arm. She pulled away and two other people joined her, protecting her. He shook his head, wagged his finger in her face, put his drink down on the nearest table, and left.

"What do you think that was about?"

"He was being a cop. Assuming she was transgender. Treating her like she was a sex worker," Andy surmised.

"Power-hungry asshole," Torbin added.

But like the others, he had done nothing wrong. At least legally.

He was a sexist, racist asshole. He could invade our space and there was nothing we could do about it.

We poured the last of the wine.

We all reviewed that evening's camera, right up until the sun rose and the bar closed at six a.m.

"Could it be a distraction?" I asked. "Pull the plug on these cameras so we assume something happened here, when it happened a long way away?"

"But the bar still has to be involved," Andy said. "Someone stole a key to get in, which means it had to be an employee..."

"Which means they are part of the robbery gang," Torbin finished for him.

I sipped my wine. It was a meaningless jumble, built on a few small things—the cut camera wire and a swirl of assumptions. Straight men having a thing for transgender women wasn't a crime. So what if I just didn't like these men? What did I have beyond that? Which brought me back to Rob's case—find who came into his bar and cut the wires.

"Let's get all the clips the police asked for," I said. "And call it a night." Then I remembered, "Oh, can I get a favor?" I told them about Mr. Big Shot PI following me. "Can I borrow your car?" Torbin had a red Mini Cooper Clubman. Not discreet, and Big Shot would probably figure it out quickly, if he was half the PI he claimed he was. But the point was to fuck with him.

"Why don't you take mine?" Andy offered. "It's been a while since I've driven stick, and I could use the practice." Even better, he had a beat-up old Subaru Forester. Less easy to follow than a distinctive red car. We traded keys.

Sadly, none of us had eaten the praline bacon brownies. I took one home and left the other two.

Chapter Fourteen

Torbin and Andy took off in my car early in the morning. It was gone by the time I headed out, coffee mug well sealed so it wouldn't spill in a car not my own. I scanned the street for the black SUV. Not here. Seemed Mr. Big Shot PI was not a morning person.

Andy's car is bigger than mine. At least, unlike Torbin's Mini, the controls made sense instead of being some random assortment of cute levers and buttons. It did mean I'd have to mind what I was doing in tight parking spaces.

No sign of a big boxy SUV. Even so, I drove an un-straight line to my office. I parked on the street, right in front of the building. Mr. Big Shot PI would not be looking for a dusty blue vehicle.

Half a cup of coffee and a whole bacon brownie got me going. I first sent the security footage to Detective Thompson. I suggested we meet later. I had questions for him that he would likely blow off over the phone. Did they have a timeline for the murdered man? Was it when Booze Boy was in the bar, or Asshole Cop? Or neither? I don't like a lot of people, but that doesn't make them criminals.

I sent a text to Dottie. I didn't want to wait until she was off work. She might be able to answer if Mrs. D. went out or if she was back in the kitchen alone.

I wasn't going to contact Mrs. D. until I heard back from Audra.

Dottie called me almost immediately. "I took the day off," she said.

"Does Mrs. D. allow that?" I kidded.

"She's not going to pay me, that's for sure. I just said I was sick. Didn't say I was sick and tired of her."

"You should get some time off—paid," I said.

"Can I get you to do me a favor?"

"I was going to ask you a favor," I said.

"Then we can trade. You first."

"Do you know the names, full names, of the men who were there when I was leaving the other day?"

"I do. Why?"

"They've been in some odd places and I would like to dig a little deeper."

"You might run into alligators and snakes."

"I might. Why do you say that?"

"Just…act like they should get what they want. If they don't, it's not fair, never their fault. Once blamed me for some missing things. Until I proved I wasn't there when they went missing."

"Stealing the good bottles?"

"That, borrowing Mrs. D.'s cars without asking, leaving a mess in the kitchen because they wanted a late-night snack for someone else— me—to clean. Never admitting it was them, happy to let her blame someone else."

"Not nice. Anything illegal? That you know of?"

"Should be illegal to be scamming off your old folks, even if they are loaded. Should be illegal to be that full of themselves. But it ain't. Stealing the booze, but given it's family, I guess that's not so illegal."

"What are their names?"

"Grandson is Brice D'Marchant, big guy is Garland Gallano, and the dirty blond is Hugh Melancon. He's not so bad, just hangs with the other two too much. And his parents are too rich. Bad combination."

"Agreed. Now I owe you a favor."

"My car is broke. In the shop. My friend Ruby is the one who is good friends with Miss Estelle. She just got a big, last-minute job, three of her workers are out—sisters, all with COVID—and she needs help. I'm doing some of the cooking but need to get it there."

"You want a ride?"

"That would be ever so helpful," she admitted.

"What time?"

"You sure you can do this?" she asked.

"I'm sure. I'll take any excuse to get away from the office."

I agreed to pick her up at one.

That gave me the morning to do the usual searches for these three. Ex-Employee was the most likely key thief. Of these three, I reminded myself. I could be wrong and needed to not forget Supplement Man and Ghost Tour Guy. It's always a big mistake to see what we want to see.

Two hours later, I had established that Booze Boy was, per his own description, a financial consultant, a small business owner, and a world traveler. Although…I could only find pictures from a vacation in Mexico. He had started a cryptocurrency business several years ago, but it had gone belly up. I was smelling Ponzi scheme, but that was instinct, not evidence. He seemed to have no visible employment for now. He drove a burnt orange Mustang, a fairly nice new car for someone with no job. He posted more pictures of him in the car than traveling the world. The latest picture had a dent in the rear fender.

The other grandchild was on his career of failing upward… or at least sideways. He had started at LSU, but transferred to UNO, taking about five years to officially flunk out of a business degree. He worked about a year in his first job in business consultant management, whatever that was. Then at another place in sales and marketing. Six-month gap after that. Then two years in his father's real estate firm. Now he listed himself as a filmmaker and influencer. He posted trailers from a film he said he was working on. Murky and confusing, not the dark and suspenseful he was going for. Low budget, as Booze Boy was one of the main actors. He had a snarky-in-a-sophomore-fashion podcast about New Orleans and which bars were unmissable. I watched two of them, but he was cliché, superficial in his descriptions. Guess I'll never be an influencer. His listed address was an apartment on the lakefront. His car was a silver two-seater BMW sports car.

Ex-Employee had an even more lackluster career path. No college degree with a few attempts, a semester here and there at some of the small technical colleges in the area. Most of what I could find was entry level: barback, bartender, waiter, construction work. He also tried a podcast, but it was just him walking around describing what he saw. It had about twelve views. Not an influencer. His car he had wrecked was a red Camaro. He seemed to not have a car now. His address was at one of the newer apartment complexes popping up along Tulane Avenue, not trendy or posh, but decent and in a changing neighborhood.

Ah, a civil case against Booze Boy for financial shenanigans. He was being sued for allegedly promising twenty percent returns but instead he'd lost everything. Case was still in process.

More interesting, he had been married when he was twenty-one and divorced when he was twenty-three.

No criminal records for any of them. But they came from the kind of families whose children got a warning, not a criminal record when caught smoking weed.

I trotted downstairs to see if the grannies had had any better luck.

Three files, not too thick. I headed back upstairs to read them at my desk. They were for the three former employees I'd identified as the most likely key thief.

Numbers can be so interesting. Ex-Employee had a healthy bank account, five thousand a month every month. Parents? Trust fund? No wonder he could play at working. A lot of withdrawals, mostly to pay credit card bills. A few other deposits, mostly from the few jobs he had. Then last month, about $9K in cash. Birthday from parents? No, he was an August baby. None of the jobs he worked would make him that kind of money.

Ghost Tour Guy was doing well, checking healthy and even had a savings account. His income was good, but varied. Deposit of anything from less than fifty to several thousand. The last few months had been good to him, over thirty thousand in the last three. Ghost touring must be good business. But he was an influencer, too. He had several social media sites, including the popular podcast one. His, at least, were entertaining. He had a good, if not entirely accurate, knowledge of New Orleans and its history and used colorful videos with his voice over, instead of being a talking head like grandson Not Nice Brice. He did product placement and showcased various businesses, bars, restaurants, shops—making it likely that money was exchanged. Still, it was quite a chunk of change in a short time.

Supplement Man was a mess. Four bank accounts, two out of state. Not much in three of them. A lot in the fourth. He also had closed about eight more in the last few years. He had over one hundred thousand in the large account. It was what the account started with but no additions since, but it had only been active a few months.

The grannies had been good.

I stretched and looked at the time. I would need to leave to meet Dottie soon. I found some string cheese and an apple in the small fridge I kept in the office. It would have to do for lunch.

I walked around the office while eating. Looked out the window. There was a large boxy SUV parked at the corner, too close to the fire hydrant to be legal.

Well, fuck. I was hoping that he was trolling, guessing I'd come here and he could pick up my tail then.

Footsteps coming slowly up the stairs.

I hopped up, locked my door, and turned off the lights, listening to see if they continued past the second floor.

There was a lot of traffic in the coffee shop, but not much up here. The grannies, as befitted computer geeks, did most of their client interaction online. I discouraged drop-in business by more than just being on the third floor. I want to know who I'm meeting before I meet them.

Yep. Mr. Big Shot PI was impatient. I might have done the same thing if I felt I really needed to see what was behind the office door. But I wasn't doing anything that affected him or his cop friend. There was nothing here for him that I could think of, but what did he think he could find?

I texted the grannies, asking for at least two of them to come up the stairs in two minutes.

The locks on my door aren't cheap, hard for even an expert to pick. There is a frosted glass pane with M. Knight Detective Agency on it, but it's thick and reinforced with wire.

He was at my door. I was standing to the side, not throwing a shadow, but I could see his backlit outline. His same shape, big and tall, with slightly stooped shoulders.

You are fucking with my day. I considered jerking the door open to see what he would do, but only some of the possible reactions would be fun. Others might be dangerous.

He jiggled the handle. Nope, not here on legitimate business, otherwise he would have knocked. Some more jiggling and a soft scraping sound. He was trying to pick the lock. If I had a choice of which cops to call, I might call them, but it might be his police contact friends who showed up, and I didn't want to be in a straight white guy vs. lesbian fight with them.

Right on cue I heard "Can we help you?" The grannies to the rescue. It was Lena, the lead granny. A second voice added, "The coffee shop is down on the first floor, if you're looking for it." Adelaide, one of the newer grannies, who did judo in her spare time. And yoga.

"Actually, I was looking for Knight," he replied.

"She's out at the moment. Can we take a message?" Lena asked.

"I didn't mean to disturb you," he said. "I can wait until she's back."

"Not disturbing us, and there is really no place to wait up here,"

Lena said, her voice clear that he was not welcome to hang out by himself up here.

"You can wait in the coffee shop if you want, but it might be a while," Adelaide offered. "We can take a message and have her call you when she gets in. What's your name?"

"That's okay," he said, realizing he was outfoxed. "I can come back at another time."

"That sounds like a good plan," Lena said. "We'll be sure to let Micky know you came by." Translated to "We will warn Micky that someone up to no good was trying to pick her lock." The grannies are about the furthest thing from born yesterday that you can find.

Heavy feet on the stairs, going down.

"The chai latte is really good, might pick one up on your way out," Adelaide said. She and Lena were clearly waiting for him to pass them and continue down the stairs.

"Might do that," he said, his voice receding. "They have nice apple pie, too."

Ah, putting on the calories while stalking me.

Once I could no longer hear his fading footsteps, I opened the door and shot them a thumbs-up. They returned the gesture, smart enough not to talk lest he hear.

I did need to leave.

I looked out the window again but didn't see him exiting. Maybe he really was getting the apple pie.

I locked my office and set the alarm. I don't usually do that if I'm in and out, but if he came back, I wanted noise. Then I quietly made my way down the stairs. They bottom out at a hallway, one way leading to a hall into the coffee shop and one to the door outside, bypassing the shop. I paused for a moment to listen near the coffee shop door. He was ordering apple pie.

I quickly exited, keeping close to the building until I could get to Andy's car. In a moment of inspiration, I rummaged in my bag of tricks that I carry with me (also, snacks like granola bars, which usually get more use) and pulled out a magnetic tracker. Letting Andy's boxy SUV cover me, I darted across the street and stuck it on the underside of his vehicle.

Then back in my car du jour, I headed for Dottie's.

No sign he was following. I made it a point to check my rearview mirror multiple times as I left the neighborhood. I took the back streets to Dottie's address just in case—even though it would be hard to be unseen on these less traveled roads.

I got to her place a little after one. I stepped out of the car, and the door immediately opened like she had been waiting for me.

"Thank you so much for doing this!" she called out, motioning me inside.

"What's going on?" I asked as I entered.

"Miss Estelle has a world of trouble; she doesn't need any more. She said she'd pay, good woman that she is, but we all gotta help no matter what." Realizing this didn't explain much, she continued, "Big client, big clean for a big party. Sisters that were going to do it got sick but thought they would be better, but they're not. They only called this morning to let her know, and the party is tonight. So, we're all helping."

She led me into her kitchen. Old-fashioned white appliances, all well used. There were several sheet pans on the kitchen table, with aromas that proved my string cheese lunch woefully inadequate.

"This smells wonderful," I admitted.

"Fried chicken, mac and cheese, and a big plate of brownies and cookies. Doing what I can."

"We load it in my car and take it to Miss Estelle's?" I asked. "Or some other location?"

"Well, it would be a help to get it to her place but might be more help to get it where it's going," she admitted.

"No problem," I said. "I'm happy to help." Not as altruistic as I sounded—this would also give me a chance to talk to Estelle and find out who Stella's friends were.

I picked up two of the sheet pans and headed out. It took two trips.

The first stop was Estelle's place a few blocks away. I followed Dottie to the door. She knocked and it was opened by a tall woman, hair and nails perfect.

"You must be Dottie!" she said. "I'm Desiree." She gave Dottie a big hug, like she was longtime family. "And you are?" she turned to me.

"Micky Knight," I said.

She gave me a big hug as well. Anyone helping Estelle was family.

"Were you a friend of Stella's?" I ventured.

"Yes, indeed I was," she answered. "Stella took me under her wing, everything from hormones to getting my GED. Miss Estelle took me in as well, let me stay in her spare bedroom for as long as I needed it. Did you know Stella?"

"Sadly, no."

Dottie cut in, "Micky is a private eye, looking into her death."

I had planned on not saying that, just hanging around and talking to people. "Well," I hedged, "not officially. Helping some of the bars to make sure they're not robbed, and if I'm asking questions, I might as well ask a few more." On the other hand, them knowing I was a PI might help, get us to the topic without needing friendly chitchat working its way around to it.

"Someone should be," Desiree said, leading us back to the kitchen where everyone else was congregated.

The kitchen was about the same age as Dottie's, what was here when Estelle bought it and little money to upgrade. But it was homey, with aromas of many good meals in the old cabinets.

Estelle was surrounded by three other women, the older woman I'd seen the last, brutal time I was here, and two other women around Desiree's age. There were more large containers: red beans and rice, sausage, gumbo, cooked greens and sweet potatoes, and a pile of cornbread.

"Oh, Dottie, you're here," Estelle exclaimed. "Thank you so much."

"My food is out in Miss Micky's car," she said.

I wagged my finger at her. "I am not old enough or respectable enough for you to call me Miss Micky. Mostly the latter."

Desiree laughed, put her arm around me, and said, "Honey, you stick with me and you will never be respectable."

"Deal," I answered. This is one of the things I love about New Orleans—how quickly we can make friends, either just for a few hours or a lifetime. But it can come easily, an unexpected grace in a hurried world.

I was introduced to the other three women: Ruby, the older woman, then Angelique and Victoria—"not Vicky, don't go there."

Thanks to Andy's Forester, I had plenty of room in the back and could take three other people.

We were going to one of the big houses near the lakefront. It wasn't old New Orleans, but still moneyed New Orleans. Opulent, mid-century mansions with expansive lawns. The more expensive were close enough to the lake to be protected by the higher elevation there, sediment left from past floods.

Not my taste but well done for its style, with a perfectly manicured lawn. On the way over, I'd gleaned that the owners were a couple in their forties, one a successful real estate developer, the other an energy lawyer. Wasn't sure who was what—or if it was a gay couple or not.

A tall, elegant woman in her forties opened the door for us. "Estelle!" she said and wrapped her in a tight hug.

I was embarrassed because it took a moment for me to realize this was the owner. The damage being raised in the white world does to you—too often you make the same assumptions the people who raised you made. There are lots of well-to-do Black people in this city, and we were at the home of one of them.

"Thank you all so much," she said to the rest of us. "I knew you'd come through, Miss Estelle, you always do."

"Close this time," Estelle admitted. "Let's get started, we're running a bit behind."

We unloaded the food and put it away. Then it was housecleaning time. Ruby stayed in the kitchen because her knees were too old for scrubbing. Angelique and Victoria worked regularly for Estelle, so they were the housecleaning experts. I mostly did what they told me.

It is not easy and it's not unskilled. My usual housecleaning was good enough for me to live in the mess I produced.

Victoria and I tackled the bathrooms, all five of them.

"You haven't done this much before, have you?" she asked.

"No, not what I'm good at," I admitted.

She nodded, pursed her lips, and then decided that two extra hands, even inexperienced ones, were better than doing it herself.

"Is it true you're the detective looking into Stella being killed?" she asked as we started on the main downstairs bathroom. "You saw it, right?"

"Yes, I was walking home from one of the bars."

"Which one?"

"Q Carré."

"You queer?"

"How'd you guess?" She handed me the toilet bowl cleaner, instructing me on the proper way to clean all the way around.

"Got good queer-dar," she said. "I sometimes go there; don't think I ever saw you."

"I may have been back in the corner."

"Naw, different times, I guess. You'd older than my usual, but I would have noticed you. Like tall women."

"You're lesbian?"

"Prefer genderqueer. Mostly women. Yeah, I'm trans, but you know gender isn't orientation. I always liked women, and I kept on liking women. It varies. Sometimes after you transition, you discover you like someone else, sometimes the same. We're all over the place."

"Just like the rest of us."

"Don't worry, I'm engaged to a wonderful woman. Not hitting on you."

"I'm too old anyway."

"Well, there is that."

Ouch. But she was in her twenties. I was too old for her. I just wanted to think I was still hot enough to attract people I'd say no to.

Then she laughed and put her hand on my arm to let me know it was okay.

"You know I think Stella was murdered, not a stupid accident like the cops said," she told me as I finished the toilet to her satisfaction.

"Why do you say that?"

"She was worried about something. I asked, but she said she couldn't talk then."

"When was this?"

"The day before she died. Her last text was a few hours before. Asking me to call her later that night. I called and called. I so want to call her one last time."

"I'm sorry," I said. "She meant a lot to you?"

Victoria hastily wiped her eyes. "Yeah. I was thrown out of my house when I was seventeen. Father a pastor and preached hellfire for two men holding hands. Not going to have something worse in his house—a 'boy/girl,' he said. Two days cold and hungry, and I did what I had to do to survive."

"Sex work?"

She pointed to the shower and handed me her chosen cleaning product.

"Yeah. I hated it, but I hated being hungry and on the streets more. Didn't get to graduate high school. No degree, no experience. Usual shit. Lucky that I didn't get busted—well, I did once but he let me blow him instead of taking me in."

"I'm sorry, that's not right." Small words for a large injustice.

"Better than OPP. No money for bail, so I could have been in there a stretch. No thank you."

"Did this cop often prey on people?"

"What do you expect? We don't want to go to jail; they don't want to do the paperwork. They let us off for two minutes' work." She smirked. "If that."

"Do you know his name?"

"Naw, not smart to know his name. Questions like that are called 'resisting arrest,' and resisting gets a trigger pulled. They get away with it all the time."

I let it go. It was wrong and illegal. Cops like that should go to jail, but neither of us had the power to make that happen.

"How did you meet Stella?"

I should have worn my crappy old shoes to clean showers. Especially ones this big.

"On the street. She saw me hanging, started talking to me like I was a real person, you know. Told me if I wanted to get out, to let her know. Gave me her phone number. I called the next day. That was about four years ago. Let me stay with her and Miss Estelle. She had rules. I had to work, I had to study for my GED. But I got room and food. And more importantly, people who cared about me."

"Stella sounds like a wonderful person."

"Whoever killed her killed a lot of other people. Who else is going to save us? Stella been there, found her way and was going to help. Shit, if it wasn't for her, I'd be on the streets. Or dead. Said if we wanted to do sex work—shit, it paid good—that's okay, but do it safe. Who else is going to save us?"

She turned to the sink and started furiously scrubbing it.

"Who wanted to hurt her?"

"Anyone that wants to keep trans people down and desperate."

"That's a lot of people," I said, speaking loudly over the running shower.

"Too damn many."

"Was she seeing anyone?" I turned the water off. The shower looked pretty clean to me. I might have to up my routine at home.

"Naw. Well, a few dates here and there, but mostly she did her school and her community work. Most were one and done."

"Did you meet any of them?"

She motioned me to follow to the next bathroom.

"Naw, not really," she said after starting me on the toilet. "Once saw a guy she had dated, big, tall ex-Marine. He looked at her, looked like he'd seen a ghost and then looked like he didn't know her. Total closet case. We laughed about it, 'cause that's all you can do."

"Maybe he was humiliated?"

"Naw, not like that. He just didn't want anyone to know he'd had some fun outside his white box."

"Anyone else?"

"Some nerdy guy, but I could have beat him up with one hand. She said she went on one date, but he wasn't into her, just into thinking he was cool and liberal 'cause he was dating a trans woman."

"You get any names? First names?"

"Naw, she just called them Man One and Man Two, that sort of thing. Nothing serious. Nothing worth getting killed over."

"People kill for too many stupid reasons."

"Not Stella. Not some stupid reason for her. They had to shut her up."

"Who?"

But Victoria had no names, just the wall of hate for people who were different and thus easy targets.

"Miss Estelle says I can stay," she said as we moved to the next bathroom. "I offered to go, but she said no. I got my GED a few months ago and Desiree is taking me on. She does nails, hair, and makeup and says she can use extra help. Maybe in five years I can have my own salon."

She talked more of her hopes and dreams, and I let her. Those precious moments in life when so much of the world is possible, before choosing one path over the others.

I wondered about myself. Was this who I wanted to be? Middle-aged? Doing the same work I'd been doing since my twenties? Or was it too late to ask those questions? I was in my late forties, worked for myself for over twenty years and built a successful business—if success was paying my bills with a little left over to cover the pleasant parts of life—travel, a good bottle of wine now and again, donations to causes I believed in. Was it enough? Could anything be enough compared to the expansive dreams from when we were young and we thought anything was possible?

We moved to the next and final bathroom.

"Would you date a trans woman?" she asked me.

"She'd have to be mature and wise, age appropriate," I answered.

She smiled. Then said, "If you met someone like that, would you?"

Would I? I'd like to think I would, but it's always easy to be the hero in our minds. "Maybe. I think it would depend on the person.

We're a lot more than our body parts. Intelligent, funny, kind. Really rich. Sure."

She laughed.

We finished the bathroom and went down to the kitchen to find the others, see what else needed to be done. My back was already aching, and I wondered if there was any face-saving way for me to help Ruby in the kitchen.

My back complaints were silenced when I realized that Estelle and Angelique had dome most of the other cleaning while Ruby had done the kitchen. Bathroom duty, nasty as it was—I don't like cleaning toilets I use, let alone ones used by other people—was relatively easy in comparison.

I was also just young and foolish enough to think I could easily keep up with women in their twenties. Probably not, but don't tell me that.

Angelique and Victoria would finish the rest of the cleaning since they had been here several times and knew their way around. Desiree was indeed a beauty expert and was with Miss Traci, doing the homeowner's hair and nails for the party. I was tasked with helping Estelle and Ruby in the kitchen, getting the food all set up for the evening.

It was a garden party, and the house had a beautiful back patio and outdoor kitchen with lots of prep space. My task was ferrying out various platters as Ruby and Estelle got them ready. Not making my back happier, but I wasn't going to complain.

I was putting the second cheese tray out when Estelle joined me with a fruit plate.

"I can do this," I said.

"So can I, and I intend to do so as long as I can. Sitting in the kitchen is how you end up sitting in the kitchen."

I vowed I would work out on a more regular basis. Especially back exercise.

I walked back with her to the kitchen where we picked up two more trays.

As we came back to the patio and arranged the food, I asked, "How are you doing?"

She shrugged, moving one of the fruit trays to a different location. "The days go by. The nights are long. Then another day goes by." She looked at me and said, "You think they might find who did this? Talked once to that new detective. He had a lot of questions and few answers."

"I think he'll try."

"You working on it?"

"I'm not police and can't do anything officially, but I can ask questions. Maybe people will talk to me when they won't talk to the police."

"Got no time for them. Law and order isn't usually what we get. Even money don't do it. Miss Traci and her husband Paul get pulled over all the time. For driving nice cars, for driving in this neighborhood. She's a lawyer and all that."

"What do you want?"

She rearranged the plates for a minute, then said, "I want Stella back, but I can't have that, can I?"

"No, I'm sorry."

She was quiet for another moment, then said, "Our hearts break, but sometimes we get blessed and find another reason for our hearts to sing. Stella gave me a reason for my heart to sing loud. Someone to ask me how my day was and to care. She said once she graduated and got a job, I could cut back, not work so hard. Just be home for her to come home to.

"After Katrina, one of my older aunties, about my age now, lost her home. Her kids talked about building back and coming home. She said no. Said 'what am I going to do with the pittance of a life I have left.' She moved to a small place in Jackson. Lived another five years just small and quiet. That's what I'll do, I'll pass the days and pray the nights aren't too dark."

"You gave so much to Stella. My family, the people who raised me, didn't want much to do with a lesbian kid. Other people did what they should have done. Cared about me, helped me get into and through college. More importantly told me I was loved for who I was, not what others wanted me to do. It doesn't sound like much, but it's so vital to those of us who don't have it."

"No one will replace Stella."

"No, not possible. That's always going to hurt. But so many people like Stella don't have the love and acceptance you gave her."

"Damn it, now you sound like her. When we took Desiree in, then Victoria, then Angelique, that's what she said. A home where they're okay to be who they are."

"Grief doesn't go away. We always carry it."

"We do. Sometimes it feels so heavy. Maybe I can help Victoria and Angelique. They can stay with me as long as they need. It matters to have a roof over your head and a bed of your own. Don't have to be fancy or nice."

"I would have been on the street if I hadn't been taken in. Young and scared."

"I want her killers to be caught. If not by the law, by life. To know that they were killed the way she was killed. Maybe it's wrong of me to wish them pain and suffering."

"Maybe it's not. It's certainly human."

"You keep asking your questions. Don't let her fade away. Maybe I've got another five years like my auntie. Maybe that will be enough time."

"Anyone I should talk to? Close friends? Was she dating anyone?"

"Desiree and she were close. Don't think she was dating anyone. But she might not have told me about that."

"Anyone she had problems with? Fights?"

"She could be tough. Fair, but no fools allowed. We had to throw one girl out. Donatella. Can't remember her last name. Doing drugs. Stella was angry she did it in my house, put us all at risk. But that was about a year ago. Didn't get along with one of the men in her classes. He was at her about men being men and some things don't change."

"Really defensive about his masculinity?"

"Yeah, called her unnatural and a freak. I told her not to let it get to her, but easy to say."

"Do you have a name?"

"Hector someone. Desiree might know."

Ruby came out with another tray. "I put the mac and cheese in the oven to warm up."

"It's fine to eat the fried chicken cold," Estelle said. "Talk to Desiree," she added as we went back in the kitchen to finish getting the food ready.

The tail end of the day was spent on finishing touches.

Traci reappeared just as we finished. Desiree had done her hair, nails, and makeup. She looked stunning, wearing a chic turquoise outfit that fit in perfectly with a garden party.

She made a point of thanking us all, shaking our hands. "Thank you so much! You are all wonderful!" Not treating us like servants as much as possible. She handed an envelope to Estelle. Quick, but a reminder that this was business.

Her husband came home just as we were leaving. He greeted us, gave Estelle a long hug.

If I had to do this kind of work, these were the people I'd want to do it for.

But I didn't have to do this. I'd been lucky. Very close to being thrown out for being gay, I instead left when I turned eighteen in my final semester of high school. But I had a place to go. An older lesbian couple took me in so I could finish high school and made sure I applied to college—and then paid my way. If that hadn't happened? Kindness, a twist of luck and fate. What if instead I'd dropped out of high school, working low-wage jobs just to survive?

We all piled into cars to go back to Estelle's place.

Once we got there, Estelle opened the envelope and paid everyone. I just shook my head—I'd been doing my other job and wasn't going to double-dip. Estelle paid a fair wage. Everyone got fifteen with four hours minimum. Traci had added a twenty percent tip.

Dottie said, "Pays better than a whole day at my regular job."

"Maybe you should work for Miss Estelle," Desiree said.

"Maybe I should," Dottie replied.

Ruby and Estelle headed into the house. They were visibly tired and ready to put their feet up. Dottie could walk home. Angelique and Victoria stayed there but got beers and hung out on the stoop chatting.

"You going anywhere near a bus stop?" Desiree asked me.

"Probably lots of bus stops. I'll take you where you're going."

"I live out in the East," she said. "That's a long ride." New Orleans East was well to the east of what most people think of as New Orleans. It's mostly reclaimed land on the other side of the Industrial Canal, bisected by the interstate highway. Mostly newer developments, built after racial segregation was officially illegal, so the houses had no "whites only" covenants attached. The Lower Ninth, an older neighborhood, was near the river and its relatively higher ground. The East was on the lake side, a swamp before the land was drained.

It wasn't a quick drive by New Orleans standards, but it would be a miserable bus ride.

Plus, it would give me plenty of time to talk to Desiree.

"Not a problem, just tell me what exit to take off I-10."

She did. I headed for Elysian Fields to catch the highway.

"Estelle said I should talk to you about Stella."

"Ah, I get a ride home if I answer questions. If I don't, I get dropped at the bus stop?"

"Nope, you get a ride home. You don't need to answer any questions, except where to let you off."

She nodded, testing me, and so far, I had passed. "You think it will do any good? You asking questions?"

"I don't know," I answered. "Maybe I'll find something, maybe I won't. But I know I won't find anything if I don't ask."

"Okay, ask away."

I turned from Claiborne onto Elysian Fields. "Can you think of anyone who might want to harm Stella?"

"Other than all those folks who want trans people wiped off the face of the earth?"

"You can include those, but are any of them here and close enough? Estelle mentioned a guy in her classes."

"Oh, year, Hector. Willing to bet he sucks dick whenever he can and then hates himself, which he projects onto anyone who isn't a closet case like his is. Stella was not in any closet. She burned those doors."

"Did he threaten her? Or just verbal abuse?"

"I was meeting her on campus, doing some work in that area, and she said she'd give me a ride home. Came up to him grabbing her by the arm, trying to push her against a wall, saying she was an abomination and was going to hell."

"He actually attacked her?"

"Was going to hurt her if I hadn't come along. I'm a good three inches taller than he is, even in flats, which I rarely wear. I started yelling, blew my whistle. He ran."

"Wow, that's scary. Did you call the police?"

"Call the police? You may be lesbian, but you are way too white. Police don't protect people like us. What are the cops going to see? Two Black trannies versus a white dude liberal enough to go to Southern? He says we attack him. Cops then smell alcohol on our breath, find a condom in our purse, and arrest us for 'crimes against nature.' Justice is for the comfortable, not the people on the wrong side of all those stupid lines, color, sex…'"

"I have a cop who is a good friend, a lesbian. I forget she's an exception. If I need the police, I call her."

"You got a tame one? Well, good for you."

"Lucky for me, finding a queer group of friends. It's what we do, isn't it? Find our community who take care of us, because the institutions too often won't. When we were just getting to be friends, she said to call her first if I needed the police. She didn't even need to say that some cops think lesbians are already outlaws, so deserve no protection."

"I spent two nights in OPP because I had grabbed a bunch of condoms from one of the bars to give out. Cop stopped me, saw that I had twenty condoms, and used that as evidence that I was a prostitute. I washed toilets, *public* toilets, before I did that. Still got busted for it, just because of who I am. Whatever you find out, if you take it to the cops, you keep me as far out of it as you can."

"I think you said your name was anonymous? At least that's all I remember."

"Yeah, I'd like that TV-style justice, her killer caught. But what if her killer is a cop? Think they might arrest him? Or find some way to blame it on us?"

"I don't know. I'd like to think they would, but they see cops as people; us not so much."

"We're not important enough to care about. Another dead transgender woman, too bad. She was a freak anyway."

I merged onto I-10. Traffic was hitting rush-hour heavy.

"Sorry," Desiree said. "I'm angry right now. Someone killed Stella thinking they could get away with it because she's Black and trans. Like me. Like my friends. Every day I got to wonder if I'm going to step into a pit of hate. Men catcalling me ugly things, adults staring at me like a fucking zoo animal—a tall woman with big hands. Then the bathroom shit. Some dried-up lady thinks I'm interested in her snatch, her ego is too big for the stall. I'm there to pee and get the fuck out."

"I'm tall and I sometimes get it. 'Are you sure you're in the right place?' They desperately need a gender-binary line, and no one is allowed to cross it."

"Stella could be mouthy. 'Can I see your gender police badge?' 'You want to see what's between my legs? Show me yours first.' She was good at that kind of stuff. I just tell them to fuck off."

"They provoke you, and when you react, it proves that you're the kind of person who tells them to fuck off."

"Well, we ain't going to solve that one. What else do you need to know?"

"Hector's last name?"

"Walker. I remember because he never walked. Always rode one of those new electric scooters all the kids use. Take a whole bike stand to lock that skinny little thing up."

"Anyone else you can think of? Estelle mentioned kicking someone out because of drugs."

"Yeah, I get why she did it. Don't be doing meth in Miss Estelle's house. But she's in prison now."

"Was Stella dating anyone?"

"No, not really. It's hard. You say up front you're transgender and people run. You wait and try to be a person and they feel you lied to them. A few here and there. She saw one man for a few weeks until she found out he was married. Also, some white guy from uptown, but he was doing it for the ride, so she dropped him."

"Any of them angry about that?"

"Enough to kill? They didn't even care about her."

"Motives are usually love or money."

"Hard to think people you had a drink with might kill your best friend."

"Evil can be banal, like the nice neighbor who helped you clean the drains."

"Maybe. The married guy was a car salesman. He might think to use a car. Could be money. She said she found out someone was cheating—money, that is. She had proof, she said. Didn't know what to do about it. If you can't go to the cops, you can't report a crime."

"What else did she tell you?"

"Just that. She was going to show me…the day after she died."

Desiree looked out the window, turning her face from me. After a moment, she said, "It was just money. Why would we care if some poor people were ripping off some rich people? I think she just wanted to talk about it, to make sure she wasn't involved and could walk away. Like I said, we don't go to the police. Take the next exit, then go right."

I confused all the drivers by signaling my intentions before exiting.

"Do you know the names of either of the men?" I asked as we waited at the stoplight at the bottom of the ramp.

"Not offhand, but Stella sent their names to me. Protection. To look out for each other. To know in case…"

The light changed and I turned right.

"Fourth block in, then another right. I'll find them and send them to you."

"Thanks, I'd appreciate that. And anything else you can think of."

"Could it be random? Some hater just went after her?"

"Possible, but she was in a car. Makes it likely it was someone she knew."

"Yeah, Stella had smarts. They might have pulled her in the car, thought to take her someplace, but she fought and they pushed her out."

"It's possible. But I can ask about the people she knew. Random strangers are harder, you know?"

"Next block, third house on the left."

I pulled in front of a tidy brick ranch with an explosion of flowers and plants in the yard.

"Not what you expected," Desiree said, reading my expression.

"Not like that." I defended myself. "You don't have a car, so I guessed your house would be more modest."

"I lent my car to my sister because she doesn't have a car. She doesn't have a car because she's not a good driver."

"She wrecked it?"

"Good guess. She hates that her trans sister is doing so much better than she is, so she resents that I had a car to lend her, so she's dragging her feet on the paperwork mess. It wasn't technically her fault, but she could have avoided it if she'd been paying attention. I do most of my work here, so can do reasonably well without a car."

I decided not to ask about the sibling relations. "What's doing well?"

"What I did today. Traci has long been a client. I do her hair and nails about once a month and for special occasions. Started doing mostly trans women, then their straight friends, now all the ladies in the neighborhood come see me. Busy all the time."

"Victoria said she might work with you."

"We been talking about it. Think she might be good at it. She doesn't want to be cleaning houses when she's older, up in her thirties."

"No, she doesn't. Let alone your forties."

"You did good, you must be in shape." She took my hand, but it was a professional appraisal. "Nice, but short for a girl. You ever want to glam up, you let me know. Friends and family discount."

"Halloween?"

She laughed and shook her head. "Or sometime you want to really impress your friends? How you look can change who you are."

"It does, doesn't it? Maybe someday when I want to try out being another person."

"We all change. Plain, no makeup to glam, hair and nails. We're all transitioning, different in a few days. Or slowly, young to old, move to a new city, get sick and get better. It's all change." She took my hand between both of hers. "I want you to find who did this to Stella. And I want you to not hurt any of us still here. I'm asking a lot, aren't I? But if you don't ask, you never get."

She let go of my hand and opened the car door.

"Thank you," I said.

She smiled, both joyful and sad, blowing me a kiss as she walked past her beautiful flowers.

CHAPTER FIFTEEN

I'd gone just a block before my phone rang. I pulled over to the curb to answer it.

"You want to meet?" Detective Thompson.

"Yeah, if possible."

"It's not possible, but I'll do it anyway. Half an hour at your office work for you?"

"Sounds good. Thanks." He hung up.

I started to pull out and the phone rang again. I pulled in again since another car was coming down the street.

"Yes?" I said, assuming he was calling back to cancel.

"Hi, Micky, this is Audra."

"Audra, hi."

"Bad time?"

"No, this is fine. Just on the phone with someone else and thought it was them calling back."

"A lot of thinking and a lot of talking, but Grandmom is getting older; someday she won't be there. No, it won't be the same. I'll never trust them to be the 'family is everything' they claim. But I had good memories in that house. The beautiful trees we climbed in the back yard, the secret passage through them into an alley, then the next street over. I would like to go back and see how tall the magnolia I planted when I was ten is now."

"I'll contact your grandmother and say you're willing to reconnect."

"Yes, please. And…tell her about me, who I am now."

"I will. It may take a day or two before I can connect with her, but I'll let you know."

Neither of us said it.

Would her grandmother still want to find her now that she was a granddaughter and not a grandson?

"Thank you. I'll be...living my life until then."

I turned my phone to silent and pulled out.

Audra was giving them another chance to reject her. I don't know if I would have. I kept lukewarm relations with my family, now mostly showing up at funerals for the older generation. Usually, Torbin and I went together. Our contact was on my terms, and I had no illusions I was loved or wanted. Just a nod to memories, the past and its claim on me.

What would it have been like, to have a childhood whole? If you're queer, or transgender, you learn to pretend, to not be who you know you are. Listen to them tell you you're too young to know what you do know. All the innocent rituals become mine fields—claim the poster on your wall is a role model, not a crush. Go to school dance, prom, in clothes you don't want to wear, with someone you're supposed to be attracted to, but you're not. Tell so many lies you begin to believe them. Sex? Actual connection? Keep it hidden. Fall in love but don't let anyone know. Pretend and lie and learn to hate yourself because you're so far from who you're supposed to be.

No wonder we're all so fucked up. Life is hard even when the world is kind and fair to you. Much harder when it's not.

I made it to my office in twenty-five minutes. Enough time for me to go to the bathroom and catch my breath before Detective Thompson arrived.

Plenty of time, it turned out. Thirty-five minutes and he still wasn't here.

I debated sending an email to Mrs. D'Marchant, but that was the cowards' way out. Much as I didn't want to, I needed to see her in person. Maybe if she could understand how she now had a granddaughter and get over the surprise/shock, and get to questions. If she was willing to understand, she needed someone to answer those questions. At least get her comfortable enough to meet Audra and then let Audra answer questions beyond me.

I shot her a quick email, asking to meet because I had an important update for her.

Still no detective. Forty minutes.

For fun, I checked the tracker I'd put on Mr. Big Shot PI's SUV.

Ah, our boy liked to gamble. He was at the casinos over in Biloxi.

Which meant I didn't need to worry about him following me that evening.

Footsteps on the stairs.

A tap on the door, and it opened. Forty-five minutes.

Another reason to be glad of the tracer on Mr. Bit Shot PI's car. I knew it couldn't be him.

"I got five minutes, so tell me what you have," Detective Thompson said as he sat down. He'd had enough time to get a large coffee from downstairs.

I swung my computer around so we could both see the screen. "Do you have a timeline for what happened to Phillip Malone, the man who died? Two suspicious people on the footage at Q Carré." I showed him first Booze Boy and then Crooked Cop.

"Why do you suspect these men? You do know one of them is a police officer, right?"

"And no cop has ever taken advantage of their authority to commit a crime, right?"

"Okay, why?"

"Cop is an asshole who harasses queer people. You can see it on this tape and other people have reported it. What's he doing at this bar at this time on the night a man was robbed and murdered?"

He just nodded, not giving anything away. "The other man?"

"He's not gay, as far as I can tell. Another night he and some of his straight friends were hitting on transgender women."

"Doesn't make him a robber. Or murderer."

"Someone cut the camera feed to the outside cameras at this bar on this night."

"Okay, okay, you have circumstances, ones that make you think hmm. Did the victim go in the bar and was he seen with any of these men?"

"Do you have a picture of him? I can look."

"You didn't get the picture from the papers?"

"Yeah, but it was grainy."

"Did you see anyone who looked like him? He was tall, six two. Nice blue blazer. Hard to miss."

"No, but I can double-check. Unless he was outside where there conveniently were no cameras."

"There could have been aliens out there, with no cameras to say one way or another."

He had a point—no picture, no proof.

"Where you able to get anything more on the cars? The ones that killed Stella?"

"Not how we do this. I ask questions. You answer them."

"Did you?"

He made a face, but answered. "SUV was a nice model Range Rover and the sedan was an even nicer Mercedes. Couldn't get plates. Piece of trash on the Rover and the license of the Benz was bent."

"Deliberate?"

"Yeah, likely. But there are over one hundred of each in the metro area. Can't search them all."

"I'll keep looking. There may be more footage of them."

"That it?" He started to stand up.

"Stella was attacked by one of her social work classmates."

He sat back down and took a big sip of his coffee. "Really?"

"Witness described it to me. He was an asshole about her being transgender, hassling her about going to hell. He grabbed Stella by the arm and tried to push her into a building, would have hurt her if the witness hadn't started yelling."

"They call the police? Any report? Can I talk to the witness?"

"No, witness doesn't want to be involved. Hasn't had a good experience with the police in the past."

"Well, shit." He slumped back in the chair and took another gulp. "If they don't talk to us, there isn't much we can do."

"His name is Hector Walker. You can talk to him. Student at Southern. As a cop you can call and ask them for info."

He nodded, but I couldn't read if he was agreeing or placating me. He finished his coffee and tossed the cup in my trash can.

"Not going to give me any insight into times?" I pushed.

"Don't really have them yet. Time of death, yeah, close on that. But when did he meet the criminals? How long was he drugged and out before he died? Still working on it. I'll send you a good picture and description. If you're in the bars, ask around." He actually smiled.

"You know any of these guys?" I asked, showing him the picture of Mr. Big Shot PI, Ex-Employee, Supplement Man, and Ghost Tour Guy.

"What's their role in this?" he asked. Not saying he didn't know them, wanting to know what I knew first.

I pointed to the last three. "All former employees of Q Carré. My best guess at suspects for stealing a key and cutting the camera lines. Other person," I jabbed my finger at Mr. Big Shot PI, "says he's a great private eye and has been following me. Also, claims lots of friends in the police department, including the one you replaced."

"He's following you? He outside now? I can go have a chat with him."

"He's over in Biloxi gambling now."

He cocked an eyebrow at me.

"Friend called and let me know."

"Friend called 'find my' tag?"

I didn't answer.

"Why is he following you?" he asked.

"No idea, except he thinks I have gay mafia powers and was solely responsible for getting his friend kicked off the case. Or he thinks I know something that I don't know."

"Or know that you know. New in town, but everything I heard was that Detective Landers got kicked off for running his mouth in a way that didn't make the police look good. He was on thin ice to begin with. Or whatever you have down here that's the equivalent to thin ice."

"Thin ice works. Every few years we get enough below freezing to have ice. But what do I know?" I mused.

"You've lived here all your life, been a part of the LGBTQ community for, what, over twenty years now?"

Really about thirty, since I knew I was queer before I graduated high school, but I didn't say that. I felt old enough as it is.

"Yeah, but what's in that?"

"Patterns and people. Straight cops and new-to-town gay ones like me won't see what you see. Maybe that's the threat."

"If he's threatened, he has to be part of either Stella's killing or the robberies."

"Or trying to protect his cop buddy and being stupid about it."

I couldn't dispute being stupid about it. "What about the other three?"

"Him," he pointed at Ghost Tour Guy, "no idea. Also him." He pointed at Ex-Employee. "This one is on our radar." Supplement Man. "Maybe drugs, maybe selling crap, always skating the line."

"Any record?"

"Beyond what you could find?"

"Always like to confirm what I look up. Stumbled over some

interesting bank account entries. Has lots of them, open and closing. Big sum in one with no explanation."

"Really? Might have to look into that. You just stumbled over this, right?"

"Sometimes you have lucky stumbles," was all I said. He let it go. Good to know. He could have pushed as to how I had information that technically I shouldn't have. But it was useful to him, so he didn't push.

"Rumor he has a gambling problem, which means he has a money problem."

"Rumor?"

"Untrustworthy source. We're looking into any sketchy characters who hang around the gay bars, and he's one of them. Give me the names of the other two as well."

I did. I noticed he also wrote down the name of the man who had attacked Stella.

"You let me know if you stumble over anything else," he said as he stood.

"Will do. Helps if it's not just a one-way street."

"Right, might maybe add a bike lane." His phone rang. He waved good-bye and answered it was he was going down the stairs. I tried to overhear, but his end was a series of "yeah" and "right."

What did I know that I knew so well I didn't even know I knew it?

"Shit, I know I'm hungry and tired," I said out loud.

My phone rang. I stared at it. A number I didn't know, but 504 area code.

What the hell. I picked up. It might help my mood to yell at a telemarketer.

"Hi, it's Desiree."

"Hi! Need another ride? Or is this about the names?"

"Not a ride, but you never know. I have the names, but I found something weird. I have an old email that I don't use much, mostly spam. It was the one I used when I first met Stella. I only check it every few weeks, mostly to clear out the junk. Well, Stella emailed me a weird video. It was from her phone, not her laptop where she usually emails me from. Probably the old email autofilled. Anyway, the video is of a drunk man, out of it, and people making fun of him. They open his phone using his fingerprint."

"Wait, did they rob him?"

"Can't tell. It's murky and dark, there are mumbled voices, but no faces. Can I send it to you?"

"Yes, please."

"She sent it the night she died. Time stamp is 11:12 p.m."

That was minutes before she died. I didn't tell Desiree that.

"Did she leave any message?" I asked.

"No, it was like she was in a hurry and I could figure it out."

"What have you figured out?"

"My guess is that it has something to do with the drugs and robbery shit. Might have been what she was worried about when she talked to me about people stealing. Like she knew she had to get this to someone else. Hit Send to the first email she thought of."

"Do you think she might have been killed for this?"

"No, she was killed because they thought she was disposable. Maybe this played into it, but she was killed because they thought no one would care."

"We do."

"They don't think we're people, either. You're a dyke and I'm as Black and trans as she was." She added, "You do anything with this, like go to the police, you leave me out, got it?"

"Of course. Let me look at it and think what to do next."

"Thank you. I'm glad—no, not glad, not the right word, but whatever, that I could give this to someone who cares." She hung up.

I impatiently checked my email, wading through spam to find the one from her.

It was a short clip, just over a minute. A man on a park bench, wan light from a streetlamp down the road. His head was lolling on his shoulder, eyes shut. A mumbled voice in the background. Then a laugh. Moving closer to the man. Two different hands came into the frame, one holding his cell phone, the other picking up the man's arm, then pressing his finger to the phone. The phone was turned to the camera to show it successfully opened. More laughter.

Slurred, "Someone can't hold his booze."

Laughter.

"Or his phone," from another voice.

Laughter.

It ended.

The laughs were chilling. They were playing a game and the drugged man was just a pawn, easy to sacrifice.

I viewed it again. Then a third time.

One of the voices sounded familiar. Or was it starting to sound familiar because I was listening to it repeatedly?

I agreed with Desiree. This was about the robberies. Were they foolish enough to film what they were doing?

They took pictures at lynchings back when you had to bring a camera with you.

They were clever enough not to film their faces, but their voices and laughter might give them away. My guess was three people besides the victim. One holding the camera, a second was the hand holding his phone, the third the one moving his finger to the phone. I could make out at least two different laughs, one a high braying, the other chuffing.

It had taken three people to kill Stella. Was she killed because she got this tape?

But it didn't reveal their identity. Was Desiree right, they found her disposable?

I sat back and rubbed my eyes.

What did I know? A swirl of clues and coincidences that didn't add up to anything I could see.

Those men shouldn't be in these bars. Was that what I was seeing? That they were out of place? Hunting something?

I couldn't discount that I didn't like them. But there are lots (lots!) of people I dislike. I rarely suspect them of murder.

I needed to keep asking questions. If I was wrong, I'd find out.

I saved the clip to my computer, then sent it to Detective Thompson from my email address with the message *Just stumbled over this. Will hang out in bars and see if I hear the voices.* I hit Send.

It was almost seven p.m. I was even more hungry and tired than before. Mr. Big Shot PI was still living the high life in Biloxi. Or is that an oxymoron, high life and Biloxi?

Burger at Q Carré. Or grilled chicken salad. Let's pretend I might be healthy. I could assume if he was out of the city, it would be quiet tonight.

I headed home, parking Andy's Subaru in front of their house. Their cats were staring at me through the window and Torbin's Mini wasn't around, so they were out.

"Daddies will be home soon to feed you," I promised the cats.

It was a pleasant evening and a nice walk to the Q.

Not driving meant I could have a drink or two if I wanted. There was a lot to do, but everything could wait until tomorrow. Nothing was going to happen tonight.

The bar was tail end of happy hour busy.

I put in my order at the bar. Peg took it since Mary wasn't around. Yeah, I got a burger. The grill smell hit me when I walked in, and salad couldn't compete.

I could view the most recent footage, see if I saw anything new. I could also sit in quiet comfort in the office since there weren't many empty seats left.

I called it quasi working, which allowed me to get a beer to go with my burger. After telling Peg to buzz me in the office when the burger was ready, I headed upstairs. I sat at the desk and took a big sip of the beer. Then I texted Rob to let him know what I was doing. It was his bar, after all.

I had finished most of the beer when Peg called.

I got the burger and another beer and went back upstairs to my hidey-hole.

I turned on the live feed in the bar to see what was going on in real time. Maybe I should copy the last few days onto my computer and bribe Torbin and Andy with food to get them to help me wade through them. Maybe I could do that tomorrow since I didn't have my computer with me.

Four hours of nonstop housework had worn me out.

It wasn't Hector, the threatening Southern student. He couldn't have been driving two cars at the same time. He was in social work. It would be hard to find anyone to help him plot and execute a murder. Not off the list, but down on it.

That left me either with my suspect pool or the great wide world.

Someone cut the camera feeds on the day a man was drugged and killed. Someone with knowledge of and access to this bar. That person had to be involved in at least the robberies, if not Stella's murder.

If I kept asking enough questions, eventually I might ask the right ones.

I texted Desiree the photos of my main suspects—Mr. Bit Shot PI, Ex-Employee, Booze Boy, and Ghost Tour Guy—and asked her if she recognized any of them.

I finished my burger and second beer. I was contemplating whether to get another beer or switch to something else when the live feed caught my attention.

Ex-Employee was at the bar, ordering a drink. Peg gave him a less than friendly look but made his drink.

He smiled at her and gave her a big tip. She shook her head but gave him a rueful smile in return and kept the tip. He found a stool at the far end of the bar and sat there, checking his phone on a regular basis. After about ten minutes, he chugged his drink and left.

Desiree texted me back. One looked vaguely familiar: Booze Boy. She had seen him once with someone Stella was dating. Another text saying she'd deleted the texts with names of old dates in them.

I texted, *Can you describe the person she was dating?*

She texted me back a photo. It was from about twenty feet away and from the side. *He didn't like his picture taken. Not with us, you know. I snapped this anyway. Safety. Names and pictures of who we date.*

Thanks, I texted back. *Can you describe him as well?*

Not too tall, about four inches shorter than I am. Brown hair in a cut that doesn't work for him, long on top and buzzed at the sides, makes him look like a mushroom. Pale white, skinny, wears nice clothes and drives a nice sports car.

I looked at the picture.

The high, braying laugh.

I glanced at my watch. It was almost ten p.m. Late, but not too late if the call was important.

"Hi, Dottie," I said when she picked up the phone. "Sorry to bother you, but a quick question."

"Sure, what you need?"

"You said Mrs. D'Marchant had two cars? Do you know what kind?"

"I have to clean them out enough, I should know. One was a Range Rover and the other a Mercedes. She occasionally sent me off in the big one if something needed to be picked up. Never the Mercedes."

"Can I text you a picture? See if it looks like them?"

I quickly scrolled through the saved clips to find the security footage of the two cars. Yes, I'm tech savvy enough to both talk and text at the same time. Which meant I couldn't be as old as my body currently felt.

"Let me take a look. Give me a minute."

I gave her a minute, trying not to impatiently tap my foot.

Finally, "Could be them. But that's Armstrong Park in the background. Mrs. D'Marchant wouldn't be driving down there."

"What about her grandson?"

She was silent for a moment. "Well, shit. Yeah, might be him. He isn't really supposed to use her cars, but 'not supposed to' never stopped him."

"Is it possible they borrowed both the cars? Him with his friends?"

"Lord, with that boy, anything is possible. Oh, he acts nice and all with his grandmother. She caught him once, cigarette smoke smell, and he apologized, blamed it on his friends and said it would never happen again. But I knew he did it again. Found a food wrapper under the seat, then sequins and glitter. I just cleaned the cars and kept my mouth shut."

"How often did this happen?"

"Mrs. D'Marchant doesn't drive much. Said she needed the two cars. One for general use and the big one for hurricanes and floods. So every few days I'd check. Knew if it was a mess, I'd get yelled at for not cleaning it, and she and him would trade excuses. Tried to accuse me once, but I had enough and proved I wasn't around. Thought she'd turn around and fuss at him, but she didn't. Just let it go. Family gets away with so much."

"You need to stop working there."

"I know. Making plans."

"Does he live there?"

"No, has an apartment by the lake, but he comes by a lot, mooching food and liquor, dropping off his laundry for me to do with all the other stuff. Made the room above the garage what he calls his film studio. Lot of expensive equipment up there. Only lets me clean if he's there. Has keys and access, so can come in and out as he likes. Thinks the world owes him everything he wants. When I gave him stink eye about his stealing her good booze, he just smiled an ugly smile and said it was going to be his soon enough anyway, he might as well take some now."

"He thinks he's entitled to it?"

"Yeah, I guess that's how to put it. If he wants it, it should be his. I blame his parents and his grandparents for letting him get that way."

"What does his film studio look like?"

"Lots of equipment, big TVs, lot of money for a waste of time."

"Why do you say that?"

"It's his excuse not to get a real job. Always going around with his phone or a camera filming things. Snuck up on me cleaning the cars. I told him to stop it, not to film me, but he just laughed and said he might make me a star and tried to keep taking my picture. I stopped moving, looked away until finally he gave up. Made a snotty comment about me giving up my chance to be in pictures."

"What kind of film did he say he was making?"

"He didn't, and I didn't ask."

"If you can, tomorrow when you're there, can you take pictures of the cars? Get the license plates?"

"Yeah, I can make it a clean the cars day. Hadn't done it on the last few days anyway."

"Don't get in trouble, but if you can that would be great."

"No promises, but I think I can do it."

I thanked her and said good-bye.

The photo looked like him. But it wasn't a great shot. Easy to argue it was someone similar.

The cars. They were smart enough not to use their own vehicles. Probably Mr. Big Shot PI's idea. Instead use Mrs. D'Marchant's available ones. If Detective Thompson was going down the list of those vehicles in the area, she would be passed by—elderly uptown lady didn't fit the profile.

Dottie said they could be the cars but wasn't certain. I was hoping if I could get pictures from her tomorrow, Detective Thompson could run a comparison, maybe see if some of the digits from the plates matched.

I was close. This wasn't strong enough evidence, especially since Grandson Not Nice Brice came from a well-to-do family. He would get the justice that money buys.

I stood and stretched. I was walking home; a real drink would be nice. I took my burger plate down to the bussing station and headed to the bar. It was busy and the bartender wasn't someone I knew well.

I walked outside to clear my head and give the scrum at the bar a chance to dissipate.

Peg was out there, sneaking a cigarette. She was older—well, about *my* age, on the butch side of butch, hair close to a crew cut, strong shoulders, wore a tie when she dressed up.

She waved at me. "Yeah, I know I should quit."

"I'm not judging."

"Thanks," she said. "Just occasionally. An excuse to come outside for a few minutes."

I heard the ding of a text message. It was from Detective Thompson. No message, just three photos of the murdered man.

"Can I ask you some questions?"

"Sure," Peg said, taking a puff of her cigarette.

I scrolled through my phone. First up, Ex-Employee. "He was just in here. Used to work here. What can you tell me about him?"

She looked at him for a moment, like she was deciding whether to be polite or honest. "He was an okay sort when we worked together. Always willing to do what you asked him to do but got off track on his own."

"Off track, how?"

"Chatting with friends at one end of the bar and not noticing other customers at the other end. Forgetting to do things on the checklist unless you told him. I suspect he had a reading problem, like dyslexia. Heart in the right place, head not so much."

"He ever do anything questionable? Shady?"

She took another drag on her cigarette. "Different folks, different strokes. But…didn't always charge his friends for drinks. Once talking about wanting to be a famous cat burglar, steal from the rich. Made it like a joke. But that was it. Typical young kid stuff."

"He ever tell you he came from a wealthy family?"

"Yeah, he mentioned it. Said they were trying tough love, since he flunked out of college, trying to get him to learn to work. Didn't seem to take since he only made it here for a few months."

"You know what happened to him after?"

"Not really, not sure what he's doing. Must be something since he can come in here and buy the good stuff. Or his parents are footing the bill, like they usually do."

"What about him?" I showed her the picture of Booze Boy.

She frowned and stubbed out her cigarette. "Seen him a few times. Mostly with Hugh." Ex-Employee.

"They friends?"

She examined the cigarette to make sure it was out before putting it in her pocket. "Maybe. Not great friends, if you ask me, more like now friends—people you drift about with. Think he," with a finger at Booze Boy, "let Hugh join in because he paid for the drinks."

"About how often did he come in?"

"Not sure, not regular, but occasionally, maybe a few times a month."

"He ever pick up anyone, leave with them?"

"Not his type of bar. He just smelled straight, avoided the men, flirting with some of the women, didn't matter if they were dykes or trans. I don't like his type in here, but the money is green."

"His type?"

"He knows it's a queer bar, but he comes here to prove he can go wherever he wants. He puts his money down and we serve him a drink."

"You ever see him do anything out of line? Get angry or threatening?"

"He was happy to let Hugh give him free drinks. Smirky, superior look. But nothing we could use to tell him not to come back. Slick like that."

"You ever see this man?" I pulled up the picture of Crooked Cop.

She scowled. "Asshole. Big bigot. You know, one of the kinds that can't stay away, like those idiots that always protest around the gay bars during Mardi Gras, where they get to watch all the shirtless men. Comes in and throws his badge around. Hassling people, asking for ID even when they're clearly over twenty-one. He likes to go after the women, especially ones like me, who don't fit his idea of what woman are supposed to look like."

"Mostly lesbians or does he go after the trans women as well?"

"Equal opportunity asshole. Asked one tall woman if she had a dick or a cunt. She told him whatever it was, it was bigger than his. Pissed him off. He started to grab her, but four of us gathered around and he thought better of it. Should not be a cop."

"How often does he come in?"

"Used to be about every week or so. I think Rob put in a complaint, and that seems to have cooled his jets. Or he's found others to harass."

"What about him?" I pulled up Mr. Big Shot PI's photo.

"He comes in on occasion. Mary and I both guessed he has a wife and kids out in the burbs but has a thing for breaking the rules."

"He hits on the transgender women?"

"He's polite about it. Nice even, takes no for an answer, but most are happy for a flirt and maybe a bit more. Okay tipper. It takes all kinds, and I don't judge people for what they do."

"Does he come in with the others?" I pointed to the previous pictures.

"I've usually seen him alone but did once see him with Hugh. And they were joined by him," she pointed to Booze Boy, "and another fellow."

"Not him?" I pointed to Crooked Cop.

"Nope, he's always alone."

"Could it be him?" I pulled up the photo Desiree had sent me.

She squinted at it. It wasn't a great photo, and the outside lights were for stumbling drunks, not close examinations. "That's Stella, right?"

"Yes, you knew her?"

"Yeah, I talked to her about maybe transitioning, you know. She helped me see I was probably better as a butch lesbian than a trans man, but it felt good to have someone to really talk about it with. Not too many people get that you don't fit in the same mold they do. Sad, real sad about what happened to her."

"Yes, it is. Evil, even."

Peg nodded. "But you asked about the guy. Looks like him. Saw her here once with him."

"Could it be someone who looks like him?"

She looked again, then said, "Maybe. All them young men look alike to me."

"Do you know about what day they came in?"

"Not sure of the date. A while ago. It was the afternoon, because Stella was only here to pick up a donation for her fundraiser. He came with her and helped carry things. I think it was a Friday, if that helps."

"It helps a lot." Much better to look for a Friday afternoon instead of scrolling through all six months of security tape. "Thanks, I appreciate your time."

"No problem, gave me a little more time in the fresh air."

"Oh, one more. Did you ever see him?" I pulled up one of the photos that Detective Thompson had just sent me.

She stared at it, then looked up at me. "Yeah, but not that it matters."

"You saw him?"

"Just briefly, nothing to help the police. He's the one that died, right?"

"Yes, he is. Tell me about seeing him."

"Like now, I was out taking a smoke break. He was outside, never went in the bar."

"Was he with anyone?"

"No, by himself. Looked at his phone a couple of times. Then got in a car, like it was his Uber picking him up. That was it."

"About what time?"

"Probably about same as now, a little after ten."

"What did the car look like?"

"Not a car, one of them big SUVs. Funny thing was, it was a real nice one, saw leather seats when he got in. Not the usual kind of car you see picking people up for money."

"Could it have been this one?" I pulled up the picture of the two cars, zooming in on the Range Rover.

"Yeah, that looks like it. Hard to say for sure."

"Do you remember the make?"

"No, but it was different from most that I've seen around."

I pulled up a picture of Mr. Big Shot PI's SUV. "Could this be it?"

"Don't think so, different shape looks like. It was dark gray, charcoal. This one looks black."

"Did you remember anything about who was driving it?"

"No, wasn't paying that much attention."

"Male? Female?"

She thought for a moment, then said, "I think it was a man just because I didn't think anything about it. Two men, no worry. Strange man getting in a car with a woman, more worry. Part of working in a bar is looking for places that might be trouble."

The things we know without even knowing.

"Could you tell if he was Black or white?"

"White, I think. Again, didn't notice a difference, so most likely they were the same. I know, not real helpful."

"Helpful enough." I couldn't think of any more questions at the moment, and Peg's break was probably long over. "Thank you. If I had other questions, is it okay if I hit you up?"

"You? Sure. But no cops. First thing they ask me is if I'm a man or a woman. Don't need that shit. When I was in my twenties, a trio of frat boys beat the crap out of me 'cause they didn't like the way I looked. Cops arrested me for disturbing the peace and let them go. Dragged me to jail with blood dripping down my face."

"I'm so sorry. No, it'll just be me."

She nodded and headed back into the bar.

I followed her. I needed a drink more than I needed fresh air.

Peg happily filled my Scotch order. I left a big tip, then headed back up to the solitude of the office.

Knowing and proving are too different things. Did I know?

Yes. Could I prove? Not so yes. Some grouping of Mr. Big Shot PI, Booze Boy, Ex-Employee, and Not Nice Brice and maybe others were involved in the drug and rob scheme. Ex-Employee likely stole the key and played out his cat burglar fantasies to come in and cut the cameras. Brice briefly dated Stella. Did he find out she was trans, figure that wouldn't do in his family, and decided to kill her? Or had she seen one of his many videos, realize what he was doing, and the gang decided to kill her? I didn't know who planned it or who was driving.

I was going to have to meet with Detective Thompson. Tomorrow first thing. And maybe pull in Joanne and Danny. I didn't have the evidence and I didn't have the official power to get the evidence. Maybe they could.

Get a search warrant for Mrs. D'Marchant's Range Rover? Find evidence on it from hitting Stella? If they were smart, they would have washed it every day since then. And if they were smart, they would all deny driving it. Claim it was stolen.

I could find the security footage of Stella and Brice together, but all it proved was that she knew him. It didn't put him near her when she was killed. And it would seem to have nothing to do with the robberies.

Peg had seen the man who was robbed and murdered get into a vehicle suspiciously like the Range Rover. Outside the bar, the night the camera wires were cut.

Coincidence isn't proof.

My head hurt. I took a long sip of Scotch. Then another.

His phone. He had filmed what looked like one of the robberies. Could the police ID the victim in it? What was on that phone? Could the police get a search warrant and seize it? Or would he be smart enough to erase everything?

I finished my drink and wanted another.

It would be better to not know than to know and not be able to do anything about it.

Rob kept a good bottle of bourbon in his bottom drawer. I'd owe him. I poured the bourbon in my Scotch glass.

Not bad. I might have to vary my whiskeys more often.

The live feed from the bar was still showing on the security cameras. It looked like another planet, all those happy and laughing people, smiling, drinking, flirting. And me, here in the office, only the flicker of the screen as illumination, knowing a woman and a man were murdered, who did it, and that they were likely to get away with it.

I finished the bourbon. I considered another but needed to be sober enough to walk home.

I watched the images of people swirling around the bar, the precision of the bartenders, Peg, Mary, and the one I didn't really know, fluids flowing into shiny glasses, mesmerizing, like a fire or ocean waves.

Ocean waves with sharks swimming in them. They returned, Booze Boy, Not Nice Brice, and Ex-Employee, pushing their way to the bar, choosing to be near Peg. They smiled at her frown. Brice had his phone out, likely capturing the scene. His magnum opus.

Peg was right. They were here because they could be. They could walk in, buy a drink, smirk at all the queer people, and walk out feeling they were better.

And they knew they wouldn't be caught.

I poured another shot of bourbon. I might owe Rob for the entire bottle before this evening was done.

I wanted to go down there and scream at them, "I know who you are and what you've done!" Raise a mob against them for their murder of a transgender woman and a gay man, robbery and drugging of others. Parasites and leeches.

But I sat in the silent office, letting the amber liquid quell my rage.

Not Nice Brice was now openly filming his friends making jokes, mugging for the camera.

Don't give up your day job robbing people for a career in acting.

He put the phone down on the bar, to take his drink and raise a cheer with his friends.

Booze Boy paid for the drinks, using a fifty-dollar bill.

Stolen was my guess.

Brice picked up the phone again, swiped at it, then had to enter his passcode as it didn't recognize his face in the dim bar lighting.

Had they cut out Mr. Big Shot PI? Him and his police contacts that might come in handy? I looked at my tracker app. He was still in Biloxi. Maybe he was the brains of the gang, smart enough to tell them not to hang out in the bars they trawled for their victims? Without his wise counsel, they were cocky enough to think they could swagger in here and party.

Or maybe this bar was convenient, the drinks reasonably priced compared to most of the French Quarter tourist spots.

They got another drink. Brice filmed Ex-Employee downing a shot. He put his phone back down again and then again had to put in his passcode to awaken it. He used his body to shield the numbers from those around him.

But not from the overhead camera.

This was illegal, and if I got caught, it would only make things worse. Not to mention possibly losing my license and being criminally charged.

What was on that phone?

I waited, watched them get another drink. They were hitting it pretty hard, shots of tequila now. It was two for one tequila night.

I sopped up the last of my bourbon with a paper towel and thew it out. Maybe a little drunk would help, but not too drunk.

I took one of the paper towels and stuffed it in my pocket. Then I mussed up my hair, so it looked different from my usual style. Not much of a disguise, but they had only seen me briefly at Mrs. Marchant's. Going out the servants' door.

Ah, a pair of lost and found sunglasses, lightly tinted enough to see. Not my style at all, cat-eyes and rhinestone encrusted. But anything would help.

I saved the clips showing him entering his passcode, then sent the clip to my phone.

Yes, I have studied how pickpockets work, what techniques they use and how to distract a mark. But it was to prevent, not perpetrate. I didn't have a partner to distract them, which was going to make it harder.

Go down to the bar and if an opportunity opens, go for it. If not, go home. Let the cops find the evidence. If they can.

I put on the sunglasses.

Yep, I could see well enough. I watched them again on the screen. Another round of shots. Two for one tequila is not the good stuff. They'd regret it in the morning. But for tonight, they were laughing and toasting each other and having a good time.

One that I hoped to end.

I put my jacket back on, glad I'd worn one, even though it wasn't really needed during the day. But its inside pockets are ever so handy. I made sure my pockets were all clear and easy to slip something into. I crammed my wallet and phone into one pant pocket to leave all the others free.

Then I headed downstairs.

The bar was crowded, almost peak time, just before midnight. My targets had taken over the corner of the L-shaped bar, with people coming and going to get to the bar or around to the dance floor. The music was loud and throbbing.

I slowly ambled over to that area, waiting as if I was trying to get to the bar to get a drink. I let several openings pass me by, like I was already impaired and not quick enough to see them before someone else stepped in. But I was waiting for the space next to Not Nice Brice to open. He was playing with his phone, taking pictures or video, putting it down only to pick it back up again. I watched to get his rhythm. He only left it on the bar for a minute or two.

The person next to him got her drinks and left.

I moved in.

Peg looked at me.

I looked back, gave them side-eye.

"What can I get you?" she asked over the roar.

"Draft is fine," I said. I wasn't going to drink it.

She nodded, knowing that wasn't what I usually drink. I'm particular about my beers and only order certain brands.

Booze Boy slammed his shot glass down on the bar and said, "Another round, all around." They laughed as if it was witty. One chuffing laugh and one high braying one.

I signaled with a slight head nod their way that Peg should serve them first.

She turned and poured the shots of tequila.

Brice put his phone down.

Someone was pushing to get to the bar, and I let them push me against him.

"Sorry," I mumbled, making my voice higher than normal.

He half turned his head, just enough to know he'd registered the contact but not enough to really look at me before turning away. This was a crowded bar, and getting jostled was expected.

Booze Boy downed his shot and slammed the glass on the bar again.

"Hey, cut that out," Peg yelled at him. "You're going to break the glass!"

"Need better glasses, then," he shot back.

"Maybe it's time to stop serving you," she said.

Mary came over and joined her. "Is there a problem here?"

Yeah, there was a problem, three drunk and now belligerent man-boys who didn't like people telling them no.

"Look, you fucking dyke," Booze Boy started.

"That's enough!" Mary cut him off.

I grabbed the phone and shoved it in my pocket.

"I paid good money for these drinks!" he shouted back, his friends chorusing him. They were angry and focused on Mary and Peg.

I walked out into the night, leaving the shouting behind.

CHAPTER SIXTEEN

Once out on the street, I crossed Rampart quickly, darting in front of a car coming too fast. I put the glasses into one of those handy jacket pockets. I would get rid of them later, in a trash can far from here.

I cut up the first side street I came to, not yet sure I wanted to go home but also wanting to get as far from the bar as possible as rapidly as I could. Not Nice Brice would notice his phone missing soon.

I circled through the side streets, going a long way around to get back to my house.

Once there, I went in only long enough to get the keys to my car, left through my mail slot by Andy.

I took a long, looping route. I considered finding a twenty-four-hour place but was worried that what I would see on the phone wasn't something I could look at with other people around.

The street was quiet, the coffee shop closed and dark. I parked around the corner, just another small gray car, leaving the spaces out front open and empty.

I didn't turn on any lights. There was enough ambient light from the street for me to find my way up the stairs. I knew them well enough to navigate the dark spots.

Once in my office, I closed all the blinds before turning on the small lamp on my desk. I needed it to make coffee, enough to counteract the booze.

At least that's what I told myself. I didn't want to see what was on that phone. It was either nothing, and I had risked this for that nothing, or it would be scenes I didn't want to witness.

I also knew I had to do it. Time was moving. By now Brice had noticed his phone was gone. I needed to know what was on it and the next steps to take soon.

I put on a pair of latex gloves—standard PI equipment, used mostly for sorting trash, sometimes my own rather than on a case. When I'd picked up the phone, I'd done my best to only grasp it by the sides, avoiding my fingertips as much as possible. I wiped those spots down.

Using my phone, I viewed the clip I'd sent, writing down the numbers, having to go through it several times to be sure I had them all. He had used his grandmother's address. Or…maybe he considered that his film studio, the place that would make him rich and famous.

I put the code in, and bingo, the phone opened up. He liked his apps; it was loaded with a jumble of them. First, I checked his text messages. A lot of them. If you're doing something illegal, do it with a phone call. Once spoken, the words dissolve into the air. The authorities can know you called someone, but they can't know what you said. Brice hadn't learned that lesson. I glanced through some of them. There were a lot to Booze Boy, some to Ex-Employee. Enough to make clear they were planning the robberies. And their gloating exulting afterward. Like it was a game on a screen and they won.

I found a thread between him and Stella. The first few were flirting, like people dating. I skipped past them to the last ones. He had sent her the clip. First, he said to ignore it, it wasn't what he wanted to send. Then he claimed it was part of a movie he was working on.

Well, that looks like an interesting movie, a lot like real life right now, she responded.

Like to take things from the headlines, he replied.

Yeah, right out of the headlines that haven't been written yet, papers not reporting, only the community. I could read her skepticism; he might have as well.

It's just a movie, not done yet, so don't talk about it. Can you delete the clip? Shouldn't have sent it.

She texted back, *Sure. It's gone.*

But it wasn't and she knew he was lying.

About a week went by and he texted her again, asking to meet. He said he needed to better explain what she had seen and didn't want to do it over text. He said he'd pick her up and she'd agreed, asking to meet downtown in the CBD after she had dinner with friends. The day she was killed.

That was their last text exchange.

Stupid of him to have not deleted this. Or arrogant.

I went to look for the videos on his phone. There was a disorganized pile of them scattering on the opening screen. Most were of him and his friends at the bar tonight, some from this afternoon, him rambling about things like Mardi Gras bead trees, magnolia trees, all superficial and banal. One of a man getting into the front seat of the Range Rover, all happy and laughing. Booze Boy handed him a drink. It ended there. Another robbery? Another friend? I kept scrolling through. Going back in time, they were organized. He had a dashboard camera, both facing forward and into the car.

One folder was titled "How to Commit a Perfect Crime."

It contained the footage he'd sent to Stella, a rougher, earlier cut. Later ones cut between scenes, showing the victim comatose on the street, then cutting back to him laughing and having a good time at a bar I didn't recognize (New Orleans had hundreds of bars, I don't know them all). Then back in the car, looked like the Range Rover. Them driving the stranger around while he was losing consciousness. Cuts between them making what they thought were witty comments.

I found the one with the man who died. I only watched enough to know it was him.

The half cup of coffee I'd managed was already roiling in my stomach. I like to think I'm tough, but cruelty and callousness bring on the nausea.

One file was titled "Trannie Trash."

"You motherfucker," I muttered out loud. He had scenes, like he was making a romantic comedy. A few snips of Stella from the distance, probably without her knowing she was being filmed. Then his narrative afterward. "I had a fun date with an exciting woman, a woman with a dick. Didn't use it, but who knows what will happen. Maybe we'll fall in love and I can bring her home to meet my parents." Followed by his high, braying laugh.

A clip of her telling him, "Hey, don't video me, that's not cool. This is not a movie."

I hit fast-forward, wanting to get through this as quickly as possible. But then it felt like I was rushing to her death, through the final moments of her life.

No, his version of her isn't her life. They met briefly, she gave him a chance to be a decent person and realized he wasn't.

The final clip was him ranting. She'd dropped him and he had thoughts.

"What a bitch! She should be begging me to come back. A freak like her isn't going to get much, especially not someone like me. I could drive a car into her and no one would care."

I stopped watching at that point. The clip went on for over ten minutes.

The next clip was a car camera. Him picking her up. Telling her to sit in the back seat as he had a cake on the front passenger seat he had picked up for his grandmother. She got in back, and Booze Boy was there.

They headed downtown, turning onto Rampart Street. She was wary, asking what was going on. They blew her off, Booze Boy offered her a drink. She refused it.

I looked at the time stamp. A few minutes before I had witnessed her killing.

I watched. Her asking where they were going, them laughing. The sudden stop. Booze Boy pushing her out.

They laughed when they saw the Range Rover hit her.

I turned it off. I had seen enough.

I stood up and walked around my office, getting a bottle of water from the small refrigerator I kept here, as if I could wash the taste out of my mouth.

I looked at my watch. It was past three in the morning.

I called Detective Thompson, but it went to voice mail. I asked him to call me ASAP. Then I texted him the same message, saying I had stumbled over something he needed to see.

I considered contacting Joanne and/or Danny but decided not to. Maybe I could convince Detective Thompson that I'd found the phone. It would be harder to fool them. They might look past it, given the evidence it contained. But they might not. Better to limit the number of people who would be questioning me.

At this hour everyone was probably asleep, phones silenced.

Maybe I should try that as well, try to get some rest.

I considered crashing there at the office but knew I was too agitated to do more than toss and turn on the not-quite-long-enough couch.

I carefully put the phone in a plastic bag, wrapped it with several paper towels, and put the bundle in an opaque grocery bag before putting it in my briefcase.

I turned out the light, carefully locked my office, and headed down the darkened stairs, letting the shadows guide me.

I waited at the outside door, hearing voices outside, stumbling home. When they passed, I headed for my car. I was being paranoid. It was late, but it was my building and I had a right to be there.

At home, I turned on only the lights I needed to not trip and kill myself.

I took a shower, a long hot one, to wash off a long day, all the sins, mine and the ones I'd witnessed. It didn't do much for the sins, but I was clean and finally feeling as tired as I should feel.

I lay down in my bed, putting my phone next to me on the nightstand, leaving the volume up.

I didn't think I would sleep, but somehow, I did.

CHAPTER SEVENTEEN

My phone woke me up shortly after six a.m.
I let it ring for a second, orienting myself to why my brain was telling me to wake up and answer it.

I picked it up, looking at the caller ID in case it was the bar asking about a missing phone.

It was Detective Thompson.

I answered.

"I got your message. What's up?"

"I stumbled on something you need to see."

"What is it?"

"A smartphone. With text messages and video."

He was silent for a moment. "Incriminating?"

"Yes."

"You stumbled on it?"

"Yes, stumbled. I can explain when we meet." I could come up with an explanation by then.

"My office in an hour?"

"Yes. Sleep is overrated. Put the coffee on."

"An hour. See you."

I threw myself out of bed and into another shower. This one to wake me up—I'd given up on washing any sins away.

Then dressing in sober, professional clothes: a charcoal suit, with white button-down shirt. My one pair of good black shoes. It might not help, but the more credible I looked, the better. It would take more makeup than I'd ever owned in my life—including Mari Gras—to cover up the drained and tired look on my face.

I stared at myself, the early morning light yellowing my skin tones, the sharp slant of sun showing the gray in my hair. Lines that wouldn't go away no matter how relaxed my face was. Soon, the half-century mark. I'd have to live to one hundred for this to be only half of my life.

I turned from the mirror. It wasn't helping.

I dithered in the kitchen, not enough time to brew and drink coffee, but my stomach needed something in it. I ended up with half a piece of bread, not enough time to toast it.

I was out of my door just before seven.

Traffic was already bad, everyone who wanted to avoid the even worse traffic in full rush hour. Parking was the usual zoo around this station. I ended up two long blocks away.

When I arrived, Detective Thompson was already there. He nodded and beckoned me to follow him to a small interview room.

Two large cups of coffee were sitting on the table. I sat behind one and took a sip to claim it.

"What do you have that can't wait?" he asked.

I reached into my briefcase and pulled out the phone. I handed it to him. He put on latex gloves to take it out of the plastic bag.

He raised a quizzical eyebrow at me.

"He used an address as his passcode," I said, reading the numbers off the sheet I'd scribbled it on.

He took the scrap of paper from me.

"How did you know his address?"

"I didn't," I confessed. "I saw him at Q Carré with some of the people I have questions about. Not doing anything suspicious, but still, why are they together? At some point, I went outside to chat with one of the bartenders on a smoke break. I saw them leave. When he got in the SUV, something shiny fell to the ground. They pulled away. I wasn't sure what it was but walked over to take a look. That's when I saw it was a phone. I didn't know his name or how to contact him, so went back to the bar and reviewed the security footage. Saw him opening the phone and was able to write down his passcode."

"Why not leave it with lost and found?"

"I'm a PI, this is what I do. I was curious who he was. I mostly wanted to open it to get his name to give it back to him. But…then I saw what was on it."

"What's on it?"

"He fancies himself a filmmaker. He taped everything he did." I took a sip of coffee. It was decent, meaning he'd picked it up along the way.

"You reviewed it all?"

"No, just enough to know what it was. That's when I called you."

"Stella's murder?"

"That and the robberies."

"Well, shit." He punched in the code.

I'd finished my coffee by the time he looked up from the phone.

"These are some sick motherfuckers, pardon my French," he said.

"I speak the same language."

He nodded grimly. I continued, "He is the grandson of Constance D'Marchant. I believe he and his friends borrowed her vehicles for their crimes. She owns both a cream-colored Mercedes sedan and a charcoal Range Rover. He doesn't live there, but he has a bunch of film equipment in a room over the garage, an amateur film studio. There may be even more stuff there." I gave him the address. He recognized it as the passcode.

"You have been busy."

"Stella should be alive. No grandmother should bury her granddaughter."

"We agree there. I need you to hang out here for a bit."

"Bathroom break?"

"Sure, down the hall. Don't wander too far."

He left the room. I gave him a beat, then followed. Cop shops are still mostly male, so the women's room was empty. I didn't desperately need to go, but better to not get to that point, given how this day might transpire. I also wanted some time to think. He wouldn't follow me in here. I didn't know if he believed my tale or not. Or if he was willing to go along with it since it solved two murders and a string of ugly robberies.

I hoped I could walk out of here a free woman.

I flushed the toilet, washed my hands, but ignored the mirror. I doubted my tired look had improved.

The small room was still empty when I returned.

It didn't stay that way for long.

It wasn't even eight a.m. and my day was already going downhill.

He brought four other people with him: An older man I didn't recognize, a younger woman carrying the phone and a laptop. And Danny and Joanne.

I wasn't sure why they were there. This wasn't their case. Well, as far as I knew. My hope was they were officially involved. Otherwise, the only reason for them to be there was as bullshit detectors.

For my pile.

The older man and the younger woman took the two remaining chairs in the room. The others stood.

"We just need to go over a few things," the older man said. He was introduced as Captain Jamal Charbonnet. "We really appreciate you coming to us. This looks like it's going to be helpful." He turned on a tape recorder and asked my name and basic information. He led me through my story as to how I had found the phone. No hard questions, just getting the supposed facts down. He asked a few more questions about how I became involved. I answered as honestly as I could about working with the bars, being a witness to Stella's murder.

Then he turned off the tape and again repeated his appreciation for my bringing this to the police.

He turned to the young woman with the laptop; she answered the question he didn't even need to ask. "Got it all downloaded."

They stood up and left, followed by Detective Thompson.

Danny gave me a look that could have been anything from "you look terrible" to "what the hell is going on," and then she left as well.

I stood up.

Joanne put her hand on my shoulder.

"Stumbled?" she questioned.

"Stumbled. Getting clumsy as I get older."

She shook her head, then said, "Don't tell me the real story until after I'm retired."

She didn't give me time to answer before she left.

Just as well. I didn't have one.

I took this as permission to go. I wanted nothing more than to go back to bed. Somehow this day didn't seem to hold much hope for that. I stopped and picked up coffee and a greasy breakfast sandwich.

I checked my phone while in line and saw both a text message and an email from Mrs. D'Marchant. She was demanding to see me ASAP to hear what I had to tell her about Peter.

"Fuck," I muttered aloud.

The man in front of me said, "Yeah, I had that kind of night, too."

She said she was available at nine thirty.

Back in my car, I guzzled both the coffee and the food. It was just a little before nine. I wanted nothing more than to blow this off.

But Mrs. D'Marchant was about to lose a grandson. She would be long dead before he got out of prison. It would take a few hours, maybe longer, before the wheels of justice would have all the paperwork signed. Right now, she didn't know.

That would change soon.

Once she knew one grandson was going to jail for murdering a transgender woman, how would she react to her other grandchild *being* a transgender woman?

I'd told Audra I would do this. I doubted there would a happy ending all around, but there might be a tentative connection that eventually could rebuild a relationship. If I didn't get it started now, Mrs. D'Marchant would be consumed by what was sure to be a worse scandal than her son's messy divorce.

I pulled out of the parking lot and headed uptown.

I swung by another coffee shop on the way and got a big cup and a donut. I'd have to count on caffeine and grease getting me through the day.

Parking was a mess, some film crew in the area taking up a good number of places. I was on the next block over, just past the corner. Not horrible, but I'd have to walk the block in front of the house and then down the side street a block to get to the servants' entrance. I assumed she'd expect me to use that one.

Another sip of coffee and a bite of donut, then I locked my car and walked around the block. Slowly enough that I arrived at the side door at nine thirty-five. She deserved courtesy and respect, not obeisance.

I rang the doorbell.

Dottie opened it, wiping her hands on a towel. She had obviously been in the kitchen and told to expect me.

We nodded at each other. I followed her cue and said nothing.

"Mrs. D'Marchant is expecting you," she said as I followed her along the hallway to the parlor where we'd first met.

"Thank you," I said as we entered.

Mrs. D'Marchant was indeed waiting for me.

"Well?" she said before I even had a chance to sit.

Dottie exited back to the kitchen.

"Good morning," I said, not letting her drive this conversation.

"I suppose you expect coffee?"

"No, I've already had coffee," I said in as bland and polite a voice as possible. She wasn't going to set the tone either.

"Is my grandson dead or alive?" she demanded.

"Alive and well."

"You could have emailed me that."

"Peter has gone through some life changes since your family asked him to leave." I wanted to say threw him out, but was threading between truth and confrontation.

She waved her hands as if that was past and didn't matter. Leave all the unpleasant pasts behind, especially the ones that damned you. "You should have brought him with you."

"There are some things you need to know before meeting."

"Really? So you can charge me a few extra hours? Or is that another day minimum?"

"It has nothing to do with my fee or what I'm charging."

"I only hired a homosexual to find my homosexual grandson. Otherwise, I'd have nothing to do with you."

Ah, cards on the table now. I had wondered if this was how she dealt with everyone she considered lesser. Maybe it was my being a woman, my skin not being clearly lily white, and I was queer, the trifecta of people she wanted to look down on.

"That's fine. Once I'm done here, we'll never see each other again." She started to speak, but I continued over her. "As I said, your grandson Peter has gone through some significant changes. You knew him as a gay man, but since he's been out of your life, he came to the realization that he is transgender and he—"

"What the hell does that mean?" she demanded.

I had to try. Maybe she could love Peter enough to accept her as Audra.

"Some people are born with the outward appearance of one sex, but everything else in them is another sex."

"Are you telling me my grandson is a cross-dresser?"

"No. Peter, after a lot of thought and working with experts, is now a woman. That is how she is living her life."

Mrs. D'Marchant stared at me, her mouth working as though too much outrage wanted to come out all at once.

"This isn't an easy or quick process. Almost all transgender people know, even when they're children, that they're different. Peter was one of those people. She now lives as a woman named Audra."

"This is nonsense! Women and men don't just switch places at the drop of a hat. I have enough granddaughters, but only two grandsons! Why are you lying to me?"

"I'm not lying. I wouldn't lie about this. Peter is now Audra. Peter is now a woman. A very lovely and kind woman."

"This cannot be real," she said, more to herself than me.

"I know this is hard, even shocking, news. It can take time to come to terms with it. Your grandchild is alive and well and happier now than before. Please give him a chance to come back into your life." I used the male pronoun, since it was how she thought of Audra and fighting about pronouns wouldn't help at this moment. I needed her to crack open the door to letting the child she had known as Peter meet her as Audra.

"No! Maybe he is as delusional as you are, living an unnatural life. Being a homosexual wasn't enough, so now he's prancing around in dresses. Some things are so unnatural and wrong that they cannot be accepted."

"I know you're angry and upset. This is an enormous change. Please don't make the same mistake twice, throwing your grandchild out of your life, without giving it time. Let the emotions cool first."

"Don't you lecture me! You're as much a pervert as he is! The only time needed is for him to come to his senses and become the man he is meant to be. If he wants to be part of our family again, that's the only way we will accept him!" Her face was red, her hands waving in the air as if clawing it.

"Don't make this about me," I said as calmly as I could. I wouldn't let her anger make me angry. Turning this into a battle would give her the excuse to be angry. And to avoid thinking about Audra and if she could love her. "Peter isn't going to change into what you want. Transgender people aren't freaks or crazy. They are born in a hard place, external features of one sex but the heart, soul, and mind of another. When they change, it means they finally stopped lying."

"I have made myself clear," she said icily, her lips in a hard line, eyes looking beyond me as if I was no longer there. "Peter is my grandson or he is nothing." She raised her voice. "Dottie! Please show this person out. Now!"

I stood up. "If you ever want to contact your grandchild, you have my number. I will—"

"Leave now! I will not be contacting you."

Dottie appeared at this door.

"Get her to leave now! Off my property. Or I will call the police!" Mrs. D'Marchant demanded.

I turned and headed out the way I had come in. Dottie trailed behind and followed me out the door. Once she had shut it behind us, she said, "Got to see you off the property." It was as sarcastic as I've ever heard her. "Some folks are just born mean and learn to be meaner."

"You need a new job."

"Don't I know it. Working on it, working hard on it. You tell Peter…guess it's not Peter now, but you tell them to come by my house for cookies. Always welcome."

"Audra. I'll let her know. Thanks, Dottie. Some people are born decent and get nicer along the way." I gave her a hug at the property line and walked away.

That was painful. I knew there was a lot of hate out there, but I had slammed right into a wall of it. As awful as it had been for me, better me than Audra. She didn't need that to be her last memory of her grandmother. Oh, maybe leopards can change their spots. Maybe over time, Mrs. D'Marchant would reconsider. She was in her early seventies. Not many years left for the mind to change. Earlier today I had almost felt sorry for her, knowing what her other grandson had done and how it would affect her family. But she was the matriarch of this copperheads' nest and she seemed to like having fangs around her.

I walked slowly, unsure of what to do next and too tired to think. I needed to blow this off so I could drive safely. Right now, my mind was churning with jumbled thoughts…from how unlikely I was to get paid to how someone could put their hate for an abstract over their love for a grandchild.

Or maybe it wasn't love at all, but a need for the world to reflect their choices back to them. If the reflection wasn't what they wanted, they threw it away.

I turned the corner only to see a big boxy black SUV parked right in front of the ornate visitors' gate to the house. My least favorite PI was standing next to it, looking at me with a smirk on his face.

"Fancy meeting you here," he called out.

"Really? I'd call it trashy." I was tempted to cross the street, but that would only goad him. He wanted to confront me. If I yelled, someone from the film crew would hear me.

"Ha ha ha, so funny."

I walked as slowly as I could in his direction. Well, really the direction of my car. He was just in my way.

"Didn't expect to see me here, did you?"

"No, did not." *Make minimal replies and keep walking. If he follows me, just keep walking, pull out your phone and dial 9-1-1.*

"Mrs. D. wanted to hire a real detective."

"Why didn't she hire you to find Peter?"

He scowled, admitting, "She did, but we were busy with other cases. Couldn't put the time into it."

Right. They hadn't been about to find him. I only nodded. It explained him following me. Somehow, I knew he'd say more.

I was right. "Yeah, my firm has worked with her for a while now. She hired me to make sure you were doing the job of finding her grandson."

"I found her grandchild. Just let her know the results. I'm sure she'll enlighten you." I veered out into the street to take a wide berth around him. If he was going to try anything, I'd have a few yards of warning. Nor did I want to be close enough to get a whiff of his night in Biloxi.

"Bet you didn't know I've been following you around."

"Bet you didn't know you were following my cousin for most of the time since we switched cars."

Not a great poker face. Enough of a downturn of his smile to let me know he hadn't figured that one out.

"Yeah, I knew that," he bluffed.

"Sure. Well, it's over. I found Peter, so you can go on to other things." I was even with his SUV now, walking past it.

"We could still solve the robberies, you know. My PI skills, your connections in the homo community."

"'Homo' is a nasty word. Sort of like prick or small dick."

"Trying to help you in your career."

"Mrs. D. is waiting for you. She doesn't like it when you're late."

A quick worried look at the house told me I was right. He looked at his watch. "Still got five minutes."

"She's going to be happy to watch you down here chatting with me." I was past him, cut to the far side of the street to let a car go by.

A quick look at the window, back to me. "I'll tell her I told you you're not a real private dick. Not even close." He snickered at his joke. "And that she made the right decision to hire me to check on you." He had to raise his voice to cover the distance.

I stopped and turned to him. "Your wife know you like to date transgender women?"

Fear, replaced by anger. "That's a lie. Don't you dare repeat that."

"Not me. Security footage. Cops are reviewing it as we speak. About the robberies." I turned away. "You have a nice day now." I kept walking.

"You're lying!" he called after me.

I just kept walking, going down the next street until he was out of sight. I'd passed my car. But if I had stopped, he might have followed me. I'd have to make sure Detective Thompson got some snips of footage from Q Carré. At the next corner, I stopped and looked back. No sign of him. He was probably getting an earful from Mrs. D. right now. Let them have their hate fest.

I slowly headed back to my car, watching for him and his SUV. And other cars as well.

It was a beautiful day, late fall in New Orleans, bright sunshine, humidity finally lower to make everything feel more clear than I've seen in months.

I leaned against my car, taking it all in, the relentless beauty of the world twined with the relentless destruction. The piece I had met today hidden by the façade of that perfect house with the perfect large green lawn, tall trees dotting the property with birds singing.

I looked away, then at my phone. Yep, an email from Mrs. D'Marchant telling me that she would not pay me for these unsatisfactory results. About what I expected. I wouldn't reply. Life would do that for me. The rest was spam. I put my phone away.

Time to get away from here, before Mr. Big Shot PI emerged. I had noticed that he went in the front door, not the servants' entrance.

Maybe this is what money buys, I thought, looking again at the expansive house. If money is all that matters.

A flash of color. Another car coming down the street.

A burnt orange Mustang.

I bent low, watching through the windows of my car. If they didn't notice me, they wouldn't recognize me. I doubted the tacky sunglasses had been enough of a disguise.

It went on until it came to the driveway of that perfect house. The driver looked like Booze Boy, and there were two other figures in the car. They had gone by so quickly and unexpectedly I couldn't be sure who the others were. A spot of bird shit on one of my windows didn't help.

I stood up enough to see over the roof of my car.

The car turned into the driveway.

I edged around my hood to get a better view.

It drove the entire length of the driveway and stopped. I caught motion just beyond the car. A garage door opening?

A faint snick, and the car disappeared. Again, motion coming down, with a quiet thump at the end. Expensive, quiet garage doors.

Booze Boy and Ex-Employee had visited here before, so that wasn't out of place. But why not park in the street? Oh, yes, my PI instincts were humming. Maybe they wanted to keep that noticeable car hidden? Knowing that Mrs. D'Marchant would not hand her grandson over to the cops. Hoping they wouldn't dare to look here?

I texted Detective Thompson. *If you're looking for some suspects, I just saw them.*

My phone rang a second later. "We're looking. Not at their apartments."

I told him what I had seen.

"You sure it's them?"

"How many burnt orange Mustangs driven by someone who looks a lot like Garland Gallano would be pulling into this driveway? With someone who has a remote garage opener like a grandson?"

"Hang tight if you can. Let me know if they move." He hung up.

The lead detective just told me I had to stay around and watch. My day was improving.

I dialed Dottie, hoping she was by herself in the kitchen.

"Yes?" she said softly.

"Do whatever you need to do to leave as quickly as you can," I instructed her. "Just get out."

"Why?" Then, "Never mind. I'll get it later." I heard voices in the background. A high, braying laugh? Or was my imagination adding that?

"I'll explain later. Just get out." I ended the call.

Then the street was quiet, only the birds singing their soundtrack to this beautiful morning.

I sat in my car, waiting, glad I had thought to go to the bathroom at the police station, otherwise the coffee would be an issue by now.

An older car pulled out from the street with the servants' entrance on it. The driver looked like Dottie.

"Yes," I muttered to myself. I'd call her later. Or she'd see the news.

My phone rang. Detective Thompson.

"They still there?"

"As far as I can tell."

"Where are you?"

"At the corner of the next block. I can see the front and the driveway. Can't see the kitchen exit on the other side of the house."

"Those the only exits you know of?"

"Probably one in the back to the yard. Doors to the second-floor veranda."

"Got it. We're about five out."

I got back out of my car to better watch the fireworks. I wasn't going to stay much beyond the first bottle rocket. It was all too possible that Mrs. D'Marchant would have the money and clout to repel the police. Or call in enough political favors. If they were arrested, I knew it would be more for the well-to-do gay male tourist than Stella. Tourism was big in this town, even gay tourists, with Mardi Gras, Southern Decadence (a big party over Labor Day weekend, at the tail end of summer when not too many other people care to slog through our humidity), and Halloween. His death was front page news, hers a small story in the metro section. The powers that be care about the front page.

There were no sirens, no warning. Only the sound of tires on the street.

Suddenly two marked cars were in front, one on the street on the far side, rapidly joined by two unmarked cars.

Showtime.

Detective Thompson got out, glanced around, and saw me. He gave a bare nod, then turned toward the house. Joanne got out of the second car, followed by Captain Jamal Charbonnet. Neither of them looked in my direction.

I again moved to the far side of my car, so it blocked all but my head. I wanted to watch, not be watched.

The three of them marched up to the front door and pounded it.

"Police! Please open the door," Detective Thompson yelled. Just like they do on TV.

He had to yell again, then Joanne and Captain Charbonnet added their voices before the door was finally opened.

It was Mrs. D'Marchant herself. Definite proof Dottie wasn't in the house. Was she just old and slow? Or was she delaying to give her grandson time to do...I didn't even know. Where was he going to go?

Oh, he was going to run. Stupid had taken over.

As she was at the door, three figures appeared at the far back end of the second-floor veranda, near the garage.

Not Nice Brice was first. Likely he had done this before, shimmying around one of the columns, hopping to the garage roof, jump from it to grab the first-floor column to slide down.

I picked up my phone but heard one of the uniformed officers yell an alarm.

Brice hit the ground, but rolled and was off running to the back of the house.

Booze Boy was next, but he wasn't good at this. He hit the garage roof at a bad angle and couldn't regain his footing, stumbling, rolling off, hitting the ground with a solid and painful thud. He tried to push himself up but fell back down again with a groan.

Unfortunately for him, Ex-Employee was following closely behind. He, too, lost his footing on the garage roof, managed to regain it enough to jump off. But this wasn't the movies, and he wasn't a stunt man. He landed close to Booze Boy, but the impact caused him to topple over, landing on Booze Boy just as he was trying again to get up.

They both collapsed in a heap.

When they looked up again, four cops were surrounding them with pointed guns.

"You're white and rich, you won't be shot," I muttered to myself.

I tried to call Detective Thompson to tell him about the back passage to the far block, but he didn't answer. He was still at the door, arguing with Mrs. D'Marchant. Mr. Big Shot PI had joined them, no doubt working his extensive police contacts.

I called Joanne.

"What?" she barked. She had stepped back, letting the others show the arrest warrants.

"Passage from the back yard to the next block over. That's probably where he went."

"What? How do you know that?"

"Talking to people. I'll explain later."

"Never mind." She hung up as she was calling to the cops on the side street, directing them to the next block.

After she instructed them, she looked around, finally spotting me. She started to head my way, stopped, shook her head, and turned back to the others.

Exit street left. I'd seen enough. At least two were in custody. Brice might get away for a bit, but he wasn't as smart as he thought he was. No car, no clothes. They'd catch him soon enough.

I got in my car, turning uptown to avoid going anywhere near that perfect house.

CHAPTER EIGHTEEN

B ut I had miles to go before I slept.

I'd made a glaring mistake. It was close to noon. Q Carré would be open.

A beautiful fall day brought people to the French Quarter.

"Don't you have to work?" I muttered as I circled around trying to find parking. I finally gave up and parked near my house. Dangerous because it was tempting to go inside and take a nap.

Instead, I forced myself to walk up Rampart Street to the bar.

Mercifully, more people were on the street than inside. Only a few customers at the back tables and Mary at the bar looking at her phone.

She glanced up at me and waved.

I waved back and headed to the office.

Rob was there.

I had hoped to find the office empty.

"Good morning to you," he said. "Or is it afternoon by now?" He looked at me and then said, "You look like you're auditioning for a zombie movie, already in makeup."

I flopped down in the chair opposite him. "It's been a long day."

"Already?"

I wavered. Exchange idle chat, or be honest.

Who better to confess your sins to than a bartender?

"They caught Stella's killer. And the drug/robbery assholes."

He put down the document he had been reading to stare at me. "What? How? That is good news!" all in a jumble.

I told him. All of it. Including that I stole the phone and it was likely to be on the bar security footage. I told him that I didn't expect him to lie or cover up for me. If asked, he should turn over the footage. Not Nice Brice would have the best lawyers, and they would be smart enough to try to get the evidence on the phone thrown out. Brice would know he last saw it here. All they needed to do was prove there was something improper about how the phone got to the cops.

After I'd finished, Rob stared at me for what felt like a full minute. Then he said, "We have a rat problem." He then clicked several keys on the security computer. "Damn buggers ate through some of the camera wires last night. No footage from the two covering the bar since sometime last night at about?"

"Ten or eleven?"

He watched the screen, looking for the time stamp.

I watched as the three of them drank their shots at the bar, the images fast-forwarding until suddenly I appeared. The sunglasses make it look not quite like me. But not quite enough. Rob skipped back a few minutes until I disappeared. A few more strokes of the keys, then he hit delete, then delete again for the trash.

He reached down behind him and, after a moment of scrabbling around, came up with a vise-grip pliers, the kind with rough teeth. He stood up and motioned me to follow him.

We headed downstairs.

As we approached the bar, he said, "I think I saw the delivery truck out back. Can you check?"

Mary nodded and headed for the rear door, with Rob slipping behind the bar, ostensibly to cover for her. He headed for the camera feeds and used the pliers to roughly tear the wires for the ones over the bar.

"Damn rats," he said when he finished.

Mary returned. "No delivery truck out back."

"Must be for all the other bars around here," Rob said as he changed places with her.

We headed back to his office.

Seated back at his desk, he said, "I will notice the blank cameras in the due course of time. Mary and I will discover the rat-chewed wires and bemoan the lost footage."

"Damn rats," I echoed.

"The means don't always justify the end. Every once in a while, they do," he said softly. "There was another robbery last night. A bar over on Bourbon Street. They're getting bolder; they had mostly hit the more out-of-the-way bars."

"Last night?" Mr. Big Shot PI had been out of town. Had they cut him out?

"Yeah, two victims, one local and one out of town. What we're heard was the tourist was going on a gay tour, so the local asked to tag along. Big SUV, with three other guys in it. Person in the rear was handing drinks forward. They both got woozy at the same time, so the local guy jumped out at the next light and stumbled home, too out of it to do anything until he woke up. His tourist friend woke up in a strange neighborhood, with someone poking him, asking if he was okay. Phone gone."

"Well, shit," I said. "About what time?"

"There were picked up around eight."

The three of them celebrating in the bar at about ten.

"Beer and a burger?" Rob offered, seeing how tired I was.

I gave him a small smile; all my face could manage. "Thanks, but maybe later. Still have a few things to do, and that would make me fall asleep." I stood up.

"Later it is, then," he said as he picked up whatever he had been reading when I interrupted him.

"Good luck with the rats." I headed downstairs and out of the bar.

The walk home helped wake me up. That, or the exercise in avoiding already drunk tourists. The ones that stop and look at our old buildings. Every ten feet, because the French Quarter has old buildings every foot. They can't stop and move to the side, they have to stop and spread over the entire sidewalk.

I was happy to turn off the busy street to my quieter one.

And then, blessedly, to enter my own little house.

My bed was calling, but not yet. I had calls I had to make.

The first was to Dottie.

"You might want to not go back there for a few days," I told her after she answered.

"Not going back for the rest of my life. Gave my notice as I walked out the door. That no-good grandson of hers and his lowlife friends run in, him babbling about being in trouble and needing help. I didn't want his trouble, so I left. Passed a few police cars on my way out. Your warning did good."

"He and his friends are in a lot of trouble."

"Maybe. It's going to be rich white boy trouble. Not poor Black kid trouble."

I couldn't argue. "What will you do now?"

"Been talking to Miss Estelle. She can't keep doing what she's doing, not at her pace and her age. She and Desiree are working together to do a whole package deal like they did for Miss Traci. I can clean and cook and learn to run things. Make it a real business. Called her as soon as I got back here. Organize a bunch of us. Hard work, but decent money."

"That's great! I'm very happy for you. I might need to talk to her about my house."

Dottie laughed. "Looks like we'll be busy, but we might work you in."

After I ended the call with Dottie, I debated what to do next. I needed to talk to Audra, but it felt too cowardly to do over the phone. Plus, she was probably still at work. It would wait until the evening.

Nap time.

But I made one more call. To her office. It went to voice mail. "You have reached Cordelia James. Please leave a message. If this if a medical emergency, please dial 9-1-1 or go to the nearest emergency room."

"Hi, this is Micky. I just wanted to update you. It'll be on the news soon enough. Stella's killers have been apprehended."

I headed up to my bedroom, changing out of my now rumpled nice professional clothes.

My phone rang.

"Micky. Hi, this is Cordelia."

"Hi," was all I managed, too tired to move my brain more quickly.

"You said you had an update?"

"Yes, it just happened today." I called her; I had to say something. Without admitting everything I had done. "The police have arrested the people who killed Stella." I gave her an edited version and that they were also the thieves. Stella had dated one of them briefly, then dumped him. His ego didn't like that, and he had given her info that made her suspect him as one of the robbers.

When I finished, she said, "How were you involved?"

"Involved?"

"It's not on the news yet. Neither Danny or Joanne have called me, so they wouldn't just contact you this quickly. That leaves being involved."

I did a tap dance about looking into security for bar owners, seeing something suspicious on the security tapes of one of them, meeting with the police detective working on it. A bartender seeing them with one of the victims. Getting the video that he had sent to Stella. Researching the cars they drove and, by coincidence, seeing one of them at a place they shouldn't have been. I was hoping if I jabbered on long enough, she would have to end the call. She was a doctor, some sick person would need her.

But she didn't. "So, you saw the police arrest them?" she said when I finally ran out of half-truths to tell.

"Yes, well, two of them. One got away, but they've probably caught him by now."

"Good, good to know. What are you not telling me?"

"I've left out the hours and hours it took to go through the security footage."

She left a silence. I knew better than to fill it. I was used to telling her everything, but that didn't apply anymore.

Finally, I said, "I didn't mean to interrupt your day, but you knew Stella…and I thought you should get more courtesy than reading it in the paper."

"Thank you," she said. "Did you tackle one of them? Get in a fight?"

"No. Was safely across the street and only watched the police. I'm too old for that."

She chuckled softly. "That's also good to hear." Then, finally, "I'll be with you in a minute." Back to me, "Are you going to the march tomorrow?"

"March?"

"Transgender Day of Remembrance."

"Oh, probably. Unless you're going."

"I had planned to. It's important but seems more important this year."

"I can skip it."

"Please don't. I'm going with some work colleagues. I know you're not telling me everything, but you had a lot to do with Stella's murderers being caught."

"I put a few things together, that's all."

"I'll see you there?"

"Yes, I'll be there."

"Good, I'll try to find you."

I put my phone down, turned the ringer off, then flopped on the bed. Why had I called her? She had asked me to get involved. And…I wanted an excuse to talk to her. I wasn't even sure why. So we could just talk to each other like normal people in the same social circle? Not do the avoidance dance we had been doing? Or…?

I didn't know.

"I'm too tired to think about this," I said to myself. Maybe I needed a cat to talk to. I should have called Stella's grandmother. She deserved to know, if not more so than Cordelia. But that wasn't my role. I had no official capacity. I hoped the police or district attorney were already there. I groaned, rolled up and texted Danny, *Someone needs to tell Miss Estelle. She shouldn't hear it on the news.*

I got an almost immediate reply. *On my way now.*

Time to nap the nap of the righteous. I lay back down, then sat up to set my alarm for around five p.m.

Then I lay back down again.

Chapter Nineteen

The sun was shining at the wrong angle for it to be morning. I was disoriented by the sharp buzz of my alarm. Then the already-too-long day came rushing back to me.

Still groggy, I heaved myself out of bed, then stumbled to the bathroom for a quick shower, to wake myself up again.

I need a haircut, I thought as I toweled it dry. Getting to be too much of a pain at this length, especially wavy as mine was, more of a soggy ball than a head of hair. I ignored the gray replacing the black.

I threw on some reasonably presentable clothes and checked my phone. Five messages. Danny, Joanne, Joanne again. Torbin and Dottie.

I went downstairs and called Dottie back.

"We're all going over to Miss Estelle's and you should be there. Not a celebration, but being around her."

"Thank you, but it should be those closest to her."

"None of that. You called me to get me out. I saw you when I was driving away. You got a story to tell that she should hear. I'm cooking up a storm. Greens, fried chicken, mac and cheese. All the good stuff. Want people there to eat it."

I agreed. That was much better dinner than anything I had here. And I would have enough time to come up with the story I wanted to tell.

I went to my liquor cabinet and took out one of the good bottles of Scotch, put it in a bag, then headed to my car. Audra should be home from work by now.

James was walking up to their door when I arrived.

He saw me as I crossed the street.

"News?" he asked.

I nodded. "Is Audra here?"

"She should be. Let's go inside."

As we entered, he called out, "Hi, honey, I'm home," in a way that told me it was the usual greeting. "I have someone here to see you."

She came into the living room from the kitchen, still in her work clothes—khaki pants, a long-sleeved T-shirt, and the kind of boots designed for stomping around the swampy coastline.

"Micky, hi," she said, her face questioning, not even allowing hope.

I pulled out the bottle of Scotch and handed it to James.

Audra understood. Her lips became a resolute line, eyes looking in the distance. "It didn't go well, I take it?" she said, more a confirmation than a question.

"For someone of her generation and mindset, it was difficult to hear. But maybe in time, she can come around and—"

"No." Audra cut me off. "She doesn't get another chance. They threw me out once. I let this door open and she slammed it shut. There won't be another time."

"Oh, honey, I'm sorry," James said, taking her hand.

"I'm not. This is who they are. Fond childhood memories blurred that, but that haze is gone." She turned to look at him. "I have a lovely life with you, our friends, our chosen family. That brittle blood tie means nothing. Let's call this a celebration, freeing me from ever looking back. Let's open that bottle!"

James gave her a big hug, then went to the kitchen for glasses.

Audra pulled me in and gave me a hug as well. "I suspect you're giving me an edited version."

I didn't confirm that. I didn't need to.

James returned and filled our glasses. I stopped him at a bare two fingers for me.

Audra raised a glass. "To the people who love us and embrace us for who we are, not who they want us to be!"

James said, "To love and life and finding the people who should be in your life!"

I touched my glass to theirs. "To happy endings, even if they are as unconventional as we are."

I stayed long enough to finish my glass and left them the bottle to get them through the night. We made plans to get together with Torbin and Andy soon. Sometimes life comes with grace; I felt like I had found new friends in an unexpected place. Audra and James were funny, smart, and kind. I could have easily stayed the evening laughing with them, in a way that hadn't happened in a long time.

As I left, I almost felt sorry for Mrs. D'Marchant. Almost. She'd chosen the grandchild that kept up the façade and turned away from the truly beautiful one.

I headed for Miss Estelle's place. I had told Dottie I would be there. And I was hungry. It had been a long time since breakfast.

As I nosed up the street, I saw Dottie walking, carrying more food containers than was sane. I stopped just in front of her and popped my trunk. She took the cue and put them in.

"It's only one more block; I could have made it," she said as she slid in the passenger's seat.

"Can't risk you tripping with that precious cargo."

There were already a number of cars parked near Estelle's house, so I only gained her a half a block, but we divided the food between us.

Desiree greeted us at the door, pointing us around to the back yard where things were set up.

We added Dottie's overflowing plates to everything else that was there. It wasn't a celebration, instead a release of tension and fear, the end of one long road. There was laughter, but it was quiet, conversations hushed. People were milling around as if unsure what was expected.

"Y'all eat," Estelle called out. "Don't let this cooking get cold."

I waited for a few people to get in line, then joined them. My stomach was screaming at the wonderful aromas. I got a lot of what Dottie had brought as I had been smelling it in my car. The grease from the fried chicken would help settle the Scotch in my empty stomach.

"I cooked that," Angelique told me, pointing to the jambalaya. She was behind me in line. I added a pile to my plate. "This is Trayvon," she said, introducing the man behind her. He was tall and skinny. "He just got out of the Air Force."

He gave me a shy smile. "Great to meet you," I said.

"Ang is a fine cook," he said.

She gave him a peck on the cheek. "Trayvon is going to help set up computer stuff for Miss Estelle. He's good at that."

"What I did in the Air Force. I got guys I know who can do stuff as well, fix things, paint. Even cook and clean."

We moved down the line. There were five desserts, and I had to choose.

"Miss Estelle is going to do what Stella was going to do, make a business of what we can all do. Make sure the money comes to us and not through other people. We been talking about it these last few days," Angelique explained.

I smiled, deciding on the bread pudding and chocolate cake.

"She made the cake, too," Trayvon said, pointing to the slice on my too-full plate. I might have to eat dessert first to get to the food under it.

"Stella's still here, isn't she?" I said, looking around at all the people gathered. Traci and her husband Paul. Ruby and what I guessed were several of her children and grandchildren. Others I didn't know. I started to wonder who was transgender, then realized it didn't matter and I had no real reason to care.

"Yeah, her memory," Trayvon said. "She was so welcoming to me."

"Her passion and vision. She gave that to us to carry," Angelique said.

I piled on one final piece of corn bread and moved on. Trayvon grabbed beers for us. I joined Dottie at her table. Let the young ones balance drinks and food on their laps. I wanted something solid for my plate.

After a few minutes of eating and drinking beer, tiredness washed over me. No celebration at having solved it, just the weariness of finishing a hard task.

It wasn't over; I knew that. There would be a trial, and they would have money and power on their side.

Ruby stood up and rapped the table to get everyone's attention. "Thank y'all all for being here. This is community for folks who care about each other. As Stella used to say, 'Love is love.' This, us here together, is love. Y'all might have heard some things, but we got a witness to what went down today, so we're going to ask her to give a talk."

I had just taken a big bite of chicken when all eyes turned to me. I tried to chew as gracefully as I could. I put down the drumstick, wiped my hands on a napkin, hurriedly swallowed, and stood up. I stayed where I was, hoping to sit down again as quickly as possible.

First, I tried to get by saying it was just luck I was there and saw it, but Dottie shot that down by pointing out I had called her before. Then I went with the ragged version I had told Cordelia. Everyone whooped and applauded when I got to seeing that burnt orange Mustang, recognizing it, and calling the cops. More laughs as I described the two of them trying to escape and landing painfully on each other. Head shakes and boos about the one who so far hadn't been caught.

"That's what I know," I finished and sat down.

"They're rich and white, right?" Desiree.

I didn't stand up. "Yes, they are."

Angry mutters.

"Justice is to protect the comfortable from the desperate," Rudy said.

"For those they make desperate," Desire amended. "You want justice, you need to believe in heaven and hell."

Estelle spoke. "Not justice. What they call law and order. More money you have, the less the laws apply to you. But…for Stella, I hope this time it's different. I hope…we get as close to justice as we can."

"You think they'll go to jail?" Dottie asked me.

"I hope they go to prison and stay there for a long time," I answered. "But…money buys good lawyers, and justice can be broken." The phone and the videos were the strongest evidence against them. If it got thrown out, they might walk.

People muttered, telling stories of being stopped three times in one day for driving while Black, being followed in stores, being denied mortgages or rentals, having to get rid of anything that said Black people live here to sell their house. Being beaten up for being transgender. Chased down the street, throwing away the nice heels you just bought to run fast enough. And never calling the police because you had to survive, and calling them usually made it worse.

I had another beer, some more chicken, and two more of the desserts, small slices.

Trayvon came and sat down beside me. "You doing okay?" he asked.

"Yes, sure."

"Just checking. You the only white lady here."

"Don't worry, I'm not a lady."

He chuckled.

"And," I continued, "this is more home than a lot of all-white gatherings I've been to." The last family funeral Torbin and I had huddled in a corner, watching as people avoided us for being the queer ones. Not everyone. Torbin's mother, my aunt Lottie, joined us, as did several of the younger cousins, but there was an underlying tension, our being accepted tentative and conditional.

"I get you," he said. "Since I've been going with Angelique, people who used to be friends look at me strange. Wondering why we're together."

"It's not any of their business," I said.

"So, you're not wondering?"

I was, but had no rational reason for wondering, so told myself not to. "Love is love."

"Ain't that the truth. We met at a game trivia night. She was good, knew a lot of the things I knew, we hit it off. I asked her out. She agreed to coffee, and I thought she was being polite and not into me. She told me then about her, that she was a woman, it just took her a while to get there. At first, I had the stupid reaction, not going there. But we'd meet at the game night and I always had such a good time with her. Finally, I asked her out on another date. We just clicked. I got someone I can talk to about anything."

"Who is also a good cook," I added, pointing to the second helping of chocolate cake on my plate.

"I'm good at the grill," he said, laughing. "We just work. That's what should matter, isn't it?"

"It is. Go for love, not respectability."

He high-fived me, then got up to fetch more beer from inside.

I finished the final bites, threw away my plate, and got another beer. What the hell, this was a party to show we had survived, still here to eat and drink and remember those who were no longer here.

I stayed long enough to offer to help clean up but was shooed off, given older-lady status.

Dottie gave me a pile of leftovers. "Take them. Someone should eat them." I offered to give her a ride home, but she refused. "Easy walk and the streets are one-way for cars, but two-way for walkers."

On the porch, Estelle was saying good-bye. Even in the wan porch light, I could see the tiredness stamped in her face. She gave me a hug around the food parcels. "Thank you," she murmured in my ear.

"I didn't do much. And…"

"They may still go free. But they won't be as free as if no one ever knew. I'd rather settle for that than never knowing. Now, if I seem the on the street, I know to spit at them."

She let go of me and turned to the next person.

I made my way to the car. I probably wasn't sober enough to drive, but it was ten blocks on slow side streets. I didn't want to walk those blocks this time of night, nor have to come back in the morning to retrieve my car.

I drove slowly and carefully. Not much traffic other than the light at Claiborne.

Then I was home and stayed awake only long enough to put the food away.

When I woke in the morning, there were an additional five messages on my phone.

"Why am I suddenly so popular?" I groused.

Shower, coffee, and then I would check them.

A piece of cold fried chicken for breakfast.

Danny, Joanne twice, Detective Thompson, someone who identified themselves as a reporter.

Not calling Joanne after she called me four times was going to be a mortal sin.

I dialed her number.

"Was about to call a welfare check on you," she answered.

"Sorry, a busy day."

"Right. So busy you couldn't call me back yesterday?"

I gave her the rundown of my yesterday, skipping my stop at Q Carré, of course. The hateful encounter with Mrs. D'Marchant, crashing out with a nap, meeting with Audra, the gathering at Estelle's. She said little, leaving silences for me to fill. "So, I didn't get home until after eleven last night, and I was still tired from the night before," I finished.

"I was wondering how the hell you ended up there at the right time," she said.

"That was mostly luck. I had left a message with Mrs. D'Marchant, and she demanded to see me then. I went to talk to her before she got lost in the mess of her other grandson. She kicked me out for giving her news she didn't want to hear. I needed to take a moment once I got outside to collect my thoughts and then bingo, saw one of their cars."

I then had to explain how I knew about their cars, searching for ones I had seen the night Stella was killed.

Joanne had a lot of questions. I did my best to answer them while navigating around the things best not confessed to an officer of the law.

I needed another cup of coffee. With a shot of whiskey.

She finally finished—or at least took a pause for now. "The official version is that you believe you stumbled over that phone. The not so official one is close to it fell off the bar into your pocket."

"I'm shocked, shocked, you would think such a thing," I said.

"Tainted evidence can't be used to convince a jury."

"There is security camera footage at the bar, you can check that." Officially, I didn't know about the rats yet.

"Right. The good news for you—and us—is that they were hiding in the so-called film studio, which allowed us to search it with a nice, legal warrant. They are beyond arrogant, filming most everything and then downloading it from his phone to the equipment there."

"You don't need to use the phone."

"Bingo. Your secrets can go to the grave."

"Cheery thought."

"Or my retirement party, which I hope comes much earlier."

Then I called Detective Thompson. He mostly told me what Joanne had, asked no questions.

"Have you caught Brice yet?" I asked.

"No," he admitted. "Still looking for him. But he can't go far. No car, monitor on his credit cards. He's probably in some rabbit hole and will eventually have to come out."

After him, I called Danny. She was mostly going to update me on what Joanne had said, ask if I'd gone to Estelle's last night and how it was. "I had hoped to get there but wasn't able to."

I gave her a quick summary, rubbing in that she missed some good food. Admitted how tired Estelle looked. How tired she had a right to be.

After Danny, I called the reporter. I had no intention of saying anything useful, but he would only call back. I stuck with a lot of "I don't know" to most of his questions, only admitting to seeing some security camera footage that I had brought to the attention of the police.

Then catching up with Torbin and Andy, again the sanitized version of what I had done. Much as I wanted to tell everything, it was an unfair burden to put on them. I wasn't going to catch anyone else in my lies.

Then I turned off my phone, made a lunch of leftovers, and went to my back patio to read a book and shut out the world. It would intrude soon enough.

CHAPTER TWENTY

The march was in the late afternoon, starting in the last of the daylight, the disappearing light taken over by candles of remembrance.

I parked along the route, closer to the finish, so I'd have less distance to walk at the end. Old-lady pragmatism. I could still tromp all over the place, but my body reminded me how creaky my knees had become the next day.

Once I got to the staging area, I was pleased to see how many people had shown up, including City Council members. Ones I had voted for. There were so many people that I didn't see anyone I recognized.

I started to wander in the crowd but a whistle blew, signaling the march was about to begin. I finally spotted Desiree. As I joined her, I saw that she was with many of the people from last night. Ruby with a cane, Angelique, Trayvon, Victoria, others I didn't know. I was introduced to a number of them, names whizzing by. Most of Stella's fellow BSW students, a brass band of all transgender people.

We started marching, the candles bright in the last fading reflection of the setting sun.

One of the things I love about New Orleans is the tradition of the jazz funeral, the somber dirge going and then the switch to more joyful music coming back; the duality of life, sadness and grief, then celebration and joy to hold them at bay.

We held hands for a while, Desiree, Trayvon, Angelique, Rudy, Estelle, others, switching as we moved around, to give everyone the warmth of contact.

We turned a corner and I got a little ahead, running into Rob and his crew from the bar.

"Come by afterward, if you want," he said. "Half the proceeds will go to Stella's project, to give trans people a safe place." He added, "Oh, have I mentioned we had a problem with rats?"

"Really? Thought we'd got rid of those."

"They come back. There is always another rat."

I spotted Cordelia several rows ahead of us, surrounded by what looked like coworkers, several still in scrubs. I looked to see if Joanne or Danny was with her but couldn't see them. Probably still working. Or they felt it would make them seem less neutral if they came. I didn't see Cordelia's partner, Nancy. Maybe she wasn't the marching type.

I had no good reason to go talk to her, so I stayed chatting with Rob, Mary, and Peg.

With them caught, it was over and it had just begun. There would be more haters, more violence, of words and body. We hadn't saved this Stella, but maybe we could save the next Stella.

Then I heard the gasp and the scream.

"Run!" someone yelled.

"No!" another person screamed.

There he was, ten feet from me.

Holding a gun, with another one strapped to his leg.

"You all are hateful people!" he screamed. "And you're going with me!" This was his way out. Suicide and take as many of us with him as possible. He lifted the gun, pointing it at the crowd.

At Estelle, at Ruby, Desiree. Rob and Mary. Cordelia.

I lunged at him, sprinting the distance between us. It felt like slow motion, all my senses on fire to detect any small opening. To stop this madness.

Joanne was right, he was arrogant. Drunk on hate and revenge. He was watching people flee and not expecting anyone to run at him.

That I was coming from behind probably saved my life.

He pulled the trigger and the night exploded.

People cried out, fear and pain.

I reached him and hit his gun hand as hard as I could, forcing the barrel down and the next flurry of bullets into the pavement.

He turned, his eyes so angry they looked hollow.

I tried to keep one hand on his gun arm, keeping him from lifting it to fire into the crowd. I used my left hand to hit him as hard as I could in the face.

It was fast. Violence often is. Too fast to think, only react.

I hit him again.

He grabbed at me, trying to claw my face.

It doesn't matter if I get hurt. If I don't stop him, he can kill dozens of people, wound many more.

I twisted away from him, trying to get directly behind him.

He struggled to lift the gun, switched to using his free hand to get the one on his hip.

I kicked him as hard as I could in the back of the knee, the place that makes the knees buckle. Then I grasped his hair, jerking his head straight back. He went to his knees.

I smashed my elbow into his face.

"Motherfucker," someone next to me said. She grabbed his arm with the gun, making it impossible for him to lift it.

But he fired again, sparks and pieces of asphalt flying.

"Get his other gun!" I yelled.

"Got it," someone else yelled.

Then the three of us shoved him face down on the street, twisting his arm to control the gun he still had.

A woman in heels stepped on his arm, digging her spikes in. "I'm two hundred and ten pounds. I can push through till I hit pavement."

He was now screaming, cursing us, demanding to be let go. Telling us to not hurt him.

"Fuck you!" I muttered at him, now with my knee in the middle of his back. "Just shut the fuck up, you little crybaby!"

The trumpet player wrenched the gun out of his hand. "Ex-Army," she said as she pointed it at his head.

Now there where whistles and sirens, men and women in uniform.

Shit, I thought. Two people had taken guns from him and were now holding them.

I jumped up, holding my hand above my head.

But I kept my foot on his back.

"It's safe!" I yelled. "He's down! No one else is a threat!" I kept repeating myself, hoping to get through the noise and chaos.

The trumpet player put the gun on the ground and also raised her hands.

The other person put the gun down as well.

We all raised our hands.

The cops roughly pulled us off him.

But no shots were fired.

"You need to call Detective Thompson," I shouted to make myself heard. "This is his case and he is looking for this man." Again, I kept repeating myself until one of the cops looked at me and seemed to understand. "He is wanted for murder."

The lights, red and blue flashes, were jarring. Like the night Stella died.

Police cars. Two ambulances.

Then I saw Cordelia with another man and a woman talking to the police. They were all well dressed. All white. A doctor and, it turned out, two lawyers.

Whatever they were saying got the police to pause from putting the handcuffs on us.

I noticed a piece of pavement lodged in the back of my hand, with blood running down my fingers.

Gawd, a fragment of a New Orleans street had entered my bloodstream.

We stood for what felt like hours. Time could no longer be measured by the ticking of a watch. I later found out it was only forty-five minutes.

We were all questioned, contact information collected, and finally, we were free to go.

I was in a daze, not sure which way to go. I looked around, the worried anxious faces. Then the relieved faces.

A hand on my shoulder.

"Are you all right?" Cordelia.

I turned to her. "I guess this proves I'm the butch." We had always joked about it, who took care of the car, who cooked.

She ignored my joke, ignored my distance. "Wait, you're bleeding."

"Blowback, hit by a piece of street. Which I'm sure has poisoned my blood and I'll turn into the creature from Lake Pontchartrain."

She lifted my hand up to examine it. "It's a nasty cut. Let's have one of the EMTs look at it."

I shook my head. "It's not bad. Take care of the seriously hurt first."

"Let me at least get some gauze from them," she said, heading to one of the ambulances.

I was reluctant to follow, too close to the jarring lights, but she quickly returned with basic first aid supplies.

As she cleaned my hand, I asked, "How many people were hurt?"

"We were lucky, thanks to some brave people. Two gunshot

wounds, but nothing life threatening. One in the leg, one in the thigh. Scrapes and bruises from people running. It could have been so much worse."

I glanced around as she worked on my hand.

Rob, Mary, and Peg. They were all okay.

The band was intact.

Audra and James in a group hug with other friends.

Desiree came up behind me and put her arms around my neck. "You are one hell of a hero. I'd marry you if I wasn't already married to a wonderful woman."

I covered one of her hands with mine. "Anyone hurt?"

"No, thank the Lord. Angelique got a cut in her leg from that asphalt spraying, but it's minor. The rest are okay. They all escorted Miss Estelle and Miss Ruby home. It's okay, Dr. C.J., you can say hello. I know you're not supposed to out in public."

"You two know each other?"

Desiree stepped away from me and run her hands down her hips. "How do you think I got this beautiful body? Medical care and magic hormones."

"Hi, Desiree," Cordelia said. "These aren't the best circumstances."

"No, sweetheart, they are not. Only good thing is I think the person hurt the most was that motherfucking piece of hippo diarrhea."

She gave both me and Cordelia a kiss on the cheek, then headed off to join her friends.

Cordelia finished the makeshift dressing on my hand. "Check this tomorrow. Keep it clean. If it's not healing quickly, get it looked at."

"Yeah, thanks," I said.

"Are you okay?" she asked again.

"Yes, fine," I said. I started crying.

Because it's Cordelia and it's what she does, she pulled my head to her shoulder and let me cry.

I let her hold me, then pulled away. I didn't have the right to ask for this comfort anymore. I hadn't been there when she needed me, and I couldn't take what I hadn't offered.

I wiped my eyes, stopping the tears.

She said, "Torbin is on his way. He's going to come get you."

"My car's not that far away." She must have called when she was at the ambulance.

"Tomorrow. You risked your life to stop a killer, got hurt, and now it's time for us to take care of you."

At that, Torbin came running through the crowd.

"Are you okay? Is everyone okay?" he said as he got to us. I don't think I'd ever seen him so worried.

Cordelia gave him the rundown.

"Andy is parked as close as we could get. Illegal, so he's with the car."

"Take Micky home," Cordelia told him. "She stopped him and saved us."

"Come on, sweetie," Torbin said, leading me away.

I took one look back at Cordelia. She was talking to the EMTs.

I stayed with Torbin and Andy. Cats on our laps, pizza ordered, cocktails consumed. We found a way to laugh and to cry and to laugh as we were crying, and we got through the night.

CHAPTER TWENTY-ONE

They were all out on bail. Even Brice, with bail set at over a million. Maybe we would get law and order, but certainly not justice.

They were good boys, from good families, their lawyers pleaded. They were white boys from rich families; they didn't seem to know the difference.

Mrs. D'Marchant was quite vocal on defending her grandson—the murdering one, not the transgender one. From *he wouldn't do anything like that* to *he was led astray* to *it was all lies by the "groomers" and he was trying to save the children from them.*

We did find out who the key thief was. It was Supplement Man, not Ex-Employee, as I'd guessed. He was their money launderer, good enough to hide from cursory scrutiny, but the police were digging deep to follow the money, and it flowed through him. Moved from the phones to one account, then quickly to another and the first account was closed and through several more accounts. The ones I had found were just the tip of the pile.

Mr. Big Shot PI was an idiot, but he wasn't involved. As my tracker on his SUV helped prove. He wanted to find the robbers to collect the hefty reward. Might have figured it out if he had looked beyond his own biases. Rumor was that he and his firm had been fired by Mrs. D'Marchant. Another rumor was that his brother-in-law was one of his police contacts, and he had heard about what was on the security footage and told his sister. Country music face-off: Stand By Her Man or D-I-V-O-R-C-E? Whomp-whomp.

I got a piece of the reward, fifty thousand of the one hundred total, since I had tackled Not Nice Brice. I gave thirty of it to Miss Estelle—not all of it, I'm not that altruistic. I let her decide how much to help with her business and how much to go to Stella's vision for the transgender community. I kept enough to repair my office roof and to get me through a few rainy days, aka months when things were slow, so I could turn down the next Mrs. D'Marchant.

Audra and James were getting married. I just received the invite in the mail yesterday.

Dottie brought by fried chicken and cookies way too often, forcing me to drag myself over to the elliptical at Torbin's almost daily. I needed to tell her to cut back. Maybe tomorrow. Or the next day. She was doing well, making more money than she had before. And much happier.

I had gone to another gathering at Estelle's last weekend. Her face was still tired; I doubted that worn-down sorrow would ever go away. She gave her acceptance, love, and generosity to everyone she could, letting them stay with her, helping them find work, with her or others, letting everyone be themselves. But none of them were Stella. Time may heal some wounds, but it leaves scabs on others. I suspected this would always be a painful scar for her. I hoped she had enough years for it to fade as much as it could.

I told Estelle what I knew, what I heard from Detective Thompson, Joanne, and Danny. Ex-Employee seemed to have remorse. His parents were lawyers, who got him good lawyers right away. It was either his guilt or their seeing the evidence against him that made him cooperate in hopes of getting a plea deal.

Booze Boy's parents were not in the same wealth category as the others, only middle managers, with a nice McMansion in the suburbs. He had scraped to make bail and was now wearing an ankle bracelet. If he avoided the death penalty, he'd be old if he ever got out.

Not Nice Brice had good lawyers. But even cynical as I was, I didn't think they would be good enough. On house arrest, staying with his grandmother. All his film equipment had been seized. He was petitioning to get it back. Danny told me not a chance until after the trial. Joanne added, by which time he'd be in jail. He had recorded a manifesto, as he called it, before he attacked the march. He was going to "kill all the groomers and perverts," be a hero—in his mind—of the so-called culture wars, or what I call civil rights for people different from those in power. It was a good fifteen-minute rant. He would be charged not only with what the others were charged with but with the attempted mass killing as well as being a fugitive. I don't believe in the death penalty, but I might have to make an exception here.

It was a beautiful sunset, the colors vibrant, from umber to purple at the horizon. I was still, watching the sky fade. The moment would pass. We are always in transit, even when we're still, traveling through time, minutes into hours, hours into the night and another day. And another. Finite time ticking away, minute by minute.

As for me? I watched the sun fade away, falling into another night. I felt old and tired, like I was fighting the same fight over and over again. Just let us be people, be who we are. But we had to keep fighting. Would there be enough years for me, for all of us, gay, lesbian, transgender, darker shades of skin, to be as fully human as we should have always been?

How many of us would time leave behind, dreams deferred, drying up in the blazing, merciless sun of lost days and years?

A faint linger of sun was all that was left in the sky, stars blurred through the haze of city lights. I tried to focus on a cluster of the dim stars, but their lights were so faint and far away, one blink of an eye and I lost them.

The sun was gone. I turned from the dark sky, going inside to the glow of an electric bulb, to pass through another night.

About the Author

J.M. Redmann has published ten novels featuring New Orleans PI Micky Knight. Her first book was published in 1990, one of the early hard-boiled lesbian detectives. Her books have won three Lambda Literary awards. *The Intersection of Law & Desire* was an Editor's Choice of the San Francisco Chronicle and a recommended book by Maureen Corrigan of NPR's Fresh Air. Two books were selected for the American Library Association GLBT Roundtable's Over the Rainbow list and *Water Mark* won a ForeWord Gold First Place mystery award. She is the co-editor with Greg Herren of three anthologies, one of which, *Night Shadows: Queer Horror*, was shortlisted for a Shirley Jackson award. Her books have been translated into German, Spanish, Dutch, Hebrew and Norwegian.

Books Available From Bold Strokes Books

A Calculated Risk by Cari Hunter. Detective Jo Shaw doesn't need complications, but the stabbing of a young woman brings plenty of those, and Jo will have to risk everything if she's going to make it through the case alive. (978-1-63679-477-8)

An Independent Woman by Kit Meredith. Alex and Rebecca's attraction won't stop smoldering, despite their reluctance to act on it and incompatible poly relationship styles. (978-1-63679-553-9)

Cherish by Kris Bryant. Josie and Olivia cherish the time spent together, but when the summer ends and their temporary romance melts into the real deal, reality gets complicated. (978-1-63679-567-6)

Cold Case Heat by Mary P. Burns. Sydney Hansen receives a threat in a very cold murder case that sends her to the police for help, where she finds more than justice with Detective Gale Sterling. (978-1-63679-374-0)

Proximity by Jordan Meadows. Joan really likes Ellie, but being alone with her could turn deadly unless she can keep her dangerous powers under control. (978-1-63679-476-1)

Sweet Spot by Kimberly Cooper Griffin. Pro surfer Shia Turning will have to take a chance if she wants to find the sweet spot. (978-1-63679-418-1)

The Haunting of Oak Springs by Crin Claxton. Ghosts and the past haunt the supernatural detective in a race to save the lesbians of Oak Springs farm. (978-1-63679-432-7)

Transitory by J.M. Redmann. The cops blow it off as a customer surprised by what was under the dress, but PI Micky Knight knows they're wrong—she either makes it her case or lets a murderer go free to kill again. (978-1-63679-251-4)

Unexpectedly Yours by Toni Logan. A private resort on a tropical island, a feisty old chief, and a kleptomaniac pet pig bring Suzanne and Allie together for unexpected love. (978-1-63679-160-9)

Crush by Ana Hartnett Reichardt. Josie Sanchez worked for years for the opportunity to create her own wine label, and nothing will stand in her way. Not even Mac, the owner's annoyingly beautiful niece Josie's forced to hire as her harvest intern. (978-1-63679-330-6)

Decadence by Ronica Black, Renee Roman & Piper Jordan. You are cordially invited to Decadence, Las Vegas's most talked about invitation-only Masquerade Ball. Come for the entertainment and stay for the erotic indulgence. We guarantee it'll be a party that lives up to its name. (978-1-63679-361-0)

Gimmicks and Glamour by Lauren Melissa Ellzey. Ashly has learned to hide her Sight, but as she speeds toward high school graduation she must protect the classmates she claims to hate from an evil that no one else sees. (978-1-63679-401-3)

Heart of Stone by Sam Ledel. Princess Keeva Glantor meets Maeve, a gorgon forced to live alone thanks to a decades-old lie, and together the two women battle forces they formerly thought to be good in the hopes of leading lives they can finally call their own. (978-1-63679-407-5)

Peaches and Cream by Georgia Beers. Adley Purcell is living her dreams owning Get the Scoop ice cream shop until national dessert chain Sweet Heaven opens less than two blocks away and Adley has to compete with the far too heavenly Sabrina James. (978-1-63679-412-9)

The Only Fish in the Sea by Angie Williams. Will love overcome years of bitter rivalry for the daughters of two crab fishing families in this queer modern-day spin on Romeo and Juliet? (978-1-63679-444-0)

Wildflower by Cathleen Collins. When a plane crash leaves eleven-year-old Lily Andrews stranded in the vast wilderness of Arkansas, will she be able to overcome the odds and make it back to civilization and the one person who holds the key to her future? (978-1-63679-621-5)

Witch Finder by Sheri Lewis Wohl. Tasmin, the Keeper of the Book of Darkness, is in terrible danger, and as a Witch Finder, Morrigan must protect her and the secrets she guards even if it costs Morrigan her life. (978-1-63679-335-1)

Digging for Heaven by Jenna Jarvis. Litz lives for dragons. Kella lives to kill them. The last thing they expect is to find each other attractive. (978-1-63679-453-2)

Forever's Promise by Missouri Vaun. Wesley Holden migrated west disguised as a man for the hope of a better life and with no designs to take a wife, but Charlotte Rose has other ideas. (978-1-63679-221-7)

Here For You by D. Jackson Leigh. A horse trainer must make a difficult business decision that could save her father's ranch from foreclosure but destroy her chance to win the heart of a feisty barrel racer vying for a spot in the National Rodeo Finals. (978-1-63679-299-6)

I Do, I Don't by Joy Argento. Creator of the romance algorithm, Nicole Hart doesn't expect to be starring in her own reality TV dating show, and falling for the show's executive producer Annie Jackson could ruin everything. (978-1-63679-420-4)

It's All in the Details by Dena Blake. Makeup artist Lane Donnelly and wedding planner Helen Trent can't stand each other, but they must set aside their differences to ensure Darcy gets the wedding of her dreams, and make a few of their own dreams come true. (978-1-63679-430-3)

Marigold by Melissa Brayden. Marigold Lavender vows to take down Alexis Wakefield, the harsh food critic who blasts her younger sister's restaurant. If only she wasn't as sexy as she is mean. (978-1-63679-436-5)

A Second Chance at Life by Genevieve McCluer. Vampires Dinah and Rachel reconnect, but a string of vampire killings begin and evidence seems to be pointing at Dinah. They must prove her innocence while finding out if the two of them are still compatible after all these years. (978-1-63679-459-4)

The Town That Built Us by Jesse J. Thoma. When her father dies, Grace Cook returns to her hometown and tries to avoid Bonnie Whitlock, the woman who pulverized her heart, only to discover her father's estate has been left to them jointly. (978-1-63679-439-6)